SHI

Tl

Jeff Carr

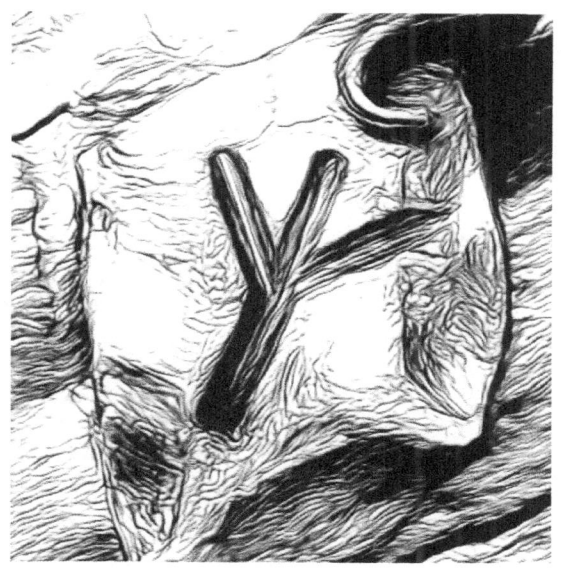

DEDICATION

This is dedicated to my family and friends, especially those who continue to support me. I couldn't do this without you.

To Sarah for putting up with me.
To Anna for being way too much like me.
To Kami for being my test subject and my biggest fan.
To Mom and Dad for being my heroes.

And finally, to my students, who constantly challenge and inspire me to be the best teacher I can be. I am honored to be a part of your story.

Remember, money doesn't buy happiness, but I'll be happy if this book makes money.

THE DARK LANDS

POLAR CAPS

SECOND REALM

MOUNT BOGDAN

LONGWELL LAGOON

SCAHILL

WESTRICH

LANGHAMMER

RAVEN TOWN

COVINGTON

THORNHILL

BERRYHILL

YARBERRY SHIRE

ISLES OF DAVENPORT

Table of Contents

A DYING WISH

My world was in a constant state of flux, a change that most could not comprehend. It had been that way for years, but only recently had I truly taken notice. The smell of the air, the way it caressed my neck, the sound of footsteps on the earth, and the pressure in the water all screamed out that something was different. As I sat here, I regretted not paying attention sooner. I should have heeded the stories and lessons he told me when I was younger and believed more deeply. Had I done so, perhaps they would still be here, fighting alongside me. Instead, I am consumed by shadow and sorrow, wishing upon dying stars that the emptiness in my heart will one day be filled.

HOME IS WHERE THE HEARTH IS

The sounds of war echoed in the air. The distant drum beats on the battlefield provided a rhythm of death and destruction. I heard voices cry out, some in agony, some in triumph. Drawing nearer was a percussion of soldiers riding beasts in armor, marching toward me in unison, accompanied by blaring trumpets. Chaos was closing in.

I peered out a circular window that reminded me of a porthole on an old submarine, and I gazed upon the fingers of light that punched through the trees, penetrating the window pane. The sun blazed just inches above the horizon, like witnessing God's descent into slumber. The once lush green and caramel fields were blackened and charred, consumed by a raging battle.

"Fire!" a demonic voice bellowed as a massive catapult unleashed its wrath, launching a flaming stone, the size of a small car, from its bowl-shaped container towards me. If I remembered anything from Mrs. Finklang's math class, I could give you its circumference for reference. However, math class, school, and innocence felt like they belonged to another world.

The small building I sheltered in was tiny in most regards. Then again, those who called this place home were equally small. One thing was for certain, it wasn't meant for humans or any figure my size. To be clear, I'm not a giant or anything like that. I'm your average-sized sixteen-year-old kid from Washington. No, not Washington, DC, not even Washington State. My name is Dean Koltien Moyers from Washington, Pennsylvania, an old mining town just outside of Pittsburgh. Although, as I tell you this part of the story, to say I was far from home would be an understatement.

"Take cover," a high-pitched, mouse-like voice screamed in a panic. Before impact, possibly before my impending doom, I observed my surroundings. The family room where I was hiding had 7-foot tall cathedral ceilings with oak trim, short for cathedral ceilings. I had mentioned that these quarters were not designed for people like me or for people in general. The walls were lined with oil pastel paintings, hanging perfectly level in four rows of eight. Each figure in the portraits appeared more unattractive than the one before. To put it politely, this family tree had no shortage of facial hair, regardless of gender.

A fresh-cut piece of wood crackled as it burned in the soot-stained fireplace to my left, startling me. I focused across the room, past a table littered with

3

weapons of all sorts - swords, arrows, spears, and even a small battle axe. I scanned beyond a homemade crib made from the Leflorian tree, a native tree that was a mix between a giant oak and a weeping willow. My gaze settled on a mirror. Its edges were blurred or foggy from the rising heat of the surrounding land, or perhaps it was just filthy; it was hard to tell. I sat there, staring at my reflection. I looked so out of place in the suit of armor that draped over my scrawny build. With one glance at me, you could tell that I was more likely to win a round of Battle Royale on my gaming PC than score a touchdown in the state championship. Yet here I was, a skinny kid from nowheresville, with a steady stream of blood running down my face. The armor was just as battered, with dents, chips, and scars in the plates that protected my body.

The metal rattled as I shifted my weight to the right, trying to ease the dull burning sensation that pierced my hip. In doing so, I accidentally bumped into an end table, causing a helmet made for me by one of the villagers to topple over. The helmet had two horns emerging from either side, curling toward the mouth. It was pretty intimidating, especially now with it being soaked in blood; someone else's, not mine.

In all my distractions, I almost lost sight of the problem at hand - the fireball. The blazing orb hurtled towards the ground, and the blast hit so near that the foundation and plaster on the walls cracked. Debris fell from the rafters, creating a cloud of dust that danced in the flames and choked the air of oxygen. My lungs wheezed with each inhale as I sucked in deep, toxic breaths. More voices now cried out from outside, voices of all ages. The death rattles of the injured swelled from beyond. That's when I felt it hit me all at once. No, not pain, not fire, or crushing stone, but anxiety, along with a sense of being completely overwhelmed.

"Your army awaits your command, Dean, I mean – Sir," the female voice called out as the front door to the cottage swung open with a bang. She entered, nearly kicking the door off of its hinges. The figure was covered head to toe in light armor and was shrouded in silhouette as she marched toward me. "Dean, you must lead them," she said in a delicate yet firm tone, with a lovely British accent.

"So many lost. For what?" I asked, more rhetorical than anything. "There's no point anymore. Is there?"

The female soldier crouched before me as the fire from beyond the cottage died down for a moment. That's when I got a good look at her. This was Liv, my friend, well, more than my friend, but for how long, I wondered. Her brown hair billowed around her shoulders. Liv was a natural beauty, even with her face covered in soot, blood, and desperation. A crest with a sun was etched into her chainmail vest. She held a hand-carved wooden bow in her right hand with an arrow quiver slung over her shoulder. Despite being only a year older than me, Liv was infinitely more mature. "Please, Dean," she said, "they need you. I need you."

"And what if I'm not strong enough?" I wiped a lone tear from my cheek.

"There may yet be a day where your strength fails you," Liv said, taking my chin in her hands. She turned my face toward her. Her eyes were haunting and magnificent, with a chestnut hue reflecting warmth and passion. "But, it is not this day."

"Wait," I said as I recognized this quote, "did you just...?" I began to ask.

Liv smiled and nodded, having used a quote from one of my favorite stories. She reached down, took hold of my gloved hand, and stood. With her aid, I lumbered to my feet. I wiped the trail of tears from my face, so my battalion wouldn't see. My battalion. That sounded so absurd, even now at the end of all things.

Liv and I stepped out of the quaint cottage, nestled into the side of a mountain, as the round, blue porthole door shut behind us. I clutched my shield tight against my hip, firmly holding my weapons. The sky ahead of us had turned an angry gray, with streaks of blood-red peeking through clouds, like rips in cloth.

Soldiers stood before me arranged in perfect formation, two lines that stretched to eternity, as straight as arrows. Some were tall. Incredibly tall, at least eight feet with pointy elf-like ears, while others were minuscule in comparison, only two to three feet in height, but stout. The tall folk were called Ravens, hailing from a tribe from many miles away. The tiny creatures were simply known as Gnomelings. This was their village, and the cozy home built into the side of the grassy mountain was where I had found solace. The Gnomelings had small, slightly pointed, upturned button noses with rosy, round cheeks. As I observed in the portraits within the cottage, some of the men had wispy mustaches that resembled whiskers, while the elders had long braided beards. Even some of the women had stubble that dangled from their chins.

I walked through the lines of soldiers with as much confidence as I could muster. The little ones saluted oddly as we passed. Some were dressed in miniature suits of armor with markings of blue and yellow on their shields, chest plates, and helmets – the colors of their village.

We reached the top of the hill that overlooked the valley. I looked into the distance, staring at the fires that raged on. The view was astonishing. Terrifying yet astonishing. Five hundred soldiers stood strong, ready to defend what was theirs, ready to defend hearth and home. They gripped their weapons as if they were extensions of their own bodies. Swords, axes, shovels, knives, picks, and more. One Gnomeling even held a small chunk of a tree with charms dangling from the branches, although I wasn't sure what she hoped to accomplish with it. The colors of their lands, the royal blues and the ripe-corn yellows, flew high on homemade flags sewn from sheets, dresses, and shirts. The faces of mostly little folk, two platoons of the Ravens, and a few other species stood shoulder to shoulder, ready to fight, prepared to die.

Beyond what somehow ended up being *my army* was the stuff from nightmares—no, worse. My nightmares usually included vivid images of clowns, zombies, and the high school bully, Rorie Henry. But this, this was beyond anything I could have dreamt. Evil beckoned. Darkness crawled across the horizon. Thousands upon thousands of enemy soldiers marched toward us. Mounted and armored rhinos with lacerating tusks led the charge in our direction. Goblins bear-crawled across the fields. If that weren't freaky enough, some even bear-crawled upside down. At least a dozen giant trolls wielded sharpened spears made from uprooted trees. The worst was still to come. A legion of armor-plated spiders with glowing red eyes scampered down the hillside from our left. Six dragons with wings like razor blades sliced through the clouds, surveying the feast below.

I tried to block out the sounds of the battlefield - the screams, grunts, and growls - but something else soon overtook the chaotic cacophony. I began clanging the hilt of my weapon against my shield in a steady rhythm. Thump, thump, thump. Liv, by my side, the only place I'd ever want her to be, joined in. Thump, thump, thump. Soon, the entire army followed our lead, creating a thundering battle cry that echoed over the hillsides. The uncertainty, anxiety, and doubt that had gripped me were replaced by focus and determination. Fear gave way to a thirst for vengeance.

I scanned the army before me, looking over the friends to either side. I felt Liv's hand rest on my shoulder, knowing it was time. "Are you ready?" I asked.

"I think so, yeah," she answered with a familiar response.

"For our friends," I said. "Our companions."

"And your dad," Liv replied.

My eyelids fluttered as they fought a barrage of tears that welled up. Choked up, I only nodded, looked out at the field, and screamed at the top of my lungs, "Charge!" The armies all around me roared in unison, a guttural call, raising their weapons toward the sky. Together we rushed toward our enemies. We rushed toward our certain deaths.

STORYTIME

Many Years Earlier...
November 1999

I remember it like it was yesterday. I sat on my father's lap in an old wooden rocking chair in the corner of my room. Like most six-year-olds around bedtime, my outfit of choice included a variety of footie pajamas. Tonight's selection was a blue Thomas the Train ensemble. My dad's name was Desmond, or Dez for short. He had medium-length hair that spiked up in the front like the brown and gray quills of a porcupine. Dad was the spitting image of Indiana Jones. With the flip of a switch or the donning of a fedora, he could go from professor to adventurer. Night after night, my dad would read to me. Tonight's tale was my all-time favorite, a story that would change my life.

"We may, Mister Frodo. We may," my dad read in a British accent as he closed a hardback edition of *The Fellowship of the Ring* and set it on my nightstand. I mention his British accent not because he was playing a part but because he was genuinely a native of Oxfordshire, a landlocked county in South East England. "The end." He removed his black-rimmed reading glasses, massaging the skin on the bridge of his nose as he let out a bear-like yawn. Dad was tired, with bags under his eyes. Due to his work as a foreman at the local coal mine, on-call work seemed to pop up regularly, sending him to the "office" at all hours of the night. But no matter how much he worked, he always made time to read to me. Some kids played catch with their dads, while others built treehouses, but we read, and we imagined together.

"What happens next, Dad?" I asked.

"Frodo and Sam journey to Mount Doom," he slid the temple tips of his glasses back over his ears and into place, "but we'll get to that tomorrow."

I shot up like a jack-in-the-box hitting its final note. I should have been tired, but ending the story on a cliffhanger seemed wrong to me. "But, but... do they make it? Does Frodo destroy the ring? Do they find Gandalf in that giant hole?" I asked in rapid-fire.

"Whoa there, Sport," my dad always called me Sport, "exactly how many cups of hot chocolate did your mom let you drink?"

A smile stretched across my face. I instinctively licked the corner of my mouth where remnants of cocoa lingered. "Just one more question," I said. Dad nodded and waited patiently. "Sam and Frodo... weren't they scared?"

"Oh, you bet they were scared," my dad said. "But you see, they were also very brave."

"Wish I was brave like Frodo," I said with a pining gasp.

My dad laughed and rubbed my head, smashing my bangs into my skull, as dads typically do. "You're plenty, brave, Dean."

"But all the kids at school make fun of me because I'm scared of Kaylynn Climer," I replied.

"Are you?" Dad asked.

"She wears a size seven shoe and can ride the big roller coasters," I said confidently. Trust me, you don't want to mess with any seven-year-old who can ride the Thunderbolt alone.

"Come on now, I'm certain she can't be that bad."

"At lunch yesterday, she brought in a hot pepper, eating it in one bite."

"She's a monster," my dad said in a deep dramatic voice like Dr. Frankenstein's. He pretended to tremble in fear, which made me burst out laughing. My laughter was so loud that it might have even woken up the dead, or worse... my mom!

"Dean!" Mom called out from the room below. I swear, that woman could hear a pin drop in my room at bedtime, even over the sounds of the vacuum, barking dogs, and late-night TV.

"That's my fault, dear; I was just finishing a story," my dad covered for me. He always covered for me.

"You do know he has school tomorrow, right?"

"She's right." Dad lifted me from his lap. He planted my feet down on the rug. "But don't you worry about being brave. When the time comes, you'll be the bravest boy in the world."

"How do you know?" I asked.

"Because bravery is in your blood." Dad walked me to my bed, pulled my covers back, then ushered me in.

11

I glanced at a scrape on my elbow from an earlier encounter. "It is?" I said in awe as I reflected on Dad's claim that bravery was actually in my blood. "How did it get in there?" I asked.

"That," he stooped down and kissed my forehead, "is also a story for another night."

As Dad walked away from my bed, he was met at the door by my mom, Isabel-Sophia, who Dad, and only Dad, affectionately called Bella. Her long black hair was naturally wavy. It seemed to shimmer in any lighting. She had olive skin and eyes that sparkled a light hazel color with enchanting blue flecks. She wore black sweatpants and an oversized black t-shirt, probably Dad's, but she still looked beautiful. Oh, and I should have mentioned she was five months pregnant. She held out the home phone's handset, saying, "It's your boss." She rolled her eyes, knowing a call at this hour meant trouble. "I told him you were busy, but he insisted."

"I'll take it in the hall," Dad said as he stepped into the second-floor hallway, closing the door behind him. Clothes hangers that hung carelessly from the door handle rattled.

Mom rested her hands on her belly. She stared into space for a moment, into another reality, until something immediately brought her attention to this one. "Oh!" she gasped. "He's kicking. Do you want to feel?"

"Uh. Sure," I said, trying to hide my apprehension. To be honest, feeling the baby kicking freaked me out. The imprints of bony feet pushing the underside of the skin on Mom's belly seemed like something out of an alien movie. This was something I wanted no part of it. But, seeing how happy it made Mom, I usually played along.

"Feel right here," she said, walking to my bedside, taking my hand, directing it to the right spot on her stomach, now the size of a basketball. I felt a sharp thud against my palm from the creature inside.

"That's so…" I couldn't finish the sentence.

"Cool, huh?" Mom suggested.

I nodded, "Yeah, cool." Not cool at all, I thought. More like disgusting.

I heard my dad talking through the door. His voice grew loud with frustration, followed by concern. "They did what?" We heard him shout. "Understood. Call Emma. Tell her we're handling it. Wake Emerson, Ellis, Mitchell, and Shreve. Tell them to gather the troops." He came back into the room with a familiar look on his face. "I have to go," he said. Mom stood and stormed out of my bedroom. Steam was practically wafting from her ears. Dad followed her, grabbed her arm, and spun her around. He was about to talk when he looked back and saw me eavesdropping. He stepped in my direction, gripping the handle and closing the door. I snuck out from under my blankets and tiptoed to the door, pressing my ear firmly against the wooden panel. "There was an accident at the mine," Dad continued. "I'm sorry, Bella, but they need me."

"Let them need someone else! Tomorrow's his first day at the new school. I wanted you to be there with us."

"And I will. As soon as I'm done," Dad tried to assure her, but even I knew this wasn't going to happen. Dad worked with the miners. He only got these types of phone calls when things went wrong. Sometimes there'd be emergencies: Trapped workers, cave-ins, explosions. Other times it was false alarms, but either way, Mom hated it, I hated it, we all hated it. In my dreams, I always pictured it like the scary chapters of a fantasy book. Dark caves. Smog. Monsters. "You knew this was part of the deal. When we moved here, you knew –"

"I die every time you get a call. Why do you have to be the one to go down there?" Mom asked.

"Because that's my job."

"Well then. I'm glad to see where we stand in your priorities," Mom shouted.

"That's not fair," Dad countered. "Bella, that's really not fair." I heard Mom's footsteps drumming away from me. I turned, pivoting on my bare heel, twisting toward my sleeping quarters when the floorboard creaked. I froze. The door handle twisted as I darted to my bed, dove headfirst onto the mattress, covered myself up in a flash, and started the worst fake snore in human history.

"I know you're awake, Sport," my dad said as he sat beside me, heaving a heavy sigh.

Fear filled my heart as I rolled over and stared up at Dad. With a tremble in my voice, I said, "Dad... I don't want you to go either. What if there are goblins down there?"

"Maybe I should have skipped the Mines of Moria chapter," Dad said in a whisper. All I heard was Moria, which set my mind racing. Suddenly I fixated on Cave Trolls–nasty giants with skin like armor. This did not help my state of panic.

"What about Moria?" I asked.

"It's nothing." Dad shifted his weight to his side, reaching deep within his pants pocket. "You know what?"

"What?"

"I was going to give you this tomorrow after you got off the school bus, but…" He pulled out a necklace with a golden chain, holding it up to the light from my ceiling fan, which made it shimmer. A jagged, oval-shaped silver charm dangled from the clasp. Etched into its center was an Algiz, or z-rune, a Norse symbol that looked like a human with raised arms (Ψ). It reminded me of a toddler's best attempt to sketch Poseidon's trident.

"Wow!" My eyes lit up as I took in the sight. It was simple yet mesmerizing.

"What does the symbol mean?" I asked.

"It means protection. It's my way of keeping a piece of me with you, even when I'm not there," Dad said, drawing a deep breath. "Do you want to hear the best part?"

I nodded.

"It's an amulet from another realm," Dad said.

"For real?" He had to be pulling my leg.

"For real." Dad smiled and held the necklace over my head. As he laid the jewelry around my neck, I craned forward like a knighted soldier. "Love you, Sport." I didn't answer. I couldn't answer. I was fixated on the amulet for an eternity. I didn't even notice that my dad got up from my bed, crossed to the door, and flipped off my light. "Goodnight," he whispered.

"Goodnight," I whispered back, laid down, and closed my eyes.

THE INCIDENT

That night I had the most vivid dream of my entire life. The whole thing felt like a movie, only now I know it was anything but. I flew overhead, staring down at a craggy mountain face with a large black mine shaft carved into it. My dad stood, reading a map, in front of a steel storage shed beneath the lumens of a beaming floodlight. I glided downward, landing at my dad's side.

"Dad!" I yelled. "Dad!" He couldn't hear me. I jumped up and down, waving my arms wildly in front of him like one of those inflatable blow-up things at a car dealer, but he didn't see me either. I tried to tug on the bottom of his jacket, but my hand went straight through.

A guy I only knew as Uncle Grant shuffled over to Dad's side. He wasn't a real uncle, just a friend of the family type who occasionally showed up for a birthday party or backyard barbeque. The steam from Grant's coffee fogged his glasses, which clung to his nose just above his bushy mustache. I could hear them talking.

"Perfect," Grant grumbled. "Reporters are here."

A motorcade of TV vans and SUVs funneled up a windy road heading in our direction. Dad pointed at a spot on the map, uninterested in the TV crews or Grant. "Here. This is where I'll go in."

"Aren't you gonna wait for the boss? I mean, Mister T's gonna be furious if we botch this on live TV."

Dad looked up from the map. He scanned the mountain, the rolling hills, and the inky pitch-black void surrounding them. He panned from left to right until he froze, his eyes locked onto something near the mine's entrance. I turned my attention in that direction and saw what had caught his eye: a wraith, six feet tall, faceless, and cloaked in black. The wraith floated two feet above the ground with only its gnarled fingers twisting from beneath the cloak. It looked like the grim reaper, only without a scythe. "This is impossible," Dad said under his breath, but loud enough for Grant to hear.

"And that's why you should wait for the boss," Grant said, unaware they were having two entirely different conversations.

"You can't be here," Dad said, speaking to the wraith.

"Shhh," the wraith shushed, placing a finger where its mouth should have been. The wraith's flesh was blue and rotting, with bones showing at the knuckles.

"What do you mean I can't be here? As a personnel supervisor, supervising personnel is part of my job duties. Especially when a team of them gets trapped beneath a dig site," Grant said, thinking Dad was talking to him. Dad didn't answer; he remained locked in a stare-down with the phantom until Grant waved his hand in front of Dad's face, snapping his focus. "Dez, are you with me, buddy?"

Dad jolted out of his gaze, looked at Grant, then back at the mine. The wraith had vanished into thin air. Dad rubbed his eyes and rolled up the map, stuffing it into his pocket. "Yeah, I'm with you."

"So, you're waiting, then?"

"No. I'm out of time," Dad said in a somber tone. I don't know why, but the way he said *I'm* out of time filled me with dread.

My dad rushed to his work truck, grabbing a helmet with a headlamp, a large flashlight, and a gym bag full of tools. He slammed the truck's crew cab door shut behind him, moving at a black Friday shopper's pace into the darkness of the cave entrance.

"Guess I'll handle the press," Grant said as he watched Dad disappear.

"Dad, wait!" I shouted, knowing he couldn't hear me, yet desperately hoping, longing that somehow he would. I raced after him.

Y

From the moment I stepped foot into the coal mine, I knew something was off. What I didn't know was how off it was. The cold air bit at my skin while a damp, foul smell filled the mine. Out of the corner of my eye, I saw the glimmer of Dad's flashlight. I gave chase, negotiating the rocky floor at my feet with the layers of collapsing earth surrounding me. I thought being in a dreamlike state would help my speed and agility, but it didn't. I kept running into walls and obstacles. I even tripped over a container that appeared to be a worker's leftover lunch: a PB&J sandwich next to a thermos.

Apparently, the only thing that I couldn't actually touch was Dad.

Eventually, I caught up to him. Dad had stopped frozen in his tracks with his bag at his feet. He seemed to be listening intently, but for what I didn't know. That was until I heard them: a series of muffled screams from trapped miners that echoed in this endless black maze of tunnels. They seemed close, yet miles away at the same time. Dad's lip stiffened. He grabbed his bag and zoomed further into the cave. His headlamp brightened everything before him as he scanned the cavern with his flashlight. As I ran with him, I could feel my feet slapping down against the ground, but they didn't make a noise. Only the crunch of Dad's boots and his panting could be heard as we wound further from the entrance. A twisting labyrinth of tunnels crisscrossed. This one seemed to go on forever until we reached what appeared to be a dead-end, but Dad didn't seem defeated. He felt around on the walls, knocking, listening, searching.

"It's here. I know it's here." Dad kept pushing, pressing, and prodding the walls until he exclaimed, "There!" A chunk of rock crumbled at his feet, and his face lit up excitedly. He kicked, hammering at the wall, exposing an entrance to a crawl space. He bent down, pushed his bag through the tiny grotto, and then scooted and slithered along the ground. The crawl space was about twelve feet long, and he could barely fit through it. I watched as he inhaled deeply, holding his breath while squeezing through the shrinking earth. Watching him made me feel claustrophobic, even though I was just a ghost or a passenger in this dream. Nevertheless, I followed his example as I held my breath, emulating the man I admired so much.

Once through, Dad's joy didn't cease. He seemed to forget all about the wraith. He bound to his feet and stood before a rusted mine shaft door sealed shut by decades of decay. What I know now, and didn't know then, was that this path hadn't been used in many years. It wasn't on any current map or blueprint of the mine. Somehow though, Dad knew which way to go. "This is it," he said in a hushed voice. He cupped his hands together, making a sort of megaphone, and announced, "Is anyone there? Please answer me." His voice reverberated off the chamber walls. We both listened hard for a moment, but his words were met by only his echo and eventually, silence. "Hello?" he called once more.

After seconds that bordered on what felt like hours, a cry of "Help!" rang out. At least three voices yelled in unison, "We're here. We're down here."

"Can you move? Can you come to my voice?" Dad asked.

"Yes! Keep talking," a lone man's voice cried out.

"That you, Palazzo?"

"Yeah, it's me, Moyers. I knew you'd find us!"

"Don't worry, I'm gonna get you home. Who else is down here with you?"

"We got Bushnell, Dennis, Wright, Garcia, Liam, Xavier, Morgan, Guimaraes, Schneider," Palazzo rattled off the roll call. I knew those names well. Bushnell and Morgan had kids my age. Liam lived next door; his daughter, Calia, had a weird addiction to ducks, but she was still my friend. Ominous thoughts started to race through my brain: *What if they didn't make it out? What if they were stuck forever? How could I look their kids in the eyes during class? What would I say?*

20

Dad gripped the mine shaft door tightly, yanking and tugging backward, but it was useless. It wouldn't budge, not even a millimeter. "I'm going to keep talking. You keep moving to me." Dad pulled a pin hammer from his bag. He tried popping the steel door loose, striking the hinges repeatedly, but again it was useless. "Keep moving. Sounds like you're almost on me." Dad dropped the hammer. He wiped his forehead as a layer of sweat started to bead up. He stooped over once more, retrieving a blowtorch from the bag. It was like Santa's magical toy sack, only with hardware store stuff, and I wondered what Dad could possibly pull out next.

A pounding on the steel door startled me. The men had reached us. "Is this it? Are you here?" Palazzo said loud and clear.

"Yeah, mate. I'm here. Gonna need you to take a step back." Dad fired up the torch and started to burn through the aged metal.

"It's working! We can see it working!" Palazzo screamed in absolute delight. A collective cheer echoed from the other side of the door. I watched as the hinge started to burn, melting away under the torch's heat. My dad worked feverishly, moving from one corner of the door to the next until he reached the final spot where the frame and door had become one due to corrosion.

"Almost there," Dad grunted as sweat streamed down his face. He blinked as a drop entered his eye. "Three, two… Got it!" With a loud groan, the door started to detach from the frame. I watched it slowly fall to the cave floor with a thud, creating a mushroom cloud of dust. As the dust cleared, a group of bright eyes and welcoming smiles emerged. The miners were covered head to toe in coal dust, but they were all alive.

21

"How'd you find us?" The man named Palazzo asked.

"It doesn't matter now," Dad said. "I hope you don't mind crawling."

"Brother, if it takes us home, we'll limbo out of this cave," Palazzo said with a huge toothy grin.

"Head straight, first right, through the crawl space. I'll meet you on the other side." The men didn't need any more instructions as they practically sprinted past Dad in the direction from where we came. Dad waited until the men were out of sight, then crouched down and exhaled heavily. I couldn't tell if he wanted to cry or catch his breath, but he was a hero, no matter how I looked at it. After a moment of quiet, Dad started to pack up his things. He placed the flashlight in the bag, followed by the hammer, and finally, the torch. He stood, about to head to the crawl space to join the miners, when we heard it... A scream followed by a deep, strange, and altogether unpleasant moan.

"Is someone still down here?" Dad whipped his attention towards the direction the miners had run. "Palazzo, is there anyone else down here?" He took out a manifest from his jacket pocket, quickly scanning a list of names, muttering them as he moved his finger down the page. The moans grew louder, more high-pitched, with a sense of desperation setting in - a clear cry for help. Dad looked into the cavernous void beyond the fallen mine door, then back at the miners crawling and running for safety. He kept turning his head back and forth until he could wait no longer. "I'm coming!" he yelled as the manifest dropped to the rocky ground.

"Dad, no! Don't go!" I yelled. Nothing about this situation felt right. The accident, the ominous presence at the entrance, and the strange noise coming from below all seemed terribly wrong. I was starting to think that this was not a dream at all.

I chased after Dad, falling farther behind. Tears flooded my eyes. Not because of the brisk air that beat against them but due to the growing fear in my heart. I wished he wouldn't have come to this place. I wished he would have waited for help. But it seemed like every time I'd wished for anything in my life, I was met with disappointment.

Minutes later, plunging into the abyss, I finally caught up to him. We'd reached a chasm in the earth that stretched beyond my line of sight - a bottomless pit that appeared to go on forever, like space or the ocean, when standing on the edge of the shore. The other side of the path was at least twenty feet from us and way beyond our reach, especially mine. I scanned all sides, but I couldn't find another way across. I looked up at Dad, fully expecting him to be plotting his course, maybe deciding between leaping the gap, swinging across it like Dr. Jones, or even vaulting across with a giant beam he'd spotted along the way. But instead, his face was frozen, as a look of terror had washed over him. The hand that held his flashlight was trembling out of control. I followed the ray of light until its beam stopped, frozen on a figure on the opposite side of the chasm. At first, I thought it must be shadow play against the cave wall, a mosaic of black paints swirling across a canvas. Suddenly, the image became clear as the wraith emerged from the darkness.

"Who are you? What do you want?" The flashlight's beam inched upward until the light landed on the creature's face, or rather, its lack of a face. The creature swayed back and forth like a bedsheet whipping about in the summer air, drying on an outdoor clothesline.

"You," the wraith hissed. "We came for you, Desmond."

"This is impossible," Dad started to say, but his words were abruptly cut off as he gasped for air, wheezing. A crimson liquid sprayed across my face. I wiped my cheek, then stared down at my red-stained fingers, slowly piecing together what had happened. A steel spear had pierced Dad's body, its blade sticking out of his back with little wings near his skin, preventing it from retracting. All at once, hundreds of ear-piercing howls echoed from the darkness below, followed by the beat of a drum. I looked down and saw a horde of skeletal figures climbing upward. They hurled themselves over each other, fighting for position, as they climbed towards Dad. Some had skin barely clinging to their bones, while others were mere skeletons. I wanted to scream, cry, and drag Dad away, but fear paralyzed me. My feet felt like cinder blocks, rooted to the ground.

The monsters rushed even faster as they began to reach us. Hand over hand, they gripped the shaft of the spear. They started yanking Dad toward them, toward the chasm. The wraith floated across the black hole, stopping in front of Dad. It reached its gangly rotting hand beneath Dad's shirt collar, searching for something. It pulled on a chain Dad was wearing. A chain that had no charm. No amulet. It was a simple gold necklace.

"Leave him alone!" I swung wildly at the wraith, but it was no use. My fists went straight through the phantom.

"Dean," Dad said, turning his focus away from the wraith, away from the monsters, and even from his wound. He looked right at me, his eyes filled with a teary mist as he smiled. In this moment of death and dread, he smiled and said, "Find me when you're ready."

"What do you mean?" I sobbed heavily, my chest rising and falling. "Ready for what?"

"I'll be waiting for you," he said in a whisper, just an instant before the monsters overtook him, dragging him into the abyss.

WON'T YOU BE MY NEIGHBOR

My eyes snapped open as I bolted upright, terrified, covered in sweat that had soaked straight through my Star Wars pillowcase. It took me a minute to adjust to my surroundings, but I quickly figured out I was back in my room. I don't know why, but my first instinct was to reach beneath my collar and pull out the necklace. I rubbed the amulet between my index finger and thumb. It seemed to soothe me. "It was just a dream," I told myself, wiping tears from my eyes. I was about to lay my head back down when the phone rang. I looked over at my alarm clock; it was 3 a.m. — no one called at three in the morning. Every kid knew this. I heard Mom stumble from her bedroom to the hallway, where the cordless phone handset sat on its base.

I heard the answer button beep as she said, "Hello." Her tired voice cracked. "Yes, this is Isabel

Moyers." Her voice changed. She was suddenly wide awake. "I'm sorry, what?"

I stood, hurrying toward my door, when I heard the phone drop and smack down against the hardwood floor. I twisted the door handle, my tiny fingers trembling as I pried the door open. Mom's scream pierced the stillness of the night as she collapsed to her knees. It was a scream that I'd never forget, and I'd never want to hear again. I ran toward her and threw my arms around her. It took her a minute to realize I was there. "Mom," I said, shaking her by her shoulders to get her attention. "Mom, what is it?" She parted her hair from her face, looking deep into my eyes.

"He fell," she said. She meant Dad. She didn't have to say his name because I already knew. I had seen it with my own eyes. I couldn't explain how, but I was there. I was in the room where it happened.

Y

The next morning, Mom dropped me off at our neighbor Esther's house. As a kid, I figured Esther must have been close to two hundred years old. Mom said she was in her eighties... Close enough. Esther would sometimes babysit me on short notice. I couldn't stand when Mom and Dad said I needed to go to the babysitter. I was nearly halfway to becoming a teenager -- clearly no longer a baby. Esther was wearing a lavender floral-print robe, had blueish-gray hair, and wore glasses so thick that each lens looked to be the size of the bottom of a coke bottle. Mom talked with Esther on the front porch for a few minutes, while I stood in Esther's front hallway. Her house smelled like cats, mainly because she had a dozen or so of them, depending on the day. Mom started to shake as she covered her face with her gloved hands. Esther pulled a handkerchief from her robe's breast pocket, handing it to Mom. It was hard to watch Mom cry, especially since she'd spent all night in tears, rotating between a sniffle and a full-body sob. Don't get me wrong, I cried too, but given my nightmare, I didn't fully comprehend what was happening. I just knew Dad was pulled into the blackness of the cave. No matter what anyone told me, I knew he was still alive. He just had to be. But when I told Mom about the dream, she just held me close, crying some more. I guess she wasn't ready to listen.

After their conversation ended, Mom came inside, kissed my forehead, and said, "No TV." This wasn't just because of the recent events. This was a common phrase Mom would utter when dropping me off at the kid-sitter's house. Kid-sitter. That sounded way better than babysitter.

"Okay," I sighed as I observed a streak of Mom's mascara smeared onto her cheekbone. Instinctively, I licked the tip of my index finger, rubbing the stained spot until it was clean, then I showed her what I had wiped off.

"Uh, gross, but thanks," she smiled half-heartedly as she smashed my winter hat down over my eyes. She crossed back through the mini-foyer and stood in the doorway with Esther again. They continued to talk while I pretended not to listen as I pulled a He-Man action figure from my backpack; the rotating battle chest Skeletor. "Not sure how long I'll be gone," Mom said.

"Take your time, Isabel," Esther said. "He can stay here as long as you need."

"Thank you, Esther," Mom said as I thumped away at Skeletor's chest with the fatty pad of my middle finger. "I just can't believe he's gone," Mom broke into another bout of tears.

"Come now." Esther embraced Mom lovingly. This was unusual for Esther. I'd never seen her show any emotion. Her routine went from watching daytime soaps to doing her crossword puzzles and pirating HBO movies of the week onto VHS tapes— all while not saying as much as a word to me. Don't get me wrong, Esther was a nice lady, but a few things about her house creeped me out. For one, her daughter lived in the basement. Let me just tell you, her daughter scared me… a lot. She was skinny and had three teeth, or at least that's all I could see. She also had tattoos all over her arms. Tattoos of odd things, such as salamanders eating KFC biscuits. She would only come up twice a day to get oatmeal (once at ten in the morning and once at noon), and she'd sniff my head when she walked by.

Other stuff in the house was peculiar too. For example, Esther had a pet parakeet named Spike. He was called Spike because his head got stuck in the cage when he was a baby. It permanently deformed upward, in a cone shape, and his feathers were spiked up in a Mohawk. Anyways, Spike wasn't exactly nice. Esther would let him out all the time and he'd bite at me. She said he was harmless, but Spike would go on the offensive, launching an all-out attack when she turned her back. Another disturbing aspect of Esther's house was her unusual obsession with gnomes. Esther's wood panel walls weren't lined with pictures of her family or friends. No, they were covered in decorative canvases of gnomes. Not just gnomes in a garden, but gnomes playing cards, gnomes drinking beer at a bar watching lady gnomes dance in their swimsuits, gnomes wrestling in oil with their butts hanging out of their pants. It was weird.

"Thanks again, Esther." Mom collected herself. She blew a wad of snot and tears into the soiled handkerchief. She looked back at me, mouthing, "I love you."

"Love you too," I said as I continued to mash away at Skeletor's chest.

Mom scurried down the front stairs and out of sight as Esther closed the door, grabbed a Kleenex from the coffee table, and wiped her eyes. "Come in here, Dean. I'll make toast." I gagged. Esther's toast was disgusting. Her toaster must have been from the eighteen-hundreds, and the setting was stuck on the highest number. The toast came out a charred black color. Esther tried to mask the snack's deformity by putting an apricot spread over it.

I took off my shoes, gloves, and coat and set them on the floor, even though I passed a coat hanger on the way in. I threw myself on the couch, which was nicotine-yellow and covered in cat stains of all sorts, but don't worry, she put a plastic sheet over it. Esther had an old tube television, the wooden box frame type with a drawer beneath the monitor and speakers on either side. A game show host reviewed the rules of a lightning round on the screen. The contestants all had big hair and terrible makeup but seemed happy. The host announced the prize was an all-expense-paid trip to Tahiti, but I didn't know where that was, nor did I care, so I pulled a few more toys from my bag and started setting up an epic battle. I positioned the heroes atop fluffy tan and brown pillows. At the base of the mini-mountain of pillows sat the villains, including their battle cats and a random t-rex that turned into a monster truck. I moved the bad guys measuredly around the tower and, in my best Skeletor voice, screeched, "We have you surrounded. Give up before it's too late."

"Never," I said as the hero, now my voice changed to a deep, brave tone.

"So be it," the villain replied as he and his minions started to scale the tower. Inch by inch, they crept until they were nearly at the top. The toy Skeletor's hand crested the edge of the top pillow, reaching for the hero's ankle, as a picture flashed into my mind... my dream. The skeletal figures that wrapped their claws around Dad, the wraith that hovered and hissed. Was I recreating the scene? "NO!" I shouted. In a fit of rage, I used the hero to kick the villains from the pillow tower. Skeletor bounced off the plastic couch cover, hitting the floor with a clunk, switching the battle armor to the most damaged setting. Before I could come to grips with what was happening subconsciously, the game show stopped broadcasting on TV. The image was replaced by bars of all different colors of the rainbow.

A shrill sound rang out through the TV speaker as a voice came over the air saying, "We interrupt your program to bring you this very important message."

The image flickered as two news anchors appeared. My eyes were glued to the screen. One anchor was a large man with a dark complexion. The other was a woman who wore excessive amounts of sky-blue makeup on her face with her hair styled in a gigantic perm.

"Breaking news out of Washington County," the man said with a solemn look on his face. "There was an incident overnight at Finley mine, where a cave-in trapped ten miners. The crew barely escaped with their lives, suffering only minor injuries, all thanks to this man." An image popped up on the screen.

"Dad!" I said in a hopeful voice. He was on TV. He looked professional, wearing his reading glasses and a black suit and tie. It must have been from a long time ago because he had way more hair in the picture than he did in real life.

"Desmond Moyers," the female news anchor continued the story, "a local foreman, husband, and father entered the mine where he freed the trapped crew. Desmond, originally from Oxfordshire, England, moved to the area earlier this year. Unfortunately, after the mining crew made it to safety, Desmond — did not return."

The camera panned back to the man. "While a body has not yet been recovered, Police Chief Randee Wiggins believes Moyers fell into a deep shaft. Wiggins claims it may take weeks to recover the body."

"Turn that off right this instant," Esther waddled into the room carrying a tray of burnt toast with the gooey apricot spread and a glass of orange juice with the pulp. Always with the pulp. She set the tray on the coffee table. "Where's the remote? Dean, turn your head away. You don't need to be watching this."

Of course, anytime anyone says "don't look," the only thing you can do is to look.

"At this point in time, funeral services have not been set," the man on TV said as Esther pressed the power button on the TV's panel, and the images on the screen compressed until only a black mirror was left.

"Body? Funeral?" I stared at my reflection on the blank TV screen. What did they mean by funeral? What did they mean, recover his body? He was dragged down by the monsters, but he wasn't dead. He couldn't be. Not really. He was my dad.

Esther turned and looked at me. Sorrow washed over her. She gingerly walked in my direction. Tears welled up in my eyes, and my hands began to shake.

"Everything will be okay," Esther said as she sat beside me.

"No!" I shouted. "He's not gone!" I leaped to my feet, sprinting out of the living room and up the stairs to the second floor. I slammed the door behind me when I reached a playroom where I'd spent most of my time whenever I had to stay here. I ran to the daybed beneath a dainty window, burying my face in a comforter.

LORD OF THE DANCE

About 10 Years Later

I sat at my desk, staring at my tablet, unsure if I could do this. Being a sixteen-year-old kid was tough enough these days, but this was real pressure.

"C'mon Moyers," I said, bouncing up and down, smacking the palms of my hands against my cheeks, trying to psych myself up. I looked around my room for some motivation, and motivation I found.

Since the first day that Dad read me *The Hobbit* and *The Fellowship of the Ring*, I was hooked on all things LOTR — that means The Lord of the Rings for the uncultured. And my room reflected my passion. My dresser held a shrine of action figures, still in their boxes, of course, while my walls were littered with posters from all the films. I had a Frodo Baggins bedspread with a matching Samwise Gamgee pillowcase. If you think that's childish, I won't tell you about my Gollum pajamas.

34

When most of my classmates turned sixteen, they got a car for their birthday, but Mom knew better. She bought me an authentic *Return of the King* film crew jacket, signed by the entire cast. She also tossed in an autographed photo of Bruce Spence, the guy who played the character, The Mouth of Sauron. Talk about obscure, but I loved it.

The desk in my room was pretty simple. Aside from a cup of mechanical pencils and my tablet, the only thing on it was a Gimli bobblehead. When I stared at these collectibles, trinkets, and characters who braved the odds to defeat evil, I thought, *I got this.*

"Alright, let's go," I said. Like the brave line of Moyers' men who came before me, I knew it was time to take action, to face my fears, and that's exactly what I did. My finger slid across the tablet screen, pressing the lime green video chat button. A ringtone sang out as I stared at the front-facing camera. Each tone made me more nervous and self-aware. I fluffed the ends of my shaggy brown hair and gritted my teeth. The blue eyes in the camera were mine, but I felt like I was staring at a stranger. I knew I needed to look more confident, but before I was satisfied with my appearance, Liv answered the call.

"Hi, Dean," she said in the sweetest British accent in recorded history. I met Liv a few years back when we became random teammates in an online role-playing game called Shire Knights. The game's premise was simple: you and a squad battle the enemies of evil trying to take over the various shires, or counties, in the UK. Each player chose their character, which ranged from archers to elves, wizards to dwarves, and any other fantasy game class you could think of. I only downloaded the game because I saw the county (or shire) Dad was from on the cover art. It was one of the counties you could defend on the free trial, and it ended up being one of the best decisions of my life. Two weeks into my trial, I was teamed up with an Elven archer whose screen name was **Oh!Livia**. Initially, she remained quiet, mainly steering clear of the toxic prepubescent trolls (not actual trolls) who made online gaming difficult for girls. After a few rounds and a victory over the actual literal trolls that had captured a village in Cornwall, we started to talk. She lived in England, not twenty miles, or maybe it was kilometers, from where Dad went to college. She was a solid year older than me, with two younger siblings, Matilda and Leah. They lived with her mother in a two-story townhome. Her dad died when she was little too, but from cancer, not from a cave-in or an army of skeletons, depending on whose side of the story you believe. As the months passed, we became great friends. It was always the highlight of my day when we had our video calls, holding them as often as possible. I told Liv everything. Even secrets or feelings I didn't tell my mom or my best friend in the States.

"Are you ready?" she asked, swiping a loose strand of hair from her face while biting her bottom lip playfully. I couldn't quite explain why, but my heart immediately leaped into my throat when she did that. I think she knew it drove me crazy because she would often do it at the most strategic times. Mom said I was crushing on Liv, but I replied, "No way. She's my BOFF: best online fantasy friend."

"Uh, yeah. Just gotta set up the song. You sure about this?" I said as I thumbed through icons on my tablet.

36

"I think so, yeah," she responded, looking slightly nervous, but she could pull it off. On the other hand, I was sweating uncontrollably, and my stomach was twisted in knots.

"Let me just hit the button here, and we'll start," I said as I opened a new app whose icon was a wooden shoe known as a clog. My task was to pick a song from a long list of options. During my scrolling, a few images with ads popped up on the screen, as they often did. "Dang it, close, c'mon, close," I said as I punched away the tiny red X's that flooded my tablet. "Got it. Finally. Here we go."

Music started to play. Drums and fiddles and a choir of bagpipes. I wondered how I got talked into this as I stared at myself in my full-length closet mirror. I looked ridiculous. My lean body barely filled out my khaki shorts and cut-off t-shirt. I also wore the chain around my neck with the amulet that Dad gave me. Truth is, I never took it off. Thanks to inheriting more of Mom's olive complexion than Dad's Elmer's glue white, I tanned easily. In certain lighting, it almost appeared as if I had a muscle or two

As the melody picked up, I considered backing out, but I didn't want Liv to think less of me. So I threw on a green vest and flexed my small muscles, giving her a "ticket to the gun show." This made her laugh. On the screen, I could see her putting on the finishing touches, puckering her ruby-red lips, as she buckled black clogs onto her feet.

"Three," I started the countdown.

"Two," Liv continued.

We skipped one, immediately starting to Riverdance to the music. I had no idea what I was doing, as I had never done an Irish dance before. But somehow, I let Liv talk me into this. She was a natural, wearing a black and green dress with lace and an embroidered pattern that ran down the side while her hair was up in a high ponytail. Meanwhile, I looked like the Dollar Store version of the Lucky Charms leprechaun, an insult to Irish folk everywhere.

Liv moved her feet and legs in double-time, clicking, stamping, and tapping the hardwood floor in her room. She knew all the steps, like the reel, the slip, the jig, and the hornpipe (I googled these). All I knew was the Macarena and the Electric slide, so I combined the two. I shuffled side to side, front to back, with my arms folded across each other. As Liv twirled, the sequins on her dress glimmered, reflecting the light from her room. The song reached its crescendo, and I hopped and clacked my heels, pretending I knew what I was doing. It wasn't actually that bad. I might have even enjoyed it. That was until…

"Holy Ghost of Saint Patrick. This is the greatest thing I've ever seen in my entire life," a voice rang out on the tablet that didn't belong to me and definitely didn't belong to Liv. "Whatever you do, don't stop until I get a screenshot."

"Dean!" Liv shouted, covered herself in embarrassment, rushed to her screen, and disconnected the call.

I darted to my tablet, shouting in panic. When I reached my screen, I saw my best friend Flynn sprawled across his bed, eating a bowl of ice cream with chocolate streaks on both sides of his mouth. "What do you think you're doing, Flynn?"

"What am I doing?" he asked with a chocolate smile. "What are you doing?" Flynn had been my best friend since first grade and had been there for every important event in my life since the day we met: He was there for me when I got into my first fight at school. He was there for me when my first girlfriend, Sydney, broke up with me because I didn't share my green Mike & Ike candy. And apparently, he was here for me now, watching me make a fool of myself in high definition.

"You weren't supposed to see that," I said, thinking that I must have accidentally three-way conferenced Flynn into the video chat during my frantic screen spamming.

"Now I can't unsee it. Thanks for that, bro." Flynn laughed and licked his spoon clean. Flynn had a full head of flowing blonde hair, and for some reason, girls loved him despite his crude sense of humor. Every girl except for Liv, probably. I'm sure she thoroughly loathed him right about now.

"How long were you watching?" I asked.

"Long enough."

"I gotta call Liv back. I'll bet my life she's mortified."

"K. Love you, bye," Flynn said as he disconnected the call.

I swiped a few times on my screen until I found the texting app, where I saw a new message from Liv.

Liv - I'm literally so embarrassed.

I had to reply quickly. Time was of the essence.

Me - I'm rlly Sry abt tht
Liv – Did you know he was watching us?
Me – No I prmise
Liv - ...
Me – Wht is it?

39

I could tell something was wrong. Liv never typed an ellipsis unless something was bothering her.

> **Me – Liv? U usd the 3 dots again**
> **Liv – It's because I'm frustrated with your grammar. Doesn't your American school teach you anything? Please type out full words & sentences? It drives me mad when you write like a toddler 💻 - Good night**
> **Me – GN**
> **Me – I mean, Good night. ☺**

DREAM A LITTLE DREAM OF ME

I tossed and turned in my sleep, having that recurring dream. The one from the mine. This time I was traveling down into the core in a minecart. The darkness was palpable as the cart twisted deeper and deeper. Although some parts of the dreams slightly changed over the years since the incident, such as my height, hairstyle, or mode of travel, I was always in those blue footie pajamas and wearing a miner's hat, covered in soot.

As the minecart door opened, I stepped out into the cave with my headlamp flickering, partially illuminating a thunderous collapse of dirt and stone. Before long, I heard a familiar scream.

It was Dad's.

I sprinted through the endless maze of the mine shaft toward my dad's call. As I ran, my feet felt weightless, and I effortlessly darted down straightaways, skillfully navigating around corners. Along the way, I passed the miners who stood motionless, their gazes fixed on me like mannequins in a department store. Finally, I skidded to a halt at the chasm, where I saw him dangling. "Dad!"

"Son." Dad's fingertips clung to the ledge of the collapsed ground, with nothing but darkness below him.

I reached down and gripped Dad's wrist. He attempted to climb up the wall, but his feet lost traction. "I won't let go, Dad," I said firmly.

"You have to!" he shouted. He shouted for me to let him go every time, but every time I refused.

"Dad, watch out!" I cried as they approached. The figures from the darkness reached out, clawing closer to him.

"Listen to me, Dean," Dad said. I was shocked as the color drained from my face. This was new. In my dreams, Dad was usually taken away without saying another word. But this time, he kept talking. "I need you to do something for me. I feel like you're finally ready."

"Ready for what?" I asked, puzzled.

"Go to Oxford," he replied.

"England?" I asked.

"Yes, where I grew up," he said.

"And do what?" Shrieking skeletons and gnarling monsters were nearly upon him. His time was running short. "Do what, Dad?" I started to sob.

"Fulfill your destiny, Dean."

"How?"

"The amulet. It will guide you."

I looked down at the amulet, which was now glowing a rose-gold hue, while the rune was lit with red streaks.

"I don't understand."

"It's time to let go," Dad whispered soothingly. He closed his eyes and smiled as a hideous face emerged from the darkness below. This creature's eyes were made of pure fire. Its teeth were as sharp as razor blades. Piercing horns protruded from its skull. Matted and tangled patches of fur barely clung to its head, neck, and shoulders. It was disgusting and ghastly, and even though I caught only a glimpse, I hated seeing it. "Goodbye, son."

"Dad?" He'd never said goodbye. Not in any other dream, not even once. This was different. Why was this different? "Dad, no!" The creature growled, causing the earth to tremble. It sounded like a chainsaw slicing through Jell-O. The beast wrapped its massive claws around Dad. It jerked him away from me, pulling him down into the pit. In the blink of an eye, they were gone. "No!" I cried out, my screams echoing in the cavernous wasteland. When my echoes ceased, a sound pinged my eardrums, faint at first, but it grew louder. An overpowering beeping filled the air, shaking the walls around me.

The walls started to crack while the floor began deteriorating. The crumbling cave was going to trap me down here. This would be my tomb. I sprinted in the direction I came from, turning corner after corner, frantically searching for the exit, but I kept ending up at the chasm. The loud beeping reverberated off the walls until I couldn't take it anymore. I cupped my hands over my ears, looking up. The ceiling splintered, about to fall on top of me, when I dropped to my knees and curled up into a ball, covering my neck, just like they teach you in an earthquake drill at school. A massive set of stalactites or stalagmites broke apart; I could never remember which was which— we'll go with stalactites.

They plunged downward, inches from puncturing my body like a voodoo doll, when I woke up to my alarm clock screaming in my ear from my nightstand. The same annoying beeps I heard in the cave. I turned and glared at my Two Towers alarm clock with a scornful grin as it continued its assault on my eardrums. I reached out, fumbling around my nightstand. I gripped the clock by the handle, then ripped it straight from the wall and hurled it across the room into a pile of dirty clothes beneath my window. I tossed my Frodo Baggins comforter aside, revealing my Gollum pajamas in all their glory. Nothing says mature teenage boy like a bug-eyed fictional creature's face covering your private areas.

I rubbed the sleep from my eyes as I groggily stumbled over to my closet and picked out my outfit for the day. But before exiting my room, I stopped at my dresser. In front of all my prized action figures, or "dolls," as my mom called them, was a collection of photographs featuring Dad and me. The first picture was of Dad pushing me on a bike, the first time I rode my Big Wheel. The next photo was of Mom, Dad, and me in front of a mine. Not *the* mine, but another one that Dad worked at when I was four. He took us inside for a tour. I thought it was cool at the time, but not anymore. I detested mines with every fiber of my being, and even thinking about them filled me with an absolute sense of dread. The last picture I looked at was my favorite. It was taken in our backyard, and I remember it like yesterday. We used to pretend we were characters from *The Fellowship,* and we'd battle goblins. Obviously, I was Aragorn. Dad was usually Legolas because he loved bows and arrows. In the photo, Dad held me tight against his chest, kissing my cheek. I can almost feel the stubble of his facial hair pressing against my skin. Right after Mom snapped this picture, we tackled our dog, Charlee, to the ground pretending he was a Hobbit.

I asked Dad, "Have you ever met a Hobbit?" His answer struck me as strange. He hesitated with a cryptic look crossing his face. The one where he was deep in concentration or appeared worried about saying the wrong thing and making Mom mad.

He looked at me and said, "Not exactly." I'll never forget the way he said it. It was weird. But I was little, and I also thought broccoli and big toes were weird. I lingered momentarily, staring at the photos. Then, I straightened them out on top of the dresser, organizing them into a line. *Go to Oxford.* I kept hearing his voice repeat in my brain. *Fulfill your destiny.* What did he mean? My destiny? But he said something else. I knew it was important, only I couldn't remember. Trying to recall the details was the worst part of my dreams. I should have written it down. I stared longingly at the photo of us wrestling with Charlee. I could almost see the picture come to life when something in the image stood out, the amulet around my dad's neck. The way the rays of sunlight shone through my window struck the picture frame; it almost gave the impression that the amulet was glowing red. That was it, that's what he told me... the amulet will guide you.

I reached under my shirt collar, pulling out the amulet. "So, are you gonna give me a sign or something?" I said to the amulet. I was definitely losing my mind, talking to an inanimate object. Get ahold of yourself, Dean. "Of course not," I said out loud as I tucked the amulet beneath my shirt. I was marching toward my bedroom door when my cell phone rang. It was Flynn. I slid the screen open to answer.

"Bro," he said as soon as I picked up.

"Why are you awake?" I asked. Flynn was never an early bird. During sleepovers, he would wake up around noon-thirty, still having the nerve to ask for breakfast.

"Remember when I told you my moms both did a DNA test? I mentioned that Mom Sheila found out her biological dad's dad was still alive and lived in England?" he asked.

"Her dad's dad? You mean, like, your great-grandpa?"

"No, dude, her dad's – dad."

"Yeah, her dad is your grandpa. Correct?"

"What are you getting at?"

"And if her dad is your grandpa, his dad would be…" I tried leading him to the answer.

"Her dad's dad?"

"Also known as your great-grandpa. Why is this so hard?" I loved Flynn and would take an arrow to the knee for him, but sometimes he was just plain dumb. How he passed elementary school was beyond my comprehension.

"Semantics," he replied. I was impressed that he used the word semantics correctly, though likely by accident. "Anyway, mom Sheila and mom Melba thought it would be a good experience for me to meet him. Maybe find out more about my past."

"That's cool. What are we talkin'? Does he do video chat, or are you goin' old school and doing the Pen Pal thing?"

"No, bro. Face to face. Like, grab a cup of coffee with the old dude."

"Nice," I replied, not fully sure why this warranted a call at nine in the morning on a Sunday. "When's he coming to town?"

"That's the thing. He's not. We're going to him. To England," Flynn answered.

"That's amazing," I shouted. Anytime anyone told me they were going to England, I was filled with two teaspoons of joy and a pinch of jealousy. "When do you go?"

"We leave in two weeks, as soon as summer break starts," Flynn said.

"You'll have to take pictures for me," I said. "You know I've always wanted to go there." Going to Europe was on my bucket list. Although that wasn't much of a boasting point because the other things on my bucket list included spending the night in a Walmart and seeing if I could balance on one foot while standing on a turtle. "What's weird though," I continued, "is last night I had a dream about…" I hesitated to finish the sentence. Not because I was embarrassed but because, as I mentioned, it was nine in the morning, and I wasn't quite ready for this much introspection.

"Dream about what?" Flynn asked.

"It's nothing," I lied.

"Obviously, it's something; otherwise, you wouldn't have brought it up."

Flynn was a lot of things, and one of those things was persistent. If I didn't tell him, he wouldn't give up. "I had a dream about my dad. In the dream, he told me to travel to Oxford," I said.

"How far is Oxford from England?"

"Oxford is in England, genius."

"Whatever, MapQuest," Flynn said, using one of my nerdy nicknames he'd come up with. MapQuest, Google, Jeeves, you name it. "How far is it from London, then?" he continued.

"I don't know," I said, though I did know. I knew quite well, in fact. Either because of tracking Dad's childhood, my obsession with all things British, or my strategic research for the Shire Knights game, I had simulated the road trip from Oxford Castle to the heart of London countless times. I knew it was fifty-six-point-one miles. I knew it took approximately one hour and fourteen minutes with the usual traffic. But I sure as heck wasn't going to let Flynn in on that nugget of information because I also knew he'd double down on his MapQuest name-calling. "Maybe an hour or two?" I said, making it sound like more of a guess.

"Then we'll make a day trip out of it," Flynn said.

"Thanks, Flynn. Even seeing a picture of it would really mean a lot," I replied.

"Picture. Why would you need a picture when you'll be there with me?" Flynn asked.

"What?" I basically shouted.

"Did I stutter? When I said we leave in two weeks, I meant us. You and me."

"You and I," I corrected. "And what do you mean? We're leaving? I'm going with you?"

"My moms talked to your mom. They decided you're coming with I."

"With me," I corrected him again, but I appreciated his effort. "Are you serious?"

"Of course, I'm serious." His voice nearly squealed with excitement. "Pack your bags, my good man; we're crossing the pond!" Flynn hung up, leaving me in a state of paralysis. I was going to England. I was going to see where my dad grew up. "I'm going to England," I repeated my thoughts aloud. Then, it hit me… I pulled the amulet from beneath my shirt and stared into the insignia, recalling my dream -- my dad's words. "No freaking way. Did you do this?" After snapping out of my daze, a thought came to mind. "Oh my God!" I hurriedly tapped my phone's screen, unlocking it with shaking hands. I swiped until I reached my messenger app, scrolled through my message history, and stopped when it reached - *Oh!Livia.* I started to text with frantic fingers.

Me – GM… Sorry, Good Morning!
Liv – It's three in the afternoon, Dean.

I often forgot about the time difference between Pennsylvania and England, causing my late-night video chat requests with Liv to be a bit awkward. Sometimes the overnight calls would get her into trouble with her mother. According to Liv, when her mom gets angry, her face turns a comical shade of red, especially her nose. Grinning from ear to ear, my fingers swiped and tapped away on the phone's keyboard. I paused, my heart racing with my thumb hovering over the send button. In slow motion, I depressed my digit on the screen and sent it.

Me – Guess who's coming to London in two weeks? ☺

I'LL NEVER LET GO, JACK!

Today was the day. I bounded down the stairs, taking two steps at a time as I headed into the kitchen. I was dressed in blue and white plaid shorts with a black hoodie. Music blared from my headphones, with my favorite composer, Howard Shore, playing. I went to the pantry, where I sorted through the cereal boxes and chose Frosted Caramel Bites. I didn't bother closing the pantry doors. Rather, I walked over to the kitchen table - a stainless steel bar with rotating stools – where I sat down, eating the cereal straight from the box with my fingers.

"Ever think about using a bowl?" Mom asked, setting a bowl, spoon, and milk carton in front of me. But with French horns and kettledrums playing loudly in my earbuds, I only heard a few syllables.

"Huh?" I replied. She plucked an earbud from my left ear, repeating herself. "No time," I answered. "Flynn'll be here any second now."

"Are you packed?"

I motioned toward the back door where my bag sat. "Yep." I set it out last night.

"I can't believe I'm letting you do this," Mom said nervously. Over the past ten days or so, Mom had struggled with the decision but ultimately admitted it was too good to pass up. She kept telling me my dad would have wanted it this way. However, her fear or hesitation seemed to go beyond just the worries of getting lost or mugged.

"You sure you don't need a ride to the airport?" Mom asked. "I could easily drop you off or maybe even walk you —"

Before she could finish, there was a loud knock on the back door attached to our kitchen. Flynn refused to use the front door for some peculiar reason, a reason he had never shared. "Flynn's driving us. His moms bought prepaid parking."

"Of course they did," Mom said with a hint of resignation.

Flynn let himself in, tossed a sack next to mine by the door, sat down, and started eating the cereal out of my box. "Hey, Mrs. M," he said between bites. He was dressed in dark blue jeans with a Tottenham Hotspur jersey, which was lily white with blue numbers and lettering. Although Flynn had no idea what Tottenham or Hotspur meant, he bought the jersey to "blend in with the locals."

"Good morning, Flynn," Mom said as she disappeared into the other room.

"Nice jersey," I said.

"It's called a kit, not a jersey." He probably googled that ten seconds before coming into the kitchen. "You'd better get that straight before we get to England."

51

"Oh great, Carneal is here," my little brother's voice rang out as he bounced down the stairs, practically skipping into the kitchen. In all the excitement, I almost forgot to introduce my troublesome little brother, Jackson, a nine-year-old on the shorter and stockier side, with a face sprinkled with freckles and hair the color of a carrot. Old ladies loved him and his dimples, but Flynn and Jackson had a strange rivalry that I could never keep up with.

"How many times have I asked you to call me Flynn, Ginger?" Flynn growled. His last name was Flynn - Carneal Landon Flynn - his family was a mix of Slavic and Irish.

"Mom, Carneal called me a ginger again," Jackson whined.

"Boys, play nice," Mom begged, though she knew this wasn't likely. "Flynn, don't be racist."

"It's okay, Mrs. M, I'm part Irish; I can say ginger," Flynn replied.

"I can't believe Mom's letting you two losers go to England," Jackson mocked.

"And I can't believe she let you stop wearing diapers," Flynn said. "You probably still take a bottle at night."

"For the record, I've leveled up to sippy cups," Jackson said.

"What are you two talking about?" Mom asked as she reappeared from the dining room, holding a small package.

"Nothing, Mommy," Jackson smiled innocently and batted his eyes. But as soon as Mom was past him, he flipped his middle finger at Flynn.

"Here, Dean. I got this for you," Mom said, handing me the package and hovering behind me.

"What is it?" I asked.

"Just a little something to keep you safe."

My mind raced. Was it a pocket knife? A can of mace, maybe? A retractable baton? The options seemed endless as I tore away at the four-by-six box. After all of the wrapping paper was thoroughly shredded, I dug my nails into the packing tape, unfolding the box flaps. I put my hand in the box and scoured around. It almost felt empty until my fingers brushed against something. I pulled out a nickel-plated whistle that dangled from a tangerine-colored string.

"It's a whistle," I said, almost questioning its existence.

"In case you need help," Mom said.

"Mom… It's —"

"It's awesome." Flynn snatched the whistle from my hands, blowing into it, causing us to cover our ears.

"I don't get it?" I said, still confused.

"Bro," Flynn said, "it's brilliant. Think about it. What if we're somewhere where they don't speak English, and we need the police?"

"We're going to England, Flynn. They invented English."

"Well, what if they don't speak American?"

Mom shook her head, grabbed the milk, and put it back in the fridge. Once he knew she was out of earshot, Jackson leaned over to Flynn and said, "American isn't a language." He next called Flynn, a word I would never utter in my home, especially in front of Mom.

"You little —" Flynn's face turned a doughy white, but Mom returned to the table before he could reply, putting her hand on Flynn's shoulder.

"Take care of my boy, Flynn."

Flynn collected himself and answered, "Course, Mrs. M. It's my mission in life."

"Bye, Carneal," Jackson said, trotting up the stairs toward his room. A Cheshire grin stretched across his face as his middle finger extended once more.

Y

The plane rides to London felt never-ending. This was only my second time on a plane, the first being a one-hour trip to Washington, DC. This time, I embarked on a grueling thirteen-hour journey with a three-hour layover at JFK Airport in New York. The layover did have its perks, though – On the way to JFK, I got to admire the breathtaking skyline of New York City. Compared to the small-town storefronts and covered bridges in Washington County, NYC was a different world. I had always wanted to visit. Mom said we would, but life got in the way. I took advantage of the layover and bought a bunch of overpriced "I Love New York" souvenirs to bring home, including bracelets and a snow globe with the Statue of Liberty in it. Most importantly, I picked out a stuffed New York Yankees monkey for Liv. In hindsight, I'm not sure why I picked out that particular gift, as I didn't know much about baseball, let alone whether Liv liked the Yankees or even monkeys, for that matter.

The longest part of our flight was a direct path from JFK to London Heathrow, where I spent eight hours on a cramped tube with wings next to Flynn and an annoying little brat. The kid kept playing the same song on repeat: "The Wheels on the Bus." But at least I had the window seat. I adjusted my body, trying to get comfortable. Easier said than done, except for this one lady across the aisle. She was draped over her seat along with the one next to her while her snore shook the entire cabin. She had a book in her hands. Some sort of post-apocalyptic story about a teen girl and a dad. If I could judge it by its cover, it looked pretty interesting. Only I can't stand reading, especially in a moving vehicle. So, I watched the extended edition of the *Fellowship of the Ring*, all five hours of it. With little else to do and not enough time for the trilogy's second film, I figured it would be a good time for a nap, so I closed my eyes.

"Ugggghhh," Flynn grunted. I paid him zero attention until he grunted a second time, more forcefully.

"What's your deal?" I asked.

"I can't sleep," Flynn said.

"Ever think about closing your eyes?"

"Yeah, I've thought of that, but lately, every time I shut my eyes, all I see is *that* image."

Baffled and slightly frustrated, I lifted my head and asked, "*What* image?"

"The image of you," Flynn started to mock my Irish Riverdance moves from the video chat, "doing this!" He kept stomping and clapping. Unsurprisingly, he knocked over a bag of pretzels and sparkling water from the tray table.

"You're a jerk, you know that?" I stared out my window, looking down at the blackness that was the Atlantic Ocean.

"What's it look like?" Flynn asked.

"Looks like nothing. Just… dark water."

"You think we'd survive if we crashed?" Flynn said, drawing the ire of everyone within four rows.

"You can't say stuff like that mid-flight," I said, giving Flynn a scornful look, apologizing with a gesture to the previously snoring lady across the aisle, who, now wide awake, stared at Flynn with her painted-on eyebrows twisted in rage.

"Lembas bread?" I heard a woman say just as a flight attendant approached with a snack cart.

"Excuse me?" I said, wondering if I was dreaming or if she just asked if I wanted Lembas Bread. Lembas was a type of elven bread from *The Lord of the Rings* universe, and it was not something that would typically be offered on the in-flight menu. I looked up to see if my ears deceived me, but to my shock, the flight attendant who stood before me was wholly unnatural and absolutely frightening. Her skin was a pale gray, while her teeth were jagged and black, with gaps between them. She extended her hand with long, sharp fingernails, offering me a leaf-covered wafer.

"Lembas bread?" The flight attendant repeated in a low, guttural voice. I rubbed my eyes and squinted hard, shaking myself as if trying to wake from a nightmare. When my vision cleared, the flight attendant was still there, but now she appeared normal, with fair skin and pearly white teeth. "Are you okay, sir?" she asked.

"What's happening?" I asked Flynn, who was staring at me as if I had a third eye. Suddenly, a jolt of electricity zapped my chest. "Ow!" I yelled as I clutched at my skin. The amulet around my neck burned me.

"Bro, are you okay?" Flynn asked.

I looked at the flight attendant for answers. "It's probably just static from the flight," she said as she offered me a bag of animal crackers.

I couldn't speak, so I just shook my head no. We sat in silence for the next few minutes. What was that all about? My mom had given me some pills to help me sleep on the flight, but maybe they were expired. After a few deep breaths, things began to calm down. That was until Flynn leaned over me, staring out my window, his full weight crushing my gut and lower extremities.

"But seriously, though," he said. "If we did crash and somehow survived, would you share your wreckage with me?"

"Not again," I moaned. "How many times do we have to go over this?"

Flynn was obsessed with the movie *Titanic,* but most of his obsession came from the ending of the movie, where Rose watched Jack slip into the bottom of the sea rather than help him onto a piece of driftwood (*spoiler alert!*).

"As many times as it takes," Flynn said. "Besides, this is about as relevant as it gets, seeing as how we're actually flying over the Atlantic."

"For the billionth time, the wreckage Rose was lying on would have sunk if it had to support the both of them."

"Doubtful," Flynn countered.

"Jack knew it. That's why he didn't even try."

"Jack was a freaking idiot," Flynn said, only he didn't say freaking. Instead, he said *the* word. The f-bomb.

"Freaking idiot, freaking idiot, freaking idiot," the annoying toddler next to Flynn repeated the phrase, bouncing up and down in his seat with each syllable. Just like Flynn, the toddler also used a barrage of genuine f-bombs, drawing the outrage of his mom to go along with a fit of laughter from everyone who could hear.

"Sorry, Flynn, but Jack was a true hero. I mean, look at the facts; he sacrificed himself so Rose could survive." I added.

"Here's some facts for you. They could have at least taken turns. Face it. Rose was selfish."

"Selfish? They both would have frozen to death."

"Ok, so why not both partially hang on, upper bodies on the wreckage, lower bodies in the water. Then they might live."

"I guess, but with their legs amputated."

"At least they'd do it together. How romantic would that be?"

I rolled my eyes and turned toward the window, hoping Flynn would get the message that this conversation was over. After a minute or twelve of uncomfortable silence, I turned back to Flynn. "Seriously though, I'm glad you brought me."

"A long time ago, I made a promise, Moyers. A promise," Flynn said. "Don't ever travel to England without your best bro. And I don't mean to." No matter how mad or annoyed I was with Flynn, he knew how to reel me back in.

When we got off the plane, I was half-expecting to see Liv waiting to meet me. When I wasn't arguing with Flynn about planes crashing or Rose from *Titanic* being a selfish snob, I thought about Liv. I envisioned what she'd wear when we met and how her hair would look. I wondered if we'd hug or shake hands or, my personal preference, stand awkwardly while doing a weird handshake-hug combo. But as I stared at the scene before me, she was nowhere in sight. The inside of the airport was massive. It reminded me of a giant shopping mall. A ray of sunlight poked through the clouds overhead, peeking through a glass ceiling in the concourse. It shone down on people of all different sizes, ages, nationalities, and races who buzzed about and took on the appearance of swarms of bees. I tried to listen to all the different accents as we passed families and herds of tourists. I was also starving, so Flynn and I stopped at one of the airport eateries, Lily's Café. Convincing Flynn to stop for food didn't prove difficult because Flynn could always eat.

Lily's Café was originally Lilly's, with two L's in the middle, but one bulb in the second L burnt out. The place was packed, and the line snaked to the airport security booth. I had my mind set on a burger, but Flynn insisted we try a local delicacy, Austin's Fish & Chips. When our order was ready, Flynn asked the server why his chips looked the same as French fries. When he demanded his money back, she called him a tosser and threw his food at him.

We made our way to baggage claim and found the yellow number eight that matched the number on our ticket. As I plucked my bags out of the sea of luggage, I had the weird sensation that someone was watching me. I looked left, then right, there, and back again and spotted something suspicious. A man wearing a long black peacoat, a black fedora, and sunglasses was staring intently at me. Despite hundreds of people passing by, he continued to stare without breaking eye contact. "Flynn." I reached back, trying to grab Flynn's sleeve without losing sight of the stranger. "Do you see this guy?" My arm was extended, and my fingers were outstretched as I searched for Flynn, but I found nothing. I fumbled about a bit more until I thought I was patting Flynn's hip or stomach, but it wasn't Flynn's voice that I heard.

"Well, begging your pardon!" a woman shrieked. I turned around, shocked to find that I had touched the bottom of an elderly woman. Her face turned red with embarrassment, while her husband's face was also red but not from embarrassment.

"Did you just grab my bird by her bum?" he said in a Paul McCartney-esque voice.

"You grabbed a bird?" Flynn appeared next to me, fashionably late. "Where is it?"

"Where were you?" I asked. "I thought you were with me. I was trying to grab you, but the old lady's…"

"Oi! I'm talkin' to you, son," the man interrupted. "Did you just grab my bird on her…?"

"Where's the bird, dude?" Flynn asked.

"Really sorry, we gotta go." I backpedaled as fast as I could. The man started to charge. And when I say charge, I don't mean very swiftly, on account of his walker. "Have a good day!" I shouted as we sprinted out of the baggage area.

BE OUR GUEST

The iconic black cab with the Union Jack symbol plastered on the side zipped along as we traversed the countryside. Flynn wouldn't tell me where we were headed, but I recognized some of the sites and towns from playing the Shire Knights game with Liv. We passed Pinewood Studios, where a ton of movies were filmed, including some James Bond films, a Tomb Raider movie, and Harry Potter, and I heard it was the filming location of *The Hobbit: An Unexpected Journey*.

Next, we traveled down windy two-lane roads, passing Gerrard's Cross and High Wycombe. Everything was green as far as the eye could see; it was beautiful and beyond what I imagined it would be, though it was off-putting at first, driving on the left side of the road.

Our driver, Nigel, was a pleasant elderly man. He had a pockmarked face with a round nose and cheeks as pink as a flamingo. During our journey, he told stories about his family, his grandkids, how his father fought against the Germans in World War Two, and how he hurt his hip in a tragic bingo accident. He shared some trivial tidbits about the stores, restaurants, and homes we drove by. He was an amazing tour guide, even if he wasn't an actual tour guide.

With giddiness, Flynn said, "We're almost there."

"Where?" I played dumb. I knew Oxford was just around the bend. If I had to guess, I would say Flynn was taking me to the home my dad grew up in. I could picture it now; the two-story brick building with a brown wooden fence outlined by trimmed hedges. Maybe even a ten-speed bike or two sitting out front between potted plants. I even remember the street. Stoney Meadows.

"Here we are. Northmoor Road," Nigel said.

"Northmoor?" I asked, surprised. Didn't he mean Stoney Meadows?

The black cab rolled to a halt, crunching gravel beneath its tires. I looked at a row of homes and a smattering of elm and thornapple trees through my window.

"C'mon, let's go," Flynn said as he exited the vehicle.

I stepped out of the car, staring at the neighborhood before me. It was your typical English suburb with cobblestone driveways, brick and plaster galore, decaying wooden peaks aimed at the heavens on each home, and a parking lane too small for any car to fit in. However, the home in front of me had a newer addition; a one-story annex made of river rock and mortar with a large round porthole window, giving a full view of the den inside. Gray smoke billowed from its brick chimney. While I was a tad disappointed not to see my dad's childhood house, I started to understand that there was a method to Flynn's travel madness and that something magical may have happened here.

"Mind telling me what this is about?" I asked.

"You mean... You don't know where we are?" Flynn sounded surprised. Almost disappointed.

"What I do know is we're in Oxford. But not at my dad's house."

"And what else is in Oxford?" he asked.

"Christ Church, Blenheim Palace, Oxford Castle, the Bodleian Library, Radcliffe Camera, museums," I rattled off names without breaking a sweat.

"Bo–ring," Flynn interrupted. "What shirt do you have on?" I stretched out my oversized plain black hoodie with a sporting logo across the chest. "No, not that shirt. The one under it. The shirt you'd never leave home without."

I smirked. Flynn knew me way too well. He knew that one of my prized possessions was what I had on beneath my hoodie. Mom bought it for me when I was ten, intentionally getting it big so I could grow into it.

I slowly lifted the bottom hem, revealing my *One Ring to Rule Them All* limited print t-shirt. It may have looked like any other shirt ever made, but when the sun hit it just right, the inscriptions on the ring revealed themselves. "Ok. What about it?" I asked.

"I can't believe you." Flynn opened his arms, aiming them toward the house with the porthole window.

"You bought me a house?" I was baffled, clueless, dumbfounded, utterly confused. Is this what Flynn felt like on a daily basis?

"No, Moyers." Flynn shook his head in disbelief. "Who wrote *The Hobbit*? *The Lord of the Rings*? The Similarities?"

"*Silmarillion*," I corrected him.

"Whatever. Question stands. Who wrote them?"

"Duh, Tolkien."

"And where did Tolkien live when he wrote the books?" Flynn asked, clearly leading me to the answer.

"Oxford," I said.

Flynn was persistent with his hand gestures, presenting the home before me in the same way a game show host would show off a showcase prize. "And that would make this house the…"

"The birthplace of the ring," I said in a hushed tone. My eyes started to mist. My knees began to weaken. I was speechless.

"Surprise!"

"My dad always told me he'd show me where it was written."

"I know, bro. I know." Flynn put his arm around my shoulders as we basked in the moment.

"Wait! What is that?" I rushed over to the concrete wall that ran parallel to the home's front gate. There, a small round light-blue plaque was anchored to the wall, partially covered by vines. I tore away at the greenery, revealing a most magical inscription. It read:

J.R.R. TOLKIEN
Author of
The Lord of the Rings

Lived here
1930 – 1947

As I stood in awe in the very place where the backdrop of most of my childhood memories had been created, a door creaked open before slamming shut, breaking the peacefulness of the moment.

"Good morning, lads," a skittish man said as he stepped out of the house, fidgeting with a pipe that hung from his lips. He had one arm hidden behind his back and looked exhausted, with purple droops hanging beneath his eyes like plastic grocery sacks.

"Good morning, sir," Flynn and I said in unison.

"Can I help the two of you with something?" he asked as he let his hidden arm loose, revealing a vintage shotgun that appeared to be freshly plucked from a museum.

"Uh, no, sir. We were just looking for a friend's house," I lied. I don't know why I lied. I never lie.

"Americans?" he asked.

"Yes," I said. My heart was beating through my shirts.

The man drew closer, so close that I could smell the coffee and maple syrup on his breath. He leaned into my ear over the fence line and whispered what I thought was the word, "Run." *Was I hearing things?* He took a step back and said, "I suppose you'd want to have a look inside, seeing as this is a famous landmark and all?"

"Oh, no, sir. We couldn't," I stammered.

"You couldn't? Or you won't?"

"What he means is, yes. We'd love to have a look inside." Flynn confidently marched to my side.

"You do see the ot-gun-shay, right?" I murmured in pig Latin, unable to peel my eyes from the double barrels.

"It'll be ine-fay," Flynn tried to reassure me.

"I also suppose," the man interrupted, "that you'd like to take some photos. Maybe even take one or two of the trinkets from my water closet?"

"I mean, if you're offering," Flynn told the man. "Wait, what's a water closet?"

"I think it's a toilet," I said, recalling Liv's mom mentioning the water closet on one of our calls.

"Well, in that case, a picture or two will be fine," Flynn corrected. "As a rule, I don't collect things from people's bathrooms."

The man propped open his gate with his boot. He mouthed something inaudible, then shifted his gaze from me to the cab. Was he actually signaling for us to leave? He wrenched his hands around the barrel of the weapon and said with a forced smile, "Maybe I can interest the both of you in a firework show?"

"You know what? Obviously, there's been some misunderstanding," Flynn said, seeing the situation escalate down a path he didn't intend.

"We'll be on our way. Thank you for your hospitality," I said as I shuffled my feet backward. Flynn and I made an about-face, spinning on our heels as we picked up the pace toward the black cab. We heard a sharp ratcheting sound behind us. I assumed the man was racking the shotgun, sending us into a full sprint.

We dove headlong into the back of the cab, motioning wildly for Nigel to drive.

"Going so soon?" Nigel said as he picked his nose. He pulled his finger out of his nostril, examining the contents.

"Go! Just go!" Flynn waved him on.

As we drove by the house, I saw the nervous homeowner standing on his porch, holding his shotgun to his chest. To his left, I caught a glimpse of another man through the porthole window that led to the den. It appeared to be… No. It couldn't be… Yes, it was. It was the same man I had seen at the airport, with the peacoat, fedora, and glasses. He turned his head to watch us zoom away, disappearing from view, as he sipped his tea. I could have sworn I saw him smile, a sinister smile, as the Tolkien home became nothing more than a faint speck on the horizon. My face was fixed on the rear passenger window, so much so that my breath fogged the glass.

"What is it?" Flynn asked.

"I don't think you'd believe me if I told you."

WE'RE NOT IN KANSAS ANYMORE

As Flynn and I walked down St. Giles street, we encountered cars, cyclists, joggers, and families out for an afternoon stroll. The buildings on either side of the road looked more like castles or museums than stores, restaurants, or apartment homes. Unlike my hometown, everything here seemed vintage or historical, with a purpose and a place in storybooks. Ivy grew on the brick and stone as if time had forgotten this stretch of England. As we stopped to wait for a car to enter a narrow driveway, I realized we'd been in England for nearly three hours, and Flynn hadn't once mentioned his mom's dad's dad.

"What time are we meeting your great-grandpa?" I asked.

"Oh my gosh. I totally forgot about him," Flynn said. Sometimes I was certain that Flynn would forget his head if it weren't attached to his body. "I guess we could check in once we get to the hotel."

"We're not staying at his house?" I asked, surprised.

"That would be weird. Mom only talked to him a handful of times online."

"And we flew across the world to meet him? Is that even safe?" It didn't seem safe. In fact, I was now more convinced than ever that we'd be the topic of an international news story.

"He's one-hundred and seven. What's he gonna do? Bite us with his fake teeth?"

"I don't know. Maybe catfish us? Lure us into his basement cages? Don't get me wrong, I love being here, but I am not spending my vacation in a basement cage."

"It'll be fine. He's only expecting a meal or two with me. Besides, we already had our suitcases sent ahead to our room at the Four Pillars. They have a pool, horses - even a free breakfast. Not that continental trash, real breakfast."

"Sounds charming," I joked.

"Speaking of charming, where's Miss Olivia Weathersby?" Flynn always liked to use Liv's full name in front of me. He thought it made her sound royal. "Figured you two would have found a way to meet up by now."

"I don't know," I said as I checked my text messages. I hadn't received a new message since we left New York, and I'd sent her at least twelve. She probably thought I was a stalker.

Flynn could see that my lack of communication with Liv bothered me, so he swiftly changed the subject. "Hey, look. It's one of those buses." I spun on my heel, staring with glee as a classic double-decker tourist bus motored our way. Suddenly, a man on a high-wheeled bicycle, towering at least six feet tall (the bike, not the man), rode in front of the bus's bumper, nearly getting squashed. The bus driver laid on the horn as she swerved, causing a few tourists to fall into each other.

I could hear the amplified voice of the tour guide who stood at the front of the bus looking out over the Sunday crowd. "To our right, you'll see a wanker who was nearly run over. And coming up on your left, you'll see the Eagle and Child Pub. This pub was a famous hangout of C.S. Lewis and J.R.R. Tolkien."

"Did you hear that?" I asked.

"Yeah. She called that guy on the bike a wanker. Classic."

"No. The pub."

"Oh, I see what you're getting at! We can buy a pint." Flynn's face lit up. Drinking wasn't my thing. Even when guys in my high school would bring it to a party, I would avoid it. But if Flynn wanted to buy a pint in Jolly Old England, he was buying one.

We rushed across the street to reach The Eagle and Child pub. Like other buildings in Oxford, it had a simple, traditional appearance, yet was grand. The name was written in Old English script on a blue sign that hung above the door. It displayed an eagle holding a swaddled baby in its talons. The sounds of fiddles and folk music could be heard from inside, along with clinking bottles and patrons singing off-key but in harmony

I stared down at my feet, practically frozen to the cement. They were here, I thought. My favorite authors. My dad. His dad. A lineage of great men stood where I'm standing. I was about to walk into the heart of something larger than myself. Flynn couldn't care less.

He nudged me aside, entering with authority, pulling me inside by my collar.

A chime echoed through the pub as the bell on the front door slammed against the weathered wood, signaling our arrival. The music died down, glasses stopped clinking, and all activity inside the establishment came to a screeching halt. The pub was at a standstill with all eyes fixated on us. As I took in the sights, my jaw dropped to the ground in disbelief. I'm not kidding. My jaw had to be halfway to the center of the earth. In my wildest dreams, I would have never imagined the images before my eyes.

"What the..." We both said simultaneously, dumbfounded by the wall-to-wall costumed patrons. Not just any costumes, but costumes from *The Lord of the Rings*. The dance floor was filled with elves, while dwarves and Halflings smoked and drank at the bar. A man in an Ent suit, a tree creature, perused the selections on the jukebox with his leaf-covered limbs dangling from his body. A group of wizards and witches huddled over a map, studying the terrain while orcs and goblins threw darts. In the corner sat three wraiths. When I saw them, my heart nearly stopped beating. They were menacing, and their faces were hidden in shadow. All three reminded me of the wraith I saw in my dream the night my dad died. Only these wraiths weren't hovering twelve inches above the ground. Instead, they wore cheap Converse shoes with long socks. I shook my head, breaking contact with the wraiths and turning to a small stage with a sign dangling above it. The sign read:

*"**Seventh-Annual Fellowship Cosplay Convention.**"*

Flynn rubbed his eyes as if he was waking from a strange dream, then, unexpectedly, he exited the bar. Within a few seconds, he re-entered just as abruptly as the first time and said, "Yep. They're still here." Apparently, he was as shocked as I was.

"Let's get a table," I said.

"Ok, but if you go all fanboy on me and start dancing with the Wizards, I'm leaving you here."

We sat at the last remaining table, a corner booth. The tabletop was made of dark oak and worn down to its final, salvageable layer. We took in the eclectic scene as the gawkers finally returned to their business while the music resumed. It's funny to think that in a place of business, the people without pointy ears, axes, and cloaks were the outcasts. This also meant the chatter, clatter, and intoxication resumed. I continued to gawk at my surroundings. The building was quite cozy, with cathedral ceilings supported by wooden beams. An inscription of a C.S. Lewis quote was etched into the archway:

"My happiest hours are spent with 3 or 4 old friends in old clothes tramping together and putting up in small pubs."

This quote rang especially true for me, considering I was with my oldest friend and wearing my oldest t-shirt. And while I didn't know what tramping meant, we were in a small pub.

The bar was stocked full of wines, beers, and ales, or at least that's what I assumed, as my knowledge of spirits was minimal at best. I once saw my mom drink one of those fruity drinks with an umbrella stuck through a cherry, but I doubt there was much of that kind of stuff here.

Not in any particular hurry, a waitress approached our table, dodging a drunken elf on the way. She wore a plaid skirt and a button-up white top with a name tag that read, "Josie." Her hair was pulled back into a braid.

"And what can I serve you two gentlemen on this fine afternoon?" she asked.

"I'll take a pint, Josie," Flynn said.

"A pint of what, exactly?" she asked.

"Surprise me," Flynn said.

"And for you?" she stared at me, tapping her pencil against her order book.

"I'll just have water," I said.

"Water," Flynn repeated. "That won't do. No, that won't do at all. Make it two pints, my lassie," Flynn said in an awful British accent, reminiscent of the character from Mary Poppins, the one who danced with the penguins.

"Two pints for the wanker," the waitress said, rolling her eyes.

"Wanker," Flynn laughed, "I really love that word."

"I don't think it was meant to be a compliment," I said, but my voice was drowned out by cheers as a woman in her twenties took the stage. As the music faded, she stood before the folk band, dressed as an elf in a long green gown. She had naturally blonde hair, not a blonde wig like some other patrons.

"Welcome, my friends, to Oxford's seventh annual Fellowship Cosplay Convention!" she boomed into the mic with a Scottish accent. The crowd erupted into applause, hooting and hollering.

A very drunk man in horse riding regalia stood atop a chair, spilling his beverage everywhere. He hiccupped, "Thank – Thank you, fair maiden, Lucy."

The elf on stage, whose name was apparently Lucy, replied, "Easy friend. We still have three days of celebration to go. You might want to pace yourself a bit." Speaking of pacing, Lucy the Elf paced across the stage. "The next seventy-two hours will be filled with drinking." The crowd roared. "Dancing." It erupted again. "The smoking of pipeweed." Another cheer. "And good times for all!" The crowd roared in approval, but as soon as the cheers reached a fever-pitch, two men dressed as orcs, monstrous mythological baddies with giant fangs and even bigger underbites, joined Lucy on stage, met by a series of playful jeers.

Our waitress came back, practically dropping our drinks down on the table. Something told me she really didn't fancy us, especially Flynn.

"I think she likes me," Flynn said, almost on cue.

The smaller of the two orcs stepped up to the microphone, announcing the rules and clues for the scavenger hunt in a scratchy voice. I backhanded Flynn so hard that his pint nearly fell from his hand before he could take a sip.

"Hey, watch it!" Flynn shouted.

"Did you hear that? There's a scavenger hunt," I said.

The second orc now leaned into the microphone, informing the crowd that copies of the rules could be found online. The orcs circulated around the room, handing out flyers, but despite my outstretched hand, they skipped us. Once all the flyers were distributed, Lucy returned to the microphone, which I presumed smelled of yeast, barley, peanuts, and spit. She asked in a sweet voice, "Is that, everyone?" I thought to myself, with a voice like that, she must be a teacher or whatever the doctors are called that look after kids.

"I have not," a gruff male voice called out. I saw a hand bouncing up and down, seeking attention. "I have not received one, my lady," the voice repeated.

"Who goes there? Show yourself," Lucy said.

The sea of cosplayers parted, revealing an armor-clad dwarf. An exceptionally drunk armor-clad dwarf who stood no more than four and a half feet tall. He climbed onto a chair to get Lucy's attention, failing to notice the parting of his fellow cosplayers.

"Well, hello there," Lucy greeted. "Why don't you come up to grab a flyer, my brave soldier?"

The dwarf's armor was magnificent. It included a steel studded leather chest plate, matching arm guards, and gauntlets. He wore a helmet with horns on both sides, just above his ears. When he tried to bow, the chair wobbled, sending him face-first into another cosplayer dressed as a wood-elf in green tights, wearing one of the light-blonde wigs I mentioned earlier.

"Whoa there, little fella, watch where you're going!" the elf barked.

The dwarf sprang upright, his head bobbing. "Little fella? Who do you think you're talking to? You wingless fairy! I suggest you get out of my way before I cut off your Spock ears with my battle-axe!" The dwarf's accent changed, revealing he was from the United States, like us.

The elf grinned as three of his friends, also dressed as elves, rushed to his side. "This just gets better and better. He's a dwarf and a Yank!" The elves laughed pompously.

Without warning, two dwarves, neither bona fide dwarves, just ones in costumes, bolted onto the scene in aid of their brethren. The older of the two crossed his arms defiantly. "No one talks to a dwarf of the mountain that way. Even if that dwarf happens to be an American!"

The drunk American dwarf nodded in agreement.

"Gentlemen, please. Good folk of Oxford and Middle Earth, I beg of you," Lucy pleaded for order but only received chaos as more costumed folk entered the fray.

"This is literally the best day of my life," I told Flynn, who was downing his pint.

"It sure is something," Flynn said with a belch.

Just before I would have sworn punches were about to fly, or maybe a barstool or two, the lights flickered and dimmed. One of the men dressed as a wizard with a giant gray cloak pounded his staff against the floorboards. "Silence!" he screamed, which got everyone's attention immediately as his voice echoed off the rafters. "Now," he lowered his voice, "can we just enjoy the party? Have the books taught us nothing if we refuse to work together?" The costumed dwarves and elves came to an understanding after a long pause as tempers in the pub lowered. The wizard turned to Lucy, rested his chin on the top of his staff, and nodded.

"How about some more music?" The crowd cheered as Lucy curtsied, exiting stage left. The folk band kicked things back off with a traditional tune.

To my surprise, the drunken dwarf stumbled his way to our table, laying his head near Flynn's arm. "I'm Roger," he said, belching into his hand. "Oops, I think some of that got in my beard." Roger wiped away at his matted brownish-red beard, cleaning out remnants of whatever he had for lunch. Then, he extended his hand to me to shake, which I reluctantly did, immediately scrubbing my palm into a wet napkin.

"I'm Dean. This is Flynn."

"Pleasure," Flynn said, refusing to shake hands.

"Heard you talkin' earlier," Roger said. "Where you from?" Roger took off his helmet. He had long brown shaggy hair with a knob pulled into a man bun up top.

"Just outside of Pittsburgh," I said. "You?"

"Cleveland," Roger replied.

"No kidding!" Flynn exclaimed. "Small world...no offense."

"Oh, look at you. Making fun of the vertically challenged guy," Roger said.

"I said no offense," Flynn tried to calm Roger but only made things worse as the dwarf reached over his head to grip the heel of his battle-axe.

At first, I thought it was a joke until Roger held the axe high in the air while grumbling obscene words. "Whoa, Roger, wait," I tried to reason with him, but before reason even reached his eardrums, the weapon's weight caused Roger to topple over again. This time his momentum took him backwards. He hit his head on the table behind us, knocking him out cold before his body hit the floor. Being my first time in a bar, I wondered if this was normal behavior. I had never seen anyone pass out like that. I looked down at Roger. He looked so peaceful in a weird drunken coma sort of way as he began to snore at the foot of our booth.

"Next time, let's go to Disney," Flynn said. I nodded as the waitress returned to our table with the bill.

"Get you lot anything else?" she asked.

Roger awakened and sprang upright as if nothing had happened, bouncing back into my sight like an old-fashioned inflatable punching clown.

"Blood sausage… Fish and Chips," Roger shouted in an insulting British accent.

"Beg your pardon?" the waitress replied.

"Pip-pip cheerio. Look at me, mates, I'm Mary Poppins!" Roger spun around in circles with his index fingers poking down atop his head.

"Boys, I think we have a problem here," the waitress called out.

"A spoonful of sugar makes the medicine go down, the medicine go down, the medicine go—" Before Roger could finish his verse, he wound up and smacked the waitress across the backside of her jeans.

"Fetch me a brew, my lovely!" he said.

She immediately returned the gesture, belting Roger right across the face, leaving a handprint on his cheek. Honestly, it served him right.

The three men cloaked in wraith costumes suddenly appeared before us, towering over Roger. Roger spun around to face them, saluted, and mockingly said, "Hallo Gov'nah!"

The first wraith, the one that appeared to be the leader, folded his arms across his chest, turning his hidden face in my direction. "I think it's time you and little mate here cleared out." The man's voice was deep. He sounded like a criminal.

"What?" I cried. "We don't even know him."

"Of course you do, Dean from Pittsburgh," Roger said to my disappointment.

"You love birds take your pet and leave, now!"

"Look, we don't want any trouble," Flynn tried to diffuse the situation.

"Pfft," Roger blew a raspberry, spraying spit all over the wraiths' cloaks. "Go back to your mom's basement with your plastic swords."

The second wraith, the biggest of the three, easily six-foot-four and three-hundred pounds, slammed his boot into the middle of Roger's chest. I watched in awe as Roger was sent airborne. He slammed into a neighboring table where chips, beer, plates, forks, and knives exploded like bomb shrapnel. The third wraith was the shortest of the three, but he was definitely not a small man. He was built like a rugby player, and I could tell his arms hidden beneath his cloak were probably the size of tree trunks. He nudged his friends aside and pulled a sword from a sheath that was draped over his shoulders. From what I knew of sword types, it appeared to be a broadsword. He held it in the air, reflections of light and candle flames flickering against the polished silver. He thrust downward with amazing speed and power, and to our shock, he cleaved the table in two!

"Well, that isn't a plastic sword," Roger said.

I stood, grabbed Flynn by the arm, scurried toward the door, and burst through. As our feet hit the pavement, I could hear one of the orcs inside roar out, "Looks like meat's back on the menu, boys!"

I ran without knowing where we were going, urging Flynn to keep up. We dashed past families and tourists while dodging oncoming traffic. I almost bowled over a girl, probably my age. I assumed she was from the pub, trying to stop me, so I juked right, dodging her like a running back in Madden. We ended up racing toward a dense thicket.

"Dean," the wind carried a voice that screamed my name, or at least that's what I thought I had heard.

"Did you hear that?" I asked Flynn.

"Hear what?" Flynn panted.

"It's probably nothing."

"Dean." I heard the voice again

"Okay. That time I heard it!" Flynn said.

"They're getting closer," I shouted. Still running at full speed, I cranked my head around, expecting to see the entirety of the pub chasing after us. The voice was definitely female. It was probably our waitress. In the chaos, Flynn either didn't pay or didn't leave a tip. But when I got a glimpse of what I thought would be a small army following us, led by the waitress, I only saw a girl. The same girl who tried to stop me in the street.

"Dean, look out!" she shouted.

"Huh?" I questioned, turning my head forward just in time to see the huge trunk of a tree. Splat! I plowed into it with so much force that I bounced off it, landing five feet back, causing acorns to rain down beside me. My ears rang so badly that it reminded me of the time I stood next to a cannon that was fired off at a high school football game. My vision blurred, and all I could make out were dark spots. I tried to stand; I felt like I could, but Flynn held me down by my shoulders. After a very woozy minute, the girl who was calling out for me came into view. She knelt down, hovering above me. She brushed her delicate hand across my forehead.

"You're bleeding," she said in an angelic voice. I recognized this voice. My eyes began to focus. The first thing I noticed was the ruby-red color of her lips. The next thing I saw was the radiant glow of her chestnut eyes. In my daze, it took me a moment, but not much longer, then it finally sank in.

"Liv," I tried to say as coherently as possible, and it was the last thing I remember saying before I passed out and the world went black around me.

BACKPACK, BACKPACK

"Why are we walking through the forest?" I asked as Liv led our way through the thick woods. I couldn't believe it. I had finally met my BOFF and most likely had post-concussion syndrome. Knowing my luck, I probably wouldn't even remember this.

"For starters," Liv said as she swept aside twigs to clear our path, "those guys might still be following us. Well, following you, technically. And this just happens to be a shortcut," she added. Liv wore distressed jeans with rips above both knees, a white tank top, and a black sweater. Her hair fell just above her shoulders, with a silver alligator clip holding it back on the side of her head. She turned to look at me, or so I thought.

"What is it?" I asked when I realized she was looking past me. I turned to see Flynn doubled over, panting with his hands on his knees.

"Can we just take a break," Flynn asked, gasping for air. "Because that was insane." I turned to Liv, who nodded in agreement, then dropped to the ground beneath a giant tree.

"What did you guys do, anyway?" Liv asked. "And where's your friend? The uh, you know—" Liv held her arm out at waist height. She meant the little guy.

"His name's Roger. But he's not our friend," Flynn said.

"Too bad the wraiths didn't believe that," I said.

"And why were wraiths chasing you?" Liv asked.

"I don't even know where to start," I said.

"You can start by telling her we made some larpers really mad." Flynn played with the dirt on the ground, collecting it in the shape of a volcano.

"Cosplayers," I corrected. "Not larpers."

"That's what I said," Flynn was lost.

Liv tossed me a bottle of water. I took a long swig, then tightened the cap, crunching and crinkling the plastic because I liked the way it sounded. I tossed the bottle back to her. "You two haven't truly met, have you?" I said as I glanced sideways at both Flynn and Liv at once.

"Not officially, though I have seen some pretty sweet dance moves."

"Don't even start," I stopped Flynn in his tracks, hoping to save us from further embarrassment, but it was too late.

"Not my proudest moment," Liv blushed, her cheeks turning a light shade of pink that was in perfect contrast to her fair skin.

"Liv, this is Flynn. Flynn, Liv." Now that introductions were out of the way, I started to regather my thoughts. I had so many questions racing through my mind: about the wraiths, about the cosplay convention, about Flynn's great-grandpa, but mostly, about Liv.

"How did you find us? How did you know we were at the pub? Why haven't you answered my texts? And are you bleeding?" Through the chaos, I just now noticed that Liv had a cut running down her forearm. Bright red blood trickled along her wrist, down the side of her hand, dripping onto the roots of a Goat Willow.

"I must have scratched it on the branches," she said, pressing a napkin against the cut on her arm. "And I didn't know you were at the pub. I was taking a walk with my granddad when I saw you, or at least I thought I saw you. I called your name. At first, you didn't turn, but I was sure it was you. Americans tend to stand out in Oxford, especially when being chased by wraiths in high tops."

"And the texts?" Flynn asked. "Moyers has been trying to reach you all day, but you just ghosted him."

"Ghosted him? Wow! Shots fired," Liv said.

"Sorry, Liv. He's just —"

"Direct?" she said.

"Protective," I said.

"Well, maybe tell your guard dog to back off a bit," Liv said. "If you must know, I haven't answered your texts because I haven't received any texts from you. I've been waiting for you to message me all day."

"I sent at least fifteen," I said.

"Three less than I sent you. Did you turn on international roaming?" she asked.

"Inter—what now?"

"Roaming, did you enable it?"

I pulled my phone from my pocket and wiped away a greasy smudge. I thumbed through my settings until I saw an unchecked box that read 'Enable International Roaming.' I pressed my finger down on the checkbox, and it turned green. Within milliseconds, our phones began to chirp with message notifications. A wave of panic hit me as I scanned through Liv's messages. I blurted out, "Don't look at the last one!" Again I was too late.

"Look, Liv, I understand if you don't want to see me, but you could at least be decent about it," she read aloud, her eyebrows pinching in anger. "Decent about it?" Her voice rose in pitch.

"I'm sorry. I thought you were ignoring me."

"Ignoring you? You're the one who —"

"Guys, I hate to interrupt," Flynn said, the thing that people always say when they have zero issues interrupting, "but do you hear that?"

"Hear what?" Liv said.

"Humming," I said as I got to my feet. There was a low-pitched hum that filled the air. It hurt to listen to, like a dull knife that pierced my ears. Another sensation soon took over as I lifted my hands to cover my ears. My chest. It burned. I clutched my hands over my heart, wincing in pain. It was almost the same feeling I had on the airplane, only ten times worse.

"What's wrong?" Liv shouted.

"Are you having a heart attack?" Flynn asked. I winced again; the pain worsened as if the prod dug deeper into my flesh. "Raise your hand and say a simple sentence," Flynn said as he rushed to my side.

"That's for a stroke, genius," Liv said.

"It feels like something's biting me!" I cried. I lifted my shirt, pulling it away from my body and chest.

"Dude, this is pretty inappropriate," Flynn shut his eyes, looking away.

85

"Look!" Liv shouted. She pointed at me in astonishment. Beneath my layers of clothing, I wore the necklace my dad gave me years ago. Dangling from the necklace was the amulet. The symbol etched into the silver amulet was glowing, like the time I saw at the house, but this was different. Much different.

At first, the colors of amber and blue glowed like the layers of a flame. Then, the amulet started to turn a shade of green. "Take out the batteries," Flynn said.

I tried to pry the amulet from my skin. Moving it an inch felt like lifting Thor's hammer or the sword from *The Sword in the Stone*, only not the one at Disney World, the real one... Want to hear something cool? When I was eight, I actually lifted that sword at Disney right out of the stone. People swarmed around me. It was kind of a big deal. Mom even took a picture of it. But I guess that should have been a story for a different time.

After I unseated the amulet from my chest, it started to move. The thing had a mind of its own. I released my grip, and shockingly, the amulet levitated. The charm shot to the right causing me to crane my neck along with it. The green color intensified. The necklace chain spun around, causing the amulet to whip to the side. The symbol turned a shade of red, and the whole thing started to pull me forward.

"It wants something," Liv said.

"The necklace?" I asked.

"Well, the charm, I believe, more so than the necklace," Liv said.

"Guys, far be it from me to be the voice of reason here," Flynn said. "But are you even listening to yourselves?"

A feeling of familiarity washed over me. An extreme case of Deja vu. It must have been pretty obvious, too, as Flynn looked at me curiously.

"What is it, Dean?" Liv asked, also taking notice.

"There's something you need to know. Something I need to tell you."

"You're a government agent?" Flynn joked.

"I'm not joking, Flynn. It's about the amulet. My dad told me it was magic."

Flynn laughed as he shook his head. But as he stared at me, waiting for me to join in the laughter, he realized I was being serious. "Magic?"

"Yeah. Real magic. He also said it was from another realm."

"Of course it is," Flynn said, clearly thinking I was out of my mind.

"He said it would guide me."

"When did he tell you that? When you were six? Bro, I can barely remember what I had for breakfast, and you remember stuff from seven years ago."

"Seven years?" Math obviously wasn't Flynn's strong suit, but I didn't have time to worry about that. "No," I said. "In a dream. He was going to tell me more about it when he..." I stopped speaking as sorrow overtook me.

"Look, bro, I get it," Flynn said. "With what happened to your dad, I understand. I mean, I was there for you during all the years of your Rings phase. I even let you dress me up as a Gork for Halloween."

"Orc," I corrected.

"Whatever," Flynn said. "I stayed by your side through high school, even though you never even kissed a girl."

"Really, dude?" My face flushed as I tried to avoid eye contact with Liv. This had turned extremely embarrassing.

"But," Flynn continued, "there are two major problems with this story you've conjured up." He paced circles around me, touching the tips of his outstretched fingers together. "One, you're following a necklace based on something you heard in a dream. And two, magic isn't real."

I crouched low to the ground and said, "Then how do you explain this?" I took the necklace from around my neck, holding the amulet inches from the ground, allowing it to dangle from its chain. The charm began to swirl wildly in a circular motion above the grass, dirt, and uprooted chunks of a tree.

"It's probably magnetic," Flynn said, sounding confident.

"Or it's magic," Liv chimed in, her eyes wide as they followed the charm like a hypnotist. The charm stopped abruptly, then pointed itself due south in a deeper shade of red. It tugged repeatedly but ultimately remained pointing south.

"It wants us to follow it." I stood up and walked behind the amulet as it guided us through the forest, swerving in and out of trees, over a dry creek bed, and into a thicket of thorn bushes. Despite getting cuts from the thorns, I was so focused on the amulet that I barely felt pain.

Suddenly, in the middle of the valley of thorns, the necklace stopped pulling me as the amulet fell limp.

"It stopped," Liv said, behind me, also covered in miniature slices from the thorns.

"I can feel it," I said.

"Feel what?" Liv asked.

"There's something here." Instinctively I dropped to my knees. I started to dig, but I had no idea why or what I was digging for. I burrowed and tunneled and pulled chunks of rock hand over fist. After my hands were thoroughly filthy and my nails were packed with mud, I felt something.

"What is it?" Liv asked.

"It's a backpack." I pulled a tattered black backpack from the ground. It was covered in mud. I unzipped it and spied another smaller bag inside. This one was of the Ziploc variety. I could see something silver shimmering inside, so I dropped the backpack at my feet, ripped the top of the Ziploc open with my teeth, and pulled out another necklace. This necklace also had an amulet hanging from a clasp with the exact same symbol as mine, though the chain was thoroughly rusted. Before I could even speak or process the strange, almost impossible, coincidence, the ground started to rumble.

Flynn took a step back. Paranoid, he scanned all around as if predators were closing in. "Earthquake?" he said, sounding as if he'd almost hoped that was the case.

"Would a magnet do that?" Liv asked sarcastically.

"You clearly haven't watched *Lost*." Flynn was enamored with *Lost*, a television show about survivors of a plane crash on a mysterious island, but that was neither here nor there.

Before Liv could answer, the two charms began to move rhythmically, almost in sync with one another. They were dancing, circling, bobbing upward and downward, zipping this way and that. I tried to pry them apart, to hold them at arm's length, but the force was too strong. As I struggled to contain them, they pulled me up, nearly lifting me off my feet, then... BAM! The amulets collided with a force that sent me flying backward. A white flash filled the air, temporarily blinding me. I squinted hard, rubbing at my eyes, and when the world came back into view, I saw that my friends had also been knocked down. I pushed off the ground with my hands, lifting myself to my feet. I moved over to Flynn, who refused my assistance. Instead, he crawled up a tree stump, lumbering upright.

I made my way to Liv and extended my hand. She grabbed onto me. I was surprised to feel how delicate her skin was.

"Are you going to lift me, or should I stand on my own?" she asked. I realized I must have looked foolish, standing frozen in the moment, thinking about her velvety skin. What a creep I must look like.

I lifted Liv off the ground with a heave, but my newfound strength surprised me. Yesterday, I could barely carry a basket of clothes up the stairs without breaking a sweat, but now I was lifting Liv with ease. I pulled her toward me with such force that she stumbled into my arms. We were so close that I regretted ordering garlic with my fish and chips, worrying that a noxious odor might be coming from my mouth. We locked eyes for a second, which seemed like an eternity. I felt sweat dripping from my palms, and after more than a decade and a half on this planet, I finally understood the meaning of "butterflies in the stomach." My heart sank into my belly, fluttering about. I think Liv must have felt the same, or perhaps my garlic breath was affecting her because she broke eye contact and stared awkwardly at the ground.

"Dean," she said with a tremble in her voice. "What happened to the second charm?"

"Huh?" I slowly glanced at my right hand. The rusty chain I pulled from the plastic bag was still within my grip, but the amulet was missing. I shifted my focus to my left hand, noticing the amulet that Dad gave me had grown. It was at least twice the size as before. It glistened as a stray ray of light penetrated the thick forest, striking it. The amulet glowed a soft purple briefly before returning to its normal polished silver finish.

"Like I said, magnets." Flynn boasted as he swiped away at the dirt that covered his jeans.

As I ignored Flynn's deduction, I realized that Liv was still close. I could feel her warm breath on the base of my neck, sending shivers down my spine. I fumbled with the chain, and charm, then stepped backward, trying to play it cool. "So, Liv, what do you think about—" I was interrupted as a noise of rustling leaves, branches, and a clamoring of footsteps echoed behind us.

"They found us," Flynn warned.

ALL ROADS LEAD TO GNOME

My legs felt heavy, and before I could move a muscle, two men burst through the trees. Well, not exactly men, but they burst through the tree line nonetheless. They crashed into me, knocking me back to the ground for what felt like the fifty-first time in the last hour. Liv was far more nimble; she sidestepped the pair and watched as I tumbled downward, landing on my rear end and skidding to a halt.

The appearance of these two strangers was… well, strange, and it must have been obvious that I was staring because the heavier of the two gave me a stern look.

"No need to be staring," he said, rubbing under his twitching nose. The two strangers who had burst into the clearing were short, even shorter than my fourth-grade brother, only they were much older. Both of the strangers had tiny packs strapped to their shoulders and wore yellow shirts with blue vests and baggy capris. The larger one was about three and a half feet tall. Judging by his appearance, he probably weighed more than me, so I could only guess one hundred and fifty pounds, while the smaller one was the same height but weighed half as much. Their curly brownish-blonde hair reminded me of spaghetti noodles. The most striking things about their appearance were their faces and feet. Their noses were almost pointy, though still human in shape, while their feet were huge. Their toes were particularly unusual, covered in thick, fur-like black hairs.

"I think I've broken something," the larger of the two groaned. He pulled a pipe from his back pocket; it was split into two. "Yep, it's broken."

"Not your father's pipe, Tubb," the smaller one said, meaning the big guy's name must have been Tubb. What an unfortunate name, I thought. "He's going to be blaming me, you know," he continued.

"Don't be a fool, Griff. He knows how clumsy I be," Tubb said, paying no attention to me, Flynn, and Liv. I felt my eyes squinting as I tried to concentrate on *what* these two were. They looked like grown-up mousey garden gnomes, had the feet of Halflings from stories Dad and I had read, and they spoke like high-pitched, miniature pirates.

Flynn wrapped his hands beneath my armpits, hoisting me to my feet.

"Look, uh, fellas," I said, trying to be sensitive to their stature as the two spun my way, perking up at attention. "Back there at the pub…"

"There be a pub?" Griff asked curiously.

"Back where's about?" Tubb chimed in.

93

"What I'm trying to say is," I continued, "we didn't want to fight anyone."

"Fight? What in Second Realm are you blathering about?" Tubb said.

"The phrase is what are you *blabbering about*," Flynn said, wrong as usual.

"I swear we didn't know about the cosplay, and we definitely didn't know the dwarf," I said.

Tubb's expression swirled with confusion as he looked around. "Didn't know you had dwarves here in these parts."

"You are from the cosplay convention, aren't you?" Liv asked.

"What be a cosplay?" Griff asked. His face was a lighter complexion compared to Tubb's. It also appeared less weathered, suggesting he might be a full decade younger than his companion.

Tubb elbowed Griff in the gut. "You guessed it, lad," he said, referring to Liv. I couldn't believe he just called her lad. "We are indeed from the convention of the cosplaying." Tubb smiled, flashing his big pearly white chompers that could probably bite through a log. "I be Tubb, and this be my companion, Griff."

"If you aren't looking for a fight, what are you doing in the woods?" Flynn asked, suddenly suspicious of the minis. "And what are you dressed up as?"

"Dressed up as?" Griff took offense. "We be Gnomelings. Tell me, what costume are you wearing? And why does it have a rooster standing on a pumpkin?" Griff asked, referring to the logo on Flynn's Tottenham kit. "Oomph!" Griff grunted as he was again elbowed in the stomach.

"What my friend be meaning is we be dressed as Gnomelings. We're looking for mushrooms for the festival."

"Never heard of a Gnomeling. And what do you mean, festival?" Liv said. "Are you talking about the scavenger hunt?" Liv, similar to Flynn, grew suspicious, though more from a curiosity standpoint.

"Aye. The hunt. Exactly. Are you three in the sca-ven-ger hunt?" Tubb said, trying to pronounce the word scavenger like this was the first time he'd ever heard it or said it.

"No. We were being chased by the wraiths," I said.

"Wraiths and dwarves? Here?!" Griff jumped behind Tubb for protection, his limbs trembling with fear.

"They aren't real wraiths. Relax," Flynn said. This brought Griff out of his temporary hiding place. "I have another question. Why do you have hair all over your feet? Is that part of your costume?"

"Body glue," Griff said without hesitation.

"Puberty," Tubb said at the exact same moment. The two shot sideways glances at one another, then Tubb corrected, "Puberty be the brand of the body glue. Lots and lots of puberty. Right Griff?"

"Right. I myself have required an entire bottle of puberty. If you'd like, we can share our puberty with you threes." He smiled at me, trying to look trustworthy, but something about these two was off, way off.

I had almost forgotten about the amulet for a moment. In a panic, I checked my pockets, then scanned the forest floor when I realized it was still in my hands. I glanced at Tubb. He was bent down, picking out the dirt between his long hairy toes. As he stood up, his eyes locked onto my amulet. "It's you," he muttered, talking only to the charm and not any of us. "You're bigger than I expected."

"What's bigger than you expected? This?" I held the amulet up.

"He must be the one," Griff whispered loud enough for me to hear. "He does look like the one."

"Shhh!" Tubb shushed. "Not another word from you. Not until we're sure. Remember the spies? The shifter of the shapes? The giant man called Gandalf that you thought was a wizard at the museum of wax?"

"He tasted like a candle," Griff nodded confidently as Tubb reached into his belt, pulling out a long wrinkled piece of parchment.

"What is that?" I asked.

"It must be from the scavenger hunt," Flynn said.

Tubb unrolled the paper, revealing a detailed, hand-drawn map. Griff rocked back and forth, seeming uneasy, almost like he was trying to keep a secret. "I fancy it's more than that," he said, teasing and squealing, much to Tubb's dismay. "If you be who I think you be, I fancy it's a map that will lead us to..."

"Griff!" Tubb growled.

Griff looked at the amulet, then the parchment, then at me. "But, Tubb, I think... I really do think it's – HIM." Only now, he was staring right at me, not the amulet, while his voice was loud enough for the entire town to hear. The way he stared felt strange. No longer looking at me like he was hiding something but staring in admiration. "I think we've found him indeed." Griff politely clapped his hands. Tubb looked up for a brief moment, then back down at the map, only for his eyes to once again lock on to me. They both slowly stood, gawking, mouths open, and I swear that Griff started to drool.

"These two are nutters," Liv said, stepping in front of me. "What's the matter with you? Snap out of it." She clapped her hands in Tubb's face.

Tubb shook himself, "Is that amulet – yours?"

"Yes," I answered. As he inched closer, the amulet started to glow again, the purple glow we had observed a few minutes earlier after the new charm had collided with the one Dad gave me.

"Give him the map, Tubb. Give it to him," Griff said. Tubb stepped forward and presented me with the map, holding it out as if it were an offering. He motioned for me to sit on the ground, so I did, flattening the map on a level plot of earth. Liv dropped to my side, followed by Flynn. They scoured the forest floor, finding four nearby rocks, placing them on the corners of the map to hold them down.

My eyes perused the parchment. It was old and worn down, and the color was the shade of a vintage newspaper. The paper had major creases, and black smudges randomly stained across it. In the world of comics, this would have been worthless. I continued to scan, spotting landmark after landmark, all here in England. Four of the landmarks had different colored X's drawn onto them. The first that caught my attention was a wooded portion, where the color of the X was violet. "Is this us? Is this where we are now?"

"It is," Liv said. "It's exactly where we are. Exactly where we—"

"Where we found the backpack with the necklace and the —" Flynn started.

"The second amulet," I finished their thoughts.

"You already had one?" Tubb asked. "Of course. That's why it wasn't on the map."

"Where did you get it?" Griff said. "The amulet you had with you when you arrived."

"My dad gave it to me when I was little."

"And what be your name?" Tubb said. "It wouldn't happen to be Dean, would it?"

"It is. This is Flynn, and that's Liv. But how did you know?" I asked.

"If your front name be Dean," Tubb continued. "What be your back name?"

Back name? I suppose he meant my last name. "Moyers," I said. "Why? What be your back name?" I had no idea why I was starting to talk like them.

"Moyers. Dean Moyers," Griff said as if he were pondering an ancient riddle.

"To break the curse. To stop destroyers. Join the charms. And find the Moyers," Tubb sang in a breathy tone.

"I am so freaking lost," Flynn said.

"As am I," Liv said.

"Me too," I said. "Can you guys just explain what the heck is happening right now? What does this mean?"

"It means it is you. I mean, you are him," Tubb said.

Griff whispered, "He has to be." His eyes widened as he stared at me like I was some sort of celebrity.

"What are you talking about? Who am I?" I asked. I felt like such an outsider in this conversation. My friends looked as puzzled as I felt.

Tubb said, "There's only one way to find out. Hold the amulet over the X's on the map." I followed his instructions, placing the amulet over the markers. The first marker had no name, but there was a sketch resembling a stone well with a wooden bucket hanging over a black hole. But nothing happened.

"Try the next one," Griff pleaded.

So I did, moving the amulet across the page like the planchette of an Ouija board, gliding effortlessly until it reached the London Eye, one of Europe's most popular tourist destinations, essentially a giant Ferris wheel. But still, nothing happened.

"What's it supposed to do?" Liv asked.

"Shhh!" Griff shushed.

"Try it," Tubb said, pointing to the last X. "Try it over Warwick Castle." The castle appeared massive on paper, and, according to the map's scale, it was located far north of our position, between us and Birmingham.

I lifted the amulet. It drifted toward the marker. "Nothing's happening," I said.

"Keep trying," Griff encouraged.

"Try what? I'm holding it over the map, just like you said, but nothing is—Wait!" I stopped as a faint sensation tickled my fingertips. "I feel something." The amulet began to shake. Griff took my hand and guided it downward, bringing the amulet closer to the paper. The silver charm scraped against the parchment, against the drawing of the castle.

"Look!" Griff shouted. "It's glowing." And indeed it was. The charm began to twirl, revolving in mesmerizing spirals. It spun so fast that it began to burn a black oval around the castle, with a thin line of smoke wafting from the parchment, creating a tiny tornado.

"Still think it's just a magnet?" Liv teased Flynn.

Words appeared on the map, just below the burnt area beneath the castle. Only, they weren't written in English or any other language I had ever seen. "There's some sort of message," I said. "You knew this would happen. How?"

"I must be guessing lucky," Tubb said.

"What is that? Arabic?" Flynn asked.

"Gnomarian," Griff said.

"Gno-what-ian?" Flynn replied.

"Gnomarian, the common tongue of all Gnomelings in Second Realm."

"I don't get it," Flynn said as he nearly went cross-eyed.

Tubb patted him on the shoulders. "Humans rarely do. Though, you are the first we be talking to in over thirty years."

"I'm sorry. What?" Flynn snapped from his daze. "Did you call us humans?"

"Yeah, guys," Liv gave Tubb a friendly nudge. "I think you can cut the act now. We told you that we're not in the scavenger hunt, so there's no need to worry about losing points for breaking character or anything like that."

I was too wrapped up in the sights before me to process the conversation. I was completely spellbound. "It's the most beautiful writing I've ever seen," I said.

Griff nodded. "Especially the double loop on the Gumbar twist"

"What's a Gumbar twist?" I had no idea, but I just had to find out.

"It's the sixth character in the alphabet," Griff boasted. "Every Gnomeling knows this."

"Gnomeling," Liv said. "There you go with that word again. What is it? I've never heard of a Gnomeling."

"Uh, don't you be worried about that. What my thick-headed friend here meant to say is, everyone in the scavenger hunt knows about the Gumbar twist. We watched a video cassette on it," Tubb corrected.

"Everyone?" Liv asked.

"Videocassette?" Flynn questioned.

"Indeed. Right after they gave us a fresh bucket of puberty," Griff added.

"What does it say?" I lifted the amulet from the paper as the spinning ceased. The glow faded.

Tubb ran his finger over the inscription. He cleared his throat and began to read. "The door is locked. But not for long. They come inside to sing death's song. Your time runs short, for this I fear. A message I give to make things clear." Tubb abruptly stopped reading as a low grumble, almost a groan, reverberated behind us. "Griff, you didn't be skipping breakfast again, did you?"

"Wasn't me," Griff said.

A loud snort startled me. I glanced to my right in time to see a blast of hot air blow Griff's curly locks of hair forward, followed by a loud thud and the sound of giant boots stomping the ground.

"Do either of you three be havin' a large elephant or a bear for a pet?" Griff asked just as a gloved metallic hand landed on my shoulder. I flinched as fingers pressed down on my muscle, rendering me immobile. I tilted my head around and caught a glimpse of the wraiths. Two of them, towering over us.

WHEN IN DOUBT, PINKY OUT

I wiggled free, and Flynn, Liv, Tubb, and Griff backed up slowly. The costumed wraiths towered over us, dressed in their customary dark cloaks. The most shocking part was that they didn't come alone; they had dark brown, mangy, and severely malnourished horses. We continued to slowly retreat, inching back until we were butted up against a large tree, all of us unprepared for the third wraith who suddenly appeared from behind us, scaring us half to death.

"Going somewhere?" the third wraith asked.

"Who are you?" I asked.

"We are the brothers Pegg," the wraith responded. He's the one I believed to be their leader. Honestly, I was surprised at how forthcoming he was, especially as he continued. "I'm William. These are my brothers, Burt and Tommy."

"Mister Bilbo's trolls?" I thought out loud.

"Who?" Tommy said.

"Nevermind." I didn't have a good feeling. This encounter seemed a bit extreme for a misunderstanding at a pub. It definitely no longer fell under the category of coincidence. Instinctively, I tucked my necklace deep into my pocket and started to refold the parchment.

"What was that you just put in your pocket?" Tommy asked.

"Just a chain I found on the street," I replied with a terrible lie. "It's rusted and worthless," I said, pulling a small portion of the chain out for them to see, keeping the amulet inside the pocket.

Burt, the giant of a wraith, marched over to Tubb's side, poking at his belly. He crept down, his hooded face inches from Tubb's. "Look at this fat little thing. I don't know what circus you crawled out of, but helping these kids was a big mistake."

Griff stood up as tall as he could on his hairy feet, staying close to Tubb's side. Curiosity got the best of him, and he stuck his finger inside Burt's dark face hole until he hit something.

"Oi. That's me stinkin' eye. What are you bloody doin'?" Burt cried.

"They aren't real. They aren't real wraiths, Tubb," Griff said with glee.

"I know," Tubb whispered. "Pipe down."

The wraith, who went by William, circled the group, stopping in front of me. "What is that you're holding?" he asked.

"A poster," I said.

"What kind of poster?"

"A soccer team," I said.

"Manchester," Flynn added.

"Which Manchester?"

"North, I think?" I said, clearly out of my depths in sporting knowledge.

"North?" Tommy barked.

"City. He meant City," Flynn corrected. "The only true Manchester soccer team."

"There you go calling it soccer. It's football." Tommy said, his voice much higher than his brothers'. "You kick a ball with your feet."

"Technically, they kick a ball with their feet in American football as well," Burt countered.

"Shut up, Burt!" William shouted in a gravelly voice. "Your brother's making a point."

"I knows he is, but I'm just saying."

With the Pegg brothers engaged in a heated debate, I knew it was time to seize the opportunity. I got Flynn's attention, then tugged on Liv's sleeve, motioning for us to slip away.

"Why can't you just admit I was right?" Tommy said. I felt like, while he was the smallest of the three, he must have been the middle sibling. He acted like a middle sibling.

"That's what this is about, ain't it?" Burt shouted. "You always have to be right."

"No. It's because I'm being reasonable. That is why mum loves me best." Tommy got in Burt's face and poked his finger into his chest, thumping his breastbone.

"I'm mum's favorite, not you," Burt cried.

"We all know that mum hated the both of you," William joined in the competition for their mother's love. "She told me last Tuesday."

We continued to slither away, crawling and ducking under branches, watching our step to avoid making noise. I stopped and peeked over a rock to ensure the little guys had followed, but they weren't with us. They were still standing petrified against the tree, clinging to each other, afraid to move.

"What are they doing?" Liv asked. "They're gonna get killed."

At the same time, the wraiths also noticed the little ones were the only two left.

"Where'd they go?" William grunted, grabbing Griff by the collar of his coat. "Where did your friends run off to?" He lifted Griff effortlessly into the air. Griff's giant hairy feet dangled five feet off the ground.

"What are we gonna do?" Flynn asked.

"I don't know," I said. "We can't just leave them."

"Well, those guys have swords, so we could just… Yeah, on second thought, let's just leave 'em." Flynn immediately turned, continuing his escape.

I heard one of the wraiths yell out, Tommy, by the sound of his nasally voice. "I guess we'll just chop off your little piggy to see if you squeal." He pried Griff's pinky finger from his clenched fist.

"Not my tea pinky," Griff begged.

Tommy pulled a small dagger from his cloak, sizing up Griff's finger. Tubb tried to rush him, but Burt stopped him with an outstretched hand.

"No!" I growled. Something came over me. Normally, I'd wait for someone else to step in. Normally, my timidity and anxiety would overwhelm me - paralyze me. When it came to trauma response, I was always the one to freeze. Never the one to fight. But something changed. I bolted toward the bite-sized hostages whom I had just met because I knew…somehow, I knew that I had to protect them.

"One…" the wraiths counted, ready to slice Griff's digit from his hand. "Two…" But before they hit three, I leaped off a rock and tackled Tommy the wraith, planting him in a cloud of dust. I bounded upright, facing off against the big one, Burt. Burt pulled his broadsword from a sheath. He thrust it upward above his head, then started to swing down. What the heck was I thinking? I was no hero. I was about to be skewered. I was about to be a kebab. But for what?

"Urghh!" Burt cried out, dropping the sword to the ground before it split me in two. Tubb had buried his fist into Burt's crotch, sending him doubled over in agonizing pain. Tommy lumbered back to an upright position, only for Flynn to tackle him to the ground again. I knew once I joined the fray, Flynn wouldn't leave. Liv barged onto the scene, picking up Tommy's dagger. She attacked William, who, unarmed, scanned the ground for a weapon. His eyes landed on Burt's sword, and he picked it up. Liv swung the dagger wildly, but William ducked and bounced back up, holding the blade's tip against Liv's gut.

"Brave," William said. "Stupid, but brave." He looked at me, pressing the pointy end of the sword harder against Liv's stomach. She winced in pain.

"Stop!" I shouted.

"Give me your prize. Give me that poster," he demanded.

"Don't. You can't, Dean," Griff said.

"If it falls into the wrong hands —" Tubb's words were cut short.

"Quiet!" William ordered. "Give it to me now, or your lady friend gets a belly piercing."

"Don't hurt her!" I said, slowly extending the map to his anxiously awaiting fingers. As his greedy metallic gloves crept closer, I heard a rustling sound encroaching, though no one else heard it. Like my strength hoisting Liv off the ground and my lack of nerves while battling the wraiths, my hearing was somehow enhanced. I thought it might be a side effect of jet lag. The rustling got louder, morphing into the sound of running with heavy panting. Now, everyone had heard it. Heads turned back and forth, trying to figure out the source of the noise. Was it another wraith? Other cosplayers? The cops? Or, my mom rushing into battle to ask why I hadn't used the whistle yet? None of that made sense. Neither did what was actually causing the commotion. It was a surprise, to say the least, as Roger - yes, Roger, our drunken dwarven *friend* from Cleveland, Ohio - crashed onto the scene, taking out William with a club to the back of his knee. William bent backward in pain, allowing Liv to wiggle free. During the chaos, Tommy broke loose of Flynn's grip. He lunged and repeatedly swung at Roger, who somehow nimbly dodged, parried, and deflected the blows. He turned to us, shouting, "Go! Now! Get to the ferry!"

BUCKLES, BERRIES, AND FERRIES

"What ferry?" I asked, confused. "Where?" I don't know why he would have expected me to know.

"Head east, push through the clearing," Roger continued fighting as Burt tried to crawl away. "Over the hill. Then take the path to the left."

"I know where it is," Liv said.

Flynn, Liv, and Tubb were back at my side. Griff lingered in the limbo between us, Roger, and the wraiths. The Pegg brothers regrouped. Despite being wounded, they popped their necks and knuckles, ready to face off against Roger and give him a proper sorting.

Roger didn't waver; instead, he acted as a one-man barrier, shielding us from our foes. "If you want them," Roger swung his arms in small circles ballistically. "Come and claim them." This was too unbelievable to be true. I might have almost cracked a smile if I wasn't scared half to death. Cosplay. Wraiths. An armored dwarf dressed as Gimli fighting and quoting my favorite movie. Two small guys with funny names that looked like a mix of gnomes, moles, and humans. Hidden messages on ancient maps. Magical amulets. What had we gotten ourselves into?

"Run!" Roger shouted as he wrestled the wraiths. "Now!" He kicked Burt in the crotch, making this the second time the wraith had been hit in the bikini area. Burt cried out, his voice sounding more like Tommy's with every strike to the groin. Roger stood over the writhing wraith, puffing his chest out—a true conqueror. Unfortunately for him, he boasted a little too long as Tommy picked up a log and popped Roger on the top of his helmet. Roger's eyes rolled into the back of his head. He hit the ground, out cold, with a thud.

"He looks like a cute little baby Gnomeling," Griff said as Roger rolled into a tight ball, then began to shiver and snore, sucking on his thumb.

"Griff, we be needing to move!" Tubb shouted.

Griff giggled to himself, amused at Roger's current state, then sprinted toward the rest of us.

We took off, at first running as a pack, wolves on the hunt, only we were the ones being hunted. As the forest grew denser, I wondered if we were actually heading east. At the moment, I was in the lead, and I prayed that someone in the group had a strong sense of direction. Otherwise, I was sure to get us lost. I peeked over my shoulder and saw that Tommy and William were right on our tails, with Burt lagging behind, limping, nursing his wounds.

"Don't be lookin' back now, human," Griff said as he and Tubb raced past me in a flash, their knees lifting so high off the ground when they ran they were practically striking their own chins. Shockingly, the pair was quite spry for their stature.

"There he goes again," Flynn said. "Calling us humans."

"He calls everyone that," Tubb added as our two tiny new friends dashed ahead, disappearing from sight. I put my head down and ran after them, faster than I'd ever run before, faster than in gym class, even faster than the time the Renfro twins from three neighborhoods over chased me on their bikes.

After what had to have been a mile, we finally reached the clearing. To my relief, it turned out my sense of direction wasn't half bad after all. I looked back to see the wraiths were gone. "Guys, wait," I said, slowing my pace while scanning the woods. There was no sign of the wraiths, only the sound of chirping birds and gusting winds. "I think we lost them." I should have known better than to say such things because at the exact moment I felt at ease, the Peggs reappeared on horseback.

"Horses! They went back for their fudging horses?" Flynn shouted, substituting fudging with the far more offensive f-word, as he had done on the plane.

The Peggs bounced around on their mangy horses' mangy saddles. The horses' hooves pounded dirt while their nostrils flared. Simultaneously, the wraiths drew their broadswords. Minutes earlier, I could have laughed at the events that were something straight out of a movie, but now... now I was plagued with dread.

"Run!" I screamed with a voice that cracked. Not my finest moment. Deep down, I hoped Liv didn't notice. We journeyed on, heading toward the path that Roger had mentioned. I could see it just on the other side of the hill, but the Peggs were getting closer. Tubb and Griff were nowhere to be seen while Flynn, Liv, and I pushed forward.

Liv was the first to reach the path, a solid thirty feet ahead of me. She didn't seem to tire at all. The ground shook as the wraiths closed in. I could feel their horses' hot breath blasting against the back of my neck. The path was too wide open. I would be run down in seconds, but I still had no idea why. *Why were they after us? What did we ever do to them?* No matter the reason, I had to act quickly, so I veered off the path. I weaved in and out of the trees, avoiding the wraiths. I was stunned at how nimbly I could pivot and turn on a dime. I almost felt athletic. The wraiths kept pace but couldn't reach me. They swung their swords, hacking at the branches, bushes, and saplings that separated us. The Peggs grumbled, cursing as they grew more stymied by the second, but they still wouldn't back down. We continued the dance for another fifty yards or so, the Peggs trying to kill us, us trying not to be killed, when I saw it: the end of the forest. The end of the path. And just beyond that, a cobblestone street and, more importantly, the ferry!

Tubb and Griff were somehow already onboard. Being as small as they were, I could barely make them out, but it appeared they were waving at us. "C'mon!" Tubb willed us on. "Your feet need to be movin' faster."

I knew I shouldn't have, but hindsight being what it is, I looked back to check on our pursuers. The mounted Pegg brothers darted out of the forest one by one, hooves clacking against the cobblestone. The lead

Pegg, at this point I didn't care which one was which, reached for me. The fingertips of his metallic glove nicked my collar. For a reason unbeknownst to me, I had a thought. One of those survival instincts, I guess. I reached down to my beltline. I unbuckled my belt, ripping it out of the loops on my shorts. The next time the wraith got close, I swung the belt, cracking it like a whip, striking the horse on the nose. I didn't want to hurt the horse, but this was war!

With all the strength I had left in me, I raced toward the Ferry, dodging the Peggs, their gloves, their horses, and their swords. The boat began to push away from the dock; a loud horn blared across the countryside. I saw Liv vault the plastic bins lining a newspaper stand, landing safely on the ferry. "Please, just a little longer," I begged the boat to delay its departure. Then, I watched Flynn take two long strides as he leaped for the boat, knocking over a merchant's box of freshly-picked strawberries. It looked like he was floating. His fingers were outstretched while his arm reached for something, anything to grip. He wasn't going to make it, until Liv wrapped her hand around his wrist, pulling him onboard. Now it was my turn, but the ferry was even farther away.

"Why aren't you moving faster?" Tubb whined as I fell farther behind. My legs felt like pudding; I was exhausted.

"Come on, Dean!" Flynn yelled, encouraging me.

"You can make it!" Liv added.

"Go, human, go!" Griff cheered, pumping both fists toward the sky, drawing a curious look from the group.

The lead wraith was beside me, but instead of cutting me down with his broadsword, he tried to grab me, like his brother before him. Just then, a strange thought crossed my mind, *they're not trying to kill me; they're trying to take me.* The razor-sharp tip of the wraith's glove tore through my clothes, scraping my shoulder, slicing into my skin. I winced and pushed forward one final time. Despite being completely gassed and out of breath, I kept moving. Now a second wraith was at my side, sandwiching me as my feet stepped off the cobblestone and onto the dock's wooden planks. I was almost there, but the ferry was lurching further away.

"Dean," Flynn screamed, holding his arm out.

"Jump!" Liv shouted, she too holding an outstretched arm.

My foot hit the edge of the dock. The Pegg brothers swiped at me one last time but narrowly missed as their horses skidded to a screeching halt. I could feel the fire burning in my calves as I planted my foot, jumping for the ferry. Time seemed to stand still as I reached out for my friends. My hand extended towards Flynn, who had wrapped his leg around the rail, leaning over the water, straining to catch me. Closer and closer, I flew. My fingertips barely brushed against Flynn's, then, as time sped up, I plunged… Like a cartoon character falling off a cliff, I plunged face-first into the muddy waters of River Cherwell. I bobbed back to the surface, spitting out a mouthful of river water.

"Well, I surely didn't see that coming," Griff made a wry face.

"Me either," Tubb added. "That be quite humiliating."

Even Flynn winced, contorting his face in embarrassment.

"A little help," I said. Without warning, I was plunked in the head by a pike pole that Liv dangled off the back of the boat.

"Sorry," she said, adding insult to injury.

I grabbed the pike pole as my friends pulled me onto the deck. Drenched, dripping, and cold, I thanked Liv for not mocking my belly flop into the water, at least not to my face. I watched in a mixture of awe, amazement, and fear as the Pegg brothers rode off down the riverbank, sheathing their swords as the sun started to set. I hoped we wouldn't have to see them again, but I knew deep down that we probably would.

WE'RE ON A BOAT

During the ferry ride, Tubb and Griff disappeared to the boat's upper deck, or at least that's what I assumed as I watched them climb the stairs hand over foot. Flynn disappeared for a few minutes as well, but when he returned, he gave me some much-needed hot chocolate, then left me alone with Liv while he went back to buy a box of something called Maltesers. Turns out, the ferry had a mini-concession stand. Flynn was a huge fan of concession stand food. Liv spoke with the ship's skipper, who graciously shared a few blankets to help keep me warm. As I dried off, I couldn't stop my teeth from chattering. Liv laughed, mocking me, but I didn't mind. Her laugh made me feel warmer inside than any blanket or cocoa ever could.

"What are the odds?" I asked.

"Of what, exactly?" Liv said.

"Us meeting in person like this. Of any of this happening, really."

"Not great," she batted her eyelids as she stared at the setting sun, an amber glow behind a thin veil of dying blues and purples.

"It's so pretty," I said in a hushed tone, staring at the sky.

"Thanks," Liv blushed and brushed a strand of hair back, tucking it behind her ear.

"I meant the sky, not you, but, uh…" I froze. *Oh no … What did I do?* She thought I was talking about her. Then, like always, I made things worse. Liv turned away, clearly not happy with me. I mean, yeah, she was pretty. She was more than pretty. Liv was stunning. She made my heart sink every time she looked at me. She made me feel like I could climb mountains. Like I could take on an army just to see her smile. But did I say anything like that? Anything romantic? No. I was a bumbling idiot who could only muster the words, "You are. I think you look just fine."

"Just fine?" Liv raised her eyebrows questioningly.

A billion thoughts raced through my brain all at once. Fix it, moron, I kept telling myself. I could feel sweat starting to build up in places I didn't know sweat could even build. "What I'm trying to say is… Well, what I would have said if I didn't… Ugh, what I meant was —"

"Yes?" Liv grew annoyed.

"All the colors in the sky can't compare to how you look."

"So I'm colorful, then?" Liv smirked.

"You're beautiful," I blurted out before I could stop myself. My face started to turn red. I could tell that

Liv was blushing too. She leaned in and kissed my cheek, causing my entire face to go numb.

"Maybe tomorrow, we could start over," I said, pulling the blanket tight under my chin. "And hopefully, I won't say anything dumb this time." Knowing me, that was unlikely.

"Start over? Why would we ever want to do that?" Liv asked. "Today is the most fun I've had in ages. A proper first date."

"Date?" I felt my cheeks flush, even brighter than before.

"What else would you call it?" Liv said. "Action, adventure, a boat ride at sunset. If we only had a bit of music. Maybe even some dancing to cap it off."

As soon as the words left her lips, I heard a sound so terrible that it could only rival my little brother Jackson playing the song "Hot Cross Buns" on his recorder. There was a nasally whine followed by high-pitched squealing and, soon after, a voice. Not the voice of an angel, but one of an off-tune Tubb. Liv glanced over to her side, bursting into a fit of laughter. Tubb and Griff were serenading us. Griff played a tune on what appeared to be a handmade flute, resembling a piece of small driftwood with holes poked in it, while Tubb held his belt tight, lifted his belly upward, and sang.

A date I had, not long ago
My love had called my name
I plopped into a river and
My heart was filled with shame.

They swayed side to side, rocking with the motion of the ferry. If their goal was to embarrass me even more, they were doing a terrific job.

> *My body aches as I shiver*
> *My fingers twitch, my body quivers*
> *But even still, she holds me near,*
> *My lady friend, I'm glad you're here.*

Ok. Maybe they just got off to a rocky start. But now, they were warming up. Liv clapped along as they continued.

> *My mother told me, Tubb, my boy*
> *One day you'll meet the Dean*
> *He'll have a lady by his side*
> *So jump on in between!*

Tubb and Griff dropped their instruments, ending the song, then hopped into our laps, snuggling against us like kittens. It was weird. Cute but weird.

"Oh my God," Flynn returned, dumping a bright red cup of candy into his mouth. His cheeks filled up with circular wax-covered balls of chocolate. "What was that awful noise?" he mumbled with his mouth full.

Tubb and Griff looked away, ashamed.

"I think it's lovely," Liv said.

With his mouth still overflowing with candy, Flynn said, "I think you're tone-deaf." He smiled with chocolatey malt plastered to his teeth.

"Guys," I said, "we're here." After the ferry docked, we let everyone else off the ship before making a move. There weren't many other passengers besides us, which was good because Tubb and Griff's concert

118

would have drawn unnecessary attention. A family of six was the first to deboard, a mom and dad and their four small children, one still in a stroller. Next were three older men. They wore sweater vests and paddy caps and puffed on cigars that smelled musty yet sweet. The last to disembark was a group of college-aged kids. As each passenger exited, I inspected the small town before us. There were shoppes, a petrol station, and a lonely-looking guy walking a long-haired dog the size of a Shetland pony. What I didn't see were wraiths, a dwarf, or horses, but I wanted to wait a few more minutes to be sure; only Tubb and Griff had other ideas. The two hurried down the ramp as they scuttled away from the ferry. Griff practically dove headfirst to the ground, dropping to his knees.

"Land!" Tubb shouted. "Sweet, glorious, land."

Griff doubled over and, with closed eyes, kissed the pavement, then retched. "Ick!" Griff spat. "This land be tasting like manure?"

"That's because it is manure, Griff," Tubb said.

The man with the dog on a leash looked on, plastic baggie in hand, standing over a steamy pile of dog droppings with a fly circling around it. The man covered his mouth to fight back a gag, then yanked the dog's leash, hurrying away. Griff stood, continuing his relentless spitting, while I decided it was safe to leave the comfort of the ferry.

From there, we were on foot to our hotel. By the time we got to the site, my feet ached, and I was ready to be off of them. The hotel was quite incredible. I fully expected a dump, but the exterior of the building was huge - steeped in old-world charm. It was a mixture of a castle and a ski resort or country club. Either way, I had to give it to Flynn; it was snazzy. The grass courtyard that led to the entrance had a humongous fountain with a statue of some naked dude in the middle.

By the time we walked in the door, night had begun to fall. Flynn and I changed into fresh clothes after we were reunited with our luggage. Flynn swapped his Tottenham jersey for a sky-blue long-sleeved shirt he bought at a beach shop over spring break. As it wasn't working out, I changed out of my lucky shirt into a plain white t-shirt. There was a cool breeze with a crisp bite, so I put on my lightweight black Adidas jacket. The jacket had stripes that ran down the arms, two side pockets, and a smaller button-up pocket on the chest for a key or other small item.

I finally had a chance to call Mom. I told her we went shopping, then got a bite to eat (not exactly a lie), and I told her we did some sightseeing (also not exactly a lie). I conveniently left out the part about almost being murdered by lunatics in grim reaper outfits.

"So, when are you visiting Flynn's great-grandpa?" Mom asked.

"Tomorrow, I think," I answered, slipping into the hallway for a little privacy, "assuming we don't get killed first," I let slip.

"I'm sorry, what?"

"It was a joke. You know how they get over here when you mention soccer or the Boston Tea Party."

"We're having tea? I adore tea," Griff said as he slid into the hall alongside me. "What is that little box in your hand?" He pointed to my phone. "And why are you talking to it?"

"Who's that?" Mom asked.

"Nobody, just the hotel manager's kid."

"Awe, you made a friend," Mom said. "What's her name?" Griff pinched his face in confusion.

"Name?" Why would mom ask this? Why did it matter? And why did I have a tough time coming up with one? "Uh, yeah, that's just, uh – Delaney."

"No, it isn't," Griff shouted.

"It's a nickname," I covered the base of the phone, snapping back at him.

"I have a nickname," Griff whispered with pride.

"She sounds cute," Mom said.

"She?" Griff squinted his beady eyes and gritted his teeth. "You be tellin' that talking rectangle it better mind its tongue before I get angry."

Instantly, I regretted having this call on the speaker. I couldn't tell if Griff was messing around or not. He swiped, leaped, and even tried climbing my leg to get to the phone.

"Alright, Mom, gotta go. Love you, bye." I hung up, shooting Griff a nasty look, only to find that he stared back at me with misty eyes. "What is your deal?" I asked.

"Oh my daisies! Your mom be trapped in the rectangle? We need to be doing something! Tell me, human, how does we save her?"

Oh my daisies was right. What was wrong with these guys? I had no idea how to address Griff, so I shook my head and crossed back into the room, letting the door slam in his face.

121

HOTEL, MOTEL, HOLIDAY INN

The Magdalen Room that Flynn had booked for us had two separate sleeping quarters, a mini-kitchen, a small dining table, and a living room with a forty-two-inch TV mounted on the wall. Tubb sat on the couch gnawing on a room-service turkey leg. His legs dangled in the air, not long enough for his feet to touch the ground. He was entranced by a dog show competition on a local television station. His eyes pinballed around the screen, following a Corgi that jumped through hoops. Tubb was bewitched, watching the Corgi swerving between obstacles.

"Remarkable creatures," Tubb said. "Can you ride them?"

"Not quite," Liv answered, not looking up at the TV. She sat at a large oak desk by the window that overlooked the horse stalls, studying the map from the forest. The living room was centered by a roaring fireplace nestled against a stone wall. The room really was top-notch; if only I could allow myself to enjoy it.

"Wait," a thought crossed my mind. "The monkey."

"Monkey?" Liv asked.

"One sec." I jetted into my bedroom. Unlike Flynn's room, which had a king-size bed along with the biggest bathtub I'd ever seen (seriously, it might as well have been a small swimming pool), mine had two double beds with a private bath. The artwork in the room consisted of horses, hounds, and riders.

I picked up my suitcase, which now felt as light as a feather, tossing it onto the bed's fluffy down comforter, unzipping in a fury. Without hesitation, I unstacked the tidily folded tops and shorts (thanks, Mom), then found the New York Yankees monkey I'd bought at the airport. Picking up a step, I rushed back through the bedroom door into the living room, holding the monkey behind my back. Liv looked up at me with a puzzled look on her face. I couldn't tell if she was more nervous or excited. "Hold out your hands," I said.

"I really don't like surprises," she said. "But alright." She shuttered her eyes, extending her hands, her fingertips anxiously wiggling.

"Open," I said, laying the monkey down gently in her palms.

"Wow," she said. "It really is a monkey." She flipped it over, checking it out on all sides. "And it's wearing baseball gear."

"Yankees," I said, trying to sound impressive.

"This may be a problem." A frown crossed Liv's face, immediately sending my heart sputtering toward my small intestine. "I'm more of a Red Sox supporter."

"Oh—well, I could see if—what I mean is, I could ask if —" I couldn't talk. I couldn't even think. Even my thoughts were stuttering. Do something, Dean, do something. Tell her it was a gag gift. Tell her that was for Jackson. Tell her you grabbed the wrong monkey. Tell her *anything*.

"I'm kidding, Dean," she said. She must have seen the hurdles of hysteria I was going through. "The Yankees are just fine." Liv looked up at me and smiled. She set the monkey down beside her, positioning its hands together on its lap. "I'll name him George."

Curious name, I thought. Embarrassingly, I let out an audible *phew*, wiping sweat from my forehead.

"I'm stepping outside for a minute," Flynn said as he exited the bedroom he claimed for himself.

"Everything alright, my tall friend?" Griff reemerged from the hall after finally figuring out how to open the door.

"Fine. Just kinda up to my ears in magic magnets and wraiths."

"Those were just humans in costume. Real wraiths would never let a Gnomeling poke their eyes. Not that they have eyes. Ouch!" Griff bellowed as Tubb's turkey leg struck him across the face.

"Eat somethin', will ya? And stop talking," Tubb said.

Griff shrugged his shoulders, diving into the meat that barely clung to the bone, tearing and gnawing.

"See what I mean?" Flynn said. "That's the fifth time you've called someone a human, and I still don't know what the heck a Gnomeling is supposed to be."

Griff didn't answer but kept eating until the bone was nearly picked clean. Tubb avoided eye contact. He fidgeted in his seat, focusing once more on the Corgis.

"Whatever," Flynn said. "I might be a minute. I gotta check in with my moms too."

"Are they stuck in a rectangle like Dean's mom?" Griff asked curiously. Flynn rolled his eyes and left the suite.

"Hey, come take a look at this," Liv said, standing and fully stretching out the parchment paper. "I found another message."

Tubb bounced off the couch, landing on his feet. He and Griff bounded to Liv's side and stood on their tiptoes to see the map.

"Where?" I nudged Griff aside, taking my place next to Liv. Her shoulder brushed against my side, causing the butterflies to return with a vengeance.

"Here, beneath Warwick Castle." She pointed to what at first looked to be a smudge, but as she tilted light from the lamp directly on the map, I could see a small inscription.

"More of that language," I said.

"Gumbar?" Liv asked Tubb and Griff.

"Gnomarian," Tubb answered.

"Can you read it?" I asked.

Tubb yanked the desk chair back and, with an oomph, hoisted his bottom onto the seat. Still too short for a good view, he sat on his stubby knees. He whispered a few words under his breath as his eyes widened as big as vinyl records.

"What does it say?" Liv moved in closer. My knees nearly collapsed.

"A charm is split. Divided by five. And only my heir will see it alive." Tubb said as he shared a knowing look with Griff. "There's more" He got closer to the paper, needing to squint to read the last portion that was written in a crease. "Collect the whole, but don't dare wait... For evil lurks to seal our fate."

Liv and I made eye contact, then we turned our attention to the little guys, but Tubb and Griff could only stare at each other. "Only the heir will see it alive," Griff said.

A pair of headlights reflected off the glass, temporarily blinding me. Shielding my eyes, I looked outside, spotting a white van. The vintage vehicle appeared to be made in the 1970s. It backfired as it raced by, heading down a hill toward our hotel. Something about the van felt odd; it was like my spidey sense was tingling, only I never knew I had spidey sense.

"Heir to what?" Liv asked.

"Do you tiny wizards suffer from mental blockage?" Griff's tone pulled my attention away from the van.

"Griff, are you sure?" Tubb asked.

"Our fates, Tubb. Our fates depend on him. You heard it. And our orders were clear."

"What orders," I asked.

"He needs to know who he is. What he is."

"They're talking about you," Liv said.

"He needs to know that he be royalty," Griff sighed.

"Royalty?" I said.

"If we don't tell him now and something happens," Griff yanked on Tubb's sleeve, "then we're dead already. So is Second Realm. So is our shire."

"The shire?" I perked up.

"Our shire. Not *the* shire. It's called Yarberry," Griff corrected.

"Okay. Fine. I'll tell him." After Tubb popped off the chair, he pulled me down to his level. "Dean Koltien Moyers."

"Your middle name is Koltien?" Liv asked.

"Don't laugh," I said in defense. Normally when someone heard my middle name, they laughed. They figured it was my grandma's name or some weird family tradition. But as I looked at Liv, I knew that wasn't the case.

"It sounds like Tolkien," she said.

"Intentional. Dad's idea," I said.

"That's brilliant," she smiled.

"Wait," I turned back to Tubb, "how did you know my middle name?"

"Middle name?" Griff asked. "What be a middle name?"

"I think that's the one between the front and back," Tubb said, then continued, "Dean, it's now being apparent that you was meant to find us. Just as you was meant to have the amulet. The same way your father, grandfather, and his grandfather was meaning to have the amulet. You see, you be a guardian. A protector. The highest knight of our shire."

"Shire... Knight..." I whispered so low that no one could hear me.

"Did he never tell you?" Griff asked. "Your father. Did he never tell you about your destiny, the amulet?"

"He tried. The night he died. My dad tried to tell me something. But he said I had to wait."

"He be dead then?" Griff asked, his face sunk in sorrow.

"That be explaining much," Tubb said. "Your father was to wait until you turned two less than a dozen. That's when the next generation's protectors are

127

told of the prophecies. That's when they reveal themselves to us. To our realm. To ensure peace. To keep order."

"That's how old your father was when we told him about his destiny," Griff said.

"You knew my dad?"

"Knew him? We fought beside him in the battle of Elrod."

"Well, he fought. We hid in a bucket," Tubb said.

"Masterful with a blade, he was," Griff added.

"He fought in a battle?" I said. "This is insane. Completely insane." Yet, I hung on every word, believing every bit of it. So much of what had happened in my life made sense now. My dreams. My tragedy. "And the amulet?"

"Its fate be our fate. If it falls into the wrong hands, Second Realm will fall under a cloud of evil for all times. Someone in your family line must have been splitting it to hide it from evil, only to be reunited in case of a great calamity," Tubb said.

"And when you didn't show up on your name day, the forces of evil took that as a sign of weakness, a sign of calamity. They declared the knights of our shires and the protectors of Second Realm... dead. And that's why we came looking. It appears the hour be late, and the only hope is to combine the five pieces. Its power alone can save us," Griff said.

"If wielded by a descendant," Tubb said.

I buried my head in my hands. Immediately, I went numb as my mind went blank. The conversation continued, but I was stuck in a fog.

"And you... you're Gnomelings. That's what you're called? That's a real thing?" Liv said.

"Indeed, lad," Griff said, taking a bow.

"Not lad. She's obviously a lady, Griff. He be a lad," Tubb pointed at me; his frustration was evident. Clearly, this wasn't the first time he'd explained this to Griff.

"My apologies, obviously a lady," Griff bowed again, this time lower.

"What's wrong with him?" Tubb asked. I felt a stubby finger poking at my temple, but I was in such a state of shock that I didn't move. "I think we killed him, Griff."

"Maybe he's hungry," Griff said. At that moment, something hit my cheek. Before I could react, something else bounced off my chin. And seconds later, I felt a warm, slimy slab of meat slide between my lips. I looked up to see Griff trying to feed me a chunk of turkey. "Here comes the dragon squirrel. Open up."

A tingling washed over my entire body. A flood of emotion took over. I lunged out of the seat, diving at Tubb and Griff, rubbing the long hair that covered their feet.

"Great work, Griff," Tubb said. "He's gone bonkers."

I grabbed two handfuls of hair, yanking upward. Tubb and Griff screamed in agony, both hopping on one foot, nursing the other.

"That really hurts," Griff said.

"It's real," I said.

"Of course it be real," Tubb said.

"And you're actually real? And there's another realm."

"I thought he'd be smarter than this," Tubb said to Griff.

I continued, "And you're not people at all. You're literally called Gnomelings." They nodded in unison.

"Is that the same as a hobbit?" Liv asked innocently.

"That be mildly racist," Tubb said.

"Dragons?" I asked.

"Real," Tubb answered.

"Goblins?"

"Real."

"Trolls?"

"Also real."

"The wraiths?"

"Real. Not the ones we fought in the forest, but speaking of them, I have a feeling they too be looking for the amulet."

"How would they know about it? The amulet? The Realm?"

Griff pondered, scratching his chin until his skin was irritated, and proclaimed, "I believe someone has told them to find it."

Ignoring Captain Obvious, I stumbled over to the couch and planted my bottom on the cushion where Tubb was sitting earlier.

It was still warm.

Gross.

"You said the amulet had to be split for a reason. But in the forest —" I said.

"You heard what it said on the map. Collect the whole. It's our only hope. It was split to keep it far from the enemy. And when we were at peace, that was perfectly perfect," Tubb said.

"But now, the enemy be too strong, and until we be meeting you here, we lost our guardian," Griff unexpectedly climbed onto the couch. He sat on my lap.

"But the wraiths, they were humans," Liv said. Griff nodded. "So, who are they working for?" She scratched her head in thought and took a seat beside me. I guess Tubb took that as a sign. He too scaled the couch and sat on her lap.

"I don't know for certain, but I fear they are minions of the Dark One or someone who be calling the Dark One master."

Before Tubb could divulge more, Flynn burst into the room. The door slammed against the rubber stopper on the wall. It bounced back, smacking against his side. "Outside. A van. White Van. Mystery Machine," he struggled to form a sentence. "The wraiths are back." His eyes locked onto mine as he did a double, more of a triple-take, staring with his jaw nearly on the floor, seeing Liv and me holding the Gnomelings in our laps. "What in the actual—"

"We can explain later," I said.

ROOM SERVICE

"Hurry, we must go," Tubb said. "Grab the map," he looked to Liv, who shoved him off her lap. He wobbled onto the couch and struggled to stand. Liv stood, rushed to the desk, then rolled the map into a tube shape. She attempted to fasten it with a hair tie when the map lifted from her hand and slammed back onto the desk.

I ran to her side and pulled the corner of the paper, trying to pry it off the tabletop, but it was stuck. Then, with tremendous force, the amulet lifted on its own from beneath my collar and tugged, jerking itself over the map. Believing that the amulet had a mind of its own, I didn't want to get in the way, so I took the chain, pulled it over my head, and let go. The amulet hovered in mid-air.

"What's it doing?" Griff asked.

"Stand back!" I ordered. The amulet pounded down against the desk. I swear the room shook. The amulet slid to the castle, the well, and finally, the London Eye. Again and again, faster and faster, the pattern repeated: castle, well, Eye, castle, well, Eye.

"First, we go to the castle, then the well, then we be going to the Eye," Griff said.

"Thanks for the recap, Dora," Flynn said. "Now, can we get the map and head out?"

"Dora? Is that another nickname? Because Dean already gave me one. It's Delaney," Griff said with pride.

"What does that even mean?" Flynn asked.

"Long story," I said. The amulet began to spin so fast that the rune etched into the silver was indistinguishable. The paper map beneath it started to smoke. It turned black as it was set ablaze, and the map turned to ash within the blink of an eye. A strong breeze whistled through a crack in the open window overlooking the stables, blowing the map remnants into the air. Tiny ashes flitted and fluttered and danced before our eyes like snowflakes until another gust of wind surged through the window, transporting the ash straight into the fireplace and up the flue.

A shrill scream came from outside the room in the direction of the lobby. Liv looked at Flynn with obvious concern. "They're still wearing the costumes?" she asked. Flynn nodded yes. "Say what you will, but these guys are committed."

"I can't see them," Griff called out from the room door. He stood atop Tubb's shoulders as he stared down periscope through the peephole.

"Of course not. That only looks straight out the door," I said.

"It's so distorted. They really do need better telescopes here."

"Call 999," Liv shouted to Flynn, who lingered beside the room's only telephone.

"Don't you mean 911?" Flynn said.

"999 is 911 here," I shouted in a panic.

"I have a better idea." Flynn rushed past me and entered my room. After a minute of drawers and doors opening and closing and what I'm pretty sure was glass breaking, Flynn emerged with a stupid grin stretching across his face.

"What did you do?" I exclaimed, tossing my arms out to the side. He smiled, then pulled the whistle my mom gave me from behind his back. Without thinking, he put the whistle between his lips, puckered, and blew. "No!" I cried out, this time with a stronger voice. I ripped the whistle from his mouth.

"Well, that did it. Now they know exactly where we are." Liv stomped in frustration.

"I thought you said it was a police whistle, like, you blow the whistle forcing them to come, like the bat signal in Batman," Flynn said.

"Nobody ever said that!" I yelled. "There's no such thing as a police whistle that's just like the bat signal." I wrenched my hands in a fit as I moved to the door, checking the peephole.

"I guess I dreamed that part," Flynn sat, sulking on the couch.

"Do you see them?" Liv asked.

"No." I craned my neck to the side as if that would help me see further down the hall. News flash, that didn't work. "Do you have a mirror?"

"No," Liv said.

"Negative," Flynn said, his forehead planted in his dejected palms.

"I do," Griff said.

"Why do you have a – You know what? I don't care why you have it; just let me see it."

Griff pulled a mirror from his back pocket, huffed on it, shined it up, wiping it clean. He held it up above his head. "Can you see it?"

"Of course, I can see it. I meant, let me have it. Give me the mirror."

"Why didn't you be saying so?" Griff hurriedly bumbled over to me, handing me the small, circular mirror. I switched off the lights and slightly cracked open the door. Holding the mirror, I angled it to see down the hallway. Despite a smudge on the upper right-hand side, the mirror was usable. I stared at the pocket mirror with reluctant anticipation, my hand trembling like a leaf, when the awful sound of marching boots approached. A set of shadows bent around the corner, oblong and horrific. It appeared to be the shadows of three people, the wraiths, or so I thought. My heart pounded as the shadows stretched further and further until three figures came into sight, only they were not what I expected.

Instead of menacing cloaked men, I saw a family: a mom and dad, both unusually tall with distinct jawlines with extremely pointy noses. I would have bet money they were twins if they didn't have a child with them. Their son, probably around six or seven years old, wore a tuxedo t-shirt that barely covered his belly. He had a significant ice cream stain crossing his chest. All three wore Royal Guard Busby hats, military headgear from the British army. Each cylindrical-shaped hat was about two feet tall and covered in black fur. The trio marched

135

and paraded down the hall, stopping at each door to salute as if they were saluting the queen. If I wasn't so worried about the family potentially being slaughtered, I might have enjoyed the show they were putting on. But, as with all good things, this lighthearted moment would soon end as the lights to the hotel flickered. The family pretending to be Buckingham palace guards spun on their heels and saw the same sight I did. Another set of shadows crept into view. This time it was going to be the wraiths; I was sure of it. Whether or not they heard Flynn blow the whistle, I didn't imagine it would be difficult to find our room. How many teens from the States would have checked in today? Then, I let my mind drift further. How did they even track us here? Of all the hotels in the area. Of all the homes and bed and breakfasts, they were only an hour behind our arrival. Was someone helping them? Their master? Were they drawn to the amulet like the wraiths of Middle Earth were drawn to the Ring of Power? Of course not, I thought. My imagination was getting the best of me.

The family froze as the shadows crept around the corner, and there they were—Burt, Tommy, and William. Still in their black cloaks, they pulled out their swords, holding them upright, their metallic-gloved hands pointing down the hall. They moved across the floor almost like ghosts, floating. They passed the ice machine, where Tommy, the smallest wraith, broke free from the pack. He approached the father, backing him up against the wall. "Room Six," he said with a hiss.

The man shook and slowly extended his arm, pointing down the hall, pointing right at me. "It's there. The room is down there. Please don't hurt me. Please don't hurt my boy."

"You and your boy?" the mom fumed as she took a stride toward her husband. She smacked him across his chest with her handbag. "What am I then, Rob? Minced pudding?"

"Shhh…" the wraith put his finger to the mom's pouty lips, tickling the coarse brown stubble above her upper lip. He hushed her into stillness. She butted her backside against the wall next to her husband.

The wraith cocked his head at an unusual angle. He stared directly at me as I quickly slipped the mirror back inside and closed the door quietly. "They're coming. What do we do?"

"I, for one, would like my mirror back," Griff said, extending his hand. I handed him the mirror, and he smiled awkwardly. "Thanks."

Holding the mirror up to his face, Griff began inspecting his teeth with it, twisting it at various angles. "What are you doing?" I asked, almost afraid of the answer. Was he trying to scare them with a toothy grin? Did he think he looked intimidating? But no, he was simply picking between his incisors.

"I left some meat in there," Griff said, pulling a slice of meat from his teeth. "Second helpings be the best helpings," He popped it back into his mouth, chewed, and swallowed.

"You're disgusting," Flynn said.

"What's the plan?" Liv asked, trying to steer the conversation back to the situation at hand.

"The window won't budge," Tubb said, standing on his tiptoes. He tried to push the window out toward the stable, but it was jammed.

"They lock hotel windows, so people don't jump out," Liv said.

"Jump out?" Flynn shook his head. "We're on the first floor!"

"Dean?" Liv said. "What do we do?" All eyes landed on me. When did this become my decision? When did I become the leader of this island of misfit toys? Just because I had this amulet didn't mean – wait. I did have a plan. Well, more of a harebrained idea, but we'll call it a plan.

"Follow me," I ordered, trying to project confidence. What we were about to attempt would work, I thought. It had to work. It worked in a movie… It worked in *the* movie. I gulped as I led my new followers into the master suite and said a quick prayer in my head to whoever might be listening.

CALLING ALL CARS

We should have called the police. Up until now, we hadn't done anything wrong. We were attacked, chased, and stalked. All we did was defend ourselves against psychopaths in black robes. But we didn't call for help. Being kids of our generation, we were typically desensitized to danger. We thought we could handle things on our own. I mean, think about it, we played most of the GTA games before middle school. We could take these guys.

Flynn lifted the comforter over the tops of the bed's throw pillows in the master suite. He tiptoed to my feet and straightened a golden bed runner over my shoes, hiding my toes from sight. "There," he said, "I can't even see you." In a hush, Flynn crept over to the bedroom's walk-in closet, where Liv waited anxiously.

She handed him a plugged-in clothes iron. He nodded, giving me a thumbs up - it was go-time, so I ducked behind my cover.

Second thoughts weren't an option, as my plan was about to be put to the ultimate test. I heard the door's key card sensor beep. Again and again, the beep cried out in failed attempts to open the room door. The Peggs must have snatched all the key cards from the front desk. It seemed they were trying them one by one. I assumed they would simply use their swords and hack away at the door like lumberjacks, but it appeared one of them may have actually had a brain. My heart practically beat through my chest as I tried to remain still. I hadn't been this nervous since my band concert at school. I played the saxophone for two years. But you'd probably guessed I was a band kid by now.

I could hear Tubb and Griff whispering as they scuttled their shoeless feet behind the standing mirror in the corner. Luckily, they were small enough to fit without being spotted, if only they would shut up.

"Will you two pipe down," Liv whispered, clearly thinking the same as me.

"Sorry," Tubb declared, "but Griff's breath be tickling my nostrils."

"It's not my fault," Griff said.

"Your breath smells like Cousin Nathan's creamed-onion pickles," Tubb belted back.

I fell nauseous at the thought of creamed onion pickles. I also grew tired of their bickering. "Why don't you both just face the other direction?" I asked.

"Oh. Good thinking, human." I could hear the Gnomelings scooting about until they were back to back.

Beep! A successful tone from the room door chimed as the handle cracked and turned. The room fell silent. The air was still. All of us waited with bated breath. I felt tiny droplets of perspiration seeping out of my pores while my hands became clammy, and my knees began to quake. I heard footsteps crunch, plopping against the floor as the Peggs moved toward us. Panic started to set in as I felt around blindly at my side in search of a weapon: a decorative candlestick. Not exactly my weapon of choice, but the plan was contrived in a pinch. Also, the toilet tank lid and scolding hot iron were already spoken for.

"You two, check in there," William said as a couple of shadows glided past the door to the suite toward the guest bedroom.

The master suite door croaked as it opened. Decked out in his wraith gear, William Pegg swiftly glided forward into our room with a sword drawn. If I didn't know better, I would have sworn his feet still weren't touching the ground as he approached the bed, stopping at the headboard.

"William," Tommy Pegg whispered through the cracked door. "There's a Tottenham kit on the bed. Looks like the friend's asleep. What should we do with him?"

"Whatever you like," William whispered back. "We only need the amulet from Moyers." I could hear Tommy and Burt clomping toward the guest bedroom.

"Nighty-night, Dean Moyers," he said with his gravelly voice. He gripped the edge of the comforter, ripping it away from the bed, fully expecting to see me sleeping. What he didn't expect was the oldest trick in the book - a layer of pillows, towels, and clothes balled together to make it look like someone was there. This was a trick that kids had been using for ages to convince their parents they were asleep while they snuck out of the house. "Huh?" William said, surprised by the body-shaped mound beneath the blanket. Through the walls, I could hear the other Pegg's swords hammering down. I could picture feathers from down pillows filling the air as the blades scraped against coils and bed springs. The mattresses were sure to be shredded to bits from fits of anger once they figured out they'd been fooled. Flynn's moms were going to freak when the hotel charged their credit card for incidentals that would surely carry a hefty price tag. But at that moment, I didn't care about damages or incidentals. I was thrilled because they fell for our trap: Split them up, dupe them, and then take them down!

"Now!" I yelled as I jumped out from behind a chair in the corner of the room that was cloaked in blankets and the bed runner that Flynn used to shield my feet. Flynn exploded out of the walk-in closet with a scalding hot iron in hand; its orangish glow illuminated the equally terrifying scowl that crossed his face. Liv followed Flynn from the closet, holding the toilet tank lid in her arms, ready to swing for the fences. Tubb and Griff shouted a menacing war cry, as much of a war cry that could come out of two Gnomelings. By the looks of it, Tubb thought he was going left, while Griff would go right; instead, they went the opposite direction, slamming into one another and falling to the ground. The collision knocked over the standing mirror, shattering it into tiny pieces.

William Pegg was too stunned by all the commotion to make a move. Rather, he spun in semi-circles, trying to make sense of the chaos surrounding him. By the time he finally got his wits back, I had wrapped my arms around his chest, holding his limbs tight against the insides of my elbows, keeping his sword hand at bay.

Liv swung away wildly, plunking the Pegg brother with the ceramic lid. In turn, the ivory weapon ricocheted against my ribcage.

"Ouch!" I winced.

"Sorry," Liv said, but it didn't stop her onslaught of wraith batting practice. The wraith's sword fell to the floor.

"Tie him up," I said to Flynn as he held the iron close to William's face.

"You move, you get pressed like a dress shirt, you get me?" Flynn grimaced. William immediately stopped struggling, feeling the intense heat. Even from my position behind him, I could feel the scalding hot metal of the iron. I swore I could smell his facial hair burning.

The Gnomelings eventually made their way back to their hairy feet and into the fray. Our tiny friends literally ran circles around the wraith's legs, pulling what they called an "elven rope" tight around the menacing figure. "We got him!" Tubb panted. They handed Flynn the loose ends of the rope, and he tied a fancy-looking knot.

I stepped back, spinning William Pegg around until he was facing me. I moved in close. So close I could smell the ale on his breath, wincing at the rancid odor. "Why are you after us?" I said. "Who sent you?"

"Dean, we have to move," Liv urged as she peeked out the master suite door.

I knew she was right, but I had to know. "I asked you a question," I said, continuing my interrogation. "Who sent you?" I jammed the hot iron in the wraith's face hole. The electromagnetic glow of the iron's heat started to dim, but I got a look at William Pegg's features. Instant regret. The shrouded blackness was preferable to the mangled mug of my newfound nemesis. He had two scars, one above his right eye, another running alongside his left cheek, and a snarling mouth with uneven teeth. He truly had the appearance of a classic villain from a horror movie.

"I ain't tellin' you a thing." His hot, rank breath was even worse when he spoke.

"Dean. I think they're coming." Liv picked up a bedside lamp. She ripped the cord from the wall, holding its neck tight, ready to swing.

"In here, boys!" William shouted for his brothers as he shouldered away from me. He began hopping for the door with the elven rope wrapped tightly from chest to knee. "I'm in —" Before he could say more, Liv smashed the lamp over his head, fracturing it, knocking the wraith out cold. William's body crumpled to the ground. Flynn looked down in awe at the lamp, only a sliver of the neck still in Liv's grip, the rest in pieces on the ground.

"Here, take it." I handed the iron back to Flynn.

"What about you? You need to protect yourself," Flynn said.

"I'll use this," I said as I bent down and picked up the sword William had dropped. I studied it for a moment, the way the moonlight shimmered off the blade, the scuff marks on the silver, and a small dent near the tip. The sword felt lighter than I expected as I tossed it back and forth between my hands. Instinctively, I twirled around, flourishing the blade like a master swordsman. The Gnomelings retreated behind Liv as the sword buzzed over the top of their heads, tracing the outline of my body as I bobbed and weaved in perfect harmony. "Whoa," I stopped, looking down at my hands as if they belonged to someone else.

"When did you learn to do that?" Flynn seemed just as astonished.

"I have no idea." I pointed down to William. "Bring him with us."

We moved into the suite's living area, knowing full well the other wraiths were sure to have heard the commotion. If not William's yell, then definitely the lamp shattering on his skull. Tubb and Griff each held a handful of rope as they dragged William behind them.

"Where do you think you're off to then?" The two upright wraiths squared up. They held their swords outstretched, tips aimed directly at us. I pulled my friends behind me, shielding them with my free arm. I dangled the sword at the wraiths, then pointed the blade downward at their brother's heart, almost daring them to try something.

"Easy now, lad," Tommy, the short wraith, said as he inched toward me.

"Don't take another step." I pressed the blade against William's skin. His chest raised and lowered with each wheezing inhale and exhale.

"You wouldn't," Burt grumbled.

"He's an American, Burt. He just might," Tommy said.

"He will," Flynn added. "Dean's had lunch detention three times," Flynn lied. It sounded ridiculous, but it seemed to have some effect on the two brothers.

"I saw a TV show about American schools, Burt. It's a bloody brutal jungle there," Tommy said.

"Tubb, do you have more rope?" I asked.

145

"Indeed, I be having as much as we need." Tubb pulled an inexplicably enormous amount of elven rope from the backpack, still slung around his shoulders. How his bag could hold that much stuff, I had no idea.

"Drop your weapons and get on your knees!" I commanded

"And if we don't?" Burt dared.

"Your mom loses a son," I poked the sword even harder into William's cloak.

Burt postured. He acted as if he were going to step toward me when Tommy gripped his shoulder. "Are you mental?" Tommy jerked Burt back. "That's our brother. Do as he says."

What they didn't know, what they couldn't know, was that I didn't want to hurt William. Not really. Even with all the adrenaline pumping through my veins, I couldn't stand the thought of stabbing someone with an authentic sword. I mean, come on, I'm the kid who cried for three days when my mom ran over a squirrel on the freeway. I'm the kid who was tormented when I watched my dad skin a fish we'd caught. How could I possibly pierce a man's skin? Even one this repulsive. Lucky for us, the Peggs didn't know about the squirrel or the fish, and I must have put on a decent poker face as they instantly backed off, tossed their swords at our feet, and dropped to their knees.

After Tubb and Griff tied the most elaborate knots I'd ever seen, we exited the room, inching down the long stretch of hallway leading to the lobby, still fearful of what else may be lurking. The hall lights flickered, casting eerie shadows across my friends' faces.

"What now?" Flynn asked.

"You remember what the map said," I responded. "We go to Warwick Castle."

"Let me see if I have this right," Liv chimed in, "A trio of nutters chase us through the woods, breaks into your hotel room, stabs the bedding because they thought we were in it, and instead of going to the police, you are going to listen to a piece of parchment paper in order to venture off to an abandoned castle?"

"Beggin' your pardon, lad, I mean, obviously a lady," Griff said, his fingers nibbling at Liv's sleeve, "I don't think you understand the urgency of the matter."

"And I don't think you understand what's the matter with your urgency," Liv fired back.

Griff's facial expressions went into a fit of mental gymnastics as he tried to work out the details of Liv's comment.

"What Griff be meaning is this," Tubb said. "Those threes, back in the room, they be just a taste of what is to come. The enemy marches across our lands, and they draw near."

Griff interjected, "And if them be willing to send assassins to your world, I fear the time of our world is in more danger than we ever imagined."

"So, what are you suggesting?" I asked, wanting someone to say it aloud.

"We unite the amulets," Tubb and Griff said in unison.

"To what end?" Liv asked.

"It will allow us passage back to Second Realm, to defeat the forces of evil that be plaguing our lands," Tubb said.

"And to be praying that they haven't awakened The Dark One," Griff said.

"The immortal," Tubb said.

"But wouldn't immortal mean it can't be defeated?" Flynn asked.

147

"Can't be defeated by mortal weapons, but if we had to, we might have time to retrieve the weapons of the guardians. Them hold magical powers that can take down even the most immortal immortal and make them mortal once more," Tubb said confidently.

"I'm so confused," Flynn said.

"Let me get this straight," I said.

"Good luck with that," Flynn said.

"Because I'm having a pretty difficult time wrapping my head around all of this," I continued.

"I think we all are," Liv said.

"You want us to go to the castle, right?" I asked.

"No. Not me. The map. The map wants *us* to go to the castle," Tubb said.

"Okay, the map wants us to go to the castle," I repeated. "Then, the map wants us to go to the well and then the London Eye, where we'll collect the pieces of the amulet. This allows us to travel to the shire."

"Our shire," Griff corrected.

"Yeah, ok, so anyway, once we're there, we have to either raise an army or collect these so-called guardian weapons to defeat the immortals? All before they wipe out all life in Second Realm? Which is kinda like Middle Earth, only real? And somehow, I'm a descendant of the guardians or protectors of your realm? Did I get everything?"

"Well, that there be an extremely high-level summary of the history of our world and your family. So I wouldn't say you got *everything*," Griff said, with his finger pressed against his bottom lip.

"But it'll do for now," Tubb interjected.

I looked at Flynn, my most trusted ally, who shrugged his shoulders as if to say, "Why not?" I turned to Liv, who still looked skeptical. Who could blame her? "What do you think?"

"I guess calling the authorities and telling them we hogtied three cloaked madmen at sword point while befriending Gnomelings in an effort to save another realm might make us appear a bit mad. Not sure I want to spend my weekend in the asylum, then."

"Is that a yes?" I asked. "We go to the castle?"

"Aye. It's a yes."

"What are we waiting for? Let's go!" I said with a confident smile. Something about this, while completely certifiable, felt amazing. I was about to embark on a real-life adventure and not the type that was coordinated by a travel agent.

"Should we be putting our hands in a circle, saying 'go humans' or doing some kind of cheer?" Griff asked, holding his tiny hand out.

But just as our excitement built, a voice interrupted from down the hall. "I don't think that will be necessary," said a man in a confident, weary, and villainous voice. "In fact, I don't think you'll stay a team for long."

Goosebumps covered my arms. Tiny hairs stood at attention on the back of my neck. The hallway lights dimmed as they began to glow a strange shade of red that filled the hallways from floor to ceiling. The man stood, blocking our path to the lobby. He was tall, roughly six-foot-five inches, and he wore all black. Black trousers, a black peacoat, black fedora, and when he smiled, I got a glimpse of his black soul. "You," I whispered.

EVERY ROSE HAS ITS THORNE

We stared down the man in black, and Flynn asked, "You know this guy

"He was at the airport. And at Tolkien's house."

"Not a friend, I presume?" Liv said.

"Doesn't appear that way," I said.

"You've bested my men," the man said, his face shrouded in shadow. "Impressive," he continued as he unsheathed a blade from under his coat. It wasn't a broadsword but something much sleeker, more elegant: a rapier. The slender, lightweight weapon had an intricate hilt resembling longitude and latitude lines on a globe. Its razor-sharp blade could easily pierce the skin of a whale shark.

"What do you think of it?" The man began to wield the sword, twisting it around his body in hypnotic patterns. "It belonged to your father."

"My father?" My heart drowned into the depths of my gut as I gripped my sword so tight that my hand started to twitch.

"Pity I had to extirpate him in that cave so many years ago."

"What does that mean? Extirpate?" Flynn asked.

"I think it means," Liv hesitated, "exterminate."

"Pretty and smart," the man said, making an awful sound with his throat like he was gargling saltwater. "You should keep this one, Dean Moyers, if I weren't about to extirpate you too."

"Take the side door. Get a car. I'll meet you out front," I said to my friends without thinking, turning back to the man, holding the wraith's sword high, ready to duel.

"Dean, no, there are five of us," Liv protested.

"Well, technically, three and a half," Flynn said, drawing a nasty look from the Gnomelings.

"I'm the only one with a sword. He'll mow us down in this hallway if we all attack." I squinted my eyes as my face pinched with fury. "I have to do this alone." I couldn't believe I had just said that.

"Not a chance," Flynn said. "We're not leaving you."

"Remember when we were six? The day you carried my bike to the top of Juliana's hill," I said.

"Yeah. I took off your training wheels," Flynn said.

"You told me you were gonna give me a push. You asked that I trust you."

"That was the first time you rode alone without falling."

"Exactly," I said. "And do you remember that same summer you ripped the water wings from my arms and threw me into the deep end of Riley's pool?" I said.

"That was the day you learned to not drown," Flynn cocked a sideways smile.

"I trusted you. Now, I'm asking you to do the same." I turned to Flynn. I don't think I've ever been as sincere as the moment I looked at him and said, "I need you to trust me."

I could tell that Flynn's first instinct was to disregard my request. Instead, he nodded, put his hand on Liv's shoulder, and said, "He'll meet us out front."

"Dean, no," Liv said.

"Liv," Flynn reassured, "he'll be fine. Let's get a car."

"What's a car?" I heard Griff ask curiously as the group's footsteps faded from earshot.

"Sacrificing yourself for your friends." The man carved an X through the air with his rapier. "Brave. Stupid, but brave."

"Who are you?" I unveiled the wraith's blade, pointing the tip at the man's heart. Rage began to pump through me. "How do you know about my dad? How do you know about the cave?"

"Silly boy," the man chuckled. "I was there. I've always been there. But you know this. You've seen me in your dreams."

"I don't understand." The bad part was that I did understand. I understood a lot of it all too well. I just didn't want to admit it.

"Oh, Dean Moyers, I wish I had time to catch you up on the history of things, but really, I grow tired of talking." The man turned sideways. He started scooting in my direction, spinning and hacking while twirling his sword. "Now, do us all a favor," he inhaled through his nose. "Say hi to your dear father when you meet him. I'd really like to go home."

Home? He meant Second Realm.

The man lunged at me, driving his sword forward and aiming at my stomach. I spun ninety degrees, dodging the sword, ending up on my tiptoes, hunching over his errant attack. He slashed upward, but again I dodged and felt a gush of wind from the swipe tickle the peach fuzz on my cheek. I bounced back a few paces and readied my sword. He was good. I knew I had to go on the offensive, so I swung from side to side, waist to head, the blade narrowly missing its target with each attempt. The mystery man had backed into the ice machine with the lid left open. He dug his free hand around, grabbing a handful of cubes. He fired them at my face, momentarily distracting me. Now he was on the attack, cleaving and stabbing away, trying to mutilate my torso, but I parried. By God, I hadn't as much as played with pretend swords since I was a kid, but I parried.

The battle raged on as we moved down the hall of flickering lights. I danced past portraits on the walls of English royalty, battles, and landmarks. Now and again, curious heads of curious hotel visitors would pop out of their rooms, then scurry back inside. The song of the swords clanging against one another was like a chorus of church bells, beautiful but ominous, for one of us was likely to never leave this place. My movements were instinctual, only I didn't know how I had these instincts. Each thrust, parry, strike, and step felt like someone or something was guiding me. I was a video game character amid a quick-time event controlled by a pre-teen. I was a marionette without strings. And I was winning.

I pushed forward, using all my strength as I wildly slashed away at my enemy, hacking downward repeatedly. We reached the last room in the corridor when the man stumbled on a pizza box a hotel guest had left outside their door. He slipped to the ground, causing his sword to drop at my feet. Before he could react, I scooped it up and held the tips of both blades to his throat.

"I'm going to give you one more chance," I said, trying to make my voice sound unwavering and deep. "Who. Are. You?! What's your name?" The man didn't answer. He only smiled. Though his face was still shrouded in shadow beneath his hat, I observed his teeth had a layer of black film on them. Not only that, but they were unusually sharp. He started to chuckle again, his throat pulsating with each grunt. "What's so funny?" I said.

"You're funny, Dean from Pittsburgh," a voice from behind surprised me. Even more surprising was the tip of a sword poking through my layers of clothes into my lower back. The Peggs had broken free of their bonds and surrounded me, with two of them crossing in front of me, standing with their backs to the glass door at the end of the hallway, which led outside.

"Finish him. Bring me the amulet," the man ordered as he lumbered to his feet, wiping himself clean and snatching the swords from my stunned hands.

"With pleasure, Mister Thorne," Burt Pegg said as he kicked the back of my knees, dropping me instantly. Mister Thorne? That was his name. Only… Why did that sound familiar? I'd heard it somewhere before. Or maybe I was losing my mind. Either way, my thoughts were put on hold as I saw the shadow of the broadsword dangle high above my head, ready to swing down like a guillotine. I closed my eyes, wishing I was somewhere else. Wishing I hadn't sent my friends away.

Wishing Flynn and the Gnomelings knew how to tie a better knot whose strength matched its appearance. But wishing got me nowhere as I looked up and watched the blade plunge downward. Time froze as images of Mom and Dad, and even my little brat of a brother flashed through my mind. Pictures of Liv and Flynn and everything that led to this point. I closed my eyes, resigned to my fate, but this was not to be my end.

"Wait!" I said, my eyes shooting open. Thorne turned to face me. "You can't kill me."

"Oh," he hesitated, signaling Burt to hold off on my execution. "Why not?"

"There's another piece of the amulet. Only I know where it is."

"You're bluffing."

I held my face as stern as possible. I'd never tell him where the amulet was, but at least I could buy some time.

The Peggs looked at their boss, waiting for his orders. Just then, a chorus of sirens filled the air. Police sirens, not the mythical sea creatures. Flashing blue and red lights reflected off the windows and glass doorways of the hotel. The wraiths looked at one another, then at Thorne. "Bring him with us," Thorne ordered.

The wraiths lifted me to my feet. Burt pushed me forward, marching me down the hall, when the screech of my mom's whistle and the buzz of a car horn rang out. I glanced up and saw headlights approaching, so I dove out of the way just as a black taxi cab barreled through the hotel's glass doors, colliding with the Peggs, sending Tommy into Burt and William into the mystery man, leaving me sitting in a fog of dust.

"Get in!" Liv yelled from the passenger seat. She had a jagged piece of broken lamp glass in her hand, holding up to the driver's neck. Without delay, I hustled around the car and dove into the open back door.

"This is a car," Griff shared with glee. "I like it." He giggled uncontrollably as he rocked back and forth on the seat cushion.

"Me too, Griff. I like it too."

STORMING THE CASTLE

I'd never seen a castle in real life. Only on TV, in movies, and at the Magic Kingdom, if that even counts. But as I stared out the taxi window, looking at Warwick Castle with its massive towers, I found the sight absolutely spellbinding. Like I had just traveled back to the middle-ages. A low layer of fog framed the entire stone structure that stood easily over one-hundred feet tall with lookout towers equipped with lit torches, large castle doors that appeared impenetrable, and what I hoped would be dungeons. And to top it off, the castle was surrounded by a dry moat. Of course, Flynn thought it would cool if the moats were filled with lava or oil and protected by crocodiles. At first, he said great white sharks, but Liv quickly pointed out that great whites don't often live in man-made freshwater moats.

On the drive to the castle, we'd caught Flynn up on the nuclear truth bomb the Gnomelings dropped on us about creatures, other realms, their mission, and my family being some sort of warrior royalty. Surprisingly Flynn took it pretty well. In fact, the only part he had trouble believing was that cave trolls didn't have sharp teeth. Tubb and Griff explained the cave trolls were toothless, and while they could crush you with the snap of their gargantuan fingers, they'd have to mush you into pulp and drink you through a straw rather than chew your bones. Mountain trolls, on the other hand, had teeth the size of elephant tusks along with huge curling horns that were super demonic.

I also shared the name Mister Thorne with my friends. Neither Liv, Flynn, nor our driver thought it sounded familiar, but for some odd reason, I couldn't shake the fact that I'd heard it before. During the drive, Liv ran through a condensed version of the castle's history. Given what had just taken place at the hotel, a lesson may have seemed odd, but what she shared could help identify potential resting places of the next piece of the amulet.

"These days, the castle is mainly a tourist trap," she said in the tone of a seasoned tour guide. "One bit of warning, though, there will definitely be security guards roaming the grounds."

"It's ginormous," Tubb said. His face, with Griff's right alongside, was planted firmly against the rear windshield. Their breath fogged it up like steam in a hot shower.

"The perimeter of the walls is roughly one hundred and thirty by eighty meters," Liv said.

Flynn's head tilted to the side as he narrowed his gaze. "Uh, yeah, so can you break that down for us? In English."

"That was English," Liv said.

"Yeah, but mathematically speaking."

"Break what down, exactly?" Liv asked.

"The one hundred and thirty by eighty meters part. Roughly how many feet is that?" Flynn asked.

"How is this conversation helping?" Liv said.

"Well, I don't know anything about the Dewey Decimal System, so putting it in feet helps me strategize and gives me a good visual representation of the castle."

"A good visual representation of the castle?" Liv grumbled. "Just look out the window. That should give you a good visual representation of the castle."

"Valid," Flynn shrugged as he took Liv's advice.

"There are two entrances to the castle," Liv continued, only slightly annoyed. "One on the north wall. The other is on the west. There used to be a drawbridge over the moat in the northeast section, but it was closed due to—" Liv looked at Flynn, who was practically salivating at hearing the word drawbridge. "Due to decay, not crocodiles. Sorry, Flynn."

"Dang," Flynn said as the cab rumbled over a bridge that crossed the River Avon.

I stared intently at its black water as Liv continued her lesson. Her voice faded until it was nothing more than muffled background noise. I fell into a trance until the cab driver announced we had reached our destination. Despite being held hostage for the first mile of our trip, the cab driver was pretty cool. Apparently, he used to work with Liv's mom at a factory up North. He even forgave her for holding a sharp object to his throat and discounted our fare. "We've parked at the

159

motte with the lights off, just as you requested," the driver said. The motte was a huge mound with a tower up top that gave defending soldiers the high ground versus their enemies. Though, now all it did was give us a hill to climb. Liv thought it would be best to sneak in on this side of the castle grounds, fearing the front entrance near The Great Hall would be swarming with security.

"Thank you," Liv said as she pulled a wad of money from her pocket, handing it to our driver. "Remember. Wait for us, and I'll pay you double when we return."

"You better. The scratches on the hood aren't going to pay for themselves."

"And not a word of this to my mum?" Liv asked skeptically.

"Now that'll cost you extra," he said, pulling his faded, sweat-stained baseball cap down over his eyes and leaning back in his seat.

We quietly exited the cab, closed the doors carefully, and crept across the road that encircled the castle. The nearest tower was up the hill directly in front of us. Looking at it now, I could see why Liv chose this path. Between us and the castle walls stood trees, bushes, shrubbery, and rows upon rows of other thick greenery. It was so dense that I could barely make out the tower overlooking the entire southwest side of the property.

"There's a gate just up the hill, to the left of Time Tower."

I nodded, pretending to have a clue where Time Tower was. "And if it's locked?" I asked.

"No worries. We can climb the walls."

"Climb the castle walls?" Flynn said reluctantly.

"Sure. Me and my mates have done it loads of times."

"Do your mates have short, chubby stumps like these guys?" Flynn asked, grabbing hold of Griff's leg, wiggling it about like a dog's chew toy.

"They'll be fine," Liv said with a snort as she laughed. "We could always toss them over." Liv led the way, disappearing into the bushes.

Griff's face was blanketed in shock. "It'll be ok," Tubb tried to reassure him.

"I'm sure she's kidding," I said, leaving the Gnomelings behind, knowing full well Liv wasn't kidding.

As I reached the top of the hill and exited the foliage, I plucked dozens of thorns from my arms and legs that left my skin looking like the aftermath of an allergy skin prick test. *Why were there so many thorn bushes in this country?*

Flynn was right on my tail, trying to catch his breath. "Did I ever tell you I hate hills?" he said, doubling over, resting his hands on his knees.

"Same," I put my hands on the top of my head, doing my best to fight off cramps like Coach Kennon taught us in third-grade soccer.

"Where's Liv?" he asked.

"Alright, gents, it looks like we're climbing," Liv appeared from around the corner.

"You've got to be joking?" Flynn said.

"Gate's locked," Liv said.

"So break it," Flynn said.

Liv rolled her eyes. "There are at least three guards patrolling right inside. They'd hear us. Hang on a second," Liv perked up as if she remembered something important.

"What is it?" I had to know.

"It's our lucky day," she smiled. "The Renaissance fair is this weekend."

"How is that lucky?" I wondered out loud. "Wouldn't the fair bring more people? More security?"

"Usually, the commons are wide open, and we would be exposed trying to cross. But because of the fair, they have tents and booths everywhere, which should give us plenty of cover. As far as security goes, I doubt they'd bring on more guards at night." Liv looked around curiously. "Where are the little ones?"

"Let's go, humans," Griff's whisper carried across the night breeze. I looked around but didn't see him – that was until I looked up. Tubb and Griff were already scaling the walls. One of them had latched their elven rope around a row of brick at the top of the tower.

"Brilliant," Liv said.

"He hooked it onto the parapet," I added.

"Para-what?" Flynn chimed in.

"Parapet. It's the short wall on the top that soldiers can see over. The raised parts are called merlons," I said.

"And the indents are crenels," Liv said. Somehow, as if it were even possible, I started crushing on Liv more each second we were together.

"Nerd alert." Flynn shook his head, rolling his eyes violently. "You two are meant for each other."

"What? We just play a lot of Shire Knights." I tried to play it cool.

"Humans!" Tubb said impatiently. The Gnomelings both stood atop the parapet, peering over at us. "Whatcha be waiting for? Someone to toss you up?" He nudged Griff with a wry smile.

Once we reached the lookout tower, we huddled up and stared out at the circular fortress surrounded by stone and echoes of the past. The ancient stronghold had three large towers with at least four other smaller vantage points. Just as Liv described, rows upon rows of tents sat in the center of the castle grounds. All of them were decorated for the fair. Torches on poles sectioned the tents off into quarters. Each section had a different color scheme. Looking at them clockwise, the tents were dark red, green, yellow, and blue. It's like they weren't even trying to hide their obvious rip-off of the Hogwarts house colors.

"So," Flynn said, "where's the next amulet?"

"No idea." I shrugged and continued to scan the area. "The last one kinda told us where to go. I figure that once we're close, it'll give us a sign."

"Tubb, Griff, you said the protectors of your realm, they – hid the amulets, right? After they split them up," Liv asked.

"That's what the stories say," Tubb said.

"So they'd be buried somewhere secret, somewhere safe?" I asked.

"If you were an amulet, where would you hide?" Flynn said.

"Guard towers," Liv said.

"The kitchen," Tubb said.

"The arsenal," Griff added.

"In the dungeon?" I questioned, drawing a collective look. "What? It's probably underground, well protected, and face it, most people are trying to escape a dungeon, not investigate it." Just thinking about the dungeon raised my heart rate until I could feel my pulse spasm through my stomach. I loved dungeons. The cages, the dim lighting, the shackles. I knew that was weird, but they reminded me of old-school video games and eighties movies.

"He's got a point," Flynn said. "Where's the dungeon?"

All eyes turned to Liv, our resident expert. "Straight through, past all of the guards."

I scanned the field before us and the castle walls that lined our path. We had two choices: sneak around the top of the castle or weave our way through the field of tents. The very second I was about to lay out my deductions, a guard climbed a ladder by the tower to our right with his flashlight in his mouth. I looked to our left, realizing our path was blocked by a half-dozen crates stacked at least ten feet high. There's no way we could climb that without being seen.

"I guess the high ground is out of the question," Liv said.

"Through the tents we go," I replied.

Sneaking past the guards proved to be an easier feat than expected. Liv's recon ended up being correct, as there were only three security officers in total. The first guard, the guy we saw climbing the ladder, was younger. I guessed he was probably an off-duty police officer or former military, judging by the way he carried himself as he surveyed the grounds. He would patrol a few yards, then scan outside the castle walls. His movements were precise yet predictable, and we timed our maneuvers to match his. Every time he'd look outside, we'd scamper from tent to tent. Once he stopped for a smoke break, we were in the clear. The second guard was an older lady. I told Flynn she was probably in her mid-forties. My mom would freak out if she heard me call someone in their forties 'old.' She sat at the northern gates rifling through paperwork, probably getting ready for a shipment for the fair, I thought. And the last guard was the size and age of Señor Tierney – our high school Spanish teacher. Tierney reminded everyone of the mayor of munchkin city in *The Wizard of Oz*, only slightly taller but with less hair. This guard, if you could call him that, was sleeping at his post, snoring so loud that he didn't even hear Griff face plant after tripping over a rope that was holding down a catapult in the middle of the grounds. And although it had never lit up or gone crazy like before, throughout our trek across the castle, I'd felt a slight vibration from the amulet. The closer we moved toward the eastern walls, the stronger the sensation.

"It must be in here," I said as we reached the entrance to the dungeon. *I knew it!*

The tiny hairs on the back of my neck stood at attention yet again.

Spidey sense.

"Down we go," Flynn said.

THE FORGOTTEN

I could feel the air get colder as we stepped inside the castle and climbed down the stone stairwell into the dungeons. Aftermarket fluorescent red and blue lights emblazoned our path, which was otherwise pitch black. Our footsteps, as quiet as they were, still echoed in the caverns below, warning anyone listening of our intrusion. Luckily, no one else was down here. As we reached the base of the dark, dank stairwell, we began to run into chambers where the prisoners of old were kept. Tiny rooms with little slits carved into the rock wall provided a hint of moonlight peering in behind the iron bars. Within each chamber sat hanging caskets, or gibbets, where bodies of prisoners were once proudly displayed. A warning for all not to suffer the same fate. They reminded me of human-sized bird cages.

"Moyers," Flynn said, pointing at my chest. "It's doing that thing again." I glanced beneath my shirt, the amulet radiated. However, it was different than before. More of a butterscotch shade of yellow compared to the purple, red, blue, and green we'd seen in the forest and at the hotel.

"We're getting close," I said. We pushed through a small corridor with ceilings no more than five feet high, into a larger room that could have only been one thing: the torture chamber. Chains with arm and ankle restraints hung from the damp and slimy walls. You could hear the water dripping from the ceiling above – the absolute definition of gloomy. Two chairs centered the room; one had four-inch spikes protruding from the seat, while the other had a cloth executioner's hood draped over the top. Swords, knives, axes, and other trade tools dangled from hooks lining each side of the room. And against the far wall sat a guillotine that was dark brown with streaks of black running down its front. "This way," I motioned to the western corner of the room, shrouded in a blanket of darkness.

"How can you be telling?" Griff asked as the group followed me. I pulled the amulet from my shirt, held it out toward the corner, then let go. Rather than drop helplessly against my chest, the amulet hovered, willing me forward. "I see," he said, gulping, with fear in his voice.

"Well, I can't see a thing," Liv said. I felt her hand on my back. She clenched my shirt tight as we paraded forward. The further we moved, the darker it became until, eventually, it was pitch black - aside from the intermittent flickering of the amulet. I reached out, feeling the cold walls to my right and left as our path constricted. The ceiling was covered in cobwebs. The occasional drop of water would splash against my skin, making me jump each time.

"How far does this go?" Flynn asked. Before answering, I bumped straight into a wall that blocked our path.

"That can't be right," I said as I walked around blindly. To my front, left, and right there was nothing but stone. No doors. No windows. No nothing. "I don't get it."

"Dean," Liv said. "Why has the amulet stopped glowing?"

She was right. Not only had the flickering stopped, leaving us in complete darkness, but it had also stopped leading us forward.

"Was it wrong? Did it take us the wrong way?" Flynn said.

"Maybe," I said. "Or maybe not." The amulet wasn't lit, but I could feel it pulling. Lightly tugging at first, then jerking slowly but deliberately. Again and again, the amulet pulled downward. "Down? Down where?" I questioned.

"I'm sorry?" Liv wondered who I was talking to.

"It's pulling me toward the ground." I realized how insane I must sound, talking to a piece of jewelry again.

"I hate to say it, bro," Flynn said, "But unless the tiny dudes have a shovel hidden in their trousers, we ain't heading down."

"I been telling you we should have brought the shovel," I heard Tubb whisper to Griff.

I stuck out my foot, scouring around along the edges of our confined space with the tips of my toes, tracing the cracks and mortar lines. Next, I began to tap my foot in beats of three against random spaces on the floor beneath us.

"I really hope you're not dancing again," Flynn said sarcastically.

"Everyone take a few steps back," I ordered. I heard my friends shuffle away. I started investigating the ground below, tapping it with my foot. The ground was solid. I spun around and inched back in the direction we had come from, continuing to tap the ground. It was still solid, and the tugging on the amulet was even stronger. "Guys, take a few more steps back." *Tap, tap, tap.*

"Do that again," Liv said. "Right there." I couldn't see her, not even the whites of her eyes, but I could hear the anticipation in her voice.

Tap, tap, tap. "It's hollow," I shouted, a little too loud for Flynn's liking.

"Shhh," Flynn warned as he backhanded me across the shoulder. "You don't want to wake Sleeping Beauty upstairs."

I dropped to the floor, exploring with my fingers. "The ground. It's different here." There was a thin layer of dirt and small rock.

I heard Liv scurrying as she dropped to the ground beside me. We frantically swept the dirt and rock aside. "Do it again," Liv said.

I tapped the ground with my fist. "It feels like wood."

"Plywood," she said.

My eager hands stirred, sliding across the floor. She was right. It was a piece of plywood. Which meant that something must be down here. "It must be covering something," I said.

"I found a crease," Liv said. "If we could pull this up, there may be a passageway underneath us."

"You two wouldn't happen to have a hammer, would you?" Flynn said. I couldn't see who he was talking to, but I guessed he was addressing Tubb and Griff.

"What be a hammer?" Griff asked.

"A tool with a stone head and claw on the back for prying," Liv said.

"Afraid not," Griff said. "But I do have a pry bar."

"Why do you have a…You know what, never mind," I said. "Just pass it forward."

"Sure thing, human. Here you go," Griff said.

Plunk. The sound of metal smacking skull rang out. "Ouch," Tubb cried. "Be careful with that."

"Sorry," Griff said.

"Here you be, Master Flynn," Tubb said in the darkness.

"Liv," Flynn said as she handed over the pry bar.

"Dean," Liv said as I reached out, blindly feeling around for the bar. My fingertips touched the cold metal. Sliding my hand forward to gain a better grip, I felt the warmth of Liv's hand. For a moment, my fingertips lingered. The touch of her skin sent shivers down my spine and sent my insides sputtering. My brain and heart instantly engaged in a battle of tug-of-war. I should probably pull away, I thought. We had work to do. What if my hand gets clammy or sweaty, and she thinks it's gross? What if she finds this weird? My heart urged me to grab her hand, but I was unsure.

Grab her hand, bro, I could hear Flynn saying like a little cartoon devil on my shoulder. I didn't know what to do, so I did nothing. I just sat there with my fingertips resting on the back of Liv's hand. That's when I felt it. With her free hand, Liv grabbed my fingers. At first, she seemed to be pulling them away, prying them off mine. I was so embarrassed. She probably thinks I'm a creep. But before I could self-impose a score of ten out of ten on the weirdo scale, Liv pulled my hand upward, interlocking her fingers with mine. At that moment, we held hands in the dungeon. At that moment, everything was perfect, as the world seemed to disappear. The room felt like it was lighting up for us. Our heart lights were shining, like in E.T., shimmering a heavenly hue, mimicking all of the stars in the sky, celebrating our affection. That's when I heard Flynn clear his throat. I looked up and saw his face and the faces of the Gnomelings. The heavenly hue wasn't the constellations rejoicing our love. It wasn't our heart lights. No, the amulet was glowing brightly again, shining a light over us and our interlocked fingers.

"So, ummm," Flynn said, "this is awkward."

"I was just," Liv stammered.

"We were — just, pry bar, but, hands, no move." I tried formulating a sentence, but words, brains, and mouths did not want to cooperate, and I sounded like a dyslexic caveman. I wondered if the amulet was intentionally embarrassing me.

"Oh, for pity's sake. How about we…" Liv motioned toward the plywood square beneath us.

"Good idea," I responded, releasing her hand and gripping the pry bar. I stood up, using the light from the glowing amulet to see. Wedging the end of the bar between the plywood and the wall, I instructed the others to step back. I tightly gripped the bar, constricting my fingers around the metal.

"Dude, I hate to say it, but maybe I should do this," Flynn said. "I mean, face it, the last time you tried to work with a power tool, you almost dismembered a finger and electrocuted Whiskers."

"How did Dean electrocute his whiskers?" Tubb asked curiously, fiddling with his own whiskers sticking off his nose.

"Whiskers is my cat," Flynn said.

"Oh my daisies," Tubb said, taking another cautious step backward, hiding behind Flynn with his eyes closed.

"Seriously, Moyers, if you want, I can—"

With an effortless heave upward, I lifted the piece of plywood clear off the floor in one swift pull.

"Dang," Flynn said. Dang was a good way to put it. That was easy. It was almost too easy, like when I lifted Liv from the ground in the forest. Maybe the angle I chose was just right, or maybe the nails weren't well-hammered, making it easy to pry away. Or maybe…just maybe…something was happening to me. My strength, spidey sense, and sword fighting skills developed so quickly since we found the amulet in the forest. But I knew there would be time to figure it out later. I gazed downward and saw a rusty metal grate with a latch on each of the four corners.

"What is it?" Griff asked. "A mine?"

"No," Liv said in awe. "I've read about this." She started to flip the latches open, one by one. "Oh my," she said.

"Oh my, what? And don't say daisies" I didn't like the sound of Liv's tone.

"There's a lower dungeon. It's a small, terrible, awful place that was used to starve and torture the worst of prisoners. Many prisoners died here. They would drop them down, covering the hole so no light, sound, or anything would come through. Occasionally, they'd dump human waste through the grate until the prisoners would suffocate on —"

"And, that's enough story time for me," Flynn interrupted.

"They called this place The Forgotten," Liv said.

I shuddered at the thought. I wished I could forget everything Liv just said. Thinking about being in that hole gave me the creeps.

"Be seeming like a perfect place to hide something, though. Doesn't it?" Tubb said, tapping his chin thoughtfully.

"It does," I agreed.

"Like another amulet, perhaps?"

I nodded regretfully.

"So you'll need to go down there to check," Griff said.

"Wait, what?" I shouted so loud that I thought I would definitely wake the sleeping guard this time.

"And there's only room for one," Flynn said, gulping as he stared into the black pit.

"The amulet. It's pointed down, right?" Liv said. I tried to come up with something, anything, which would keep me from going alone into a place called The Forgotten.

"Maybe there's a lower level. Another stairwell somewhere," I said.

"There isn't." Liv put her hand on my shoulder. What I wouldn't give to go back in time, even two minutes ago when we held hands. That felt amazing, magical even. Instead, her hand on my shoulder now appeared to be one of those "Good luck. Don't die in there" moments.

Y

I held the elven rope as tight as possible, so tight that the twine burned my hands. I could feel my skin chafing.

"See anything yet?" Flynn's words echoed around me in this potential chamber of secrets.

"No. Not yet." I must have been fifteen feet down into the hole, but I wanted to be home, away from here. I loved castles and knights. I loved stories of dungeons and what lurked beneath, but this... this was NOT OK! I'd been down here for thirty seconds and was already losing my mind. I could only imagine the madness if someone were put down here for days, weeks, or worse.

I had to be getting close to the floor, so I stretched, reaching my leg downward. There was only air and dangling for a second, but then I felt it; my foot brushed against something. I thought it was the ground, but as I planted the toe of my shoe, it moved -- the ground moved. I screamed a high-pitched shrill.

"Are you alright?" Liv asked.

"Hang on." I collected myself, put the rope between my knees, and held on tight with my right hand. With my left, I grabbed the amulet. Lucky for me, it was lighting up again, so I decided to use it the same way you'd use a flashlight. I aimed it toward the ground, worried what I would see. But there it was... actual solid ground. I breathed a sigh of relief, lowered both feet, touched down, and scanned the floor. It was filthy with black mold and other fungi growing everywhere. Not to mention it smelled disgusting. "I'm good. I just slipped," I reassured my friends. I spotted my shoe had come untied. That was it. I must have stepped on one of the knots of my laces. I always put a few knots on the laces, so they didn't slip back through the top hole. That had to be why I felt something move. *What a chicken*, I mocked myself. Crying over a shoelace. It's not like there was a giant— "Snake!" I shouted at the top of my lungs as a gigantic snake slithered between my feet.

SNAKES - WHY DID IT HAVE TO BE SNAKES?

The freakish serpent must have been ten feet long as it hoisted itself in the air. I leapt skyward, pulling down on the rope as hard as possible. Pulling it straight out of Flynn's unprepared hands. I panicked as the entire rope fell down on top of me. The snake hissed, then flashed its fangs, lunging at me, trying its best to strike. I started to dance, tiptoeing around in fear - fear of it touching me, fear of it biting me. I liked to think that I wasn't afraid of too much, even though I ended up being afraid of a lot (dolls, clowns, school bullies, frogs... yes, frogs), but snakes were definitely high on my list. My mom always told me I was overreacting, but I was certain I had ophidiophobia: an unhealthy fear of snakes. I hated their soulless, black, beady eyes, their scales, the way they moved, the way they hissed, and their sharp teeth. I hated how they shed their skin, leaving a memory of themselves wherever they felt necessary. I hated real snakes, plastic snakes, stuffed animal snakes, and I especially hated those wooden toy ones that wriggled around in your hand with the most subtle movements. I even hated fictitious snakes - they all creeped me out.

"Human?!" the Gnomelings cried.

"Moyers!" Flynn shouted, probably ready to jump in to rescue me.

"Dean!" Liv's voice trembled.

I backed into the corner and gathered whatever wits I had left. I gripped the rope like a whip. I started flailing and wailing it around like a pool noodle. I must have looked ridiculous, but lucky for me, no one could see it. Even if I hit the snake, it wouldn't have done much more than annoy the serpent. I switched from a two-handed swing to a one-handed grip, taking the amulet in my free hand. As I panned side to side, I caught a glimpse of the snake's ninety-nine-foot tail slithering away, disappearing into a hole in the wall.

"Get yourself together, Dean," I said out loud. Still, on guard, I held the rope and amulet tight. At any second, that snake could come charging back at me, only it didn't. In fact, I could hear its nasty squirming moving further away. Now what? I thought as I looked at my surroundings. This place was cramped - like, claustrophobia city. Like, buried alive type of cramped. Why would the amulet lead me here? I started checking for loose bricks or rocks, hoping there'd be something hidden yet obvious. The thought even crossed my mind that there may be a secret lever to pull that would lead to an even more secret room, but none of the above was true. Instead, it was just me, the rocks, the smell, and that hole with that snake.

Frustration mounted. I defiantly gazed at the amulet, waiting for further instructions, but the blasted thing still pointed down. "How much further down do you want me to go?" I said with the same attitude that usually got Flynn in trouble with teachers at school. "Here," I dropped to the ground of the cramped space, "is this down enough for you?" I decided to take it one step further. I contorted my body until my chest was between my knees and my cheek was firmly pressed against the moldy floor. "How about this? Is this better?"

The amulet sprang to life on cue as if it were listening. It lifted from the ground, and with the chain outstretched, it pulled directly into the snake hole.

"No way." I tried to return to my knees in retreat, but the amulet tugged on my neck so hard that it jerked me back to the floor. "I am not sticking my hand in there!"

"Uh, Moyers. Who you talking to?"

I didn't answer Flynn. Instead, I just kept up with my one-sided debate with the charm. "Listen. I get that it's my destiny and all, but maybe you didn't see the monster that slithered its way in there. So, unless you have a gigantic snake trap I can use, I suggest we try to find another way."

"Your friend is wonkier than a bucket of poodle noodles," Griff said.

"Guys, I'm coming up." Resisting the amulet's power, I stood, wound the elven rope around my arm, and bundled it up, keeping a few feet of slack for myself. "Catch the rope," I said as I heaved it upward.

"Got it," Flynn said.

"Did you get the amulet?" Liv said.

Without a response, I tugged the rope and put my feet against the wall, starting my ascent. I thought my friends would understand. They were my friends, after all. We'd figure something out. Maybe one of them could reach into the hole. Someone who didn't have a deathly fear of snakes. But it wasn't them I had to convince. The amulet was *not* pleased. It began to glow more aggressively. The butterscotch yellow had a hint of amber with a layer of red around it. "Don't get mad at me," I said. "Let someone else have a try. Someone not named…"

As I was about to say my name, I noticed something odd. Something I hadn't seen on the way down. There was a carving into an off-colored brick in front of me, with symbols or hieroglyphics etched into the stone. They were identical to the ones we saw on the Gnomelings' map.

I lowered my feet back onto the ground. I pushed closer to the symbols until the glow of the amulet revealed some sort of message. "Tubb, Griff," I called. "I think I found some Gnomarian writing. Can you translate something if I tell you some symbols?"

"Try us," said Tubb.

I traced my fingers along the symbols etched into the rock. There was something enchanting about the fine detail. "There's an X. Do you know what an X is?"

"Of course, we know what an X is," Griff said loudly. "What's an X?" I heard him whisper.

"It's a sort of diagonal cross," Liv shared.

"What next?" Tubb said.

"A fork. A pitchfork, maybe. Almost like the one carved into the amulet. Except it has a flat line at the base and an extra prong at the top."

179

"Is that all?" Tubb asked.

"No, there's one more symbol. It's a bird. Some sort of bird. I've seen this before. It's a dove."

"You be certain?" Tubb asked.

"Positive. My dad had a tattoo of a small dove between his thumb and index finger. The same one," I said, thinking this couldn't be a coincidence.

"Dean, the message means Desmond was here," Tubb said.

"You're pulling my leg."

"How can he pull the leg of Dean when Dean is down there, and we be up here?" Griff asked.

Why would someone carve that into a rock? Here of all places. Unless—unless my dad was down here, I thought. He left me a note! He must have written it even if it wasn't meant for me. Electricity jolted through me at the thought of my Dad being here. "Ok. But why does a dove mean Desmond?"

"When a guardian is born, they get a symbol. Your grandfather, whose symbol was a lion, chose the dove for your father," Tubb said. "He was a peace bringer."

"So what's Dean's?" Flynn asked." What did his dad choose for him?"

"A fanged coiler," Griff said.

"Sounds intimidating. What is it?" Liv asked.

"I think you call them snakes," Tubb said.

I stared at the markings on the stone, still shell-shocked, still in awe. My dad was here. Right here. Standing where I'm standing. I wondered if he was afraid too. Wait… "Did you just say my symbol is a snake?" Are you kidding me? Of all the animals, I got a snake.

"To be fair, a fanged coiler sounds way cooler," Liv said.

Animal nomenclature aside, I was left with a choice to make. I knew what Dad would do, so I knew what I had to do. I couldn't back down. I wondered if I did, would he see me. Would Dad know I was a failure? A sudden burst of adrenaline surged through me, and I went for it. I dropped back to the floor, sticking my hand inside the unknown.

It was NASTY! My fingers searched and scoured, yet all I found was wetness, clumps of who knows what, and tangles of hair and spider webs. At one point, I swear I squeezed a mushy clump of rat poop. Honestly, I wanted to vomit. "C'mon," I willed myself to keep looking. I pushed my body flat against the ground until my shoulder was pressed firmly against the wall, and my arm was entirely in the hole. My fingers clawed, reaching out until I felt something. Not the rat poop, hair, dirt, or shedding snake skin, but something smooth and square. It kissed the edges of my fingertips. I couldn't get a good enough grip, so I flipped it in my direction. That did the trick. Right when I was ready to take hold of it- "Ouch!" Something bit me. That stinking snake. It bit me. I flicked my fingers, trying to ward off the devil. I could hear it hissing. I could feel it slithering all over the exposed skin of my arm. I wanted to back away, but there was something special about this tiny square thing.

With a grunt and a lunge, I dug deep, sinking my arm as far as it would go, willing myself until I could feel the small item in my grip. It was a box. A smooth box. And it was mine. *Chomp!* The beast bit down again. This time it was worse. I could feel the fangs dig into my flesh. It hurt even more as the fangs exited my skin. I could feel the warm blood pour out of my fresh wound. I screamed in pain as I retracted my hand, still holding the box tight.

"Dean!" my friends cried out again.

"I'm fine," I reassured them as I got to my feet. The snake slithered out of its hole and wound circles around me, gnashing its teeth. "Not this time, you ugly-fanged coiler," I said as I kicked the snake in the head. End over end, the snake spun before hitting the rock wall, dropping to the ground in a heap. "Get me out of here," I yelled to my friends, tucking the small box into my pocket and grabbing the rope.

As I ascended, I stared down at the snake, wondering if I had killed it. It looked so pathetic, lying there, so pitiful and lifeless. I almost felt sorry for it, until the monster twitched, jolted up, and sprung at me! I pulled my knees to my chest, narrowly avoiding its bite. The snake slithered back into its hole as I willed myself up the rope.

Did I mention I hate snakes?

ANOTHER BRICK IN THE WALL

"What is it?" Flynn hovered over me. The others soon joined him as I sat on one of the executioner's chairs, the one without the spikes.

"You're bleeding," Liv said as she took a square of cloth from her pocket, patting my wound dry. "Are these teeth marks?"

"I'm alright. Just a scratch."

"It has to be the amulet, right?" Liv asked as she got a better look at the box.

"I don't know," I said, uncertain. My amulet had gone wild the last time we found a part of the artifact. The way it behaved in The Forgotten was more like it was leading me to another clue. I didn't want to mention it to Flynn, Liv, or the Gnomelings, but I felt a strong connection to the amulet that hung around my neck. It was almost as if I could sense its emotions, and, more importantly, that it *had* emotions.

The tiny box was perfectly square and as smooth as silk. I felt around the object until I found a groove on the backside. I dug my fingernails into the groove and pried the box open. Inside was a piece of paper, rolled up like a scroll. "Move. I need the light," I said to Flynn. He ducked to the side, letting the gleam of the blue lights of the room shine down over my shoulder. I unrolled the paper with great anticipation. Did my dad write this? Likely not. This paper looked ancient. Maybe my grandfather or even his grandfather. When fully opened, the paper was still only about three inches long. There were numbers written on it, followed by a single word: Trebuchet.

"What's a trebuchet?" I asked, certain I had butchered the pronunciation.

"Isn't that a country in South America?" Flynn said.

"That's Paraguay," I said.

"My uncle Wippledunk played an instrument called a trebuchet back when he was in the band that sang at the Dancing Dingle," Griff said.

"He played the flute, Griff," Tubb said.

"Then what be a trebuchet?" Griff asked.

"That be what we're trying to figure out."

"You guys," Liv's voice rang out. "I know this!" We all turned and faced her expectantly. "It's another word for catapult. Outside of the castle, we drove by a massive catapult. Inside the grounds, by the tents, we saw another. Only smaller."

"Some of us saw it closer than others," Griff said, rubbing his chin, which still stung.

We crept back outside, keeping a close watch for the guards. The coast looked clear. One after another, we weaved between the tents until we reached the catapult. It was big, but not as big as the one outside of the castle. That one was old and was probably used in a siege against real soldiers. This one was likely used for party games or demonstrations. Still, it must have been fifteen feet tall and made of solid wood. There were ropes, levers, and cranks all around it. How could something so primitive be so complex?

"Do you know how to use this long-neck thing?" Tubb looked up at us.

"Don't look at me," Flynn said, focusing on Liv. "She's the one who knew all about the castle."

"From the internet, Flynn," Liv said. "They didn't let us shoot flaming fireballs in school."

"Look here," I held the scroll up to the moonlight. "The numbers." I read down the paper. *43° NE. Angle 20°. 60 inches. 80 pounds.* That had to mean something.

"Human," Griff whispered. "I have a directional circle. Maybe that will help."

"A what?" I asked. Griff reached into his endless backpack, plucking out a compass.

"Forty-three degrees northeast," Griff said as he spun clockwise until the arrow of the compass teetered between forty and forty-five degrees northeast.

"That must be where we aim." I handed Liv the scroll, bent down, and gripped one of two handles attached to the base of the trebuchet. The entire structure appeared to be on a rotating track. "Flynn, help me move this thing." Flynn and I pushed the trebuchet until we were in line with Griff. We lowered the handles until the device locked in place. The catapult was pointed at the castle wall.

"The amulet must be hidden inside the wall somewhere," I said.

"Then we have to break it open," Liv said. "Angle twenty degrees. That might be the firing angle. Look," she said. "Along the arm." There were numbers. Liv climbed the rear of the catapult and grabbed hold of a lever. She pulled down until the lever stopped at the number marked twenty.

"Sixty inches," I said. "What has to be sixty inches?" We all studied the mechanism. A rope wound was tight, tied to the top of the trebuchet arm. It looked pretty long. "Griff," I turned to my companion, "can you climb up there and get that rope?"

"Can a horned peanut grow under a pumpkin bush?" he asked as if I had any clue what he was saying. "Of course," he reassured, then scaled the catapult. He nimbly reached the top and untied the rope, sending the loose end down to us. He untied the rest, climbed down, and draped it over the knob of the release arm.

"Sixty inches. That's about—" Flynn stopped to do some mental math. "Five feet." He smiled, proud of himself.

"And how many meters is that?" Liv said sarcastically. "You know, so I can strategize and get a visual representation," she mocked.

"And here I was starting to like you," Flynn said.

Liv smirked as she gripped the dangling rope as Griff finished his descent.

"I'm roughly sixty-five inches tall," Liv said. "So that would make sixty right about... here." She slid her hand up the rope, holding it tight.

"Great. What do we do with it?" Flynn asked.

"That must be where we attach the weapon," I said.

"Weapon?" Flynn said.

I searched the grounds. There were a few loose piles of wood and even a tent full of carnival game prizes, but nothing that would bust open a castle wall. "We need something heavy."

"Something like this?" Tubb said. He was lugging a bowling ball in our direction.

"Did you have that in your pack too?" Flynn asked.

"No. There's a bunch of them. Stacked right over there." Sure enough, we turned to see a stack of black bowling balls. Apparently, acquiring these was easier than having actual cannon balls for festival decorations.

"Give it to me," I ordered and returned to Liv. We tied the rope around the ball the best we could, making sure it would hold. Next, we double-checked the other end to ensure the rope wouldn't slip, fray, or snap.

"What now?" Liv said.

"Eighty pounds," I said.

"Here. On this side. There's a weight. Looks like a barbell weight sitting in this box." Flynn waved us over. He was right. On the far end of the trebuchet sat a small box. There was a large weight that read 10 lbs. along with two smaller weights.

"It's a counterweight. Its force flings the stone." Liv was brilliant.

"I can fetch more of those black orbs," Tubb said.

"That might work," I said. I gave Tubb a nod. He ran back and forth, retrieving bowling ball after bowling ball until we had seven in place on the counterweight slot along with the existing weights, trying our best to tie them down. The box, however, was overflowing. "Let's give it a try."

187

We all moved out of the way, everyone but Liv, that is. She pulled down on the rope, freeing it, setting the catapult into action. With all the bowling balls, the counterweight swung downward, thrusting the arm of the trebuchet with it. "It's gonna work," Liv said as the arm started to gain momentum. Just as it spun toward its peak, one bowling ball wobbled loose, followed by another, then another, all falling to the ground with a thud. Within a fraction of a second, all but a single bowling ball and the original weights had escaped, causing the arm's momentum to stop completely. The bowling ball we used for ammo didn't as much as budge from its resting place.

"They're too... round," I said. "We need something heavy with a flat bottom. Something that won't wobble loose." We sat and thought. We thought and sat. We looked around, but even with all the chunks of wood and carnival prizes strewn about, we either didn't have enough weight or risked overfilling the narrow counterweight box. Surely we didn't come this far to stop now.

"If only your brother, Jackson were here," Flynn said. "I'd gladly pick him up and toss him in the box."

That's when it hit me. "You're a genius," I said.

"I am?" Flynn said.

"Oh, Griff," I called out. Griff stirred. "Do you enjoy rides?"

"Oh, you betcha. I be loving rides. All kinds. Merri-go-circles. Spinning ferrets. Unicycle flyers. Horse dancing. But best of all, I love —Wait..." A concerned look crossed his face as if he were starting to put the pieces of a puzzle together. "Why do you be asking?"

Using an old leather belt found inside one of the tents, we strapped Griff to the counterweight box.

"Are you sure this be safe? Despite my rugged exterior, I am rather delicate." Nothing about Griff was rugged. But lucky for us, he was the right weight.

"You'll be fine. Just one jerk, a quick spin around, and it'll be all over." Or at least I hoped. I suddenly felt faint and dizzy. I prayed I wasn't sending Griff on a one-way trip to the afterlife.

Griff put his hands together and looked at the sky in a quick wish for good fortune.

"Ready?" Liv asked as she placed her hand around the rope. The ammo lay in the tray at the base of the catapult. Flynn double-checked the angles, then shot Liv a confident thumbs up.

"Griff?" I said. He gulped, closed his eyes, and shook yes.

Tubb buried his head between his knees. "I can't watch."

"If something happens to me," Griff looked at Tubb, "you can have my toenail collection."

"On three," I started. "One."

"Two," Flynn said.

"Three!" Liv jerked the rope back like she was starting a wind-up toy and let go.

The arm groaned as it whipped upward. The rope and ammunition stretched out until they were taut. The force of Griff as the counterweight flung the bowling ball ammunition into the air. We watched as the rope released from the arm while the ball soared toward the heavens. Well, everyone watched except for Griff; he was too busy being launched backward after slipping from his constraint, crashing headlong into a tent. Higher and higher, the ball climbed until it hit its apex, shot downward, then smashed into the castle wall with a booming *thud*. The impact was precise and exactly what we needed, causing a chunk of the castle wall to collapse. But it was also the last thing we needed as the beams of flashlights, and the sound of guard whistles approached.

"They heard us," Liv said.

"It sounded like a car crash," I said.

"Should we use our whistle too?" Flynn asked.

"NO!" Liv and I shouted in one voice.

"Tubb, get Griff," I said. With a nod, Tubb was off and running. I was still amazed at the Gnomelings' speed, despite their appearance. "Liv, Flynn, on me!" We rushed to the castle wall, searching through the rubble. I almost didn't notice the amulet around my neck, but it was spinning, glowing greens and blues, just like in the forest. "It's here!" I yelled.

"Did it work?" a woozy Griff said, barely keeping his footing. He had a welt on his head the size of a small cucumber.

"I think that did the trick!" I was elated. I frantically tossed aside chunks of stone, digging and clawing until I felt something. A cloth sack that vibrated and pulsated as it started to glow. "Got it!" I emerged from the rubble. I opened the sack to reveal the next part of the amulet. A broad smile crossed my face as I backpedaled past my friends. As before, the amulets converged with a blast of light, slightly growing in size. I held the amulet to the sky in celebration. "We did it!" But my friends didn't seem to share in my excitement. Their expressions were not ones of joy but of sheer terror. "The guards," I said to myself. Only, it wasn't the guards they were afraid of. Little did I know, the guards never made it to us. They were knocked out cold. All of them. Even sleeping beauty.

As I turned around, I came face to face with three sharp blades belonging to the three cloaked brothers dressed as wraiths. "Not you again," I said. The air in my lungs deflated.

"How did you find us?" I asked. I wasn't sure they'd tell me, but I had to know.

"You five are about as loud as a football crowd on Sunday mornings. Talking in the hall about the castle. We just had to figure out which castle you meant."

I felt so stupid. How could we be so careless?

"Hand it over," William Pegg roared as Burt and Tommy circled our position. They aimed their swords at Flynn and Liv. William trained his sword toward me, inches from my neck.

"Not a chance," I said as another faint spell took hold of me. My weak knees nearly caused me to topple over. I looked down at the wound on my arm from the snake bite. It wasn't bleeding, but it oozed a clear, goopy liquid.

"Don't think you're in any position to bargain, lad," Tommy said to me as he dug the tip of his blade into Liv's lower back.

"She's not a lad," Griff defended Liv valiantly. "She's obviously a lady!"

Tommy shrugged.

I wrapped my fingers tight around the charm and grumbled, "This amulet is mine. My own. My..."

"So help me, if you say precious, I'm going to be sick," Griff said.

"My family's!" I finished, to Griff's relief.

"I've heard enough," Burt said. "I'll kill this one first." He lifted his blade skyward above Flynn's head, showing me without words that he meant business. "You have two seconds before I —"

"Before you what?" a familiar man's voice came from behind the Peggs. William spun around, and his face was blasted by the beam of a flashlight. "Castle security," the man's voice said. "And you're under arrest."

Burt shielded his eyes while the rest of us got a better look at our savior. It wasn't any of the guards we'd seen. Not the former cop, the old lady, or the sleeping Spanish teacher. No, it was...

"Roger!" Flynn shouted with glee.

"Backup has arrived!" Our dwarf friend from the pub shouted as he stood before us with a flashlight, security uniform, and a taser gun which he held in his left hand, contacts aimed directly at Tommy. "Are you ready to ride the lightning, wraith?" Roger asked as he took aim, squinting with a sharpshooter's eye.

"You wouldn't," Tommy dared.

He would.

Without hesitation, Roger fired. The contacts of the taser stuck inside the hidden face of Tommy's cloak. Tommy fell to the ground with a grunt as his body began to twitch.

Roger reached around his back, pulling a second taser from his belt like an old-west gunslinger. He took aim and fired another shot, this time at Burt. But he missed the face opening. Instead, the taser connected down low, about waist high.

Burt chuckled, his laughter echoing off the castle walls. "Came up short, yet again," he mocked Roger's size and efforts.

"I wouldn't be so sure," Roger retorted with a wink, motioning for Burt to look down. Burt's eyes traced the contacts of the taser. A look of shock crossed his face as he realized his bone-dry wool cloak had started to spark. Within seconds, it was ablaze.

"Fire!" Burt yelled as he burst into flames. He dropped his sword, waving his arms hysterically. As he ran towards the exit in the direction of the lake, his cloak began to shred and burn away.

"What the?" Flynn's jaw dropped as he saw Burt was practically naked beneath the cloak, aside from plain, white underwear.

Flynn and Liv picked up Tommy and Burt's swords. Together, they converged on William, who, unrelenting, held his blade firm, trained on my throat.

"Drop it," said Roger.

"I'm taking that amulet," said William.

"Then you'll have to kill me for it," I said. "Only…"

"Let me guess. Only there's another piece, right?"

William took the words right out of my mouth. But how did he know? "The thing is, you and your mates are terrible at secrets. When you aren't blurting them out loud, you're leaving them behind."

What was he talking about?

"After you tried to run us over, we found part of your map in the fireplace at the hotel. The one you tried to burn. We know all about the Eye. And we don't need you no more." The Eye? He didn't say anything about the well. Maybe they don't know about the well. My scheming was short-lived, however, as William tightened his grip, his bare hand wrapped around the sword's hilt. "Besides. I don't care what the boss wants no more. You hurt my brothers. So for me, this gig is over. That's where I draw the line. And now I'm gonna hurt you back." With one swipe, he was going to dice me like an onion. I knew I had to do something. I stared down at his hand, unsure of what came over me, and I chomped down into his meaty flesh, biting, gnawing, and tearing with my teeth as hard as I could. Maybe I had more in common with a fanged coiler than I thought.

"You bit me!" William screamed as he released me. I quickly rolled to the side.

"Ahhhh," Liv charged, trying to catch William off guard, but William swung his sword mightily. He slammed it against Liv's blade with such force that the impact knocked the sword out of her hand, sending it clear across the courtyard. Liv gave chase. William spun to face Flynn. They squared off, swords clanking as they danced. With each strike, William cursed. He lobbed a variety of bad words, some I didn't even know existed. Flynn lunged forward in an attempt to skewer William, but William saw it coming. Their swords ended up locked at the hilts. They both lost their grip when they tried to free the blades, and the swords clanked to the ground. William, being resourceful, landed a right hook that struck Flynn across the face, knocking him out cold.

"Flynn!" I ran towards Flynn, but William stopped me in my tracks. He snatched the amulet from my neck, snapping the chain. Instantly, something inside me changed. The adrenalin that rivered through my veins slowed to a sluggish halt. The extra dose of strength I acquired via the amulet was gone. I felt...ordinary. I swung at him with a clenched fist, but I was too weak. I fell face-first to the ground. It was like all of a sudden, I could feel everything. Every sore muscle. Every nick, scratch, and cut. The wound from the snake burned and throbbed. Worst of all, I could hear the Pegg brother laughing at me, mocking me. It took all my energy to get to my feet again. I balled up both fists and swore I would pummel him, even though I couldn't see straight.

"Goodbye, Dean from Pittsburgh." I heard the wraith say. That's when I felt a burning, pinching sensation that started off dull but became unbearable. I looked down to see a small knife lodged in my stomach. A ring of blood stained my shirt. As I fell to the floor, the side of my head smacked against a rock. With blurred vision, I watched the wraith escaping into the night. Escaping with my amulet.

"Dean!!" Liv cried.

"Human!" the Gnomelings shouted. I heard my heart beating in my temples. The pain was unrelenting.

"What do we do?" Tubb sobbed.

"The police are on their way," Roger said.

"There's no time. He'll die before they get him to a hospital," Liv said.

"Flynn," I wanted to check on him but could barely speak. "Is Flynn—?"

"He'll be fine," Liv reassured me. "Try not to talk." She turned and looked at the Gnomelings, placing a hand on each of their shoulders. "Do you know how to fix him? Any sort of medicine? Or spell?"

"No, but I once made a honey cake out of cram and dwarf roots," Griff said.

"What does that even mean?" Liv asked.

"I don't know," Griff said. "I talk nonsense when I be nervous. And right abouts now, I'm being very nervous." Griff began to shake.

I could tell by their tone that this was bad, really bad. Their voices started to trail off. Everything started to go fuzzy. A chill passed through my body.

"What do you suggest?" Roger asked Liv.

"My granddad is a surgeon. His house is nearby. Help me carry him to the cab." And that was the last thing I heard before the world went black.

THE MAN AND THE MYTH

The moving trucks left a cloud of black exhaust smoke as they rounded the cul-de-sac and rumbled out of our subdivision. Dad pulled the 'SOLD' sign from the lawn of our new home while Mom stood on the porch. She nursed a glass of sun tea, with beads of moisture sweating on the outside of the glass, trickling down to the floor of the wooden deck. I tiptoed over to her and let my hand slide into hers. I rested my head against her pregnant belly. I didn't understand much about birth or babies or the storks who dropped them off at our doorstep, but I knew my brother, Jackson, was sleeping inside my mom's stomach, and I always did my best not to wake him up. Anytime I was around mom, I was as gentle as I could be. As gentle as any five-year-old has ever been.

"You're going to be such a good big brother," my mom massaged the back of my hand with her thumb. As soon as the diesel engines of the moving trucks were out of earshot, I heard another car approaching. I wondered if it was a neighbor. A black Oldsmobile rolled to a stop right in front of our house. There was only one person inside. It was a man who looked older than my dad but not as old as my grandpa. This was generally how I determined age as a kid. This man had thinning hair atop his bald head and wore big, dark aviator sunglasses.

"Who's that, Mommy?" I asked.

"That's Daddy's new boss. The one who found us the house so Daddy could be near his new job," she replied. This guy was the reason we left St. Louis. The reason I left my best friend, Addie, my kindergarten, with all my teachers, and everything I knew.

"Does he have any kids?" I asked. If he was going to ruin my life, the best he could do was to have a kid my age to play with.

"I think so. Why don't you go say hi," she said, nudging me down the stairs.

I didn't want to. I wasn't particularly keen on rubbing elbows with my dad's boss, especially since I was still upset about having to move in the first place. But my mom shooed me along and slowly hobbled down the steps after me. The man crossed to the trunk of his car. He lifted it open, pulled out a black duffle bag, slammed the trunk closed, then met my dad at the curb. They shook hands. My dad seemed to like him, so I figured he must be friendly.

"Boss, this is my son, Dean," my dad introduced me. I put my hand against my forehead as a visor to shield my eyes from the sun.

"Ah, Dean," the man said with a gravelly voice. "I've heard so much about you, young man." I pretended to smile. Technically, I did smile, but I was pretending to care. "How old are you now, Dean?"

"Five and a half," I said. Every kid knew how important that half a year was, as it separated the men from the boys.

"Five and a half," he repeated. I got the feeling he was mocking me. "I can only presume you plan on following in your father's footsteps when you get older? Working in the mines?"

"No, sir." I shook my head.

"You're not?"

"I'm going to live in a faraway land and be a hero. I'll fight dragons and monsters and save the world one day," I said confidently.

"Kids, huh?" my dad said. "When I was his age, I wanted to be a pickle."

The man faked a laugh as the smile on his face faded. His upper lip twitched in a strange pattern that reminded me of a fly rubbing its limbs together. I remember how he moved in closer, close enough to feel his breath on my ear. It made me so uncomfortable. "So, you want to be a hero? Not if I have anything to do with it, Dean," he whispered as he started to laugh again.

"Alright, Dean," my father said. "How about you go check out the treehouse? Let Mister Thorne and I catch up on work stuff."

The world turned black around me as my parents, and my house disappeared. Yet, Mister Thorne remained, draped in a black cloak and holding a sword in his hands, the tip of the blade piercing the cold ground beneath his feet. His eyes were narrow and gray, and his teeth were chiseled.

I ran as fast as my tiny legs would carry me, but I didn't seem to move an inch. He reached to grab me. His skin was rotting, and his veins were exposed where his flesh had deteriorated. I tried to scream, but nothing came out. I was paralyzed. Mister Thorne's charred fingernails inched closer. He wiggled his fingers, rotating his hand like a wizard maneuvering a magic wand, and before I knew it, he was spinning me in circles. He started to laugh. It sounded like a choir of screeching demons were crying out along with him, creating a symphony of dread.

Although I couldn't see the ground, I could feel my heels digging further into the dirt as I was pulled into his grasp. I leaned my head back to evade, whipping it from side to side, but it was useless. Thorne put his icy palm on my forehead. I closed my eyes and prayed for this nightmare to end. Pain shot through every centimeter of my body until I could feel no more.

Ψ

It seemed as though hours had passed when I opened my eyes. I was no longer shrouded in shadows. Green fields surrounded me in every direction. The song of a sparrow sang out from the top of a nearby tree. I stood and wiped webs and black spots from my clothes. Was I back in England? I was a teenager again, so maybe this wasn't a dream. It sure didn't feel real at all. I felt light, almost as if I could float or glide across the ground.

"Flynn! Liv!" I shouted, but no one answered. Smoke billowed on the horizon over mounds and hills of grass and trees. A series of screams sang my name, sending chills down my spine. Not the cries of banshees, demons, or even Mister Thorne, but the pain from innocents - women and children.

I scuttled up the first hill, then down the other side, climbing peaks and navigating valleys until the source of the smoke and the screams were in sight. A village with small homes built into hills was set ablaze. In the center of the town was a lake, its water stained red, with figures floating on its surface. Young, old, it didn't matter. Death was indiscriminate. I ran until I arrived at the heart of the village. Gnomelings and taller elf-like creatures battled against a malice I'd never imagined seeing. Goblins with greenish-black flesh, sharp teeth, and claws for nails were striking down all in their path. The way they moved and fought made it seem like they were possessed by a powerful source of evil. They slashed away, shredding Gnomelings, tearing flesh from bone, and did so with villainous pleasure.

"NO!" I screamed and picked up a spear that lay in the dirt. I attacked the creatures without hesitation, pushing back the horde of goblins. Fueled by rage, I fought hard, and I was winning. I was winning until I saw them. Tubb and Griff lay motionless on the ground, their eyes wide open, staring at the sky with a permanent look of shock on their faces. They were...they were dead. I heard a familiar voice wailing to my right. "Liv." I darted toward her, making my way around a burning wagon, but I was too late. Arrows, at least six, had pierced a plate of armor that covered her body. A trickle of blood seeped from the corner of her mouth as she dropped to her knees, falling face-first onto the ground.

"Dean! Help me!" Flynn hollered. I spun on my back heel and saw him. He was on his back, holding a battered shield, parrying blow after blow from the giant club of a cave troll. The troll lifted his club over his head and swung down with all his might. Flynn stopped moving. He stopped crying out for help. He stopped everything.

A sinister voice whispered into my ear, "You failed them, Dean Moyers. And just think… You thought you would save the world."

"Who are you? Why are you doing this to me?" I said.

Without warning, a massive hand gripped my throat, hoisting me in the air. My feet dangled. I kicked as I tried to break free, but it was no use. A familiar face came into view - Thorne. His beady black eyes and rotting mouth were unmistakable. The amulet draped around his neck was glowing a bright white. Suddenly, Thorne's head snapped back. I saw something happening to him. He was transforming - his jaw started to open while his face stretched. Horns swelled from his skull. His eyes turned to a glowing, flame-colored red. His nose bulged, his cheekbones protruded, and his features became sharp and menacing until he was no longer human. His body was also outstretched, transforming his slender frame into a massive, muscular beast. He had turned into a Minotaur: 50% bull - 50% man - 100% horrifying. He snarled and growled as his spit, snot, and stench washed over me.

"Now, you join your friends." Thorne, or the Minotaur, or whatever this thing was, tossed me to the ground, where I crumpled into a heap. He stood over me and lifted a massive sledgehammer high in the air. I shielded myself with my hands, holding my arms outstretched to stop the blow. Was this my end?

"Dean. Wake up." A call tickled my eardrum. The voice was…

"Dad?"

"Dean, wake up." The voice grew louder and more urgent. "You must wake up now. There's still time."

"Dad, you don't understand. Thorne has the amulet. My friends are– they're dead."

"Find me in the depths of Chalice Well," he said.

A blinding blast of light shone down from the heavens over me as the Minotaur began to swing, only the light blinded him as well. He grunted and turned his head away from the sun's rays that burned his corneas. I squinted as beams of light poured through the cracks between my fingers.

"Wake up." My dad's voice faded.

"Wake up." It was replaced with that of another.

DOCTOR WHO?

"Wake up, young man," an unfamiliar voice said. A man's voice. One that did not belong to my father. Rays of the sun prismed in through stained glass windows, blinding me as I slowly opened my eyes. And just as in my dream, I held my hand out to shield the light. I twisted to the side, finally able to focus, getting a good look at my surroundings. I was lying on a hulking bed with white sheets, white pillows, and a white comforter - Pretty much white everything except for the red stains that tainted the white bandages wrapped around my body.

A man carrying a clipboard walked out of the room briefly, then returned with a few small medical tools and a bottle of pills. He was an older guy with a big head of frizzy white and gray hair with a bushy mustache. More of the Albert Einstein look than Santa Claus.

"Ah. Gracious. At last. You're awake," the man's voice was soothing.

"Where am I?" I didn't recognize anything. It felt like a church or a hospital, but I knew it was neither. There were too many potted plants and King George the Third oil paintings.

"You are in the home of Doctor Winfred Anders. That's me. This is my home," the old man said, almost as if he were trying to convince both himself and me that it was true.

"Doctor Who? How did I get here?"

"My granddaughter, Olivia, brought you."

"Liv!" I tried to sit up. This was a truly awful idea. My side burned, and it felt like something was tearing.

"Easy now." Doctor Anders helped lower me back onto the mattress, double-checking my bandages. "Do you remember what happened to you?"

"I was—we were attacked and—there were wraiths. Then, this guy named Thorne turns into a Minotaur. Or at least in my dream he did. Oh, and we were trying to find fragments of a magic amulet that will help save my friends. They're called Gnomelings. They're from another realm. Well, I think they are."

Doctor Anders twisted an extension on a cylindrical object, which activated a tiny light. He checked my eyes, moving the light from side to side, and said, "Hmm. Perhaps you hit your head harder than I thought." He had a point. If I didn't experience these events first-hand, I wouldn't have believed a word that spewed from my mouth.

"Get some rest," he said, removing the light from my eyes and writing some notes on a clipboard.

I closed my eyes and instantly drifted back off to sleep. The next time I awoke, Anders was finishing up checking my pulse. There was a gentle knock on the door. A heartbeat later, Liv entered with her arms behind her back. She stood and observed for a moment as the doctor finished examining my wounds.

"Am I going to be alright?" I asked.

"In time, you'll be as good as new. Luckily for you, the blade missed all of your vital organs."

"Will I have to go to the hospital?" I asked.

"No, Dean. I have everything you need. I wouldn't send my dog, Gus, to the local hospital."

Staring at the bandages on my stomach, I nearly forgot about the snake bite. I lifted my arm to see the two puncture marks, nearly healed. "The snake. It bit me," I said to the surprise of Liv.

Anders, however, was not surprised. "I put you on a combination of Cloxacillin and Piperacillin." The look on my face told him he may as well have been speaking a foreign language. "Antibiotics," he cleared up.

"Makes sense."

The doctor looked back, smiling amicably at his granddaughter. "I'll leave you two alone."

"Thank you, sir," I said.

"Thank Olivia. Her quick thinking saved your life."

The door closed behind Doctor Anders as he left the room. Liv stepped to my bedside and carefully sat down. She had workout pants on, I think they were called leggings, to go along with a sporty sweatshirt that hung off one shoulder. There's no other way to put it, so I'll just be honest. To say she was a sight for sore eyes (and every sore muscle and wound in my body) would have been the understatement of the century. The light from the stained glass window reflected off her face. It was mesmerizing.

"Hey," I said.

"Hey," she replied.

Hey? The girl I've had a crush on for... well, pretty much forever... saves my life, and all I can say is hey? Good thing Flynn didn't hear that otherwise, he'd tell me I have absolutely zero flirting game – and he'd be right.

"What I meant to say was —"

"It's fine," Liv said.

"No. I need to." She nodded, and I continued. "You... You saved me. Thank you."

"Someone had to. God knows I couldn't leave it to Tubb and Griff. They'd likely stuff your wound with honey cake and dwarf root. Though I still don't quite know what that is."

I laughed. It hurt to laugh. It hurt to breathe. I wanted to sit up. I wanted to stand. Laying down on my back made me feel helpless. Liv noticed. "Here, let me help," she said as she stood, crossing to a nearby dresser where she grabbed some extra pillows. She helped me sit up, then stuffed the extra cushions behind my back.

"How long was I out?" I asked, almost afraid to hear the answer.

"Four whole days and one night." It was worse than I thought. My dreams came and went in a flash, but I never imagined being out for days.

Voices yelling outside the room elevated. Before long, a commotion took over. "What's that about?" I was sure I didn't want to know.

"The Gnomelings. They've been eating since we arrived. They truly are remarkable creatures."

"Oh yeah?"

"They told me all about their home. The plants they harvest for food and others for their pipes. They told me about brown ales, black ales, yellow ales, and all sorts of brews. They also shared how they generally eat four meals before noon." Liv smiled with the corner of her lip. "Oh, and who can forget about their detailed instructions on brushing foot hair so it is not tangled."

"Did they brush your foot hair?" The words left my mouth before I could consider what I was saying.

"Excuse me?" Liv stole her hand away from mine.

Great job, Dean. You blew it again. We were holding hands, you idiot! *Fix it ... fix it*, I thought. "No, what I meant to say was, did they uh —"

"I will have you know that I've been an experienced foot hair brusher since I got my first foot hairs." Liv gripped the cuff of her sock and slowly pulled it off her foot. My entire existence was spiraling. What have I done? Now my dream girlfriend thinks I'm a jerk or she truly has thick wads of brown foot hair. I didn't know what would be worse. As she yanked the sock completely off, I was relieved to see that she was Gnomeling foot hair free and messing with me again. "But I did paint my nails two nights ago. Do you like the color?"

"I love the color."

I didn't even look at the color. She could have painted them with flames or skull decals, and I would have said, "I love the color," just to get out of the mess I was in. If living with my mom taught me anything, it was that women were always right about everything. Even when they weren't.

"Would you like to see them?" she asked.

"Your toes?"

"The Gnomelings." Liv exhaled. Someone needed to put a gag in my mouth, so I stopped talking. Maybe Doctor Anders had some medicine to knock me out for another four whole days and a night.

"Of course, I'd like to see Tubb and Griff."

Liv disappeared from the room as the commotion outside ceased. The parading pitter-patter of hairy feet (not Liv's) made its way toward me. The solid wood door groaned as Tubb slowly pushed his way in, followed closely by Griff. The Gnomelings crept toward me as if their footsteps would reopen my wounds. They wore their patented yellow shirts, blue vests, and baggy capris, only clean. This meant they either did laundry or had a change of clothes in their endless pit of a backpack.

"You're alive! We be so pleased!" Overjoyed, Griff held his hands over his mouth when he spoke.

"I be so pleased too," I said. Again, why was I talking like them? Maybe Doctor Anders was right about me hitting my head too hard.

"The medicine human said you was lucky to survive, but we tolds him it was your destiny." Griff patted my leg. I guess that was supposed to make me feel better. I figured the medicine human meant Anders. "At first, he thought we were off our bongos, but now he knows about your destiny and believes us."

"Well, I'm okay now. The doctor said so." The Gnomelings climbed onto the bed, sitting on either side of me, resting their heads against my shoulders. Like the last time, it was weird but comforting. "Thanks, you guys." Liv reentered the room, taking a seat next to the bed. She giggled and snorted when she saw the Gnomelings lying by my side. I paused, taking in the moment, then a thought entered my mind. I hadn't

209

asked about Flynn. He must be a hot mess right now. I knew I would be if this happened to him, only he was way more protective of me.

"Flynn, where is he?"

"Look over there," Liv nodded, motioning to Flynn, nestled in the corner of the room, draped in blankets. It appeared he was out cold, with drool dripping down his shirt. "He's been there every day. He sleeps there, eats there. He said he felt guilty. I guess about what had happened. I told him it wasn't his fault. I mean, he took a wallop to the skull and got knocked out cold. But even so, he never left your side for a second. He's just a big puppy, isn't he?"

"I heard that," Flynn's eyes fluttered open as he wiped the drool from his chin. "Welcome back, Moyers." Flynn stood and stretched, popping his neck and back. "Have any good dreams while you were away?" He wore the same clothes as before, but they were still filthy.

"The opposite, actually," I was itching to share what I'd seen. "The guy in black from the hotel. Mister Thorne. I told you that name sounded really familiar. Turns out he was my dad's boss. He moved us to Pennsylvania. I remembered it in my dreams."

"Why would he do that?" Liv asked.

"To keep tabs on us is all I can figure. Maybe he was suspicious about Dad and the amulet. Then, one day he decided to make his move. Maybe killing him would allow the dark forces to take over. But when Dad was in the cave, and the amulet wasn't, he assumed the amulet was gone for good. Either way, it can't be a coincidence that the night my dad talks about my destiny, telling me the truth, is the night he —" I didn't want to say it again. Even though years had passed, saying my dad had died still cut me to my core. Cut me deeper than any blade ever could. "It also explains how he knew we were here. I just can't figure out how he's tracked us every step of the way."

The more I thought about it, the more some things made sense, while others were as clear as a mud puddle after a thunderstorm. It was like trying to solve a Rubik's cube, only with one side missing the stickers. I speculated that Thorne didn't know I had the amulet as a kid, at least not for a while, so I was no threat to him. That was until we came here, and the wraiths spotted us with the amulet and the map. But did he know about the amulet being split into chunks before I blurted it out at the hotel? He must have thought it odd that I was going to England around the same time the Gnomelings said it was my 'coming of age' or sixteenth name day or whatever they called it. My head started to spin. I was in no shape to solve the world's problems in my current condition, even another world's, so I resigned to being an utter failure. "And now he has everything that he wants." I slouched my shoulders in defeat.

"Not everything," Flynn said.

"He knows about the Eye but doesn't know about the well," Liv added. "Or at least not yet." Liv made a face I hadn't seen before. She seemed scared. No, nervous. No... suspicious. But of what?

"Although," Flynn interrupted, "we don't know which well holds the next part of the amulet." He marched to the stained glass window by the bedside, staring at a Hawk-moth sucking sugar water from a feeder. "There must be thousands of wells around. The map wasn't specific."

"Chalice Well," I said.

"In Glastonbury?" Liv said.

"I guess. My dad told me to go there."

"When you were little?" Liv asked.

"No. In my dream, he told me to find him in Chalice Well."

"Geez, dude. What *else* did you dream about?" Flynn said.

I looked over the faces of my friends, recalling my dream. Seeing their lifeless eyes and hearing their screams was too much to bear, so I lied. Lying was becoming a habit for me. "That's about it. Everything else is kind of a blur," I said.

A couple of days later, I felt pretty decent. There was still a sharp ache when I coughed or laughed, but overall I was in a good mood, and the pain was manageable. I stood up by myself and, for the first time, was able to put on a shirt without help or putting myself through absolute agony. After I was dressed, a knock came from the door. Doctor Anders pushed his bushy hair in, peeking through the gap between the door and the frame. "She's almost here," he said.

"Who's almost here?" I asked.

"You'll see," Anders laughed, more of a squeal, but I think a laugh is what he was after. With the help of Flynn, Doctor Anders moved me to a wheelchair, despite the fact I was insistent I could walk on my own. The chair was on the aging side of the furniture spectrum. Its armrests were made of wood, topped with leather-coated foam padding. The padding of one of the armrests was cracked, and the foam poked out, tickling my elbow.

They ushered me into the living room. Tubb sat at a large wooden table with old topographical maps strewn about, along with empty bowls, plates, and pitchers. "Master Tubb has a brilliant mind," Doctor Anders said. "He's a natural cartographer."

"A cartogra-what?" I inquired.

"Map maker. He's memorized the legend and nearly all the shires in the UK," Anders boasted. "There's ninety-two of them, so that is no small feat."

"How about Griff?" I wondered aloud. I knew Tubb was the brains of the operation. In our short amount of time together, he seemed the most logical and prepared of the two.

"Griff?" Anders pondered but was quick to compliment. "Griff is spirited and endearing."

"I heard that," Griff scowled.

"It was a compliment, Griff," Tubb said without taking his eyes from a large map.

"Oh, yeah. I know'd that," Griff picked up a container of some sort of juice. He chugged until it started to drip down his chin, then set the cup back on the table. He looked over at us and belched. "Compliments to the chef."

Anders looked down at me and said, "Store-bought apple juice," with a shrug. "He loves it."

As the doctor wheeled me to the table, I took in his curious interior decorating decisions. Doctor Anders was definitely a collector—of history, culture, and perhaps even dead animals judging by the collection of mounted heads above his mantelpiece: deer, birds, a bear, and even a stuffed raccoon rowing in a mini-canoe. If it weren't so adorably comical, I might have been terrified.

"I founded it! Chalice Well. It's in Glass-tone-berry," Tubb tried his best pronouncing Glastonbury.

"I could have told you that," Liv said as she entered the room, carrying a home phone handset. "In fact, I'm ninety-nine percent certain I did tell you that."

"Well, either ways, I founded it." Tubb remained proud, stoic.

Liv stopped at my side. She put her hand over mine as it sat on the wheelchair armrest. "How are you feeling?"

"Fine, I just wish—" I was interrupted by a loud thumping on the front door. Doctor Anders must have had one of those iron door knockers. Knowing what I know about the Doc, it was probably in the shape of a bear or a lion.

"There she is." Liv's hand slid off of mine, tracing a line from knuckles to fingernails with the delicate tips of her fingers, causing goosebumps to spread across my entire body.

"There who is? Why are you guys being so secretive?" I asked.

Liv made a path through the living room, past the foyer, and I heard her open the door, allowing the light to stream in from outside.

"Such a pleasure to meet you," Liv said. I could see her with another person, presumably a girl or a woman, based on the figure of the shadow and the way Liv referred to this mystery person as *she*. "He's in here," Liv said. Did she mean me? Who would be here to see me? Was it someone from Second Realm? One of Tubb and Griff's friends? Another guardian or knight of their shire? Oh, I know. It had to have been a soldier. Doctor Anders must have gotten someone from the military to help us. Or maybe it was a historian or someone who worked at the museum. Anders had all these maps tossed around his house; perhaps someone was going to help us find a way to— "Mom?" My jaw nearly hit the table in shock as *my mother* marched into the living room with tired legs. She made a beeline directly toward me, stood at the foot of my chair, and folded her arms the way she does when she's mad. No, when she's furious.

THE FELLOWSHIP

"Do you know how long it took me to get here?" Mom asked.

"Uh–" I couldn't even reply. My vocal cords were paralyzed. I was either too afraid to say anything, or I was afraid of saying the wrong thing.

"Thirteen hours, young man. Thirteen hours on a plane next to Smelly Mc-no-deodorant. Thirteen hours with no inflight movie. And why?"

"Why?" I knew why.

"Because my baby was…he was…stabbed!" Mom started to sob, dropped to her knees, and enveloped me in the biggest bear hug I've ever felt. A hug that nearly lifted my feet right out of a pair of slippers that the doc had given me.

"I'm alright, Mom. Really, I am."

"Alright? Dean, you could have been killed." Mom got to her feet. She looked like she had just woken up, but not from the long flight. With her baggy sweatpants and paint-speckled "Salt Life" t-shirt, it appeared she was sleeping when she got the call about my *incident* and ran out of the house immediately. I also noticed she didn't have a bag with her, which confirmed my deduction. Her black hair was tied up in a messy bun. She also wasn't wearing make-up, not that she needed it. My mom was the type of person who could roll out of a dumpster for a bed and still look amazing.

She turned to Flynn after wiping a few errant tears from her cheek. "You," Mom's tone changed entirely. She was about to lay into him; I was sure of it. After all, before we left for our flight, Mom told Flynn, "Take care of my boy." I wanted to say something, to spare Flynn the tongue-lashing he was about to receive, when Mom leaped in his direction and, to my amazement, gave Flynn a hug bigger than the one she'd given me.

"Where's the little terrorist?" Flynn asked Mom, meaning my brother, Jackson. "He still looking for his Lucky Charms?" Another redhead joke.

Mom let out a sigh and a laugh as she patted Flynn on the shoulders. "He's with Esther." Esther, our neighbor, was older than father time himself, and apparently, she was still babysitting. And yes, I have zero issues calling it babysitting when it comes to Jackson.

"Thank you. Thank you for watching out for him. Thank you for calling me," Mom turned to Doctor Anders, hugging him, followed by Liv one more time. After she and Liv broke their embrace, Tubb and Griff were lined up with arms wide open, waiting their turn. Mom looked beyond confused. She looked absolutely bumfuzzled (a synonym for confused that I learned in English class). "I'm sorry," she turned to me for

217

answers. "Who are these two?"

"The bigger one is Tubb. The other is Griff."

"You can call me Delaney," Griff stepped forward and curtsied. "I be so happy you escaped the tiny rectangle."

I shook my head in disbelief, though I should have expected that. "They're our friends. They're called Gnomelings."

"I know what they are," Mom said.

"You do?" I asked.

"Of course I do. Only they're more hideous in person than I'd imagined," Mom said with a pinch of unexpected honesty. We'll chalk it up to jetlag.

"You be far too kind," Griff blushed. Tubb rolled his eyes at his kinfolk.

"They grow on you," Liv said.

The corners of Tubb's mouth twisted downward while his eyes drooped. Mom could see that she had hurt his feelings. "I'm sorry, that was harsh. You're both adorable and hideous. Like a bulldog." Mom corrected herself. Griff was puzzled by the adjustment in Mom's vocabulary, so he did what Griff does. He hugged Mom's leg.

"He's not going to do anything weird, is he?" Mom asked, looking down at Griff.

Ɏ

Hours passed, and we caught Mom up on our journey. We told her everything, everything except for how I'd seen Thorne turn into a Minotaur in my dream. Aside from my groggy confession to Doctor Anders, I hadn't shared that with anyone. Especially the bad parts. Surprisingly, Mom wasn't surprised at most of what we discussed. In fact, she already knew much of what we had learned. "Your dad," she shared, "he told me a long time ago about Second Realm. About how his family line were protectors. He said one day he would take you. That you may need to travel back if anything bad happened. At first, I thought he was crazy. I almost filed for divorce and called the police. I mean, it's not exactly what you expect to hear over family dinner. But the more he explained, the more he'd shown me, the more I realized he was telling the truth."

The way Mom told her stories somehow made everything even more real. "Did you know about Thorne?" I asked.

"No. I never liked the man but couldn't pinpoint why. He always seemed —"

"Bongos," Tubb said.

"Creepy," Liv said.

"Spirited and endearing," Griff said, still unsure what to make of the new words he'd learned.

"What? No." I gave Mom a look to ignore Griff and keep on. "Thorne always seemed like he was scheming. Like he was up to something bad. I assumed it was shady business deals, but I never got the impression he was evil."

"Do you think Dad knew?"

"It's hard to tell. But as the saying goes, keep your friends close—"

"And your peanut butter moist," Tubb added with a cocky smile.

"Where did you find these two?" Mom asked as the Gnomelings blushed, batting their eyelids at her affectionately. Holy cheese balls. Were Tubb and Griff smitten with my mother? Were they – flirting with her?

Gross.

"So what happens now?" I asked, fearing what she was about to say. I didn't want to go home. We'd come too far to stop now.

"The obvious answer is to get you back to Pennsylvania," she said. I knew she would say that.

"Mom!" I protested.

"But..." she started.

"But?" I asked.

"But, knowing this is what your father wanted. What he needed. You can stay."

"I can?" This wasn't real life, was it? My mom was the same mom who wrapped me in bubble wrap and made me wear a motorcycle helmet on my tricycle.

"You can. But I'm staying too."

"You are?"

"Your mother and I discussed this at great length," Doctor Anders joined in. "She will stay with me here, where we will help you on your mission, quest, thing."

"You'll be our command unit," Flynn said with a weird grin. "We'll be call sign Falcon. You can be call sign Mother Bird."

Mom laughed. It was nice seeing her. I still couldn't believe she was here.

"Wait," she said as she scanned the room, counting heads. "Liv, you said on the phone that someone else helped save you. Some night watchman?"

"Roger, yes," Liv answered.

Roger... I'd forgotten about Roger. He was there too. Saving us for the second time. When I was stabbed, he came to help. Just mentioning Roger's name sent a jolt through my memory banks. Images came flashing back at once: images of Roger using a taser on the wraiths, burning one of them pretty bad. But where was he? Why was he there in the first place? And why did they call him the night watchman?

Turns out Liv was about to explain. "Roger worked security at the castle. He came in late for his night shift because he was a little –"

"Drunk," Flynn said.

"Woozy," Liv sugarcoated.

"Did he or did he not help save my son? I want to thank him," Mom stood as if she were willing him to appear out of thin air.

"That may be a bit difficult," Liv said.

"How so?" Mom asked.

"He's currently at a hearing," Liv said. Mom shrugged. "A disciplinary hearing to see if he can keep his job or if they're going to fire him. Or arrest him."

"Arrest him for what? Being a hero? Unacceptable." Mom stood for the flag. She stood at work. And for some reason, she always stood when she ate pizza. But she wasn't going to stand for this.

"After he set the Pegg brothers on fire and helped us to the car, Roger found a stash of brandy in a tent. He drank it all, then dressed up in the costumes used in the Renaissance Fair."

"Oh my," Mom said.

"He did say he looked voluptuous in the fair maiden dress," Liv said.

"Oh my," Mom said again.

"Did we mention he was a dwarf with a giant beard, and he tried to ride the pigs from a nearby farm while wearing said maiden dress?" Flynn chimed in.

"Oh...My," she said one final time but reconsidered. "It doesn't matter. Dress or no dress. Beard or no beard. Pig riding or no pig riding. Roger is a hero, and I'd like to meet him."

It wasn't until later that night that Mom got her wish. While we were game planning, studying roads in and out of Glastonbury, the loud hollow knocker on the door echoed through Anders' home. I'd finally convinced my mom and the doc to let me get out of the wheelchair. Mom and I walked to the front door, arm in arm. "After you," she said, motioning for me to open the door for our guest. I gripped the cold wrought iron handle, pulling the door ajar. There he stood. Mom's hero with hands resting on his hips like a conquering soldier. Roger was wearing a suit equipped with a hot pink bow tie. He smiled a ridiculous toothy smile, framing his pearly white teeth against the backdrop of the night sky as if he were posing on the red carpet.

"You must be Roger?" Mom said.

"The one and only," Roger boastfully replied. "And you are?"

"Isabel. Dean's mom."

"Isabel from Pittsburgh. Mother of Dean from Pittsburgh," Roger charmed. He reached out, taking Mom's hand and kissing her knuckles. He kissed them a little too long, then said, "It's an honor to make your acquaintance."

"The honor is all mine. You saved my son's life. I cannot express how much I am in your debt."

"To look upon beauty such as yours is more reward than this humble servant could ever ask," Roger said.

"Okay, this is getting a little weird." Roger and Mom both looked at me. "Did I say that out loud? Sorry, it's just—"

"Guys. I think we've figured it out!" Liv shouted from the other room. Thank God. I couldn't have walked away from Roger and Mom faster. What was going on? First, the Gnomelings, now, Roger. Mom was like a contestant on the oddball version of that show, *The Bachelorette.*

"There's a path. A backdoor, in a sense, that will allow you to get onto the property without being seen." Doctor Anders traced his index finger over a faded beige line on the map. It weaved in and out of green spaces, most likely a wooded area or countryside, then fed to the back of a spot marked **The Well**.

"And why do we need to go through the back door?" Flynn asked.

"Just because the wraiths and Thorne think the last piece of the amulet is at the Eye, it wouldn't hurt to show some extra precaution," Liv said. "I mean, Dean was already stabbed."

"And poisoned," I added, wishing I wouldn't have. Wishing I could rewind and lodge my foot directly into my big mouth.

"Poisoned?" Mom belted. "You never told me he was poisoned," she turned to Liv.

"I didn't know." The look on Liv's face told Mom she was telling the truth.

"Either way, the point stands. Olivia's right. You need to be safe." Anders added with emphasis.

"So what be our plans?" Tubb asked.

"It seems fairly straightforward," Anders exclaimed, raising his index finger. "Roger, Flynn, Dean, Olivia, and the little ones retrieve the amulet from the well. Isabel and I will help navigate. Once you arrive, we'll head to the Eye and scout it out. The wraiths, as you call them, and this Thorne fellow won't be looking out for us, giving us the advantage."

The next morning, the plan was set into motion. Mom was not only on board but helping. I couldn't believe it. When I saw her enter the home, I thought we were done for.

As Tubb, Griff, and Roger loaded the car, Flynn and Liv helped Doctor Anders pack a bag full of wraps, Band-Aids, along with other medical supplies. I needed a minute to collect my thoughts, so I headed back to the garden on the other side of my recovery room. I sat on a large stone that Anders called his *thinking stone*, watching the Hawk moths buzz around.

A screen door creaked open as Mom came outside, inhaling the scents of nature, the scents of the Doctor's gardenias, daisies, carnations, and tulips. She was holding something in her hands as she came to sit next to me on the bench.

"I brought this for you," she said.

"What is it?" I asked as I eyed a rectangular package wrapped in brown paper, tied together with frayed twine. It was long but thin.

"Your father planned on giving this to you when the time was right. After he… passed…I lost track of it. I knew I needed to find it when I got Liv's call. I knew you needed to see it."

Mom handed me the package. I untied the twine, digging my nails into the overlaps in the paper. "It's a picture frame," I said.

The wooden frame was cracked along the side. The rear kickstand seemed to be faded from the sun like it had been sitting in a window for a decade. With rapt attention and anticipation causing my hands to shake, I flipped the frame over and stared past the glass protector at something beyond my wildest dreams. Tears filled my eyes until they overflowed, droplets pitter-pattered against the glass.

"Is this really real? I mean, it's not photoshopped?" I asked. Thinking this couldn't be possible, but knowing deep down that it was.

"It's really real," now my mom started to cry. In the picture was my grandpa. I never knew him. He died before I was born. But I'd heard stories. Beside him sat my dad, with the amulet draped over his neck. The one he had given to me when I was little. They stood atop a hill looking over a valley with dirt roads that corkscrewed toward a lake. Along the dirt path sat tiny houses built into the hillside, all with round doors and round windows with gardens that bloomed the biggest flowers I'd ever seen. Flanking my dad and his dad was a family of Gnomelings. Two adults were accompanied by fourteen children.

"My pip-pop and me-mop," Griff pointed at the adults. At some point, he and Tubb had come outside. Even they were crying. "And here," he slid his finger across the glass, tracing a path in the dust to the smallest of the Gnomeling children, "here be me and Tubb."

Mom collected herself. "Your dad planned on taking you when you were that age, but he never got the chance," she said, putting her arm around my shoulder. Tubb and Griff situated themselves between us, one on each side, while Roger borrowed a stool to peek over Mom's shoulder, either to look at the photo or smell Mom's hair; I couldn't decide which. Flynn and Liv bookended the group and shared a smile.

"Wait. Just wait right there," Doctor Anders called out from behind us. "I must capture this." He bumbled back inside to a nearby chest on the floor, rummaging through its contents until he pulled out a vintage Polaroid-type camera. Now on a mission, the doctor grabbed a handful of hardcover books from a shelf, stacked them on the outdoor picnic table, and propped the camera up. "That should do. Now let me find this timer mechanism," his every thought now coming out as words. "Ah, there!" He rushed back to the group, positioned himself to the right of Roger, putting his arm around Liv. "Smile, everyone!"

All of us humans joined in, saying a collective "Cheese" as the camera flashed. Within seconds, the tiny motor in the camera began to whine and whirl. We all walked to the other end of the table, wanting to see the picture develop. The square of black photo paper slowly escaped the device as Roger hunched over the paper, blowing on it, urging the developing process on. Before we knew it, the magic had happened. And aside from Roger still sniffing Mom, Flynn's eyes being closed, and Tubb and Griff looking in opposite directions (later, they admitted they were looking for the cheese we'd mentioned), it was perfect.

"Eight. Eight companions," Liv said.

"We're an elf short of a fellowship," I said. Liv laughed. A good thirty seconds later, Roger laughed too. He was probably under the influence of some sort of alcoholic beverage, so his brain waves were moving a little slowly. Or, as Dad always said, the wheel's still turning, but the hamster might be dead.

"Are you ready to go, Dean?" Mom asked.

"Let's go find the well," I said. "Let's go find dad."

ALL'S WELL THAT ENDS WELL

It was mid-afternoon. To Flynn's dismay, Liv drove us to the well. Flynn argued that he had always wanted to drive on the wrong side of the road, but since the Mini-Cooper belonged to her grandfather, Liv decided to not take any chances. "I'm just saying," Flynn was just saying, "I'm an excellent driver. I think I could get us there in good time." That was a blatant lie. Flynn once crashed his mom's minivan into a tree, trying to race a squirrel.

"Enough already," I said. We'd only been on the road for an hour, and I was beyond done with this conversation. Besides, Liv was doing an excellent job of driving, and I had to say we were making great time, though I never realized just how badly she was speeding. We zoomed down a winding country road with fields hemming us in on all sides. There were cottages with faded paints of earthy colors, brick walls lining the roads, and barns with plenty of—

"Sheep!" Roger lunged forward, shouting from the back seat. He, Flynn, Tubb, and Griff were crammed into a space that would normally only be comfortable for two. Liv swerved to the right, narrowly avoiding five sheep that meandered onto the road. What Liv didn't see coming was the --"Shepherd!" Roger warned as Liv whipped the wheel back to the left.

Tires screeched as smoke spewed. I turned to the back window just in time to see the shepherd getting smaller from our viewpoint. He was cursing while waving his arms wildly, either telling us we were number one or flipping us off.

"Will you get that thing out of my face?" Flynn said. I took my eyes off the road, laughing at my friends' predicament. Tubb, who was evidently not well-versed in seatbelt safety, had been tossed across the back seat while dodging the flock and its shepherd. His hairy foot wound up directly beneath Flynn's nose, tickling them both simultaneously.

"I can't help it," Tubb said. He wiggled and giggled, squirming between the seat, Griff, and Flynn. "This vroom vroom machine be too small."

"If you don't approve of the *vroom vroom machine*," Liv mocked, "you are free to walk the rest of the way. It's only fifteen kilometers."

"I could make it," Tubb boasted. "My physique is primed for long-distance travel."

"There's no food or drink on this road for as far as the eye can see," Liv smirked at Tubb through the rearview mirror.

"No food?" Tubb said. "I think we're being just fine here, thank you." Roger helped free Tubb from his predicament. The group looked like they were engaged in a backseat game of twister.

Liv's cell phone chimed to an 8-bit tune of Howard Shore's *The Lord of the Rings* theme. Our eyes met, and we shared a smile. "That's your ringtone?" I asked, a bit surprised, although I should have expected it.

"One ringtone to rule them all," she said. I thought to myself, could she be any more perfect?

"Hi, Granddad," she answered the phone, putting it on speaker, placing it in the cup holder while Flynn urged Liv to use the call signs he came up with.

"Hello? Are you there? Hello? Olivia?" We could hear Doctor Anders' voice on the phone, but it was distant. It sounded like he was in the middle of a wind tunnel.

"You need to use the call signs. The code names we came up with. Remember?" Flynn was adamant about this, but he was the only one, so he took matters into his own hands. "Go ahead, Mother Bird. Falcon is ready to transmit."

"Hello?" Anders said again, still sounding far away.

"Oh, not again," Liv sighed. She slapped her palm against her forehead. "Granddad, you have to turn the phone around. How many times do we need to go over this?"

"Do this. Spin it around. You see, it's upside down," my mom's voice came through the speaker.

"Olivia? Can you hear me?" Now Anders was loud and clear.

"Yes, we can hear you." Liv covered the base of the phone, turning to me. "How does he practice medicine if he can't work a cell phone?"

"Great! Are you ready for directions?" the doc said even louder, the volume increasing with each word.

"Ready." I pulled a map from the glove box, unfolding it across my lap and smoothing its wrinkled edges and ends against my legs.

"Have you reached the church? Saint Kaleb."

"We have. Just now." Saint Kaleb Church was right outside my window but disappearing quickly, with Liv picking up speed. The church was lined with a picket fence surrounding the structure and bordered by daisies and sunflowers.

"Alright, give me a second. Ah! Of course," Doctor Anders said as if a light bulb had gone off in his brain. "Dear me," he hesitated. "You'll want to turn right a few meters *before* you reach the church… I fear you've missed it."

Why the doc insisted on giving directions when we could have just printed some off MapQuest or Google is beyond me. "Turning around now," Liv said as she cranked the wheel, pulling a U-turn into oncoming traffic, sending the Gnomelings flailing across the back seat again.

"I don't think I'm enjoying cars no more," Griff said with Tubb's bottom smashing his cheek into the seat cushion.

Tubb's stomach growled so loudly that it scared the devil out of Liv. She nearly jumped out of her seat, accidentally jerking the wheel, causing the car to hop the curb and smash through the corner of the picket fence, sending stakes skyward.

"Oops," Liv said casually.

"Oops? What's oops?" Mom asked.

"Nothing. Keep reading," I played it cool. "We're on the dirt road now."

"Perfect. You'll need to keep a sharp eye out for – U--ll Not --- ss." Most of what Anders said was inaudible. What did come through sounded like he was talking underwater.

"Sorry, didn't catch that. The phone was breaking up. Try again," I said.

"I said, you need to turn —U–shall–ot---Pass." He was still breaking up.

"Try one more time, Granddad." I saw Liv looking in the rearview at Flynn, who had his arms crossed again. "I mean, Mother Bird." She mouthed, "*Happy?*" to Flynn.

He was.

The more Doctor Anders talked, the choppier it got, but we were able to decipher a few keywords as he repeated himself. "You shall not pass?" I asked. "We shall not pass what? I don't understand."

"The road!" Anders screamed as if his volume was the problem. "You need to turn onto the road called Euschalnot Pass." He even spelled it aloud for good measure.

As soon as he finished his sentence, we blazed past an old wooden street sign hammered to a post that read, "***Euschalnot Pass***."

"It's right there!" Roger lunged toward the front seat, pointing out the windshield. Unfortunately, Roger's sudden movement scared Liv yet again. With everything going on, I couldn't blame her for being skittish. She whipped the wheel to the right this time, slamming on the brakes. The car fishtailed, wiping out the "Euschalnot Pass" street sign with the back end, sending Roger head over feet onto the vehicle's dashboard.

A swirling sandstorm of dirt and debris surrounded the car as we came to a halt. We sat in stillness, but only briefly, as Griff broke the silence with a flatulent squeal that escaped his bottom.

"Seriously?" Flynn scrunched up his nose in disgust.

"It happens when I'm flurried." Griff winced, rubbed his tummy, and wished to disappear.

Twenty minutes of accident-free driving later, and after thoroughly airing Griff's stench from the car, we arrived at the rear of the property of Chalice Well. My mom and Doctor Anders told us to call when we were leaving, once we'd acquired the amulet, or in case of any trouble. They were taking the long ride to London to scout out the south bank of the River Thames (which I found out was pronounced 'temz' - not 'Thames' like 'flames') and the London Eye. The London Eye was the largest observation wheel in the world that gave a panoramic view of London. It was also the resting place of the final piece of the divided charm, aside from the one we'd soon hoped to find.

Liv and Flynn ran a quick recon mission. When they returned, they told us the coast was relatively clear, aside from a family finishing a tour. However, when they came back, they exchanged insults. Things started to get personal.

"What I'm telling you is, you probably could use lessons." Flynn mocked Liv's driving, pretending to jerk a steering wheel from left to right.

"I don't see your car here. Is that because you have to be an adult to rent one? Not an insolent child?" Liv rolled her eyes, marching to my side. "Shall we begin the search?"

"Sure," I said. Chalice Well was over two thousand years old. Doctor Anders explained that the well may have marked the site where Joseph of Arimathea hid the cup that caught the blood of Jesus Christ at the Crucifixion, otherwise known as the Holy Grail (which I was far too familiar with due to my Indiana Jones phase). Some said this is why the water of Chalice Well had a hint of red.

Once the tour had cleared, we roamed the property. I led the way with Liv at my side. "What was that about back there with Flynn?" I asked.

"He's just angry with me because Griff's rolling about gave him a bruise on his cheek, or his ego, I can't remember," Liv said.

Weird, I thought. Flynn was probably the worst driver ever, so I wouldn't have expected him to criticize Liv. I shrugged it off as we passed a fountain, a lion's head. Tubb and Griff had dropped to all fours, scooping water into their hands, slurping it out as if they had just crossed the Sahara Desert.

"This," Roger said. "This is why we can't go anywhere nice."

"What you be meaning?" Tubb lifted his head, water dripping down his chin.

"Were you raised in a barn? Drinking like that."

"Yes," Griff answered plainly.

"Well, you look the part."

"Better to look like a barn animal than to be riding one," Tubb said. Only, was it?

"Give 'em a break, Rog," I said.

"Yeah, bro," Flynn added. "You have no room to talk. You had chunks of vomit on your doublet the first time we met you."

"That was a chicken burger," Roger clapped back. "And it was armor, not a doublet."

"Chicken vomit, maybe, doublet boy," Flynn said.

"Boy?" Roger fumed.

I tuned out the banter and continued walking, taking in the sights. The property was beautiful. Full of flowers of every color and magnificent shrubs, bushes, and plants galore. There were statues of religious figures, lit candles, endless gardens, and plenty of benches deliberately situated for relaxation, prayer, or meditation. Mom would have loved this place. I envisioned her parked on one of the benches for hours, just reading a book.

There was a faint rush of water in the distance, so I decided to head in that direction. I discovered a shallow spring at a place named Arthur's Court. It consisted of two perfectly circular pools fed by a stream of water that trickled down a rock path. The largest bird bath in the country. There was a staircase to our left. I had a gut feeling about following the source of the water. With my friends following close behind, we climbed the stairs, finally spotting the reason we came: The Well.

The lid of Chalice Well was propped open for viewing. Beneath the lid sat the well itself. It was protected by reinforced steel. There was no way I could slip between the grooves. It was made in such a manner that even a baby couldn't fall into the depths. Liv, Flynn, Roger, Tubb, and Griff stood, staring into the core.

"Well, what are we waiting for?" Roger asked. He fell to his knees and started to yank on the rebar. It wouldn't budge, not even an inch.

"You're not Superman, ya dumb lump," Flynn sighed. "You can't just bend steel."

"Dumb lump? I don't see you coming up with any suggestions." Roger scoffed, wiping his hands on his pants as he stood.

"I don't know. Maybe there's another way in?" Flynn said.

"Another way in? To a well?" Liv said. "Are you really that daft?"

"Whoa! What's with the name-calling, Paddington? I'm just trying to help." Flynn squinted. His eyes became narrow. He made this face whenever he got defensive.

"Oh, so since Paddington lives in England, that is supposed to be an insult? Even your American jokes are boring."

"Let's just try to relax, humans," Tubb said.

"Relax?" Flynn turned his attention to Tubb. "You want us to relax? We just drove here in a piece of junk on wheels with no AC, where I had to smell your feet and your... odor... for two hours! And you want me to relax?"

"Don't talk to him that way," Liv said.

"I'll talk to him however I want." Flynn shot back.

"Guys, c'mon," I said, but it was pointless. My feeble voice was drowned out.

"You had your own seat," Flynn continued. "You didn't have the toddlers in tiaras sitting on your lap asking for a tummy rub and snacks."

"I am not a toddler," Roger said. "I have a beard."

"Oh, we know," Liv said, now ready to attack Roger. "We can smell the food you haven't cleaned out of it since nineteen-eighty-eight."

It went on like this for hours, but the hours felt like days. Something was different. Something had changed. We had been together for almost a week, and we hadn't had so much as a minor disagreement, at least not one that led to an argument, but this... It's almost as if my friends' minds were poisoned. Even the sky seemed to change. Dark clouds rolled in from out of nowhere. I scanned my friends' faces. Envy. Wrath. Greed. As plain as day.

It took me forever, but I finally convinced them to help me search for another path or way to break into the well. However, even then, Flynn and Liv would constantly argue over which direction to take. While looking for clues near the statues, Roger and the Gnomelings would bicker and complain if they disagreed on the most impressive statue. The biggest argument came when they debated over who would win in a fight: a single gargoyle or a group of fairies. I couldn't handle the tension. "Stop fighting," I would say, but my pleas fell on deaf ears. So, slowly, I distanced myself from the group, from my fellowship, and not one of them noticed. They were all too self-absorbed to see that I was gone.

Eventually, I walked back to the well where I sat, resting my feet on the steel bars that covered the opening. Even with the space between us friends, I could still hear their voices, bitter and vindictive. My heart started to break right at that moment. "Why are they acting like this?" I said aloud, my lip quivering, tears forming, ready to pour. For the first time in a long time, I felt alone.

"It's Thorne," a whisper cried out. "He's made it to the Eye." My dad's voice was coming from inside the well.

"Dad?" I looked over the edge of the well opening but saw only a dark ripple of water a few feet below.

"The nearer he draws to forging the pieces of the amulet together, the worse the conflict with your friends will be. You must stop him. Evil will always try to corrupt. Once your friends turn on one another, once you're divided, it will only be a matter of time before Thorne gets what he wants." There was a pause as a light wind blew. The cold air sent a shiver down my spine. "Your instincts will betray you. Good, evil, right, wrong, life, death - everything will begin to blur."

"Do you think we can win?" I asked.

"It's possible. But there is an ever-growing shadow that hinders my sight. The same shadow that didn't allow me to see Thorne for who he was all those years ago. Thorne and his minions seem to run with the wind at their backs. They seem to be a step ahead. I fear someone you love is in grave danger."

"Who, Dad? Who's in danger? Is it Mom? Liv? Flynn?"

"I'm afraid I don't know. The evil I speak of gains strength by the second," Dad said. "Do you remember what I always told you about evil, Dean?"

"That it sucks?" Probably not the answer he was looking for, but evil did indeed suck.

"Yes, but what else? How do you defeat it? What is the recipe?"

I thought back to my childhood. To our imaginary battles in the backyard. To our movie nights. To the talks at the dinner table about bullies. And then, I remembered something he'd told me. A slogan of sorts.

"Companions. Trust. Faith. This is the recipe for defeating evil."

"Very good. Now use it," he said. "The words I have given you. Use them to claim the next fragment of the amulet. It's here. Which means there's still hope."

"Okay," I groaned. "How do you expect me to do that? The well it's blocked. You're down there, and I'm up…"

"Companions, trust, and faith," Dad repeated the phrase three times, more deliberate with each pass. But his repetition didn't really help my situation, at least in my mind.

"Please, Dad. I don't understand. Those are just words!" I waited for an answer that didn't come. "Dad?" Silence. Pure silence. What was I to do? "What do you want from me?" My hands gripped the cold steel that covered the well; sparks flew. I jumped back, looking at my palms, expecting to see them covered in welts, only that didn't hurt. "Do that again!" I commanded, but nothing happened. I lowered myself toward the steel grate. "Show me how!" The steel barrier sparked once more. A silver shower of sparks burst from its edges. "Companions, trust, faith," I said as a flood of memories from our adventures came rushing back. I knew what had to be done. Or at least, I'd hoped I did.

I corralled my friends, who never stopped whining or arguing until we reached the well, where I used my big boy voice, "Will you guys just shut up!" They were stunned into silence. "I need you all to think about what we've gone through together. Stop fighting and think. Realistically, there's no way we should have succeeded. We were outnumbered." Flynn nodded. "Overmatched." Roger grinned. "In a strange land."

Tubb shook his head while Griff picked lint from his belly button and smelled it. "And the only way we'd succeeded was by taking on the odds together." Liv's scowl at Flynn turned into a look of remorse. "Listen, I don't know what lies within me, but I do know that I can't do any of this without you. You make me whole. You are my companions. I trust you with my life. Now more than ever, we need to have faith in each other, not fight each other. What did the guy in the bar say? Have the stories taught us nothing if we refuse to work together?"

Shame overcame our fellowship. Shoulders slumped, heads dropped, but I wouldn't have it. "No!" I shouted. "You will not hang your heads! We are not defeated!" I turned to my right and took Liv by the hand; our fingers slid together perfectly. I turned left and, to his shock, grabbed Roger by the hand, though I definitely didn't interlock fingers with him. It was more of a bro-type of handholding. After a second of uncomfortable eye contact, everyone else got the hint. We all interlocked hands, forming a circle together around the well. "The Shire Knights will prevail!" I said with conviction.

"The Shire Knights?" Flynn questioned, looking at the group. "That's us, huh?"

"That's us," I nodded.

"The Shire Knights," Liv said even louder.

"The Shire Knights," Roger grumbled.

"The Shire Knights," the Gnomelings cheered.

And within an instant, we were chanting the words, *The Shire Knights* together. Once our chant faded, everyone turned their eyes to me as if to say, what now?

I let my hand slip free of my friends' grip. I took a slight step forward, then hung a dangling foot over the steel grate that protected the well. "I'm going in."

Flynn looked puzzled. "Dean, I don't know what you're planning, but —" he started.

"Have faith," I interrupted. Without hesitation, I took a step toward the pit of the well. My foot went straight through the steel bars that seemed to disappear, magically bending around me.

I LIKE WARM HUGS

The drop should have been about eight feet. In my head, as I imagined this playing out, I figured I would float on the surface of the shallow pool, scanning bricks for clues like it was with Warwick Castle. But instead, I was sent into a spiraling freefall. I fell so far that my stomach felt like it was trying to escape through my throat. A gush of wind beat against my face as the water below rushed to meet me. When I hit the water, the impact was jarring. I plunged so deep that the pressure on my ears was agonizing.

The water was itself ice cold. It barely warmed as I swam up toward the surface. I reached the top, opening my eyes, expecting to see a circular well with my friends staring down, just a few feet above me, through an open lid. But that wasn't the case. Instead, I found myself in a coal-black cavern. I squinted as I gazed upward at the opening to the well, just a pinhole of light a mile away, filtering through the darkness. I swam to dry land, spitting out a mouthful of stagnant water that flooded my cheeks and nostrils when panic washed over me. Instinctively, I patted at my chest and neck, fearing the amulet had sunk to the bottom of the water or snagged in the fall, but I quickly remembered Thorne had it. "Flynn! Liv!" I shouted, but the only thing that answered was the echo of my own voice.

Once my heart rate returned to a normal rhythm, I scouted out the area. The ground was littered with coins that sparkled and shimmered. I hunched over to retrieve one of the coins. Not the brightest or biggest, but one that looked the most unique. "Edward the Confessor," I mumbled. It was the size of a nickel but thicker. The front had a man's face, with a cross carved into the back. I stuffed it into the front chest pocket of my jacket and buttoned it closed, then I looked around, spotting so many more. There must have been hundreds of these things down here.

No, thousands. I considered picking them all up, scooping them into my hands, filling my pockets until they overflowed. I could be rich. Instead, I thought back to when I was little when my parents would take me to Tarpon Springs, Florida. There was this fountain there with a statue of a dolphin that spits water from its mouth. Each year I would take a penny, or a quarter, or even a token from Chuck-E-Cheese and throw it in the fountain, making the same wish again and again. I wished that one day I would be brave. As I scanned the smattering of coins at my feet, I realized these were someone's wishes too. Someone's dreams. Someone's hope for a loved one to stop being sick. Someone's desire to be a big brother or sister. Who was I to take them? So, I moved on.

I wished beyond a wish that I had the amulet dangling in front of me, hoping once more for its guidance. But even if I did, the blasted thing would have probably sat dormant with its spiteful sense of humor. Honestly, if it weren't important to the survival of a Gnomeling race and their entire realm, I'd probably chuck it into the depths of the Atlantic and be done with it.

Behind me was the water I'd swam out of. In front of me lay two paths. One was to my right, the other to my left. But which way should I go? Whenever faced with this decision in video games, I'd always go left. It seemed to be a logical conclusion, so I took a step in that direction. The air in the left tunnel gave off a strange sensation. It was warm and inviting. The further I walked into it, the more the scent of cinnamon rolls snaked into my nostrils. A tunnel in the core of a cave should *not* hold the smell of cinnamon rolls. I began to doubt my decision. I tried to turn back, but my feet didn't want to move. That's when I heard them, voices singing out. Sweet harmonic voices coming from the shadows before me. They were sirens calling to me. This time, the actual mythical sirens, not police sirens. They wanted me to join them. I felt like... yes, I needed to join them. So, I took a step forward, followed by another. As I moved further into the blackness, the voices grew louder. Good memories blistered my heart. Mom. Dad. Carnivals. Kindergarten graduation. Meeting my best friend, Flynn. After that, I thought of Liv. Liv and her smile. The way her hand fit in mine. The way her hair blew around in the breeze. The way she was willing to fight and die to help me defeat the wraiths and Thorne.

Wait! Something snapped in my brain. Thorne! The man in the black fedora. The man with the rotten teeth. The man who was responsible for my father's demise. The man who turned into a Minotaur in my dream — My dream! He was going to kill my friends. Dad said the closer he got to the bound amulet, the more confusing things would become. This was a trap! I spun around, ready to run, but my feet barely budged. Footsteps and screams now surrounded me out of nowhere. I kept pushing on, willing my heels from the ground until I felt it: my left foot started to break free of an invisible stranglehold. Barely, but it was lifting. Just a little more, I thought, when something jerked me back to the earth. As I turned, I saw two skeletal hands reaching from the floor. They gripped me around my ankles, holding me fast so I couldn't move. "Help," I screamed. "Somebody help me." It was no use. Now, more hands were emerging. Tens of them, decrepit and rotting but strong enough to hold me in place. They inched up my ankles, knees, and thighs; I was consumed. I closed my eyes and prayed. That's when the words popped into my head.

"Companions, trust, faith," I whispered first, then repeated it louder with each pass. I needed to focus on what was real - on what mattered. The amulet gave me power. It taught me to swordfight. It gave me the ability. But my friends... My friends gave me the strength to use it. That's when I heard them. Their voices were as clear as a bell, as clear as the sirens' call, only real. It sounded as if they were directly above me, only a few feet away. I closed my eyes and listened.

"I'm sure he's fine. Dean knows how to swim." It was Flynn.

"Maybe this is his Jedi Trial. His Dagobah," Liv said.

"What's a Jedi?" Griff's voice echoed in the cavern. "And what be a Dagobah?"

"I don't know that we have time to explain all that," Flynn said.

"Dagobah is a planet," Liv said, never failing to seize an opportunity to show off her knowledge of anything pop culture. "Jedi trial refers to a man named Luke. He once entered a cave with fear in his heart. He confronted his fear, fighting an evil man named Vader, but really he was just battling the fear within himself."

"That was deep," Flynn said. "Now I see why Dean loves you."

"Loves me?" Liv was caught off guard.

"What's a Luke Vader?" Tubb said but was thoroughly ignored.

"He never told me he loved me," Liv said.

"He won't. His feelings for you are the fear he brings to the cave. You're his Jedi trial." Flynn sounded more coherent than I'd ever heard in our friendship. "Some people share an ice cream. Others hold hands during a movie. But you two... you two dance on the internet or play an online dork game until you fall asleep with your foreheads plastered to your screens. If that ain't love, I don't know what is."

I heard someone bumbling, snorting, and sobbing. Quickly, I realized it was Roger when he blurted out, "That was the most beautiful thing I've ever heard."

Roger was right. Flynn was right. I loved Liv. I needed to get the amulet, get out of here, and tell her as much. Determination and willpower surged through me. Then, as if I was fired from a cannon, my legs started to move. Faster and faster, I pushed against whatever evil lurked down the path until I was free, back where I started, back at the crossroads. I was running down the path to the right when I felt the amulet starting to work, even though I didn't have it with me. Thorne did. Why did I have to keep reminding myself? But still, it seemed as if I could feel the weight of it around my neck. Mom told me once about this condition called Phantom Limbs, where people who lose arms or legs can still feel them after they're gone. I must have had phantom amulet because I swore I could feel it tugging on me right then and there, telling me where to go. This charm, this amulet wasn't just an object; it was part of me. My bloodline. My destiny. So, I pretended to hold it out at arm's length. I let this phantom amulet guide me and be my eyes.

Suddenly, my fingertips glowed a beautiful sage-colored green as I was shot off into the dark, dragged by an unseen force. I rocketed through twisting tunnels, spinning and swerving as my screams echoed off the walls. Until, finally – whap! I slammed into a muddy wall. The glow of my hands alternated between purple and green, pointing at a soft patch of soil before me. "You want me to dig?" I asked the mysterious force that remained glowing steadily. "Fine. Let's do it."

I wiped muck from my face and forced my fingers into the muddy wall. It was surprisingly soft and crumbly. I dug frantically, working my way deeper into the dirt. A deafening rumble shattered the silence, followed by colossal explosions that rocked the ground beneath our feet. The earth trembled and quaked as the walls began to crumble and cave in, filling the air with choking dust and debris. The mud fell along my sides, almost melting around my body. Before long, the dirt had completely covered me. I found myself in a clearing in front of a pedestal, which was ten feet away. I stepped into the clearing, my shoes sloshing around in the mud. My whole body quivered as I was being pulled toward the next piece of the puzzle that rested in a glass case atop the pedestal: the next piece of the amulet. I reached down to grab it, squinting my eyes, when BOOM!

As soon as my fingertips made contact, the amulet seemed to explode with a flash of blinding light. Even with my eyes shut, I could see the surge of luminescence surrounding me. The strange thing is, I don't remember putting the amulet on. I don't even remember this fragment of the amulet having a chain as it sat on its pedestal. But sure enough, I could feel it. Somehow after the explosion of light, this portion of the charm dangled from a chain that hung around my neck.

The world tremored again. This time it started to split at my feet. I knew it was time to leave. When I reached the pool of water near my entry point, I looked up. I could see shadows of my friends peeking over the opening, but they were still so far out of reach.

"Flynn, Liv!" I cried out. "I've got it! I've got the amulet. Help me get out of here!" But it was no use. I could yell until I was blue in the face, and my lungs collapsed, but there was still no way they would hear me. Another violent jolt shook the ground, and I watched in horror as the ceiling overhead began to crack and crumble. Panic seized me as I frantically searched for an escape route. My mind raced, and I considered darting down the left tunnel.

My heart hammered in my chest as I contemplated the grim possibility of being trapped here. Was this what it all amounted to? All the risks and sacrifices, only to end up buried alive beneath tons of rubble? I refused to give up hope, though. I had to keep fighting, keep searching for a way out, no matter how slim the chances may seem. I was not going to end up like Dad. That's it... "Dad," I called out for him as a tear escaped my watery eye, trickling down my face in between the dirt and grime. "Dad, help me. I don't wanna die here." I broke down as the earth continued to disintegrate. Just then, a cool breeze blew as a glowing light surrounded me, a halo of protection.

"You won't, son," my dad's voice was clearer than ever. I couldn't see him, but I could hear him. He was nowhere and everywhere all at once, whispering in my ears.

"But I'm stuck!" I said, taking in the foreboding and imminent collapse. "I'm going to be buried alive."

"Do you trust me?" Dad asked.

"Of course I trust you," I said.

"Then close your eyes." The ground shook again, more violently than before. Huge rocks and chunks of soil and clay started an avalanche.

"Dad!" I cried out as the falling terrain blocked the pinhole of light from above.

"Close your eyes," he repeated.

I did as he asked and felt a warmth surrounding me, something I hadn't felt in so many years. It was a hug. A hug from my dad. He was shielding me from the earthquake.

"A great darkness is near, Dean. You must stop it. You are the keeper of the light. Do you understand?"

"Yes," I replied.

The rumbling continued as the world broke apart, but I felt nothing. No pain, no rocks smashing or hammering down, crushing my bones. I should have been a goner, but I was safe. Eventually, the thunderous percussion of collapsing earth ceased, leaving a high-pitched ringing in my ears. I was afraid to look, to open my eyes.

"Dean, there is something else I need to tell you. And it's going to be difficult."

"What is it?"

"My part in your story is over. I must leave you."

My eyes shot open. Dad held me in his massive arms, a place where I felt safe. A place I longed to be. The halo of light started to fade. I looked around and found myself in a field of grass, with the blades kissing the skin of my lower legs. And that's when I got a good look at him. Dad looked exactly as I remembered, only his eyes seemed different. They were old, maybe a thousand years old. Eyes that had seen much, perhaps too much. Eyes that had gone to a place I wasn't ready to see. His words hit me hard. "What do you mean? Over?" I asked.

"My journey ends here and now, and you will not see me again. At least not for a long while."

"No!" I shouted. "I want you to stay. I need you to stay. I want to be with you."

"And I, with you. But that is not the way it's written."

"I don't care how it's written!" I tried to pull away. I wanted to pout, to beat my message into his chest with clenched, bare fists until he had no choice but to stay with me, but I wasn't strong enough. He pulled me in closer, resting his face on mine. The stubble of his beard itched my cheek, but I didn't care. I missed that feeling and would give anything to keep it a little longer. I could smell his cologne. Instantly, it took me back to a more innocent time. What I wouldn't have given to bottle that smell. My God, I missed him. A river of tears flooded my dad's eyes as I burst into heart-rending sobs, shaking uncontrollably. Years of pain and yearning for his presence exploded within my soul. "Dad, I need you. Please come back. I've missed you so much," I pleaded. The thought of losing him again was unbearable.

"I've missed you too, Sport. And when all this is over, when your story ends, we'll be together once again. I promise."

"No, please don't go. Please, Dad, come home!"

"I am home," he said, pointing at my heart. "This is where I'll stay as long as you'll have me."

And without another word. Without another sound. Without another heartbeat in my chest or another tear splashing against the ground. My dad was gone, vanished into thin air. I fell to my knees and cried to the heavens until I could cry no more.

DUCK TALES

It was becoming a recurring theme of my journey to wake up in a strange place, or at least somewhere other than I expected. When I came to, I was lying in the grass, still on the property of Chalice Well, though no longer in the well itself.

"What happened?" I stared up at my friends who were hovering over me.

"You um..." Flynn tried his best to explain, "You kinda levitated, then fell in the well like you were David Blaine or David Copperfield... Whichever David is the magician."

"They're both magicians," I said, rubbing my temples the way Mom does when she gets migraines.

"Then we heard you screaming for help. Followed by this weird flash of light, which we assumed had something to do with the amulet since we can't seem to find a piece of the amulet without there being some sort of explosion. Long story short, you ended up here."

I couldn't see straight as I sat upright. My head was still spinning in circles.

"Take it slow," Liv said, kneeling beside me, placing her hand on my cheek.

"Liv," I said.

"Yes, Dean."

"There's something I need to tell you." A look of concern crossed her face.

"What is it?" she asked.

"Flynn was right about what he said back there," I said, even though I wasn't entirely sure if the conversation I overheard was real or if I had imagined it.

"He was?" Liv asked curiously. I hoped she didn't think I was talking about her driving.

"I was?" Flynn said, just as confused.

"About my Jedi trial," I clarified. Liv's expression changed to one of shock. She looked up at Flynn in disbelief.

"How did…? How could you possibly have…?" Liv stammered.

"I don't know, but I heard everything. And, I wanted to tell you that I…I…" I paused. Of course, I paused. This was such a Dean thing to do. The words stuck in my throat. They were right there! So many times, I wanted to say this simple phrase. So many times, I'd chickened out. We'd been talking online for so long, and aside from Flynn, I'd never known someone so well. And I couldn't think of anyone else I'd rather have here with me than her. The tide was turning, and I was about to chicken out again, but I remembered the coin I never threw back. As I patted my hand against my pocket, feeling the outline of the coin, I thought, maybe this could be my wish. My wish for bravery.

"It's alright, Dean. We've had a long week. I don't want you to feel —"

"Oomph!" Flynn gave me a swift kick on the back of the leg. He nodded as I looked into his eyes, telling me without words to go for it. So I did.

"I love you." I said it. Gathering all the courage hidden in my body, I finally said it. "I love you, Liv. I've always loved you. I understand if you don't feel this way too, but—"

"I love you too, Dean." Without hesitation, Liv took her free hand and placed it on my other cheek. She leaned in, and we shared the most perfect kiss of all time. The kind of kiss that puts storybook kisses to shame. The kind of kiss that made Roger blush. The kind of kiss that made Tubb and Griff cheer and chest bump. The kind of kiss that went on for seven minutes and thirteen seconds until Flynn started to tap on my shoulder, pointing at the time.

"We still do have a world to save, right?" Liv broke the embrace, slid her hands down my shoulders, then my arms, eventually resting her hands in mine. With a cat-like smile, Flynn rolled his eyes. "How about you help lover boy here to his feet? Let me go get the car?" Flynn held out an open hand. He was practically begging Liv to throw him the keys.

Liv looked at me, then shrugged. She pulled her car keys from her pocket and said, "I guess you've earned a chance to drive on the wrong side of the road." She tossed the keys to Flynn.

"Be back in a sec," he said, snatching the keys out of midair, pumping his fist in victory.

Y

On the drive to the London Eye, a lot had transpired. Mom and Doctor Anders told us they had spotted Thorne, but he didn't have the Pegg brothers with him. This made perfect sense. Burt would have had third-degree burns, while William told me he was done with his gig just moments before he stabbed me. In place of the Peggs, Mom mentioned that Thorne had upgraded his minions, with at least five more on the payroll. Four were described as being on the smaller side - taller than the Gnomelings but shorter than Roger. They couldn't get a good look at their faces, but Mom said she knew they were ugly and hairy. According to Doctor Anders, the other one was a gigantic security officer that seemed more like a professional wrestler than a policeman. As far as Mom could tell, they hadn't located the amulet yet.

During the drive, our seating accommodations were a little less cozy for me. Liv sat up front with Flynn, leaving Roger, Tubb, Griff, and me in the back seat. I told them all about what had happened in the well, including how I saw my dad. Eventually, I shared my dream and informed them about Thorne's transformation into a Minotaur and the fate I saw for each of them.

"Well, there be good news, and there is being the bad news," Tubb explained. "The good news is that Thorne truly must be an agent of evil that comes directly from our realm. He isn't really a man at all. This human body must be his shifting shapes form. This means he must be an assassin sent by the Dark One. A spy in the network of evil."

"And that's good news, how?" I asked, as I couldn't think of any scenario where *that* was the good news.

"As I was saying, Thorne can only transform into his true self if he's Second Realm," Tubb stated.

"He must be stuck here without a way back," Griff said. "He must be requiring the amulet to open a portal."

"How did you plan on getting back home?" I asked. Up until this point, the thought didn't even cross my mind. "If you didn't find me or the amulet, how would that have worked?" Tubb took a big inhale, sinking down into his shoulders. "You would have been stuck, too," I said. He nodded, sulking in somber silence.

"So," Liv interjected. "If Thorne doesn't get all the pieces of the amulet, that means he can't go full beast mode in London?"

"In theory," Tubb said. "But if the theory is wrong, he can mush us into a pulp, then scramble our insides like pudding."

"So, what's the bad news?" I asked.

Tubb hesitated.

"Tubb," I gave a stern look. "What is it?"

"Well… If Thorne is an assassin for the Dark One, as I now be suspecting… With most of the amulet complete, he can conjure up enough magic to summon help."

"What kind of help," Liv asked.

"The bad kind," Griff gulped.

"Another minotaur?" I feared.

"No," Tubb said. "Unless one be holding the whole amulet, with all the pieces, only things native to this realm can pass through. That's why we see Thorne as a human."

"But he could send other things? Right? So what other things do you have in your realm that he can bring here?" I said.

"Demons, ogres, or goblins could come through as humans, but only a few at a time," Tubb said.

"His new guards," I said, hoping I was wrong.

"As far as creatures go, there be spiders, elephants, but those are too big to fit through the portal... Oh my daisies, maybe the corneaducks."

Griff gulped once more, "I don't be liking corneaducks."

"What's a corneaduck?" Liv asked. The way the name sounded, it reminded me of a dinosaur.

"A sort of bird," Tubb said.

"Birds?" Flynn wondered. "What could be so bad about birds?"

Tubb wrung his nervous fingers together. "Let's just be saying they're named corneaducks because they have some very specific diets."

"Which would be?" I was sure I didn't want to know.

"The cornea."

"They eat eyeballs?"

"Technically, they be picking them out so they can feed them to their babies. Then, the babies eat the eyeballs," Griff clarified.

"From people?" I asked. I don't know why I did. The more I asked, the more I wanted to forget.

"Mostly," I shuddered at the thought. "But, if you had a surplus of Walruswolf eyes, they make a great substitute," Griff said.

"Sorry. Fresh out." Suddenly spiders and elephants didn't sound so bad. "Hopefully, Thorne doesn't have a clue about this piece of the amulet." I gripped the amulet tight, taking a deep breath. "I mean, he wouldn't call for corneaducks if he thought he was about to win. Right?" My friends shrugged, their shoulders lifting to their ears. "Anything else you want to share about the eye-eating birds?"

Before Tubb or Griff could reply, a chime rang out from inside the car. Liv leaned across the front seat to get a better view of the dashboard. "Oh, bollocks!" She slapped her hand against the ceiling in frustration. "We need petrol." I glanced over Flynn's shoulder and saw the low fuel indicator was on. To be honest, I was grateful for the distraction. Thinking about demons, goblins, or birds that plucked eyes from humans made me a little uneasy. We were still a few miles outside London, unwilling to risk running out of fuel, so we stopped at the next filling station. And, of course, Liv had to explain to Flynn why she said petrol and not gas, even though, to his point, gas was easier to say, plus it had fewer letters.

When we stopped to pump, Liv let Flynn fill up the tank. For some Flynn-like reason, this made him happy. Liv suggested we check in with my mom one last time before rolling into London. I said, why not, and grabbed the phone from inside the car.

"That's odd," I said, looking down at the display. "There's no signal."

"Happens here a lot," Liv took the phone to double-check. "Signal's pretty spotty until you get closer to the river." After scanning the neighborhood, Liv pointed. "There. Let's walk to that hill to see if we can get a bar or two." So, that's exactly what we did. The two of us moseyed across the street through a playground to the top of a hill. Flynn pumped petrol, then joined Roger and the Gnomelings inside the filling station store for some pre-battle snacks. I could almost picture Tubb and Griff drooling over the nacho cheese dispenser. Roger would most likely be flirting with the cashier, assuming he was done thinking about Mom. I'm going to say this again… Gross.

Once we reached the top of a small hill, I tried the phone again and, for a moment, received a signal. "Worth a shot," I said, phoning Mom. It rang for a split second, then disconnected. I tried again, moving left, right, up, and down the hill. This pattern carried on for minutes. Signal. No signal.

"Try holding it up higher," Liv said. What a ridiculous idea. As if the extra three feet of elevation would get a strong sig—

"Hey, it's working," I said as an extra bar popped onto the meter, staying put.

"Put it on speaker so we can hear," Liv inched closer, positioning her ear toward the sky.

I tapped my thumb on the speaker icon. The phone began to chime. *Ring, ring, ring, ring…* Six more times, it rang, each sound causing more anxiety than the one before. "C'mon, pick up," I urged. Finally, someone picked up when I was certain the call would be forwarded to voicemail. "Hello? Mom? Doctor Anders?" No reply, only silence followed by a staticky noise.

"What is that?" Liv craned her neck further, trying to hear.

"It sounds like water. Like running water," I said.

"The river. The River Thames," Liv's expression turned serious.

Suddenly, chills ran through me at warp speed. I was filled with an overwhelming fear that something was wrong, terribly wrong. "Mom!" I was shouting into the phone at this point. "Mom, are you alright? Please, answer me."

She didn't answer, but someone else did. A sinister laugh resonated through the phone's speaker. Soft at first, then growing louder. I immediately recognized Thorne from how he greeted me, saying, "Hello, Dean."

"Where's my mom? Where's Doctor Anders?" I asked into the phone.

"Don't worry, they're with me. We're just getting to know each other. Say, Sport... why don't you join us?" That really struck a nerve. I despised this guy already, but to call me Sport the way my Dad did crossed a line. If I ever saw him again, I'd knock his teeth out and shove them up his— "Perhaps bring the piece of the amulet that you found in the well," Thorne continued. "Or perhaps I'll simply take it from you."

"I don't know what you're talking about," I said, trying to play dumb.

"Oh, but you do know what I'm talking about, don't you? You went into the depths of Chalice Well. You've found *my* Holy Grail."

How did he know that? How could he possibly know? If Mom or Doc Anders gave us up, I couldn't bear to think about what kind of torture he must have put them through. Then, I wondered if he could sense the amulet. Similar to the way I could feel its power within me, even after it was taken. "Thorne, I swear if you so much as—"

"Dean, while I would love to hear everything you plan on doing to me, I grow tired of this conversation.

I'll have all of the pieces of the amulet soon enough, and you will have lost. Just like dear old Dad." The call disconnected.

"Thorne!" I shouted, then redialed, but it went straight to voicemail. I tried again—the same thing happened. I wondered if he shut the phone off or chucked it into the river.

"This is wrong! This is so messed up! How could everything be going against us?" At this point, I was salty, bitter, angry, disheartened, and, more than anything, worried about Mom. I lost my dad to this man, this shifter of shapes, as Tubb and Griff put it, but I couldn't bear to lose her too.

"Dean," Liv said. Her voice quivered. I assumed it was because of the phone call.

"I know. I know. We'll figure something out," I said, trying to comfort her.

"No, Dean, look," she said, pointing upward, toward the east. Something bizarre stood out. A dark cloud. A dark cloud was moving in our direction, moving against the wind, against the other clouds.

"What the flippers?" Only I didn't say flippers. I was now saying words I normally didn't say. "That is *not* normal."

"I've got a bad feeling about this," Liv said.

"Get to the car!" I looked at Liv. She shook her head in agreement. We darted down the hill, taking off toward the car as fast as our feet could carry us. I reached the passenger door, yanking up on the handle. "It's locked."

"Where's Flynn?"

A bell jingled as the convenience store front door opened. Flynn, Roger, Tubb, and Griff strutted out, looking like a bunch of tourists. They had handfuls of paper sacks filled to the brim with junk food. Tubb was munching on a foot-long beef snack while Griff gnawed on a pickle on a stick. Roger downed an energy drink while Flynn brought up the rear wearing a bright, tri-colored jester's hat. I glanced back up at the sky; the cloud was encroaching. Only, it wasn't a cloud at all. Piece by piece, the dark object started to break apart and fan out.

At that point, Tubb must have followed our gaze to the sky because he dropped everything in his hands and belted out, "Corneaducks! Run!" The rest of the group looked up, seeing the nightmare headed our way. A few of the birds began to swoop down in our direction. Their features started to take shape. They looked like pelicans, only with talons instead of webbed feet, and their bills were even more pointy and razor-sharp. The birds all had gray feathers with red streaks on their wings with a lightning bolt shape that stretched across their faces. Here's the kicker… they only had a single eye positioned in the center of their elongated foreheads. Maybe that's why they were on the hunt for corneas. If you asked the devil himself to design a bird, this would be it.

Flynn was almost at the car, still carrying bags full of junk food, scouring the depths of his pockets with a free finger or two. Liv slammed her hand against the hood and demanded, "Keys! Now!"

"I'm trying. You're pressuring me!" Flynn yelled after he put a candy bar in his mouth to free up another finger.

"Of course, I'm pressuring you! These things are going to eat our eyeballs!" Liv shouted back.

"Drop the stuff, Flynn. They're almost on us!" I started to jiggle on the handle, nerves taking over.

Flynn did as I asked, dropping his goodies. A glass Hawaiian Punch bottle hit a rock and shattered, the fruit juice staining the ground orange. Flynn continued rummaging through his pockets for the car keys as Liv yelled, "Watch out!"

Just then, a corneaduck swooped down, its beak aimed at my head. The shadow of its wingspan blanketed the entire car in the darkness. Adjusting like an F-15 lining up its target, this bird was going to eat my eye, and I liked my eyes. I ducked at the last second. A gust of wind blew my hair back as the demon bird zipped past.

"It's stuck," Flynn shouted. "The key is stuck on my pants." The key chain was snagged on the thread of his pocket. He tugged upward, tearing the thread free. "Here. Catch." He tossed the keys over the car. I watched in slow motion as they floated to Liv. She held her outstretched hand over the hood, about to clasp the keys when a corneaduck plucked them out of midair and disappeared.

"Are you freaking kidding me?" Liv screeched.

"Cover your eyes," Tubb hollered.

"Help! Help me" It was Griff. He was huddled up into a ball beneath the back tire. Three birds dove at him in sequence. The first bird missed as Griff tucked his knees tight against his chest. The second bird missed too but didn't have time to evade. Its bill got stuck in the tire, piercing the rubber, causing air to leak. The third corneaduck learned from its friends' mistakes, changing its course. It snagged Griff's ankle and pulled him from beneath the car. These things were strong. Judging by our trials at the trebuchet, Griff weighed right at eighty pounds, but this bird, this creature, was pulling him like he was nothing more than a plaything.

"Griff!" Tubb shouted. With help from another corneaduck, the bird started to lift Griff into the air. Tubb dove headfirst, clutching Griff around his wrists, yanking him back to the earth. "Hang on!"

"Gnomelings!" I cried out and ran to help them, but it was too late. At least ten other birds joined the fray, taking hold of the Gnomelings by their legs. They carried them into the sky. Carried them out of sight.

"Get back, you monsters," I spun to see Roger battling with a half-dozen birds. With his right arm, he shielded his eyes, tucking them neatly against his inner elbow. He picked up a stick with his left hand and swung it at the creatures. He was no match. The birds zigged, zagged, plucked, and bit. Tiny wounds started to speckle Roger's body, forming tiny crimson polka dots across both arms, legs, stomach, and back. Eventually, they corralled him, grabbed hold of him by his double-knotted boot laces and wrists, and shuttled him away as well.

"What do we do?" Liv dodged a battalion of birds as they dive-bombed, taking aim at our heads. With each attack, the birds let out a shrill shriek that violated my eardrums. Their clamoring was pure torture.

"Make a run for the store. It's our only chance," I suggested. I saw a hundred merciless corneaducks circling above us like vultures as I looked up. Flynn took the lead, followed by Liv, and I brought up the rear. We rushed into the store and slammed the door shut behind us.

I SHOT A BIRD IN LONDON
JUST TO WATCH IT DYE

A petrified convenience store clerk of no more than eighteen, crouched behind the counter with her hands over her ears, trying to block out the screeches of the corneaducks. She didn't know exactly what was happening, but she could tell it was bad. She wore a black skull cap over her blonde hair, denim overalls, and combat boots and appeared ready for battle or a heavy metal concert.

"Barricade the doors," I ordered. Flynn and Liv took action, sliding displays and candy shelves in front of the doors. But I knew this would only provide us time to think, a temporary solution to a permanent problem. I knew this because the entire store was protected by a rickety screen door with floor-to-ceiling windows covered by ads. Once the birds figured this out, it would only be a matter of time before they burst through. "Does this place have a back door?" I asked the clerk.

"Through the coolers. But it doesn't open because the lock's busted," she answered.

Crack! A corneaduck smacked against the window, splintering it into a spider web of glass. *Crack* Another strike to our left. Then one to our right. They were testing the glass for weak points. I told Flynn and Liv to look for anything we could use as weapons. When they returned, Flynn had a gallon of milk; Liv had a plunger. The sad thing is that both of their items were better than mine. All I could find was a plastic back scratcher.

"Too bad you don't sell guns and ammunition," Liv said, narrowing her eyes as she turned to the clerk desperately.

"Actually...," the clerk replied.

"Actually, what?" Liv, Flynn, and I said all at once.

"In the store room. We used to sell some gear. The boss decided it was dangerous with the number of kids that shopped here. You see, a few years back—"

"Yeah, honestly, we don't care about any of this. Can you just show us what you have?" I interrupted. I felt bad. This girl seemed nice enough, but there were more pressing matters, specifically, the cannibal birds.

"Rude," she scoffed, then marched to a slim door behind the counter. Just as she reached for the handle, the corneaducks launched another strike. This time a few of their beaks broke through the windows, but they didn't completely shatter. Reminiscent of the ones stuck in the tire, these were stuck in the glass. The clerk yelped and scurried even faster to open the storeroom door.

We followed close behind as she pulled a string that dangled from a light on the ceiling. The room was about ten by six. It consisted of old milk crates full of muscle-car magazines, a couple tires, and boxes covered in mildew. Posters of beer ads from the 1980s lined the walls, barely hanging on, secured by pushpins. The clerk rolled a tire out the door. A rush of excitement and adrenaline surged through me as I tried to guess what we'd find - pistols, AKs, maybe even an RPG. But my excitement faded faster than you could say Chuck Norris when she took the lids off, revealing a boatload of... well -

"Paintball stuff?" Flynn's face pinched in disappointment.

"You're one to complain. What are you going to do? Soak them to death with whole milk?" the clerk shot back.

Getting over my initial disappointment, I said, "These'll work." I drew a paintball gun from the box. The barrel was long and sleek. It had an ammo hopper, which could hold at least two hundred paintballs attached to the top. I would have thought this was awesome if I weren't scared out of my wits. I always wanted to play paintball but was terrified of getting shot. Bruises looked awful on my skin.

"You have grenades?" Liv's voice rose with elation as she took two paint grenades from the box. They could have been the twins of real grenades, only they had a splash of neon pink on the pins and were full of paint instead of TNT.

"Still want your milk, pretty boy," the clerk shot Flynn a dirty look.

"Why are you still here?" Flynn snapped back, then turned his attention to the boxes. "Oh yeah. Come to daddy," he set his milk down on the ground, removing two revolvers, the paintball equivalent of the fifty-caliber hand cannons we'd use in *Call of Duty*.

"We can use these too!" I blurted out. My hands were shaking with sheer elation as I tore paintball masks from the belly of the box. The masks had plastic protection covering our foreheads, cheeks, and necks, with a protective plastic shield covering the eyes. If the psycho birds could poke their way through glass or rubber tires, these wouldn't do much, but it was better than nothing.

Our joy was short-lived as more of the corneaducks rallied around our stronghold. They dived-bombed the store strategically, piercing the windows until the cracks began to spread. Soon, the only thing keeping us from them would splinter into a million pieces. We stacked up against the barricaded doors, readying our weapons. I crammed as many paintballs as I could into the hopper until it resembled an overflowing gumball machine. Most of the paintballs were blue, but there was a smattering of yellows and greens and a pink one or two. Liv also readied her paintball guns, then snapped the paint grenades onto her belt. Flynn loaded a magazine, racking the slide to chamber a neon orb of destruction.

"Let's do this!" the clerk stacked up at our side, lowering a protective mask over her face. She racked a paintball shotgun that must have been buried deep in the box because I would have totally snagged that one. Flynn looked as if he was about to make a smart-mouth comment to the girl but decided against it. He must have been thinking the same thing as me: we could use all the help we could get. I took my cue from our new friend and slid the mask down, so the foam rested on my nose. I could see clearly through the protective lens for a second, but I must have been breathing heavily because the mask started to fog up.

"What's the plan, boss?" Flynn asked as he adjusted his jester's cap to fit snugly beneath his paintball mask.

"I think we should fan out. Into some sort of formation. Make it harder for them to attack." I said.

"Good idea," Liv said.

"I'll make a break for the car and take cover behind it. Flynn, you go right; defend our position from the pumps."

"Why do I have to go behind the pumps?"

"Your gun has the least amount of ammo," I said. "If you run out, just spray them with gas."

"Petrol," the clerk corrected. Even through my foggy lenses, I could see Flynn roll his eyes, mocking her. "I'll go with him," the clerk said. She pulled a lighter from her pocket, flicking it until a flame rose two inches from the opening. Having an open flame next to a stockpile of petrol was a terrible idea, but the crazy look in the clerk's eyes made me a little nervous, so I focused on Liv.

"Liv, I need you to stay here. Once we're out, close the door."

"What?" Liv pulled away. "No way."

"They're not after you." I reached beneath the collar of my shirt. "They're after me." I retrieved the amulet. "They're after this."

"Don't you think I know that?" Liv said.

"Please, I can't stand to think of anything bad happening to you. We've come too far."

"Which is exactly why this is a terrible plan."

"Guys," Flynn shook me by my shoulder.

268

"Liv, listen," I said, ignoring Flynn. "At least let me get to the car."

"Dean," Flynn shook me again.

"Then, if we can take a few out, I'll give you a signal that it's clear."

"Not a chance," Liv folded her arms across her chest.

"Seriously, you two. Will you be quiet and listen to me?" Flynn stood between us, holding us both apart at arm's length. He looked both of us over, his head drooped in exhaustion. "Can I talk now?" I shook yes. Flynn lifted his chin, staring at the amulet. "I have an idea."

Flynn shared a plan that seemed to fall between insane and ingenious, only Liv wasn't a fan. The way Flynn saw it, the birds were after me. They knew that I had the amulet. So why not throw them off the scent?

"This is a truly awful idea," Liv voiced her frustration. "First, Dean wants me to sit still and play the role of the precious princess trapped in the tower. And now you want to take the amulet yourself. Thinking these birds will fall for it."

"It worked for the treasure hunters on this TV show I watched," Flynn stomped on the ground.

"That was fiction, Flynn. This is real life," Liv shot back. "And what if you get caught? Dean has proven he can handle the amulet. He's stronger with it. What if you get corrupted?"

"Please," Flynn huffed. "You said it yourself. This is real life. Not some movie. I'm not going to turn to the dark side." Flynn spun on his heel to face me. I knew what he was about to say. What he was about to do. He was going to make me choose. The idea of giving up the amulet was hard for me, but it wasn't the worst thing ever. Besides, my plan already had us splitting up, drawing them in different directions and weakening their numbers.

On top of that, I believed in Flynn. Unlike Liv's hesitation, I wasn't worried about the amulet corrupting him. Sure, I was a little concerned he might lose his way, ending up on a train to Germany, but that was about it. Flynn was my best friend. He'd been there for me since first grade. And the look on his face at that moment told me I had to trust him

"Fine," I said, pulling the amulet over my neck, resting it in Flynn's hands. "We split up. Draw them away from the group. Keep the amulet out of their hands. I mean, beaks."

"I don't like this one bit," Liv said firmly. She squinted her eyes, causing her nose to scrunch. "What if one of you gets taken? Even if that doesn't happen, what if this plan works, and they all go after Dean, and we can't help him? What then? If, by some miracle, we can take them down separately, where will we meet up? Do either of you even know where the Eye is?" Her voice was filled with doubt. She clearly had the same concerns about Flynn's navigational skills as I did.

"No, but you do, Olivia Emily Weathersby," Flynn said.

"Just Liv is fine," she replied.

"Irregardless," Flynn said.

"Irregardless is not a real word," Liv said.

"As I was saying," Flynn continued, "I know we can count on you. Dean trusts you, so I trust you," Flynn smiled, laying it on thick. He always knew how to turn on the charm when he needed to. Deep down, Flynn was starting to grow on her, or at the very least, she saw what I saw in him.

"Pardon me," the clerk joined the conversation. "At any point today do I get to set these storks on fire?" she asked, fiddling with her lighter.

"If you want to roast them without us, be our guest," Liv stepped aside, motioning for the clerk to walk out the door. "Otherwise, do us a favor and kindly stop speaking." Liv went into command mode. It was exciting to watch her think through a plan. She grabbed a dry-erase board from the counter along with a blue marker and started diagraming our paths. For the most part, I had been calling the shots. Everyone had looked to me for answers. But with Liv's knowledge of the city, this mission was right up her alley. Literally. "Flynn," she said. "You head east. And before you ask what direction that is, it's straight that way." Liv pointed east.

"But what if I get turned around? Or confused?" Flynn doubted his sense of direction. I mean, he did go missing in our school once. A custodian found him two hours after dismissal rummaging around inside a closet. He thought there may have been a hidden door back to the classroom.

"Opposite the sun," Liv said. "You'll run into Buckingham Palace. Huge building."

Flynn still looked puzzled.

"Bigger than an ASDA. Can't miss it," Liv added.

"What's ASDA?" Flynn asked.

"The UK version of Walmart," I said.

Flynn nodded as if this extra info cleared things up.

"When you reach Westminster Bridge," Liv continued, "you'll have to be on the lookout."

"Easy-peasy," Flynn gave a thumbs-up.

"Dean. You head north, toward Paddington."

"Paddington's real?" Flynn asked.

"The station, not the bear," Liv answered. "Cut through Soho, then cross at the Golden Jubilee."

"Got it," I made mental notes. North. Paddington. Soho, then Jubilee. "And you?" I asked.

"For starters, I will not be locking myself in here while you're out there. But I will lay down suppressing fire. Once you two fan out, I'll head southeast, then cross the Lambeth Bridge. We'll meet up at the South Bank Lion. It's a statue at the edge of Westminster. South means down, Flynn."

"Never eat soggy waffles," Flynn traced the compass rose in the air with his fingertip.

"It's gonna be dark soon," I snuck a peek at the dying sunlight through one of the holes left by the birds. For a split second, I forgot about them. I thought maybe they had given up, had been called back to their master, or just got bored and took a nap, but then I heard the low buzz of the swarming again. They would never leave without us or the amulet.

"Are you certain about this?" Liv whispered in my ear, making sure Flynn didn't hear.

"I am. Sam took the ring for Frodo for a short time, and that worked out. Flynn is my Sam. That means this will work out too." I looked deep into Liv's eyes. For the first time on our journey together, I couldn't get a read on her. I didn't know exactly what she was thinking, what was running through her brilliant mind. "Ready?" I said.

"I think so, yeah," Liv said. "You?"

"As I'm going to be."

Liv nodded as a shiver rose up her body. "It's so cold in here." It was probably because Tubb, Griff, or Roger left the cooler doors open.

"Here. Take this," I said, removing my jacket, placing it over Liv's shoulder. A chivalrous act if I do say so myself. Admittedly, I'm a slow learner, but the approving nod from Flynn let me know that this move was indeed smooth.

"Thanks," Liv placed her head on my shoulder. Now I had shivers running through my body, but not from being cold. I hoped in my heart that I would never get used to or grow tired of this feeling with her.

"And what about me? What shall I do?" the clerk blurted out as she lifted her mask and wiped the fog from the shield. She had apparently found a jar of shoe polish and used it to paint thumb-sized lines beneath her eyes that resembled war paint.

"I'm sorry. Do you even have a name?" Flynn said.

"Sure I do," she said. "It's Tiggy. But friends call me Mia."

"Tiggy?" Flynn sniggered. I elbowed him in the gut. "That's a lovely name," he added, causing her to blush. "Got any more of that black stuff?"

Mia handed Flynn the polish. Flynn drew a pattern on his forehead. He was going for a diamond, but it looked like a cabin missing a few logs. He handed the polish to me. Like Mia, I kept it simple, tracing a line beneath each eye. I passed it to Liv. Beneath her left eye, she traced the letter K, and beneath her right, the letter S, both backward from her perspective, but to us, we saw S K.

"Shire Knights," I approved. I looked at Flynn and could smell his brain working overtime. It was only a matter of seconds before he questioned the spelling of knights and why it didn't start with an N. But, before he had the chance, Liv popped the cap back on the polish, tossing it to Mia, who caught it in her gloved hands.

"Mia, you make sure all of England has enough cooked birds for the Holidays!" Liv's eyes became narrow and fierce. Mia nodded as she slammed her mask back down over her face. It was go time!

ᚤ

Looking back now, it was easy for me to regret giving Flynn the amulet. As I said before, it wasn't that I feared he'd take it and go all evil overlord. He was Flynn. That wasn't in his genes. But suddenly, as we burst out of the convenience store, I felt a sense of dread. I felt like I might never hold the amulet again. Even worse, I felt this might be the last time I saw my friends alive. Maybe Liv was right. With the amulet dangling around my neck, I was confident, formidable in battle, able to see the big picture. I knew that I was part of something greater. That I had a purpose. Without it, I felt like... Dean from just outside of Pittsburgh. Not even Pittsburgh itself. A small-town nobody, too weak to stand up for himself, not smart enough to figure things out on his own. A high school kid who owned footie pajamas and, up until he found the map, the Gnomelings, and the amulet fragments, had never so much as had a real girlfriend. But here I was, kicking open the flimsy screen door to a rundown petrol station, paintball gun firmly in my grasp, about to unload on birds with one eye and beaks as sharp as bayonets.

At first, the plan mostly went as expected. Flynn raced out of the store, across the lot, hunkering down along a petrol pump. Mia joined him shortly after, though she didn't last long. After she set a couple of the demon fowl ablaze, she was stabbed in the butt by a bird. The corneaduck's beak was lodged in her rear end, and its body bobbed up and down like a lawn dart. She extracted the beak from her skin and pants, then rushed to her car and drove away. It would have been nice to know she had a car. This whole ordeal could have gone down much differently. Looking back, we should have just asked Mia if she had a car. She might have been able to drive us to the London Eye.

Once the dust settled from Mia's tires burning rubber, Flynn bolted away, heading in the opposite direction of the sun, just as Liv instructed. Before we lost sight of him, he must have shot five or six birds from the sky with remarkable accuracy. The corneaducks reacted to our strategy. They began to split into mini-squadrons to take passes at our skulls. Liv screamed for me to run as she laid down covering fire. I could hear the barrage of paintballs whizzing past me. Paintballs pinged the eyes of corneaduck after corneaduck, blinding them upon impact. They howled in glorious agony. Some wounded birds nosedived into the ground, others smacked into billboards, while others flew wildly away with no sense of direction. I wish I could have stayed to see Liv use the paint grenade, that would have been epic, but I followed orders, heading north, hoping beyond hope that everyone was safe.

I looked over my shoulder and checked my six. There was still a gaggle of the birds on my tail, at least twenty. I ducked behind trees, taking a few potshots. My first hit went straight into a corneaducks throat as it opened its beak to squawk at me. I could hear it choking on paint as it slammed into a brick building.

Before long, I got the hang of my aim. This was the first gun I'd ever shot that didn't have Nerf bullets for ammunition. I sprinted in and out of residential neighborhoods, hopping fences, firing the weapon, dodging dogs on leashes and old ladies with brooms, but the whole time I kept my eye trained on the ducks. Eventually, I reached a place called Ladbroke Square. The remaining birds, around ten of them, circled overhead. I could tell they were planning an attack as they squawked, fanning out in a V formation, then darted downward. I ran out into the open and unloaded. Splat! One duck down. Another. I was taking them out slowly but surely, but they moved faster than I could shoot. I stared down at the gun, spotting a switch that alternated between SA and FA. "F A," I said. "Fully automatic!" I flipped the switch and held down the trigger. The paintball gun became a turret. Shot after shot made contact. I dotted their eyes and wings, although even with my decent accuracy, I still missed quite a bit, splattering historic buildings with neon colors. I'm pretty sure I even busted a window in a library that appeared to be at least two hundred years old. "Whoops," I said.

WHISTLE WHILE YOU WORK

As night fell, ominous clouds obscured the moon's light. Overhead, the fluorescent street lights flickered. My spirits were high, although my ammo was running low. I hadn't seen any villains for at least ten minutes. The absence of their cries gave me a sense of peace.

Typically, the dark scared me. Everything bad that had ever happened to me happened in the shadows. Only now, the dark was my ally. I moved swiftly through shrubbery and gardens in Hyde Park, Green Park, St. James's Park, and any other park that helped me avoid the carnivorous beasts that might still be on my tail, lurking, waiting for me to make a mistake. Thankfully, I managed to stay unharmed and unnoticed for the most part. That was until I reached the Equestrian Statue of Charles I.

I took a break, leaning up against the concrete base of the statue. Once I was certain the birds were nowhere around, I allowed myself a second to take in the sights. Charles I was depicted in the statue wearing a suit of armor, holding a baton in his right hand. With black hair and a pointy beard, he looked like the spitting image of William Shakespeare. Beyond the statue, a row of luminous storefront signs lit up the square. It reminded me of Piccadilly Circus with its double-decker buses, cabs, and bicyclists winding rhythmically through the roundabout. The buildings appeared like stacks of cereal boxes in a pantry, unlike the skyscrapers in the heart of London. Street performers amazed tourists with their dance moves. A pair of illusionists named Harper and Brookelyn, who may have been identical twins, wowed a small audience with magic tricks. A singer named Aniyah Lin (apparently popular on YouTube) belted out a pitchy rendition of a popular song. There were so many people buzzing about that it took me a moment to realize that many of them were murmuring and pointing directly at me. At first, I was unsure of what was happening. Did they spot the enemy? Was an attack about to happen? It wasn't until a traffic officer screamed, "You there. In the mask. Drop that weapon!" that I realized they were staring at the paintball gun draped over my shoulder. They must have thought I was a terrorist.

"This?" I said after lifting my mask from my face. "Oh, no, this isn't what you think. It's just a —" I pulled the gun over my head, holding it in my hands. I was just trying to show him how harmless it was, but seeing as it was nighttime and I had a jet-black, fully automatic weapon, he must have thought I was aiming it at him.

"Everyone get down!" The officer dived forward and crawled on his belly alongside a parked car. He lifted a whistle from his yellow vest pocket as he peeked out from behind the tire, blowing with so much force that saliva sprayed everything and everyone within ten feet.

"Gun!" A woman screamed.

"Mummy! Daddy!" a child cried out in fear.

I froze. I wanted to plead my case, and I wanted to run, but my legs and mouth refused to obey my brain's commands as if they were on strike. Within seconds, three more officers joined in, surrounding me, blowing their whistles at me. Luckily for me, officers in the UK are usually not armed with guns, so I avoided a showdown. But they were relentless with their whistle-blowing. If I had my whistle, I could have joined the fun.

"Hands on your head!"

"Get on the ground!"

"Drop the weapon!"

"Freeze!"

"Hands up!"

"On the ground!"

"Don't move!"

The officers' commands were so utterly confusing that I couldn't keep up. In the chaos, I threw the gun, then fell to the ground in surrender. Nearly cross-eyed from the officers' shouting, I lay on my back with my hands raised like a mummy. Police swarmed as people were taking videos and pictures. I was going to be in the news. Headlines ran through my mind:

AMERICAN TOURIST AIMS WEAPON AT TODDLERS. NEWS AT TEN!

EYE SEE LONDON

I looked around my holding cell. Sterile walls with random splotches and stains of all sizes and colors. I didn't even want to guess who or what made them. Benches lined the entire room, with a singular toilet tucked not so discreetly in the corner of the cell. Yep, prison life was tough so far. All two hours of it. In that one-hundred-and-twenty-minute span, I had three cellmates. Two were sleeping on the benches, both snoring. Gigantic men with long hair. The third was a guy named Kevin. I know his name was Kevin because he wore a mechanic's uniform with a name tag. He smelled like a dumpster, had chunks of dried lettuce in his beard, and his arms were tiny, like a T-Rex. With an unknown vendetta, Kevin stared right through me. To be honest, it was pretty intimidating, but if prison shows and surviving middle school taught me anything, it was that I couldn't look weak. So I stared right back at him. Neither of us blinked. It went on forever. A stalemate. My goal was to establish my dominance within the prison. After twenty minutes of this staring contest, my confidence grew, but I realized that mere eye contact wouldn't be enough to secure my safety. I needed to assert my position as the alpha. Without hesitation, I asked, "What do you think you're staring at, Kevin?" I smirked with a hint of sass.

"Huh?" Kevin grunted, looking side to side. He scanned the room as if he didn't know where the voice was coming from.

"Leave him alone," an officer said as he entered the cell carrying a thick pair of black glasses and a walking cane. "Time to go, Kevin. You made bail."

Kevin held out his hands, fumbling for the glasses. He put them on, reached for the stick, expanded it, and tapped his way out the open cell door.

"Who does that?" the officer asked, turning his attention to me. "Who picks a fight with a blind guy? Typical American."

After shame washed over me and another one of my non-blind cellmates was released, they finally called my name. I was escorted to interrogation. Two detectives, DCI Lanie Buck and DS Kelsi Downes introduced themselves. Their breath smelled of coffee and black licorice. They grilled me on my situation. Buck had blonde hair with ice-blue eyes. She was the bad cop in this policing power couple. She found a way to insult me and make me second guess my life choices all in the same breath. The sad truth is, even when she asked me, "Tell me your full name and date of birth," my mind went blank. Lanie Buck had surely made grown men cry in this very room. I was a goner.

Detective Kelsi Downes, a skilled and charming officer, began her questioning with precision. She effortlessly disarmed me with her friendly demeanor, and I found myself ready to divulge any information she requested, if only to avoid another frightening encounter with DCI Buck. Downes' hair was a dark shade of brown. She had curls that would make Shirley Temple jealous. Eventually, after I nearly wet myself from fear, the dynamic duo gave me a chance to explain.

"If you lie to us," Buck started.

"We'll know," Downes finished.

They took a seat across from me at the stark metal table. I imagined the countless thieves or murderers who must have occupied the same seat, facing these experienced torturers. I understood the importance of honesty and the need to choose my words carefully. The lie I was about to tell came easily, almost seamlessly. As you know, I wasn't skilled at deception, but my freedom was at stake this time.

"My friends and I were playing a game of paintball," I told the detectives. "I must have gotten lost. When I came out into the square, I was amazed by how beautiful your country was. The statues. The culture. I was in shock. I totally forgot that I had the paintball gun with me."

The two detectives looked at one another. Buck raised a curious eyebrow and said, "Keep talking."

Confident I had their attention, I sealed the deal with a calculated comment, "It may seem crazy, but consider this, I'm just a stupid American." Buck grinned and broadened her shoulders in a show of triumph.

"Well done, son," Detective Downes said as she leaned in, patting me on the shoulder in approval. My half-truth, or half-lie, depending on the perspective, proved to be a resounding success. It appeared that my admission had given them a sense of pride, a form of retaliation for the events of 1776.

Once the cops were convinced that I was telling the truth (or at least a version of the truth), they allowed me to make a phone call. I made three. One to Mom, one to Liv, and one to Flynn, but no one answered. This made me nervous. The cops played it off by explaining that it was after midnight and they were probably sleeping. But I knew the truth. There were only a few reasons why no one would pick up, and none were good. After completing all the required paperwork, the cops granted me my freedom. Unfortunately, they took possession of my paintball gun with all the ammunition.

Y

As soon as my feet hit the pavement, I took off in a sprint. The station was located near the London Eye, the only positive aspect of the ordeal. My pulse was off the charts. My hands were trembling. I worried about the fate of my friends and my Mom. Then, my worries broadened to the fate of Second Realm and all of its creatures, lost because I couldn't defeat Thorne. Lost because I was caught by the police with a paintball gun. I must have been the worst hero ever, even worse than George Clooney's Batman. "Positive thoughts, Dean. Think positive thoughts," I told myself as I reached Jubilee Park and Garden. The wide-open park offered little cover as I approached the London Eye. I crouched behind a park bench to survey the area. The clouds had mostly cleared, and the moon cast a bright light on the

Eye. The London Eye was a sight to behold. It was much larger looking in person. It appeared twice as big as the Statue of Liberty and nearly as tall as the Arch in Saint Louis. Surrounding the magnificent Ferris wheel were capsules that resembled Tylenol pills, only with glass walls for scenic viewing. Each capsule could hold up to twenty-five people. Only there were no people in sight. A sign at the base of the Eye showed the tourist attraction closed at six in the evening.

"Where are you guys?" I whispered, my anxiety was nearly crippling me. All I wanted to do was curl up into a little ball, make myself invisible, or maybe just cry myself into a deep sleep, hoping when I woke, this was all just a crazy dream. Maybe I would wake up in the woods near Oxford, and I'd just been knocked unconscious the whole time after slamming into that tree. But I knew better, and I knew that giving up now wasn't an option. Dad wouldn't quit, and neither would I. But what now? Wait! I had an idea, an epiphany. I'm brilliant, I thought. I pulled my phone back out. My fingers swiped and tapped until I located the *Find my Family* app. When Mom installed the app, it made me feel like such a loser, but now I was thankful she did. I scrolled down, clicked on 'Mom's Phone,' and hit the circular **Find** button.

Scanning...

Scanning...

Scanning...

Located...

A map slowly loaded on the screen. A steady blue dot represented me. A yellow flashing arrow pointed to the location of Mom's phone. It was pointed right at the Eye. But where? I didn't see her until – the Eye started moving. It rotated slowly. I watched, inspecting each capsule as it passed, and that's when I saw them. About halfway down on the right side (3pm if you imagined the Eye as a clock), there was a capsule full of people. All bound, hands tied behind their backs. The first person I spotted was Liv. No! She was caught. Then, next to her, I saw Mom, Anders, Tubb, Griff, and Roger. But no Flynn. Could he be on another capsule? Was he taken? But then reality set in. It was Flynn. He probably got lost.

I looked back to Liv, Mom, and the rest. Not only were they tied up, but they were gagged too. Each appeared to have a balled-up ankle sock stuffed into their mouth. Liv had a cut above her right eye. Tubb had a bruise the color of an eggplant plastered over his cheekbone. Griff was bleeding from his nose. Roger's face was so swollen that it appeared he had been stung by a swarm of bees. I'd imagined he put up a fight trying to protect Mom.

The wheel slowed as the capsule came to a grinding halt at the base of the ride. I paused for a moment, forgetting to breathe. No one else seemed to be around. This had to be a trap; in my bones, I knew it was. But my bones weren't calling the shots around here, nor was my brain. Anyone with a brain would have stopped me from doing what I was about to do, but my heart willed me to my feet. Before I knew it, I was sprinting toward the capsule at full speed, toward Liv. When I reached the capsule door, I could hear everyone inside screaming from beneath their gags. I knew what they were saying; they were telling me to stay back and warning me this was a trap, but that didn't matter. All that mattered was freeing them. I wouldn't sit back and hide. Dad wouldn't hide.

I swung the capsule door open and pulled a wad of cloth from Liv's mouth.

"Dean, it's a —" she started to warn me.

"I know." I loosened her restraints, a poorly tied knot that looked exactly like the knot used to tie up William Pegg in the hotel. Next, I moved to Mom, freeing her as fast as my fingers could untie. Then, I gripped the rope around Roger's wrists. The instant my fingertips touched the rope, I felt cold steel press against the back of my head.

"Dean!" Mom said. Liv's eyes widened.

"Back away slowly," a gravelly voice commanded. It wasn't Thorne's voice, so I knew it must have been one of his henchmen.

"No," I mustered all my strength to show defiance. But that defiance lasted as long as it took for the gun to be cocked.

"Try again," the man said. I turned and faced the monster. He was humongous. His arms were bigger than my entire body. He was ugly, too. Not that I can brag, but this guy was hideous. His nose was permanently off-center, making his eyes appear at different heights. And his head had to have weighed thirty pounds. Anders was right; he looked like a professional wrestler and undoubtedly one of the villains.

"You fell for my little trap," Thorne said, stepping from the shadows into the light.

"I knew it was a trap," I boasted as if that made my situation any less awful.

"Search him," Thorne snapped his fingers. Within seconds, the rest of his minions scampered out from behind nearby trees and shrubs. I couldn't see their faces, but judging by their stature and how they moved, I could tell they weren't quite human. They were hunched over, dragging their knuckles on the ground as they raced toward us. Their breathing was off too, like gremlins with asthma.

"Goblins," I whispered loudly enough for Thorne to hear me.

"Hellions, actually," Thorne corrected me. I didn't know what a hellion was, but I was sure I hated them. After a thorough patting down, one of the goblin-ish creatures, or hellions as Thorne called them, shook his head no, indicating his search came up empty.

"Where is it?" Thorne asked.

"Where's what?" I played dumb.

"Don't play dumb with me, boy!" Thorne's eyes glowed a shade of crimson as his voice became deeper and more guttural with each word. This was not good. His power must have been growing, being in possession of the amulet. What would happen if he got the whole thing? Would he turn into that creature, making my nightmare become a reality? Would he kill Liv and Flynn?

"Flynn," Thorne hissed. I must have been thinking out loud again. "You gave it to him. Didn't you?"

I stood defiant, not giving him the satisfaction of knowing he was right. But this was good news for me. Perhaps, Flynn wasn't lost after all. He was probably hiding. He must have seen the others captured and knew he couldn't let our part of the amulet fall into Thorne's hands. A wry smile inched across my face.

"Is this funny to you?" Thorne asked. "Remove the girl and the mother from the Eye." The hellions pulled Liv and Mom off the capsule one by one. As the hellions moved in and out of the light, I got a better look at them. Their skin was a puke shade of green. Their fingernails and teeth were razor-sharp, and they were all dressed in blue coveralls.

"I liked the wraiths better," I said, scanning the area. "They here too?"

Thorne nodded. "Somewhere at the bottom of the river." The look on his face told me he was serious. "It's so hard to find good help these days. Especially from humans."

I looked over at Mom. An absolute fear washed over her. "What do you want from us?" she said.

Thorne fidgeted with the amulet that hung around his neck. It didn't glow. Not like when I had it. And even though I wasn't wearing it, I could almost feel it. Just like in the well, it was calling out to me with a magnetic vibration.

Thorne must have sensed it too, because he looked into my eyes and said, "It appears the amulet still hasn't accepted that I am its rightful owner." He stepped toward the open capsule door. "I need you to join me. Get a bird's eye view, if you will. Help me find the next piece."

"And if I refuse?"

Thorne nodded to his brute. The oversized rhino on two legs took his aim away from me, pulling Liv into the middle of the square. He pointed his weapon at her heart. The gun looked old and vintage, but that didn't make it any less terrifying.

"Don't!" I screamed. I looked at Liv, who had tears in her eyes. I looked back at the capsule at Roger and the Gnomelings. I saw the panic on their faces. "Help me," I whispered, begging Dad to show up. Wishing that he'd tell me what to do. But I was met only by silence and by Thorne's stupid face.

"What's it going to be, Dean?" Thorne said as he waited at the threshold.

Without a word, I joined him at the steps of the Eye. He pulled a lever and pressed a button, and the ride moved, wheeling the next open capsule down to us, sending the one with Roger, Anders, and the Gnomelings back into the sky. We boarded the Eye, and the doors closed behind us. I looked out the glass hopelessly as the Eye started up again. Even if I helped Thorne find this piece, he wouldn't have the entire amulet. There was still a chance. Flynn. Flynn was out there somewhere.

YOU GIVE LOVE A BAD NAME

It took me until the third rotation of the Eye before my senses locked onto the next piece of the amulet. Beneath a row of benches, a faint yellow glow outlined a brick on a cobblestone pathway. "If I tell you where it is, do you promise to let them go?" I asked.

"I'm a villain, Dean. I make no promises that I can't break."

"Then, I'm not talking."

Thorne shrugged. "So be it." He pulled a two-way radio from his pocket and pressed the black button on the side. The radio chirped. "Shoot the girl," he said. "And if you don't hear my voice in the next sixty seconds, shoot the mom too."

"No!" I looked out the looking glass of the Eye as we reached the summit. I could make out the gigantic henchman, who looked supersized even from this high up. His arm was still outstretched, and the gun was still trained on Liv's heart. "Stop!"

"Hold," Thorne chirped into the walkie again. He raised his eyes to meet mine. "Where is it? Where is the final piece?"

Defeated, I sighed and said, "There." I pointed toward the benches. "Beneath the bricks below the middle bench. Nearest the grass."

"You're sure?" Thorne asked.

"Just leave them alone. This is between us," I said as I slumped my shoulders, hanging my head. I thought of Flynn. Now praying he wasn't anywhere near us. Maybe it was best if he forgot about us and saved himself, keeping the amulet far away from Thorne and his goons. If he was smart, he'd be halfway home, planning a life in witness protection. But if there were two things I knew about Flynn, he wasn't smart, and he was loyal to a fault. It was more likely he was about to rush in with his paintball gun, ready to take on the small army below.

Thorne spoke into the walkie once more. This time, I didn't understand a syllable. He was speaking in another language, one I'd never heard before. It was clear he had given an order as two of the hellion henchmen broke away from standing guard and raced to the bench. They picked it up, heaving it into the river. The pair dropped to the ground, digging and clawing at the bricks, tunneling into the earth. The faint yellow glow became a radiant beam of light.

As the Eye stopped and we stepped off, the hellions returned to Thorne with his prize. "I've been coming here every May for the past seventeen years. I've sat on that very bench, never knowing how close this truly was." Thorne held the amulet piece to the one hanging around his neck. With a blast of light, the pieces merged, and for a brief moment, I saw Thorne in his true form. I saw the Minotaur. He was menacing, hideous, and far beyond any terror that a nightmare could conjure.

Thorne laughed as he stared at me, my knees buckling and lips trembling. "What's the matter, boy? No joke? No snarky comments? Aren't you going to beg me to let you go again?"

"I'll never beg," I said in a child's voice, trying to find my courage.

"What was that?"

"I said," I straightened my legs, inhaled, and puffed my chest out, "I'm not going to beg." This time my confidence grew. "I'm not going to cry. I'm not going to help you ever again."

"Is that what you think?"

"What I think is that Flynn is long gone. He hid the last piece of the amulet somewhere you'll never find it. With the pieces you have now, you'll never return to Second Realm, but even if you do, you won't be strong enough to rule." The London Eye whirled and whined as the capsule carrying my friends was again front and center.

"You're right about the last part," Thorne said. "I do need the whole amulet to cross over and take my true form. Only in the realm can I sustain it. But... Do you really think your friend is outside my grasp?"

I nodded.

"Foolish boy. Nothing is outside of my grasp."

"Dean," Liv said, but my eyes were locked on Thorne.

"Flynn is the bravest, noblest, most courageous person I know," I said.

"Dean–" Liv tried to interrupt one more time.

"He'll never let you find him. He's probably already hidden the amulet or destroyed it forever."

"Or maybe," now Thorne was the one smirking, "maybe Flynn is standing right behind you."

"Yeah, right," I scoffed.

"Maybe," Thorne outstretched his hand, "your friend isn't at all who you thought he was."

Time stood still as Flynn walked right past me, arm extended, handing over the last piece of the amulet.

"Flynn?" I stared at him in disbelief, my mind struggling to process. Was this some kind of trick or illusion? Mind control, maybe?

"Well done, my son," Thorne patted Flynn on the back.

"Son?" I echoed, my confusion deepening.

"Now it's time that I tell you something about Flynn." Thorne put an approving arm around Flynn's shoulder.

What was going on? Surely that wasn't the real piece of the amulet. He must have switched it out, right? The thoughts raced through my mind.

"Remember when I came to visit you when you moved into your home so many years ago?" Thorne asked. Of course, I remembered. "I had your family moved near me. Near us," Thorne looked at Flynn with a smile. "So my son and I could keep an eye on you." Thorne broke his embrace with Flynn and started pacing. "I made sure you two would be in the same grade. In the same class. I told Flynn that his entire mission in life was to stay close to you, Dean Moyers.

In case you ever found out about who you were. What you were."

"But Flynn didn't have a dad," I corrected. "Only his moms?"

"Pawns in my game," Thorne stroked the point of his chin. "I was always around. Watching. Whispering. Making sure my son stayed on task."

"Flynn. He's lying. Tell me he's lying."

"Everything you thought was true about your friend, Flynn, is the real lie."

Flynn still wouldn't make eye contact.

"And this trip to England," Thorne boasted. "Did you actually believe Flynn was reuniting with a long-lost relative? Didn't you wonder why you never met him? Why Flynn didn't have as much as a picture? A name, even. Are you so blinded by 'friendship' that you couldn't see this coming?"

"Will you look at me?" I begged.

"When I got word your little friends had crossed over through the portal, I knew it was time to bring you home. I knew you would lead me to my prize," Thorne said, rubbing the amulet between his fingers. He kept talking, revealing more of his master plan, but I no longer cared. All I cared about was Flynn and his betrayal.

"I said, look at me!" I shouted at Flynn.

Flynn startled, turned to me slowly and said, "I'm sorry, Dean. I really am."

"Is it true? Was all of it a game to you?"

"You don't understand," Flynn said. "He's my dad. I didn't have a choice."

"Your dad," I said. "And what about my dad, Flynn? What about him? Did my dad have a choice when Thorne had him killed? Did you know about it?"

"No."

"You knew this whole time, didn't you?"

"No," Flynn said again, "I didn't. I promise."

"There's no promise in this world that you can make that I'd believe now!" I thought back on every moment we had ever shared, my life with him literally flashing before my eyes. All the laughs, the tears, the memories blended into a fit of rage. How could this be happening? No matter what they said, this had to be a joke, a devious attempt to fool Thorne. But the more I thought back on our journey, Thorne always seemed to be right on our tails or one step ahead: seeing him at the airport, Tolkien's estate, the Pegg brothers finding us at the hotel when Flynn went outside to get air, at Warwick castle, they found us again. Then, after I escaped the well, Flynn went to get the car by himself. The odds were impossible, but they found us. They always found us. The Pegg brothers said we left a piece of the map at the hotel, but I watched that map burn up and fly away. It was Flynn. It was him the entire time. And how convenient it was for him to ask for the amulet when we were one step away from our goal. Why didn't I just listen to Liv?

"You're a liar!" I roared. "I hate you!"

"Dean," Flynn pleaded, "I still tried to protect you, even though I was helping my father. You have to know that. Please try to understand."

The time for understanding was over. I lunged at Flynn with my fists clenched and a fire brewing in my belly. I leaped toward him, ready to ram my shoulder into his gut and pummel his backstabbing face, when – THUD! A set of knuckles the size of pumpkins struck me across my mouth. I crumpled to the ground as Thorne's brutish goon chuckled, rubbing his hand.

"Stay down," Flynn urged as he crouched beside me.

"You were my friend," I muttered as blood poured from my busted lip. "My best friend." I tried to get back to my feet, but the world spun. I could hear Liv cursing, Mom crying, and Roger and the rest grunting and fighting to escape their restraints.

"Sorry, I don't have the time to listen to you whine. I really do have a realm to claim as my own and an army to summon from the Dark Lands. The Dark One has foreseen it," Thorne stated as he held the final piece of the amulet in his right hand and the rest in his left. This was the third time I'd heard of the Dark One, and if Thorne's evil wasn't the worst kind out there, I secretly hoped I'd never have to encounter whatever or whoever this Dark One was. "Shall we get this over with?" he said.

A rainbow of colors flashed as the ground shook. A noise rang out so awful that everyone aside from Thorne covered their ears and prayed their brains didn't explode from their ear canals. Despite the pain, the pressure, and the ringing, I looked up, watching as the colors and flashing lights stopped. Suddenly an orb of darkness expanded over Thorne's head. Matter seemed to bend; everything looked twisted and misshapen. Then, BOOM! An explosion rocked the earth. Thorne was sent flying backward. Concrete and cobblestone blasted skyward. Chunks of rock rained down like shrapnel. I ducked, covering my head until the falling debris had stopped.

My sight was still blurry after the massive right hook from Thorne's goon, but Thorne appeared to be different now. He was starting to transform. He let out a howl as two horns extended from his skull through the flesh. The features on his face began to distort as his muscles expanded and ripped through his shirt. "Yes!" he cried out. His minions surrounded him, holding their arms up in praise like he was some sort of God.

"Stop him, Dean," I turned my head to see Liv pleading. "Stop him!"

"How?" I asked. What was I to do? He had the amulet. The whole amulet. What did I have?

"Remember the well. You must believe," Liv said.

What were the words Dad gave me? "Companions, trust, faith," I said to myself. Only now, that was only a half-truth. The words felt empty. I couldn't trust. Especially after Flynn, my companion, caused me to lose my faith.

Liv must have seen me struggling with my thoughts because she said it again. "Believe! Believe in me! Believe in your dad."

I thought hard. Of Liv. Our kiss. Of Dad and the last time we spoke. The hug that I never thought I'd get. The goodbye that eluded me my entire life. "Companions, trust, faith," I said again. This time with meaning. Again and again, I repeated the phrase until, all of a sudden, Thorne's transformation stopped midway. The amulet glowed a rose-gold hue while the rune was illuminating with red streaks, the exact same look as the first time I held it.

"What's happening?" Thorne wailed as the horns started to bore back down into his skull. The amulet lifted from his chest and started yanking, tugging... Toward me.

"Companions, trust, faith," I kept saying it.

"Shut him up!" Thorne growled as he held onto the amulet for dear life.

One of the hellions, the smallest of the bunch, pounced in my direction, claws bearing down. I closed my eyes, holding open my hand. "Now would be a good time for a little help, Dad." And with those words, I felt my hands clench around the hilt of a sword. A sword that appeared out of thin air. It was something out of a movie. It was as if the amulet willed a sword into my hands, as if it wanted me to win. I glanced down at the weapon. The sword's hilt was black, while the pommel was made up of a gem with the same symbol as the amulet etched into its heart. It was everything I needed at that moment and more.

"How is that possible?" Thorne asked.

I swung down, slashing the first hellion across its chest. It must have had chest plate armor underneath its coveralls because I heard a clank upon impact. But the impact was immense, and the creature screeched in agony before crawling away.

"Stop him!" Thorne shouted. The rest of the hellions approached. I fended them off one by one as I marched towards Thorne. Their armor protected them, but I managed to hurt them enough to scare them into hiding. When I finally had a clear shot at Thorne, I saw something so shocking it made me feel like my heart had dropped to the pit of my stomach.

"Not. Another. Step," Thorne said, holding the gun he took from his goon. It was aimed at Liv, stopping me cold in my tracks. The brute wrapped his mammoth arm around Mom's neck in a chokehold, strangling the life out of her. Mom's feet barely scraped the ground as she tried to kick her way free.

"Put the gun down, Thorne," I said, tightening my fingers around the leather grip of the sword, pointing the tip in his direction. "Are you going to let him do this, Flynn?" I asked, looking at Flynn standing at Thorne's side. He kept glancing from me to Liv to Mom and back to Thorne. "Does my mom mean nothing to you?"

"Grab his sword," Thorne said to Flynn.

"Remember when you broke your wrist skateboarding?" I said. "Who took you to the hospital?" Flynn looked at Mom. "That's right. She did."

"Don't listen to him, son. Just get the sword."

"And who taught you how to dance for the spring formal?" I said. "Not him! Not your dad! It was my mom. Are you just gonna stand there?" I could see the impact of my words. The emotion played out across Flynn's face like a game of charades. Anger, sadness, confusion. Thorne saw it too.

"Not another word, Moyers. I'm warning you!" Thorne roared.

"I know you, Flynn." I ignored Thorne's warning. "You didn't have a choice, right? I understand. I actually understand. I would do anything for my dad. But you have to see what is real. This…" I motioned toward the space between the two of us… "This is real. But him," I pointed back to Thorne. "He made you—"

My grand speech was cut short by the sound of a gunshot. Stopped by the sound of my mom screaming. A scream I hadn't heard her scream since the night my dad died. Stopped by the sound of Liv's body crumpling to the pavement.

HAVE A NICE TRIP, SEE YOU NEXT FALL

"Put him with the others," Thorne stood over Liv's body, smoke still steaming from the barrel of the gun. "Take them up top and toss them in the River."

"And the woman?" The brute was talking about Mom.

"Throw her in first," Thorne said with a sadistic smile. "Make the chosen one watch as I destroy everything that matters to him."

I wanted to scream. I wanted to cry. I wanted to punch something. I wanted to punch Thorne. But all I could do was stare at Liv. Her body was doubled over. She looked so small and innocent and helpless. I leaped toward her, reaching my hands out to grab her. To shake her. To tell her to wake up. To tell her to stay with me. To tell her that everything would be alright. Instead,

I was met by the meaty hands of the brute as he gripped his paws around my neck.

"This is your fault!" All my anger was aimed at Flynn. His face was one of pure shock. "You did this!" I screamed at the top of my lungs.

My cries must have struck a nerve because he marched over to Thorne and grabbed him by the collar of his black coat. "You said you wouldn't hurt them. You promised," Flynn's voice was shaky.

"I did what was necessary," Thorne said.

Flynn stepped back and swung wildly, cracking Thorne across the jaw. "You lied to me!"

"I told you. That's what villains do," Thorne grinned and wiped his lip. "Get in the car, son. Hopefully, the drive to Black Lake gives you time to reflect on your loyalties."

My legs scraped the ground as the brute dragged me against my will toward the Eye's capsule. I watched Flynn storm off to the car. Looking at him now was like looking at a stranger - someone I thought I knew from a past life. Turns out, I knew nothing. How much of what we shared was real? Was he ever my friend, or was it all a game to him?

"Have a seat," the brute tossed me into an open space between Roger and Anders. Mom was chucked to the floor by a group of three hellions. Her face slammed against the carbon steel. "Going up," the brute said; his accent sounded Russian. He grinned and pointed toward another hellion who stood at a control panel. Within seconds, the Eye groaned, and we ascended toward the clouds, high above the river, where we were destined to be thrown into the water. From that height, it would be like hitting concrete upon impact.

As we slowly ascended, I saw Thorne slipping into the backseat of a black Town Car while his hellions scampered away, disappearing into bushes. I saw Liv's body alone on the pavement. Why did she have to go? The first girl I'd ever cared about. She was perfect. She was beautiful. She was brave. And we were meant for each other. The more I stared down at Liv, the higher we got and the smaller she appeared. I was a sniveling mess, and my heart hurt so badly that I wished I would die right there at that moment. That the brute would crush me with his fists and not even wait until we reached the top of the ride.

In the middle of my grief-stricken reflection, I heard a high-pitched throat-clearing ahem from my right. I assumed it was Tubb or Griff. I figured they were going to tell me to be strong. Be brave. Suck it up and be a man, even though all I wanted to be right now was a time traveler. I sniffled once, twice, three more times, then stared down at Liv. Now just a speck in the universe.

After I couldn't take it anymore, I looked at Mom, sadness overwhelming me. If there was one person who could understand the pain that ravaged every inch of my body right now, it would be Mom. When we lost dad, I would hear her crying in her room at night. She would never cry in front of me. She was strong for me. This thought, this singular moment, gave me the courage to fight back. I needed to be strong for Mom. He took Liv from me. But he won't get the satisfaction of taking mom, Roger, Tubb, Griff, Anders... Anders. I was so consumed with my feelings that I hadn't given two seconds of thought about what he must be going through – seeing his granddaughter mercilessly gunned down before his eyes. I turned to check on him, but he wasn't there. I mean, physically, he was there. He was sitting on the bench with his head pressed so hard against the window that I could have sworn he was attached. But mentally, the guy was checked out. Who could blame him?

"Ahem," the throat clearing returned. This time it was at least twice as loud. I looked over to the bench across from me and saw Griff. He dangled his fingers in front of him, free of the restraints. I perked up, burrowing my face into my shoulder and wiping my eyes. Then I silently mouthed the word, "How?"

Griff, with a gag still firmly implanted into his mouth, motioned behind him, leaning slightly to the side. I noticed a screw that had come loose in the bench seat of the capsule. Griff must have sawed himself free, but how could I help? He must have known exactly what I was thinking because he turned his eyes to Tubb, sitting two seats to his left, then to the brute, then to Tubb, then to the brute again. Finally, his eyes landed on me. He motioned with his hands, pointing back and forth between their seats. Going out on a huge limb, I guessed he wanted me to distract the brute so they could switch spots. I looked up at the monstrous murderer that was salivating at the opportunity to fire us out of the capsule. He was staring out the window, not worried about us at all. "Swap seats?" I whispered. Griff shook his head fervently in agreement.

"What did you say?" the brute grumbled. Uh-oh. He heard me. Think fast, Dean.

"Ummm, I said you're weak," I responded, hoping to steal his undivided attention. He walked down the capsule, stopping between my feet, then backhanded me across the face. Maybe I got too much attention, but it was working. With the brute's back turned to the

Gnomelings, Tubb and Griff swiftly swapped places. Tubb was now sawing back and forth with his stubby arms, trying to break free. I knew that if we were going to get out of there, I had to keep up the distraction. I also knew this would hurt badly, but I kept mocking him anyway. "That's all you got, you big fat coward," I said, instantly bracing myself for the next blow. The second smack stung, but I didn't cry out. In fact, I didn't react at all. All my anger towards Thorne and his son, Flynn, was now directed at this monstrous man. Or at least I think he was a man.

"No one calls me fat, boy," the brute growled, his voice becoming increasingly shaky.

"I didn't call you fat boy. I just called you plain old fat!" Whap! Another smack across the face. I could feel a welt rising as my head throbbed.

"You know what the worst part about you is?" I continued. "You attack kids. You work for a guy who shoots unarmed girls. And look at you," I laid it on thick. "Seriously, how does it feel to be that ugly?" He pretended not to care. He was about to spin toward my small companions in the middle of their jailbreak, so I kept his focus on me. "And how did you even get here, to London? Did Thorne walk you on a leash, or did someone leave your cage open, and you snuck out?"

His face flushed with fury as he swung his fist, smashing his hand into the Plexiglas partition behind me, splintering it. "That's enough out of you!"

Only it wasn't enough out of me. I wasn't finished. Not even close. "You're so incredibly ugly that when your mom dropped you off at school, she was arrested for littering."

"Huh?"

"Too dumb to understand the joke?" I said. Steam poured from the brute's ears. I stole a glance behind him, trying not to give away our plan. Roger had snuck across the aisle and was busy sawing away while Tubb and Griff untied everyone's leg restraints. "How about this one? You're so ugly, your mom had to put meat around your neck so the dog would play with you?" Another backhand across the mouth, but still, I showed no fear. "You're nothing more than a pathetic sidekick. You'll never be important. You'll never be anything at all. Just a big, dumb loser." That last line was meant to be a zinger, but it was hard to think of top-notch insults when my ears rang.

"I've heard enough of this," the brute roared. Mom let out a muffled scream in protest as the brute called down to the remaining hellion for the ride to stop. I felt nauseous. Thorne ordered Mom to be thrown in first. Over my dead body, I thought... Only that's exactly how I feared it would end up.

The entire capsule jerked as it stopped abruptly, sending us swaying back and forth. I quickly peered outside. We had reached the very top, the dead center. The brute approached the side opposite the capsule doors. He didn't just break open the window, he ripped the entire structure apart, tearing metal from its hinges and firing the remains into the river below. Anders had backed himself into a corner, reeling from the shock. Mom was still bound and gagged but had her feet on the seat. At first glance, it appeared she was backing away, but I knew she was getting ready to kick like a wild stallion. "Now, who wants to see mom fly?" The brute turned in our direction but realized that something was amiss. More like someone was missing. "Where are they? Where are the little ones? Is this more of your magic?" Tubb and Griff were — gone. Vanished from their seats.

"Not magic," Tubb said, running circles around the brute.

"This is a fellowship!" Griff added, running in the opposite direction, sending the brute spinning in spirals, trying to keep pace with their blinding speed. After several laps around the brute, Tubb and Griff stopped behind him.

The brute, dizzy and unsteady, twisted on his size twenty-three clodhoppers and came face to face with the fiercest Gnomelings I'd ever known. Sure, they were the only ones I'd ever known, but I doubted any others could match their bravery.

"I'm gonna rip you to pieces and hang you from my wall with my other trophies. Starting with your hairy little feet."

"Nobody be touching our puberty, bucket head!" Tubb gritted his teeth.

"Charge!" Griff yowled as the Gnomelings went into attack mode. They slid around the monster, attacking his legs with kicks to the backs of his knees to make him buckle. Tubb tucked his chin into his chest and headbutted the brute's butt, causing him to lurch forward, while Griff leaped off one foot and delivered an uppercut to the brute's jaw. How was this happening? How could these two take on someone this size? I was so enthralled by the spectacle before me that I failed to see that Mom was now free of her restraints while Roger was sitting right next to me.

"Psst," Roger whispered in my ear. His breath was awful, reeking of expired cheese. He looked down at my hands. I felt Roger go to work on the knot as I tilted forward.

"And what do you think you Gnomelings will actually do against a panzer?" Tubb and Griff glanced at one another. Aside from a tank I'd seen in military movies, I didn't know exactly what a panzer was, but I had a feeling this guy was some sort of mutant. The brute, the panzer, ripped off one sleeve at a time, revealing his hulking biceps. His skin was strange and deteriorated, like cracks on a desert floor.

"Whatever they have to do to buy time," Anders said. The panzer wrenched back, turning toward the bench where Anders sat. Anders positioned himself in an old-time boxing stance. His feet were shoulder-width apart, his arms were low — halfway between his waist and chest — and his hands made small circles. "Time for you to take on someone your own size," Anders stiffened his lips to show the panzer he meant business. Only, the panzer started to laugh hysterically, then swung his club of a fist, sending Anders airborne to the back of the capsule. Anders smacked into the window with a thud, cracking the glass.

"Next time, send two your size," the panzer said, cracking his knuckles.

"How about just one. Only with swords," I said in my best superhero voice as I held out my hand, trying to recreate the magic from the base of the Eye. I willed the sword to materialize, twitching my fingers like a Jedi summoning a lightsaber. Only my Jedi training must have been incomplete because nothing was happening. I desperately stretched my fingers open, but the power I felt when I was near the amulet was gone. I was an empty shell washed up on shore. The kind you put your ear up to hear the waves, but all I heard now was the panzer laughing at my ridiculous pose.

"You're not so strong without the amulet, are you?" he said, mocking me. "We will be crossing over to Second Realm before daybreak. I can feel it. And soon, when Black Lake closes, no one will be left to remember you."

So what if I didn't have the amulet. So what if I didn't have the sword. Thinking of Liv ignited a fire in my soul, and I wouldn't go down without a fight. Before I could budge or take a swing, the Gnomelings stealthily scampered behind the panzer, crouching directly behind his knees, and immediately, I knew what to do. It was the second oldest trick in the book, used by nerds like me against bullies for a millennium. You didn't need a sword or an army. You didn't need to be the biggest, strongest, or fastest. You just needed a friend to duck down behind your enemy and an unsuspecting shove to send them toppling over.

"Any last words?" the panzer cranked his neck from side to side, making the most awful popping sounds.

"Enjoy your flight," I said as I lowered my shoulder and charged toward the monster. The amusement on his face quickly faded as he flexed his muscles and braced for impact. With each step, I gained momentum and lunged toward his sternum. My shoulder slammed into his chest, like hitting a brick wall. He didn't budge. I hopped three paces back, then charged again. Over and over, until finally, on my last effort, before I passed out from exhaustion, I managed to send the giant tank stumbling back towards the hunched-over Gnomelings. As he tripped over my companions, his arms flailed in an attempt to regain his balance. But his momentum was too great, and with the capsule walls torn off, he had nothing to grab onto. He toppled over, bouncing not once but twice, before plunging downward and falling into the River Thames, screaming all the way. I rushed to the opening and peered over the edge just in time to see a splash that must have been thirty feet high. The panzer's massive body disappeared into the water. I waited for a while, expecting him to surface, but he never did.

"He sank to the floor," Tubb was at my side, rubbing his hip, his skin red and raised.

Mom and Roger joined me at the opening, staring down at the murky water below, watching the dying wake caused by the panzer's impact. I saw Roger take Mom's hand out of the corner of my eye. I hoped it was out of shock, but Mom didn't immediately retract. In fact, it took her a good twenty seconds to pull her hand away.

"How do we get down?" Anders asked, sitting on the bench, nursing a nosebleed.

"The hellions be gone. Griff's going to start the wheel," Tubb said.

"Hate to break it to you, Griff, but we're four-hundred feet in the air."

"Four-hundred and forty-three," Anders said.

I turned around, expecting to see Griff, but he was nowhere in sight.

"Where'd he go?" I asked.

"You be forgetting about the elven rope," Tubb smirked. He pointed out the window to our right. I walked to the edge of the Eye, where I saw Griff lowering himself from beam to beam, swinging, flipping, and sliding down with a gymnast's grace and ability.

"When this is all over, you're going to have to tell me where you're keeping all this stuff," I said as I stared out at the lights of the sleeping city, wondering what would happen next.

DYING IS EASY, YOUNG MAN, LIV'ING IS HARDER

Once Griff figured out how to not only start up the Eye but to stop it, we disembarked. From the entrance to the ride, I could see Liv. Making my way to her body was the longest minute of my life. Anders stumbled along behind me and sobbed, sneezing into an old handkerchief. At one point, Mom had to help him walk.

I knelt down alongside Liv, reaching out to touch her. My hand lingered over her shoulder, then her head, and finally, I brushed her hair, splitting the strands with my quaking fingertips. My eyes were so full that I appeared to be looking at her through goldfish bowls. "I'm so sorry," I said, my voice cracking with each

310

syllable. "I should have never left you." I thought I was going to be sick. Losing my dad was hard, but I was little. This was so much different, knowing what loss really was. "I love you, Liv." I rested my hand on the side of her face. Liv's skin was cold, amplified by the river breeze. The tip of my index finger slid to the base of her chin, just above her jaw. "You'll always have my heart," I cried as Anders gingerly knelt at my side. My body started to shake. My arms began to spasm. And as soon as I said the word heart, I felt a heartbeat throb in my finger. Only, it wasn't my heartbeat. "What?" I muttered, realizing that my finger rested directly on Liv's vein. Her artery. I could feel her pulse. She had a pulse. "She has a pulse," I said aloud this time.

"What did you say, human?" Tubb asked.

"Liv," I shouted as I rolled her over onto her back. Anders put his fingers to her neck, confirming my diagnosis. There was a streak of blood that stained her shirt, just below her chest, but not what I would have expected to see from a gunshot. "Liv!" I shook her, begging her to wake. "Liv, wake up!" By now, Mom, Roger, and the Gnomelings stood over me, watching, praying. I leaned in, ready to start CPR, only I didn't know CPR, but I had to try. I remembered our first kiss and figured it was probably the same, but I'd blow air into her mouth this time.

"Pinch her nostrils," Anders said.

I squeezed her nose shut, placing my thumb on her chin, drawing her mouth open. My lips touched hers. They were soft and delicate and tasted of strawberries even in the grips of death itself. I inhaled, ready to breathe life into Liv's lungs, but as soon as I was about to exhale, I felt her lips move. They closed over mine.

Before I knew it, Liv was planting the biggest kiss ever on me.

Anders screamed a victorious scream. Mom began to cry, shaking my shoulders, further slamming my face into Liv's. Tubb and Griff jumped around wildly. Roger puckered up, then closed his eyes, expecting mom to return the favor. Thankfully she ignored him.

After a moment of bliss, I broke our embrace. "How?" I said. I helped Liv sit up. She rubbed what I expected to be a gunshot wound, a bullet hole. But when she pulled the collar of her shirt down and wiped away a smattering of dry blood, there was only a bruise with some scraping.

"That's not possible," Anders said. "The bullet never entered her body."

Still wearing my jacket, Liv pulled the flap toward her, unbuttoning the chest pocket. "It's possible if you have this." She reached inside the pocket, dug around, and slid out a coin.

"Edward the Confessor," I said, staring at the bent and dented coin I *borrowed* from Chalice Well.

"Help me up," Liv said. I stood and hoisted Liv to her feet. She stared at the broken glass from the Eye's capsule and said, "What did I miss?"

"Thorne is crossing over. We're running out of time."

"Flynn?" she asked.

All I could do was shake my head.

"I'm so sorry." Liv tried to comfort me, even though she was the one who had just been shot. "What do we do now?"

"The Black Lake." I spun to Anders. "Do you know where it is?"

"I do. But Thorne took our car when they captured us." Anders turned his head in shame.

"We could call a taxi," Mom said.

"The pubs have closed, and the cabs have scattered," Anders said. "Either way, it's doubtful they'd take the fare. Black Lake is simply too far."

A headache was eminent. I dug my fingers into my temples. "The panzer said he could feel the portal closing."

"We don't have a car. We can't afford the time it takes to call for one. So that leaves us with just one choice," Liv said. "We appropriate one."

"You mean steal one?" I asked.

"Yes, I mean stealing one. Only respectfully," she answered.

"And does any of yous be knowing how to appropriate a car?" Griff asked.

We turned our eyes to Liv. "Don't look at me," she said. "It's just an idea."

"Do you vow that you won't judge me, my lady?" Roger said, taking a knee before Mom.

"O-kay…" Mom said, clearly uncertain of what Roger was doing on one knee.

"I can appropriate a vehicle for your son."

"We would be honored if you could do that for us," Mom said.

Eager to get a move on, I agreed. I didn't have time to worry about Roger proposing to my mother. "We need to hurry!"

We scoured the parking lot to the Eye, looking for a car to borrow for the night. From there, we moved to a nearby neighborhood and business district. Roger gave us very specific instructions for our heist. The car had to be modern, and it had to be a Cadillac. This put us in a sticky situation as there weren't a lot of Cadillac dealers in the area.

"What are we looking for again?" Tubb asked.

"It has a shield logo on the front."

"Roger, Roger," Tubb said with a smile and continued his search.

Roger huffed gruffly, not amused.

My nerves were getting the best of me. I don't know if it was paranoia or a sixth sense, but I swore I felt the connection to the amulet fading, passing more with each second, to the point it was almost erased. I wondered if that meant the portal was closed for good. If we didn't quickly find a car to steal, we'd be out of luck.

"I've got one!" Liv shouted, alleviating my fear for the moment. "Only, I'm not so sure we should take it."

I bolted across the street, jumping over a man asleep on the curb. I spotted Liv below a street light. The halo of the lamp's glow gleamed over her. She stood in front of a morgue where a jet-black Cadillac was parked. The only thing was... it was a hearse, and a casket was in the back.

"What do we do now?" I asked. We couldn't steal a hearse. Not with a body inside.

"Where's the driver?" Roger asked.

Liv stood on her tiptoes and snuck a peek inside the morgue's window. "It appears he's finishing up paperwork. Probably taking her to a church or morning service."

"You sure we need a Cadillac?" I asked.

"I only know how to hotwire the XT5s. XT5s are found in Cadillacs. And this here," he slapped the hood, "is a Cadillac."

So we made our choice. We hijacked a hearse with a corpse resting in a casket in the back. Not an ideal situation, but these were desperate times.

INTO THE THICK OF IT

Three hours.

That's how long it took us to drive from London to Black Lake, and the entire ride felt like an eternity. The bond with the amulet seemed to fade more with each passing second. I tried my best not to think about Flynn, but that's all I could think about. There were moments when Liv, Mom, Roger, or Anders would try to get my attention, but all I heard was Flynn saying, "He's my dad. I didn't have a choice." His voice rattled around in my brain like a bad song stuck on repeat.

Black Lake was a nature preserve in Frodsham. It looked like a swamp with an oversized puddle of black water sitting in a field.

We parked the car at the water's edge but left it running. Headlights cut through an eerie mist. Willow trees, gnarled and bowed, gently kissed the ground. Long shadows played tricks on our eyes. Tubb and Griff shuffled out of the back of the hearse. Since they were small, we made them ride in the back with the casket. We also chose them because they had no idea what a casket was.

"I can't be believing that lady slept the entire ride," Tubb stated.

Griff wrinkled his nose. "I can't believe she smelled like Me-Mop's cleaning liquid."

"You opened the box?" Roger asked.

"You smelled her?" I added.

"Tell me you didn't touch her," Liv said.

"Well, I be trying to open her eyes, but she must have been really sleepy because..." Griff rambled.

"Stop. Just stop talking," I said. We didn't have time for this, and I really didn't want to know the rest of Griff's story.

"So, Gnomelings," Liv said.

"Yes, female human," Tubb said.

"What do we do now? How do we pass through the portal?"

"And where exactly is the portal?" Mom said.

"If the portal be open still. It's right down there," Griff said.

"That's where we climbed out of." The Gnomelings both pointed to the middle of the lake.

"And if it's closed?" Liv asked.

"Then we swim out," I said.

"I cannot swim," Roger said. Why was that not a surprise?

"Don't worry. I was a lifeguard in high school," Mom said. "I'll save you." Roger batted his eyes. I wished Mom wouldn't have said that.

My attention drifted to the lake as I walked to its banks. I placed my hand over the water, hovering just inches above it.

"Feel anything?" Liv asked.

"I do," I said. "Only barely." There was a faint buzzing sensation flowing through my hand. "If we don't do this now, it's game over." The thought of Mom, Roger, and Anders being tied up on the Eye, Flynn's betrayal, and Liv's near-death experience flashed through my mind. I took Liv's hand, saying, "You can't come."

She pulled away. "Excuse me?"

"You don't know what it was like. Seeing you hurt. I can't do that again," I said.

"You can't do that? I was the one who was shot."

"I know, but—"

"But nothing, Dean." Liv crossed her arms, scowling at me. "I did this for you. I am doing this for you. You have no right to tell me that I cannot finish this with you."

I felt so much shame. All I wanted to do was protect her. Before I could apologize or make her more upset, her expression softened. "You're right, though."

"So, you'll stay?" I said, relieved.

"Absolutely not. But, Grandad stays. In fact, I think your mum should stay too."

That we agreed on. "What about Roger?" I asked.

"He can't swim, remember. Besides, he won't leave your mum's side for a second," Liv said. "He's too smitten with her to break eye contact."

I glanced over at Roger. He was still staring at Mom. "What do we do? They won't approve of this."

"I have an idea," Liv said. She laid out the plan, and before long, it was time to act.

Y

"Mom. Can you, the doc, and Roger help me get this casket out of the back?" I asked, setting phase one of Liv's plan into action.

"Can I ask why?" Mom replied.

"If we pass through the portal," Liv said, "this lady may never come back. At least here, someone might find her. They could give her a proper burial."

Mom thought about it for a second and said, "I guess you're right."

"Plus, we don't need the Gnomelings poking at a dead body anymore," Liv said.

"Dead body?" Tubb said.

"She be dead?" Griff gulped.

Mom nodded as the Gnomelings turned a paler shade of white than the corpse in the casket.

"That explains so much," Griff said.

We slid the wooden coffin down the rollers, out of the back of the car.

"Where do we put it?" Mom asked.

"Can you guys take it from here? Just set her over by those trees?" I let go of my handle and pointed to a row of pine trees about thirty feet away. "Tubb, Griff. See those flowers in the back of the car? I'm gonna need you to grab those so we can leave them with the casket."

"I don't be seeing no flowers," Griff squinted his eyes, glaring into the back of the hearse.

"They're in there," Liv said as she moved to the driver's side door.

"What color are they?" Tubb asked.

"What does it matter?" Liv was getting frustrated.

"White. They're white," I said. "Just hard to see from your angle."

"We do be having a bad angle," Tubb agreed. "Let's go, Griff."

Tubb and Griff hoisted themselves up into the back of the hearse. As soon as their hairy feet were clear, I slammed the door shut behind them. "Go," I shouted at Liv, then sprinted around the passenger side, opened the door, and took a glance back at Mom. She, Anders, and Roger had just set the casket down and were staring at us.

Mom cocked her head to the side, looked back at the casket, then at me again. She knew. It took her about one second to figure out what we were up to. "Please, don't!"

"I'm sorry, Mom."

"But, Dean." The way she said my name nearly broke me.

"What's he doing?" Roger asked.

"He's leaving," Mom said.

Without another glance, I entered the hearse. I could hear Tubb and Griff in the back bumbling about. We'd be through to Second Realm before they figured out there were no flowers.

"Hit it," I said to Liv. She slapped the gear shift into drive and slammed her foot on the pedal. The tires spun in the dirt, kicking up mud. I looked in the passenger mirror, where I saw Mom running toward us. I knew at that moment that I had absolutely broken her heart, but I couldn't let her go with me. Here she'd be far from Thorne. Here she'd be safe.

"There we go," Liv said as the tires finally gained traction. We hurtled towards the lake, our hearts pounding with adrenaline. Liv took one hand off the wheel and held it out to me. I looked down and grabbed it, intertwining my fingers with hers. In that fleeting moment, we locked eyes, seeking solace amid chaos, just as the front tires touched the water.

The moment we hit the lake, the world around us disappeared. The bumper submerged, sending a wave over the windshield. I closed my eyes and prayed. I prayed for my mom, for the portal to still be open. I prayed that the Gnomelings would stop screaming about the missing flowers. Above all, I prayed that we wouldn't drown in Black Lake in a Cadillac hearse.

When I opened my eyes again, horror overtook me. The murky water engulfed the hood, and the windshield flooded soon after. To make matters worse, water began seeping in through the vents. If cold, damp, and claustrophobic had a smell and a feel, this was it.

"I don't think it's working!" Liv yelped, lifting her feet from the floorboard that was filling fast with freezing water. Just then, the engine sputtered and died.

"What's that?" I pointed at a pulsating blue light in the distance. With each passing second, it grew closer.

"A reflection from the headlights?" Liv said.

"It's the portal," I felt a spark of hope, but it was quickly quenched by the gushing of water through the vents.

The lake couldn't have been more than fifteen feet deep, but as the seconds turned to minutes, we sank at least the length of a football field.

As we dove deeper, the moonlight faded, and the portal lights drew closer. The beam shrank into a tiny dot, only to expand into rings of prismatic colors - pinks, yellows, browns, and blues. Finally, a blinding white light appeared, forcing me to turn my head away.

Tubb and Griff's panicked voices echoed from the back of the hearse. I felt the air being squeezed out of the car all at once. My chest tightened with each gasp for breath. Holding Liv's hand, I could feel her pulse racing. Did we make a mistake? Had the portal closed? Were we being transported? It was impossible to tell, for everything suddenly went dark. It felt like we were floating on a cloud, then, just as suddenly, we could breathe again.

THE CAKE IS A LIE

Something gripped the car and pulled us through a vacuum of water, space, and time. Shimmering metal prongs wrapped around the vehicle, reminding me of the bear claw machine in the grocery store as it dragged us horizontally. Luminous gold circular strips guided our path that led toward a curtained waterfall.

"Is this it?" Liv said as she fixed her hair, brushing a wild strand from her eyes. "Are we through the portal?"

I turned around in my seat, checking on Tubb and Griff, who were catching their breath, both slumped against the sidewall of the hearse. A quick thumbs up from Tubb reassured me. "Looks like it," I said.

As we approached the waterfall, a hand emerged from its center, followed by a second that gripped a walking stick. Then, the rest of the figure emerged: a delicate, shrouded creature that appeared female, cloaked in mystery and brown fabric. She waved her walking stick above her head, shutting off the waterworks, revealing a metal platform beneath her feet with a conveyor belt leading upward behind her. She pulled her hood back from her face. Small in stature, her facial features resembled that of an elf. Her ears were pointed, but her nose was not, and her eyes were a stunning shade of bluish-green. As for her feet, I couldn't tell if they were covered in hair, the same as Tubb and Griff's, because she wore long boots that stretched from toe to knee. She was short, but not Gnomeling short. She was Autumn Bartlow short (about four-eleven if you don't happen to know Autumn Bartlow).

The car came to an abrupt stop. Tubb toppled over, smacking the partition that separated us with a thud.

"Ouch," he whined and rubbed his head.

We exited the hearse as water poured off the floorboards, draining onto a spongy surface that was the ground – like a rock bed, only much squishier. Our Gnomeling friends raced around the back of the hearse and slid on their knees before the cloaked woman. They bowed their heads in respect, then looked up at her longingly.

"Should we bow too?" Liv asked as she took her place at my side.

"Dean Moyers," the woman said to my shock. She looked no older than twenty-five, but I'd later find out she was well over one hundred years old. Time obviously hit different here. "It has been so long since I last laid eyes upon you in person. And that was for a brief moment on the day of your birth."

The woman...elf...person, approached me slowly, running her hand down my arm, sending goosebumps crawling across my body. Liv sneered at her. I would have sworn I heard her growl if I didn't know better. I felt a sudden flush of embarrassment, wondering if Liv was jealous. This was a new experience - to have a girl show jealousy over me. I kinda enjoyed it. I cleared my throat and asked the woman who she was.

"My name is Avaleigh Palada-Veurink. You may call me Ava for short."

"Thanks for clearing that up because I was not going to remember your full name," Liv said, her tone laced with sarcasm. She was jealous.

"Is," I looked around, suddenly terrified at the prospect that we may not be alone, "Thorne here?"

"No," Ava said. "I sensed he crossed over some time ago, but his heart led him down another path. While your heart is pure, leading you to us."

"And who exactly is us? What are you?" Liv asked.

"I am a mage, a seer, and I stand before you as a representative of the Shire of Yarberry within Second Realm," she said. "I am here to guide you to our world."

"You mean this, isn't it?" I asked. "Your world?"

"Oh, no," Griff chimed in, wobbling himself upright on the unstable ground. "We still be in limbo. Halfways between your worlds and ours'es."

"This place," Ava continued, turning her back and leading us down the tunnel, "is nothing more than ripples on the surface of a pond."

"And how far do these ripples go?" I asked.

Ava took my hand. Liv fumed. "To the edge of time and back again," Ava said. "But for you, only the bat of an eye. The inhale before a breath. The fraction of —"

"Can we just get moving? Lately, I have a distaste for riddles." Liv grabbed my other hand and started pulling us both forward.

"There is little need for envy," Ava said, turning to face Liv. "The love of my life has long since passed, and it is not Dean Moyers. He is yours, and I wish only the best for you."

"Envy. Who said I was envious?" Liv tried to play it cool, but her tone was defensive. She was so envious.

Ava ignored Liv's response as she continued speaking. "As for you, Dean, you should consider yourself lucky to have someone like Liv by your side. She is fierce and loyal and will not hesitate to defend you."

I couldn't help but grin at Ava's words. Liv scowled and kicked me in the shin.

"Hey!" I protested, rubbing my sore leg. "What was that for?"

"For grinning like an idiot," Liv replied, but I could tell she was trying not to smile.

Y

We walked for what seemed like miles through black caverns and tunnels. Definitely more than a bat of an eye, that's for sure. Eventually, we reached a huge wooden doorway that reminded me of one they used to keep the dinosaurs inside *Jurassic Park*. Beyond the door was a spiral staircase that stretched into heaven, or at least that's what it looked like. Seriously, this thing was so massive that it made climbing the stairs up the

Empire State Building look like a leisurely stroll in the park.

"Please tell me you have an elevator?" I said.

"What be an elevator?" Griff asked.

"A box attached to cables that go up and down tall buildings, so you don't have to walk the whole thing."

"Oh, that sounds lovely," Griff said. "But no. We be walking the rest of the way."

"If it makes you feel better, Griff and I had to walk down these steps," Tubb said.

"No, Tubb, that does not make us feel better at all," Liv said.

"The good news be that the exercise builds up an appetite," Griff said as he passed by, rubbing his stomach, rattling off names of cakes he had baked in the last year. He and Tubb bounded up the stairs effortlessly. I can't quite explain it, but the Gnomelings just being here gave them a double shot of adrenaline, like when I snuck a drink of Mom's coffee before school. The same went for Ava. Even though she walked with a staff or a cane, the closer we were to the top, the faster she moved. They were so far ahead of us that they were nearly out of sight. The hike gave me time to reflect. It also gave me sore calves with blisters on my feet. And all of it left me wondering, did I make the right decision, leaving Mom behind? She must have been worried sick. Though I'm certain Roger was more than willing to lend a comforting hand.

"Worried about your mum?" Liv said. "I'm worried about Granddad."

"You can read me that easily?" I asked.

"Like a picture book," Liv said.

"Then what does this expression mean?" I said, lowering my chin, lifting my eyes to meet hers.

I tried my best to look serious or romantic, but I don't think it worked because Liv said, "Do you have to use the toilet?"

"What? No!" Now I was doubly embarrassed, as Liv laughed as she sped ahead.

"Human!" Tubb shouted at me. "Need to be speeding up your steps. We're almost there."

Onward we moved. Upward we climbed until we reached yet another tunnel. Stairs and tunnels. Stairs and tunnels. Two hours inside a new realm or dimension, and all I saw were stairs and tunnels. We found ourselves in an oval-shaped room when we reached Ava, Tubb, and Griff. There were orange tubes that lined the ceiling and slithering, slimy creatures that hung from the walls – they were slugs the size of Chihuahuas.

"What's in the pipes?" Liv asked.

"Lava," Ava said. "It flows from the mountain through our village." Ava pointed her walking stick upward. A ray of light extended from it, casting a glow upon even more pipes and tubing, all filled with flowing orange goo. "It's not the same as your lava. It's much cooler and has nutrients that feed the very life of Second Realm." She lowered her staff and walked to a black tarp, parting it to the side, revealing another room that had two more enormous doors that appeared to be carved from stone. The doors were decorated in Gnomarian script, with the symbol from the amulet everywhere. Around the writing stood images of creatures etched into the rock - elves, dwarves, Gnomelings, and other things that didn't look familiar. But front and center stood two humans in full battle gear. One was a male, holding a staff with an amulet dangling from his chest. The other was a female who wore a silver crown and held a bow and arrow. At first glance, I was convinced…

"That's us," Liv whispered, stealing the thoughts from my head.

"It can't be. Can it?" I turned to Ava.

"Not exactly." The doors opened as Ava waved her stick. "Each generation has a new guardian. These images were shaped three thousand years ago." She looked us over closely. "Though the resemblance is striking."

The doors gave way to some sort of laboratory. Four water columns descended through the ceiling, gathering in a pool at the center of the room. The water was musty -- a shade of greenish-brown. Rows upon rows of tables were covered in glass containers, beakers, and jars. One wall was lined with a stack of ovens and bellow-fed burners being manned by a small army of Gnomelings decked out in lab gear - goggles, lab coats, gloves. Another wall was home to what looked to be a million books, charts, and documents. Enough to be the history of all of Second Realm, even though I had no idea how far back their history actually went.

The bite-sized scientists scurried about, failing to notice our presence. At least at first. They gathered samples from the water pool, moved over to the stoves, placed the beakers and cylinders over an open flame, then watched in disappointment as the water materialized into smoke, flame, and ash.

"What does it mean?" I asked.

"Our land is dying." Ava took a glass container of the cloudy liquid, stirring it with her finger. "Look within." She held the water up to my face.

"Pond water?" I said.

"Look closer."

I stared for a minute, noticing nothing but floating chunks with particles that swirled around. "Wait," I said. Images. Figures. Shapes. They started to come to life in the water. I saw beasts storming villages. Fire ravaging homes. I saw children screaming with fear in their eyes to go along with the soot covering their faces. Monsters wreaked havoc.

Then, just as in my dream, vision, or whatever you wanted to call it, I saw my friends. Tubb and Griff were tossed around by a pair of dragons who played catch with their bodies. Liv lay motionless, pierced with arrows longer than her body. Flynn, yes, even Flynn, was broken, his body bent unnaturally, clobbered by a cave troll.

"I've seen this before. Can it be changed?" I said.

"This is only a glimpse of what the future holds for our land and people if we do not deviate from our current paths," Ava replied.

"But we're here now. I am a guardian. A protector of the Realm. A Shire Knight." That was more of a statement than a question. "And I can defeat Thorne. I can get the amulet back. That counts as far as deviating from the path, right?"

"For all of our sakes, I hope so." Ava was now flanked by at least a dozen Gnomeling scientists. They stared upward at me, batting their big eyes, gawking. Turns out, I was a bit of a celebrity. "What do you say we show you a land worth saving?"

OH MY DAISIES!

Around twists, turns, nooks, and crannies, we finally made our way through the labyrinth within the laboratory and eventually ended up outside. Word of our arrival had spread, and columns of Gnomelings were standing, staring at us in awe, touching our arms and hands as we walked past. Equally awe-inspiring was the landscape that captivated my imagination.

Spectacular, mesmerizing, amazing, jaw-dropping... words couldn't quite capture the sights before me. The grassy hills were greener than anything I'd ever seen as if they were painted with a special shade of emerald that only existed in this realm. Flags of blue and yellow flew high above their shire while colorful banners adorned the marketplace. Gigantic oaks, willow trees, and Leflorians (a cross-breed of oaks and willows) framed their village – a perfect painting. Bob Ross would have been proud. The bubbly white clouds floated carelessly across the picturesque blue sky. There were two lakes within my sightline. One was larger, and at least ten Gnomelings sat around fishing on homemade wooden rocking chairs. The second lake was much smaller. At the moment, it was occupied by three Gnomeling girls who were chasing a duck. A regular duck. Not the murderous kind with one eye. One thing was for sure: This place was magical, beautiful, innocent, and perfect, and I couldn't believe I was here.

Ava stepped between Liv and me, taking our hands in hers once more. "Welcome to Yarberry Shire," she smiled, but only temporarily. "I wasn't born here, but the people took me in. You see, Dean, this is but a part of our Realm that needs saving. Beyond our shire lies forests, rivers, lakes, and majestic mountains, but also a darkness that moves quickly. The one you call Thorne shall seek this land for his own use and will murder and enslave the innocents as an offering to the Dark One."

"Who is this, Dark One?" Liv asked.

"An ancient evil which lies beneath the dying soil. A place called the Dark Lands. Thorne, along with others, claims to do her bidding."

"The Dark One is a girl?" I raised my eyebrows in curiosity.

"Don't be sexist," Liv said.

"I'm not. I just assumed."

"That's the problem with boys," Liv said. "Always assuming."

"Thorne and his minions move this way," Ava proceeded. "Even as we speak." I was happy for the interruption, as the banter with Liv was leading me down a rabbit hole of gendered stereotypes. "Look around. Talk to the people here. We will convene in the meeting house at sundown. A plan must be formed."

"The meeting house?" I said, looking around at all the labeled buildings, only I didn't read fluent Gnomarian.

"The large domed building at the top of the hill."

I scanned the landscape, landing on a circular-shaped dome with a stick roof. "Got it. The super-dome at sundown."

As Ava gingerly sauntered down a dirt path, my gaze roamed the town before me. Gnomeling women picked vegetables, men carried barrels up and down hills in wheelbarrows, and the children...let me tell you about the Gnomeling children. They were nearly identical to Tubb, Griff, or the other Gnomelings but way cuter. Picture the most adorable baby you've ever seen. Human or animal. Now, multiply that adorableness by twenty-thousand. That's a Gnomeling baby. Short, chunky, with button noses, bright eyes, and hairy little feet with fat little toes.

Life was plentiful here. I'd never felt more alive than in this very moment. Liv leaned in and brushed against my arm. She must have felt it too. Then we both felt something else. Thud! Something. No. Someone just slammed into our legs. Someone no taller than my knee. It was a Gnomeling child. He looked like a bowling ball with a baby face and stubby little arms and legs. "Watch where you be going, you oversized bumbledorf. I —" His words cut short as he opened his mouth so wide that his jaw nearly touched the floor. "Oh my daisies! It's you! It's really you!"

"I'm sorry. Do I know you?" I asked.

"You don't be knowing me. But everyone be knowing you. Sir Dean Moyers of the Realm of Pittsburgh."

"Just outside of Pittsburgh, actually," Liv added as the tiny orb with limbs climbed up my body like I was nothing more than a jungle gym until his face was the same height as mine.

"And you. You be Miss Olivia of England-Shire. I've read all about you in school this year. You two be my heroes." He squeezed my head until I thought my eyeballs would pop out of their sockets. "Pinch me. For I must be in the most glorious of slumber dreams." He let go of my face, then, with his left foot, pushed off of my chest and leaped at Liv, latching onto her shoulders, hugging her tight.

"It's a pleasure to meet you," Liv said.

"What's your name?" I asked.

The Gnomeling slid down Liv's side, landing on his feet, then he rested his hands on his hips, framing his body against the picturesque backdrop. "The name's Pint."

"Because you're small?" Liv said, crouching down to Pint's level.

Pint chuckled, "No, because my parents be naming my eldest brothers Quart, Pitcher, and Gallon."

"Well," Liv said, placing her palm on his cheek, "I think Pint is a lovely name." Pint blushed, his cheeks turning the color of an Arizona sunrise.

"Can I be showing you something?" Pint asked, bouncing with excitement. "Pretty please?"

"I don't know, Pint. We probably should be moving along. Lots to see, you know?" I said.

Pint's chin sunk into his chest as his eyes welled up with an incredible amount of tears.

333

"You know what?" Liv said. "I think we have plenty of time."

Pint sniffled, wiping his eyes with the back of his chubby little fingers, and took off in a flash. Well, it was more of a waddle down the hill, but I'm sure in tiny Gnomeling speed, it was a hasty getaway.

We entered a Gnomeling home that was exactly how I'd read about in *The Hobbit* or *The Lord of the Rings*: Houses built into hills, perfectly round porthole doors, and lots of pegs for hats and coats. The kitchen was packed with pastries, cheeses, and freshly brewed beverages that were all the color of tea. The entire path of the home formed a perfect circle, beginning and ending at the front door. Every fifteen feet or so, another door led to a different room, including bedrooms, washrooms, playrooms. If you imagined the path as a clock, the front door would be 6 o'clock, whereas Pint's room was around 11 o'clock. Pint's door was painted half blue and half yellow, the colors of Yarberry. We'd learned that each shire had its own symbol, mascot, and colors. Their mascot was a badger. Their symbol was... you guessed it. The symbol from my amulet, which was now Thorne's. Before we entered Pint's room, I asked him if other shires had guardians or amulets, but he said they didn't. The Gnomelings of Yarberry long ago were the ones who discovered the amulet and the protectors. One protector to save them all.

"Are you ready for this?" Pint asked as he pushed the door open to his room. He led us inside, making us cover our eyes with our hands. "Don't be peeking."

"We're not," Liv said.

"Oof," I said, kicking something hard on the ground. Something that let out a yelp.

"Don't be worrying about Allison. She'll be fine," Pint said. "Capybaras be rather resilient. Right, Allison?" I heard a growl. Allison didn't seem happy.

"Here we be," Pint said as we stopped. "Ready?"

"Sure," I said.

"Liv? You ready?" I asked.

"I think so, yeah," she said.

"Go ahead. Open," Pint said.

Slowly, I pried my eyes apart. From wall to wall, floor to ceiling, everything in Pint's room was... me. This was my room, only in reverse. Where I had posters of "The Shire" or "Mt. Doom," Pint had a Pittsburgh Steelers poster and my High School pennant. Where I had a collectible action figure of Gollum holding the Ring of Power, Pint had a clay model of me holding the amulet. On the opposite wall were paintings and hand-woven textile pictures, all with a familiar theme.

"Look at this," Liv weaved her way in and out of piles of dirty laundry, mostly consisting of hats. She stopped at an oil painting of us sharing our first kiss. "How?" she asked. "This just happened the other day."

"Didn't Ava be telling you? Time moves differently here. Since the trouble began, we meets every night of the week at the center of town, and the elders be sharing stories with moving pictures of your battles," Pint said.

"Are you spying on us? With cameras or something?" Liv asked. "Oh God, you don't have one in my room, do you?" Liv's voice trailed off into a mumbling panic.

"The water. They see us the way I saw the vision in the water," I said.

Pint nodded. "This one," he motioned to a charcoal-etched image that hung above his bed, "is my favorite." I stared with wonder at the sketch of me, Flynn, Liv, and Roger fighting the Peggs in the forest. "Though, I don't care for how Mister Flynn be treating you."

"Neither do I, Pint. Neither do I." I plopped my hand on Pint's head, mashing his curls into his scalp. "Don't take this the wrong way, but why do you have all this stuff? Of me. Of us?" He twisted his head, staring up at me, batting his bulbous eyes.

"Because... You be my hero! You, Dean Koltien Moyers, fought the beast." He must have meant Thorne. "And you have traveled here to save our people and our shire. You be the first guardian I will ever meet. And...I...I love you." Pint wrapped his summer sausage-sized arms around my leg and began to sob.

Liv let out a snort. From her angle, it appeared he was humping my leg like a dog. "Shhh," I whispered, then patted his head again. His cheeks flushed with joy.

"Can you lead us to the meeting house?" I said. Pint broke away, wiped his face, and nodded. "Anything for my hero and Princess Liv."

"Princess? I can get used to that," Liv smiled. We each reached down, taking one of Pint's hands in our own, and together we walked toward the dome, toward news of our fate. Of course, with someone Pint's size dangling between us, Liv and I couldn't help but swing him around a few times.

I HATE MEETINGS

I don't remember a lot about Dad's job, aside from the nights he was called away from home. Especially *that* night. But one thing I did recall was his absolute hatred for meetings. I'd hear him scream from his office, "Why can't they just send a letter?" Mom was the same. Some days she'd call me and tell me she was running late; she'd always say, "I have a meeting," in a tone that definitely didn't advertise she was having a good time. I didn't have a ton of experience with meetings. We'd have the occasional morning meeting with our first-hour teacher in school. It usually consisted of her yelling at us for another class's behavior or telling us about the lunch changes.

This meeting, however, was much different. As I approached the building, I was struck by how low the dome roof was. Inside, it felt even more cramped, the ceiling right on top of us. But that's to be expected when the average height in Yarberry Shire is no more than a yardstick. Ava stood at the front of the room at a large wooden table that sat upon a raised platform. She wasn't alone either. She was joined by an elder Gnomeling named Cliff. Cliff was Griff's grandfather, or as Griff called him, Pip-pop. Apparently, every boy's name in their family rhymed. There was Cliff, Griff, Sniff, Whiff, Spiff, and Biff. If I knew one thing for certain about Gnomelings, it was that their naming skills were pretty unremarkable. Alongside Cliff was a towering figure, at least eight feet tall. I'm guessing he could probably dunk a basketball without jumping. He had to duck to get through the doorway and hunched over the entire time inside. His features were equally strange, with a long pointy nose like a beak and elf-like ears. The sides of his head were shaved, and he had long, flowing blonde hair up top like a Mohawk mullet.

"Thems be called the Ravens," Griff said as he took his place at my side, hands firmly planted in his pockets. He had a pipe dangling from his lips, but it was empty. "They live in a village to the west. Hundreds of 'em. Strange folk." Griff noticed me staring at the pipe with curiosity. "Oh, don't worry. I don't use it. I just hold it. Makes me look official."

"Officially brainless," Tubb said as he stepped into the room, patting Griff on the back, knocking the pipe from his mouth and sending it clamoring to the floor.

I turned my focus back to the Raven. There was something else odd about him. He had a thin layer of skin that dangled from the bottom of his arms, and when he held his arms out at his sides, they looked like wings. "Can they fly?"

"Oh no," Griff said as he wiped the pipe's mouthpiece off on his sleeve and reinserted it between his teeth. "Thems lost the ability to fly ages ago."

"But the flaps be sounding funny when they wave them abouts," Tubb added.

"Master Moyers," Tubb's pip-pop, Cliff bellowed from the stage. "We would be honored if you would join us."

"Up there?" I asked. What a dumb question. Of course, he meant up there.

He nodded as his eyes grew narrow.

"Got it." Trying to play it cool, I walked confidently as I approached the stage. Maybe I should have borrowed Griff's pipe to look "official." While Cliff was the wise town leader, the Raven was surely a warrior. The closer I got to him (I was assuming his gender at this point, but seriously don't tell Liv), the more intimidating he became. Shrapnel scars ran down his jawline, and a finger was missing from his left hand—unless the Ravens only had four fingers on their left hands, which remained to be seen.

"My name is Klavos," the Raven said as he stretched out his five-fingered right hand for me to shake.

I obliged.

"Klavos is the leader of Raven Town," Cliff said. "He and his kin are prepared to fight alongside us.

He, I thought. I knew he was a he. Take that, Olivia. Not sure why my thoughts carried such sass, but back to the story.

"It is a pleasure to meet you, Dean Moyers." Klavos's grip nearly crushed the bones in my hand. "I met your father and grandfather many moons ago. I only hope you can live up to their standards."

"You and me both, birdman," I let slip under my breath, hoping Klavos didn't hear me.

"Shall we begin?" Ava said as she unrolled a large piece of parchment which turned out to be a map. Another map written in Gnomarian. The landmarks that crowded the paper were easy enough to follow. Rivers of blood, lakes of fire, mountains with dragons hovering, and a black lagoon with skeletal hands extending outwardly... you know, the normal map stuff. "As it stands, our armies are not enough to defeat Thorne."

"The Ravens of Raven Town disagree," Klavos started.

Ava grew frustrated. "If we do not call on additional aid, we will fall."

"You've seen it?" Klavos asked. Ava nodded yes.

"I've already dispatched messenger coneys seeking the aid of Berryhill, and our finest swimmers have reached the Isles of Davenport beneath the sunken ship, but I have not heard back," Cliff said.

I wondered what messenger coneys were, but before I could even ask, Tubb put two fingers above his head to imply ears and stuck out his front teeth. "Rabbits," I whispered to myself. They have messenger rabbits.

"That will not be enough," Ava said.

"Our fellow flock from the north will come to our aid if we signal them. I'm sure of it," Klavos boasted.

"That will not be enough," Ava restated.

"What else is there to do?" Tubb asked.

"Call on the forces of Mount Bogdan," Ava said.

"Impossible," Klavos said.

"Agreed. They will never help us," Cliff said.

"Why not?" I asked.

"The dwarves of Mount Bogdan are selfish. Only caring for their gold and gems," Klavos said.

"Then what do you suggest?" Ava paced.

"What about your people?" Liv turned to Ava. "On the way here, a Gnomeling, Pint is his name, told us of your magic."

"I am all that's left of my kind. A remnant from the third age," Ava held her staff in front of her face and traced her fingers along symbols etched into the wood.

"That's a weapon. Isn't it?" I asked. For some reason, now being up close, I got the feeling it was more of a weapon than a walking stick.

"It is my staff. My caduceus."

"Is it magic?" Liv said.

"Indeed."

Just then, a thought crossed my mind. Well, more like it plowed right into my temporal lobe. "The carving in the door where we first crossed over. There was a picture of me, well, not really me, but of a guardian. He was holding a staff. The same as yours."

"Your memory serves you well. Along with your keen observation," Ava said.

"Then that's it! I need one of those weapons," I said. "It must be a sign." Not even sure if that was possible. "If we can't call on any more allies, then we need better weapons."

"Ha!" Klavos belted out a laugh that may as well have been a slap in the face. "You know nothing, boy. You cannot just find more caduceus rods. They were forged by the great wizards of old. Five of them. And only two remain. That one," he flapped his flappy non-flying arm toward Ava, "belongs to her. Only she can wield it."

"Then where's the other one?" Liv said.

Ava pointed the tip of her staff at the black lagoon on the map. "Here," she said. "Protected by Chief Troll of Fallert's Crossing. Buried in the muck of Longwell Lagoon."

"So let's go get it."

"One does not simply go get it," Cliff said. "Chief Troll is the fiercest of his species and the last of his line of cave trolls. And the caduceus rod is his prize possession. It never leaves his side."

"We have to try," I said. "Don't we?"

Ava thought about this for some time. She mulled it over while pacing, pausing, and starting back at the map. "Attacking head-on would leave us weak, and the most important battle is yet to come."

"What do you have in mind?" Klavos asked. We could see the wheels turning in Ava's brain.

"We send in one, maybe two, of our stealthiest warriors. We steal the weapon from beneath his nose." The resemblance of this plan to Bilbo's plight in the Hobbit was uncanny.

"His nose being the optimal word," Cliff added as he stroked his long white beard. It just now dawned on me that Cliff reminded me of those gnomes people buy for their garden decorations. In fact, all the elder Gnomelings looked like traditional garden gnomes. "Chief Troll will smell us a mile away. Creatures of Second Realm have been trying to get the caduceus from him since he won it at The Battle of Frerichs."

"Then we send someone whose scent is unfamiliar." Ava turned to Liv and me as a pitiful smile wiped her face.

"Us?" Liv said.

"It may be our only hope," Ava said.

"Is it strong enough to win?" I asked.

"The caduceus held by the Chief is the strongest known to man," Ava said. "Stronger than my own."

"Can it defeat the amulet?" I said.

"If the amulet is held by its rightful heir," Ava nodded to me, "No. But, since Thorne is not the rightful heir, there is hope. If only a fool's hope."

"Well, I never got the best grades, so a fool's hope is alright by me," I said, turning to Liv, holding out my hand.

"Me too." She took my hand in hers, and that settled that. We would ride out at dawn. The meeting itself kept on for hours. Strategies were put into place to brace for Thorne's attack. Upon arriving in Second Realm, he wasted no time. Although he had traveled through the portal only a few hours before us in our world, he had a two-day head start here in Second Realm. Ava attempted to explain the time variance, but it went way over my head. She gave up after Liv told her I still couldn't remember the time differences between Pennsylvania and England.

News of his invasion spread quickly. Thorne led his army from town to town, from north to south, plundering and pillaging everything in his path, with his sights set firmly on Yarberry Shire. That would be the place for the last stand of the free peoples of Second Realm. Cliff crunched the numbers and determined that Thorne's army would arrive within a fortnight. It was then that I learned a fortnight was two weeks. Two weeks to find a weapon strong enough to defeat Thorne. Two weeks to raise an army. Two weeks before what could be the end of the world as we knew it.

A HORSE WITH NO NAME

The next morning Liv and I saddled up on two ponies. Liv's pony was named Stump. Stump was an appropriate name because this horse had the build of a glob of grape jelly. My horse was simply named Horse. I think it bears repeating; the Gnomelings really could use a lesson or two on naming things. Ava, Cliff, Tubb, Griff, Pint, and a smattering of locals met us at the trail leading out of Yarberry Shire to see us off.

"Ava," I said as I fastened Horse's saddle. We'd been here for less than a day, and everything came at us so fast that Flynn, my old friend, hadn't crossed my mind until now.

"Yes, Dean?"

"Flynn. Is he here? Did he cross over with Thorne?"

"Uncertain. However, if he did or did not, I believe your paths will intersect once more before all is settled."

"Did you know?" I asked bluntly.

"Elaborate," she said, though I was sure she already knew what I was about to ask.

"If Flynn was my friend since forever, and you've been watching me since forever, did you know he was Thorne's son? Did you know he would betray me?"

"Being a seer does not grant me sight onto all things," Ava explained. "Thorne is an agent of darkness. He shielded Flynn from us."

That was a relief to hear. Otherwise, I would have had a hundred more questions, and none of them would have been polite.

"Any other questions?" Ava said.

"Actually, I have one," Liv said.

"Go on," Ava said.

"Earlier today. At least, I think that was still today. Pint called me Princess Liv. Am I some sort of royalty here? Not that I need to be, it's just…"

"Pint has a habit of spoiling news that doesn't need to be spoiled," Ava interrupted. "Now is not the time to be troubled by such things. You should focus on the task at hand."

Liv spun in her saddle with a smile as wide as the Mississippi River. "She didn't say no!"

"Best of luck being to you, Dean. Bring me back something from Chief Troll's lair," Pint shouted as he hopped up and down, cheering for us.

I nodded as confidently as I could.

"Remember what we discussed," Cliff said. "Stay downwind."

"Does someone have a flurried tummy?" Griff said, sniffing the air.

"No, genius," Tubb smacked Griff on the back of the head. "The plan. The plan is for Liv and Dean to

345

stay downwind. So Chief Troll doesn't smell them coming. Remember?"

"Oh, right. Got it! Stay downwind, humans," Griff yelled as he waved wildly.

And with that, we were off. I pulled my phone from my pocket to check it one last time before leaving our friends behind. No signal. What did I expect, really? Liv and I were alone in another land, and I didn't exactly see any cell towers here. But I had to be sure that Mom hadn't tried to call or text. I missed her terribly, yet I was confident we had made the right decision. If you had told me two weeks ago that I'd be off horseback riding across the countryside with Liv, I wouldn't have believed it. If I was told the countryside would be in another realm on the way to steal a weapon from the chief of all trolls, I would have thought you were insane.

THE CHIEF TROLL'S LAIR

The journey on horseback from Yarberry Shire to our destination was grueling. Longwell Lagoon - the name had a nice ring to it, sounding like a vacation spot or a place to stop over on a Caribbean cruise. But if Ava and Cliff's stories were true, it could be the last place we'd want to see, yet the only place we had to reach. The road wound on, heading fairly, but not quite straight into the Lagoon itself, passing in between Thornhill, Covington, and Westrich along our way. They called it a lagoon, but in truth, it was a pit of nasty, toxic, black substances. The tar that bubbled up from the ground emitted a gaseous odor resembling spoiled milk.

"Do you think we're nearly there?" Liv asked.

"Judging by all the dead things on the side of the road, I'd say we were," I said. Everything around us was dead, including the trees, grass, and critters. The sun even hid behind dark clouds to avoid illuminating this dismal place, and a thunderstorm crashed our party. The air was thick with the scent of wet earth. Thunder rumbled like a warning. Liv and I rode side by side as the rain hammered down.

"Great," I said. This was all we needed. It was strange, though. As the drops pelted against my skin, soaking me to my core, Liv seemed almost immune, untouched by the raindrops dancing around her like playful sprites.

I couldn't help feeling a twinge of envy as I watched her, wondering how it was possible. Was she some kind of rain goddess, impervious to the elements? Or was I just a magnet for bad luck? Either way, I couldn't deny that something special about her set her apart from the rest of us. As the storm raged on, I couldn't help but feel a sense of awe and wonder mixed with a healthy dose of fear.

"Lovely little abode," Liv commented as we reached a rocky hillside covered in thorns. After dismounting Stump, she pulled a sheath of arrows from a sack, slinging a quiver over her shoulder. Weapons she received courtesy of Klavos and the Ravens of Raven Town. She snuck alongside the rock-faced hill. She pulled a strand of dead vines away, revealing an ominous passageway. "Ava said there was only one way in and one way out. Guess this is it. At least it'll be dry," Liv looked at me pitifully.

"Should we knock first? Or just go in?" I tried to play it cool as I hopped off of Horse, but the odor escaping from the open passageway was enough to make me sick.

"Why ruin the surprise. Let's go steal the magic staff thing and hop back on our trusty steeds and head back."

Trusty steeds. That was funny. Doubly funny because Stump and Horse bolted their way into the shadows behind us the second our feet touched the ground.

"You two better be here when we're done!" I ordered with a whisper.

"You didn't bring a weapon?" Liv asked.

"I didn't know we were allowed to."

"Allowed? Dean, we're Shire Knights. You don't have to ask permission."

Now I felt stupid. Stupid and unarmed.

"Don't worry." Liv leaned in, kissing my cheek. "I'll protect you."

Y

The inside of Chief Troll's lair was about as foul as the outside. The passages were a huge, cavernous maze. Dead tree roots were gnarled, twisting in and out of the ground. And the only thing that told us we were on the right path was the smell. The worse the smell, the closer we got.

"What did Ava tell us about the Chief?" Liv said as she ducked under a jagged stone that pierced the ceiling of our confines.

"That we should be careful; otherwise, he'd use our spines as toothpicks."

"No. The other thing."

"Stay downwind."

"Right." Liv licked her fingers, holding them high in the air to test for a draft. "How can you tell which way is downwind inside a cave?"

"Good question," I thought. I had no idea what the answer was. Suddenly, a noise came from just ahead of us. I gave Liv the signal to stay put and decided to check it out. As lightly as I could walk on the crumbly surface, I snuck through the corridor and crouched behind a boulder. Peeking over the top, I could see a makeshift throne planted in front of a roaring fire. It must have been the Chief's lair. Through a putrid green mist that hung in the air, I could see rotting carcasses on the floor, mostly animals. Mounted on the wall were trophies from Chief Troll's kills, including deer, elephants, and a few unrecognizable creatures. The room was peppered with swords, skulls, chests of clothes, and other treasures. At first, the room appeared devoid of living things until the ground quaked.

"Do you see anything?" Liv asked as she sneaked up to my side.

"I told you to stay back."

"Stay back? I'm the only one with a weapon. I think I should take point."

Suddenly, a scratchy deep voice echoed through the lair. "Max? Harlie-beth? Is that you?" The thunderous footsteps of Chief Troll shook the ground, causing debris to fall from all around us. I panned left and right, wondering where the monster was, when the backside of a gigantic cave troll appeared, stopping right before us. And when I say backside, I mean its butt was right in our faces. Luckily, he wore some sort of animal hides that covered its unmentionables.

"What is that smell?" the Chief said. Instinctively, I lifted my shirt collar to ensure I didn't have body odor. After convincing myself that I smelled pretty normal, considering the circumstances, I prayed we were somehow downwind.

"Ewww," the troll said. He lifted his foot as a slimy green goo connected his toes to the floor. He reached down, picking off a decomposing creature's guts from between his toes. He lifted the carcass to his nose, smelled it, then gagged. "You're a nasty bugger, aren't you?" he asked just before opening his mouth, tossing the dead thing inside, gnashing the bones with his gums.

Liv covered her mouth, trying her best not to retch as the troll marched across his lair and took a seat in his chair. When he sat, the earth shook. It felt as if the whole place was going to cave in. The Chief was at least twenty-five feet tall. His skin was hard and coarse, a layer of leather over body armor. His mouth was rank, and even though he was toothless (just as Tubb and Griff had said), I knew he could crush our bodies by way of chomping. There was one thing about the Chief that stood out above the rest. Not his height, weight, or dental hygiene... but his eyes. They were a cloudy, milky shade of blue, marbles floating in a glass of two-percent milk.

"He's blind," Liv said.

Liv was right. I'd seen eyes like his when Mom made me volunteer at the nursing home last winter. I helped this one resident, Miss Victoria Deville. Sweet old lady. She smelled like cough drops and Vicks vapor rub and she was blind as a bat. His eyes looked exactly the same as hers. I smiled as I felt a glimmer of hope for the first time on this trek, but I didn't want to get ahead of myself. I mean, the dude was still the size of a shipping container. He could crush me with his pinkies. "Where do you think he's holding the rod?" My eyes panned across the room, surveying the bubbling black lagoon with all the dead things that dotted the hideous hideout.

"There," Liv said in a hush as she pointed to the Chief's throne. Right beside him was a basket. Sticking out of the basket were spears, animal bones, and a staff. Wooden, ancient, with a light green gem resting in the woven peak of the scepter. It was definitely the caduceus I'd seen etched on the wall back in Yarberry.

What are we waiting for? I thought. I stood as silent as possible. Liv started to sneak forward, but I grabbed her by the shoulder. I pointed to a patch of high ground to our right, motioning a shooting stance. I wanted her to cover me while I moved in. As she said, she had the only weapon. Liv nodded, then tiptoed toward the elevated earth that overlooked the Chief's throne and the murky muck of Longwell Lagoon. She gave me a thumbs up after climbing onto a perch for overwatch. Time to move, Dean.

I snuck out from behind my hiding place, dancing around anything on the ground that would make a sound or suck my body into the tar pit. The room was massive from ground level. It would take me longer than anticipated to reach the Chief. I stared into the Lagoon and wasn't quite prepared for what I saw. Death, death, and more death. Bodies. Some new, most old. Skeletons stacked upon skeletons of all sorts of creatures. This wasn't just a lair. It was a graveyard. It was a reminder to anyone who dared step foot here that things would not end well. Yet here I was, heading toward the giant troll. One thing was for sure: If mom knew what I was doing right now, she'd kill me way faster than the Chief ever could.

Mere feet away from the caduceus, from my prize, I glanced up at Liv. She had repositioned herself, now with a much better vantage point. At first, she looked poised, unwavering, exactly how you'd want your source of covering fire to look. But that all changed fast. Liv's expression went from confident to panic. She frantically pointed toward Chief Troll. Behind him, on the opposite side of the caduceus, something lingered in the shadows. At first, I didn't see what, but after a second, it became clear: a goblin.

A goblin with mangy black hair and puke green skin snuck from behind the Chief, creeping towards a chest at the Chief's side. The chest contained jewels, coins, necklaces, and a diamond the size of a honeydew melon. The goblin inched closer to the treasure chest, then stopped on a dime. He saw me, I saw him, and we just stared at one another. My fingertips reached for the caduceus as he reached for the diamond. The two of us, human of Earth and goblin of Second Realm, were frozen in a stalemate. But who would move first? I wondered if he was a threat. I wondered if he wondered the same thing about me. And for that moment, we both forgot the one thing we should never have forgotten. The Chief. The gigantic troll purred, sniffed, and wrinkled his nose as a putrid odor snaked inside his nostrils.

"You think I don't know you're there?" Chief Troll said in an angry grumble. I looked at the goblin, then up at Liv. "I smelled you when you walked in. Think you're clever, do you? Think because I'm blind, you can steal from me?"

It was a standoff. Who would move first? Who was Chief Troll talking to? Me? Liv? The goblin? All three of us? Just then, Ava's words returned to me. "We send someone whose scent is unfamiliar." Of course. He had to smell the goblin. I'd bet my PlayStation 2 that the

Chief had smelled, smashed, and swallowed hundreds of goblins in his day. This was my chance. My one chance to make my move before the goblin set things into motion that couldn't be undone. I wouldn't sit by idly and let this smelly, green creep ruin my day.

I stepped forward just as the Chief slammed his massive fists down on his throne, splintering the throne's armrests into a billion pieces. "I hate goblins," the Chief said. What a relief. He had no idea I was here. Chief Troll stood, swiping his arm side to side, sweeping the goblin off his feet. I rolled across the ground, barely dodging the Chief's hand, and snatched the caduceus. He hadn't even noticed.

"Hey! Wait. He's stealing—" that rat of a goblin was about to snitch on me. Only he never got the chance as Chief Troll tossed him up in the air and swallowed him whole. Liv waved me on as I pranced around the bubbling, black muck, heading out of the lair.

When I met Liv in the winding tunnels, I hadn't sensed what she immediately noticed.

"Your hand," she said. "It's glowing."

Sure enough, as I looked down at the hand that gripped the staff; it was glowing a faint shade of bluish-green.

"Does that mean it works?" Liv said.

"I'm not sure. But Ava said that if I make the connection, I can use it for all kinds of things," I said as we left the foul air behind us, hopefully making our way to the safety of our horses and back to Yarberry Shire.

"Too bad you can't do some sort of mind control on stinky back there."

I stopped in my tracks.

A few seconds later, Liv realized I wasn't by her side. She pivoted back in my direction.

"What do you mean?" I asked.

"I mean, it's too bad you can't control Chief Troll's mind," Liv said. "Get him to fight for us."

I looked down at the caduceus, the magic rod. The gem woven into its peak began to glow brighter. "What if I can?"

"Dean, I was half joking. Let's take it back to Ava. Let her teach you how to use it."

"If you were half joking, that means you're half serious."

"I really wasn't."

"You heard them," I said. "We need allies and weapons. And what better weapon than a ten-ton monster?" I looked over the caduceus, mesmerized by its gaze. "How hard can it be? Let me try," I said as I focused my energy, tilting the head of the staff, pointing it at a small rock on the ground at Liv's feet.

"What are you doing?" Liv asked, staring down with a worried look on her face.

"Trust me. Just gonna pick this rock up and move it around. Easy-peasy."

"You know who else probably thought that magic rod was easy to use?"

"Who?" I said.

"The person who had it last," Liv folded her arms across her chest. "The person that Chief Troll probably ate and digested and whose bones are now being used as ornaments."

"Watch and learn," I said. I scrunched my face, focusing all my thoughts on moving the rock. At first, I felt a pulsating beat coming from the grip right before the entire thing began to glow. The next thing I knew, a blast of light shot from its peak and shattered the rock into a zillion pebbles.

"Seriously?" Liv shouted, jumping out of the way. "I thought you were picking it up. Not blasting it to oblivion, nearly taking my legs off."

"Probably just a learning curve," I said.

"Probably a bad idea that can only get worse. I trust you see that now."

"We came this far," I said.

"For the weapon. Not the Chief."

"Liv, I can feel it. I know I can do this. We can at least talk to him. Try to convince him. I'm not saying I want to use this against him or fight him. But I have to give it a shot."

"And if it doesn't work? If he refuses to listen?"

"Then we run."

"And if he chases us?"

"We run faster."

"This is a terrible idea," Liv said.

"This was your idea," I replied with a charming smile.

"You're going to be the death of me, Dean Moyers," Liv said as she rolled her eyes.

"Not today," I set off back into the stink.

As we crossed the threshold into the lair, I once again tried my best to remain undetected. I also made sure to keep my distance.

"Ahem," I cleared my throat. Initially, the Chief didn't hear me as he bent over, picking up remnants of his broken throne, tossing the pieces into a burlap sack. "AHEM!" I cleared it again, this time louder.

"Wha—?" Chief Troll stood upright and spun in our direction. "Who's there?" he said, sniffing the air.

"I have your caduceus," I exclaimed in a deeper tone than I'd normally speak, trying to sound intimidating or regal. Liv shook her head in embarrassment.

"What in the world is a caw-dew-see-us?" he pronounced awfully.

"Your staff," I said.

No reaction.

"Your scepter."

Still no reaction.

"The glowing stick that has magic powers," Liv shouted.

"Curious," the Chief dropped his bag full of sticks and bones and crushed rock. "For one. Why would you take my magic stick?" He took a step in our direction. "For two. Why did your voice change? Unless there's more than one of you." He took another stride; this time, his foot splashed in the black of the Lagoon, splattering the walls with goo. "And for three. Saying you did take my magic stick. Why are you still here telling me about it?"

"One. I need the weapon to fight the army of a bad guy named Thorne." The Chief's expression turned more serious when I said the name, Thorne. "Two. There are two of us. My name is Dean Moyers." The Chief's eyebrow raised.

"Moyers, eh?" he said.

"You know my name. And you know that if I'm here, this is serious. Thorne's army is marching across the land. They're killing everything in their path."

"And three," Liv said. "We need your help." She crossed her fingers for good luck.

"Ha!" he patted his big belly, laughing. "A Moyers needs my help. The Chief helps no one but himself.

357

And he is especially not going to help you. Dean Moyers." He took another step toward us, at least in our general direction. His head still twisted from side to side as his fingers felt around blindly at the air.

"Why? Why won't you help us?" Liv asked.

"Because, when I was younger. At the height of my power. A human came into my lair. He stole something from me that didn't belong to him. Then, when I tracked him down, he stabbed me right in the eyes, taking my sight and sword." Chief Troll started to sniff the air. "His name was Moyers too. Joseph Moyers."

"My great-grandpa," I said. If my great-grandpa Joe did this, that means Chief Troll was really old.

The Chief sniffed more frantically, then stopped as he whipped his head in my direction, staring at me with his dead eyes. "There you are!" He growled and slammed his fist down.

"Move!" I pushed Liv left, and I jumped right.

"If Joseph Moyers was your great-grandpa, I'm definitely gonna eat you!"

Chief Troll wildly swung his open palms from side to side, attempting to clobber us. I slid under one attack but, in doing so, ended up right in front of his nasty foot, which still had gloop stuck in between his toes. Liv fired an arrow, but it only bounced off his forehead. So much for being armed. He sniffed again, smiling, then lifted his colossal foot. He started to stomp downward. I looked in all directions but knew I didn't have time to move. Not before he would crush me.

"The caduceus. Dean, use it!" Liv shrieked.

I raised the staff above my head and closed my eyes, bracing for impact, but nothing happened. Was I dead? Did he crush me that quick? Funny, because I didn't feel a thing.

"Put me down!" the Chief bellowed. I opened my eyes, shocked to see the troll hovering above me with zero control of his body. "I order you to put me down at once, you tall Gnomeling!"

"I'm not a Gnomeling. I'm a human," I said, barely able to believe this weapon was working. I didn't know how I was controlling it, only that I was. I waved the caduceus back and forth, and the Chief floated in whatever direction I pointed. "Say it! Say, human."

"Fine. Fine. You're a human. Whatever that means."

"I'm not letting you down until you agree to help us."

"And why should I?"

"Good question," Liv interrupted. She picked up a spear from the ground and aimed it at the Chief. "Why should I not send your tongue straight out of the back of your mouth?"

Ava was right – Liv was fierce, and I liked it.

"This one's feisty," the Chief said. "Tell me, then, what do I care about Thorne and his 'army?'" The Chief used air quotes around the word "army" as he dangled in zero gravity. I don't know how to explain it, but watching a troll with fingers the size of telephone booths do air quotes made me smile. Maybe he wasn't actually all bad, despite all the dead bodies that littered his lair. "What does a war between the free folk and Thorne matter to the Chief?"

"What does it matter? Listen," Liv said. She was hot. Not in the physical sense, though I do think she's pretty hot; let me tell you, she was fuming mad. "I came here in a hearse, almost drowned in a lake, watched my boyfriend almost die—" (Boyfriend... *She called me her boyfriend*) "— and why? Because some madman will

359

destroy an entire planet, realm, or whatever this place is. Do you think he's just going to stop with Yarberry? Do you think he'll leave you be once he defeats the free folk? Let you live your stinky, smelly, slimy days in peace in this disgusting pit of despair?"

"You don't need to get personal," the Chief said, genuinely offended.

"No! When they're done with the little folk, they'll come after you next. They'll come after everyone, leaving nothing to chance. How's that for getting personal?" Liv's nostrils flared.

"She's right," I said. "And what side of the story do you want to be on? Do you want the songs to sing of your glory? The day Chief Troll, the mightiest warrior in Second Realm, came to the rescue? A hero?"

"Hero, huh?" the Chief scratched his chin in thought, still floating in the air.

"Or do you want them to call you a coward? A washed-up, mindless has-been who did nothing and lost everything?" I lowered the caduceus, dropping the Chief in the black vat of scum. I would say I set him down gently, but I was trying to make a point and released him when he was a few feet from the ground. The muck splashed everywhere. "Make your choice, Chief," I planted the staff into the goop, gritting my teeth. The gem turned an angry shade of orangish-red. I turned my back to him. "You have until sunrise in one fortnight's time."

"That means two weeks," Liv said with a reassuring nod. She took my hand in hers, our fingers interlaced, and we walked away, praying with each step that he didn't pummel us on our way out the door.

DANGER IS MY MIDDLE NAME

Thirteen days and twenty-three hours had passed since our arrival in Second Realm. During that time, I trained with Ava on the caduceus. She even showed me some sacred scrolls that would be useful if I got the amulet back from Thorne. The scrolls contained spells that I could use to cast on the enemy - spells to drive them mad, control their thoughts, or even make them drop into a little ball and start sucking their thumbs if that's what I wanted them to do.

The Gnomelings of Yarberry spent the fortnight preparing for battle. They made spears and arrows from chopping down trees. They melted down metals to forge small daggers and swords. Cliff, Tubb, and Griff trained the farmer folk day in and day out. We even heard that Pint was studying my swordplay against

Thorne, using it as a model to teach the other Gnomeling children how to defend themselves if the worst came to worst.

Updates brought by messenger coneys arrived sporadically, some sharing news of complete chaos across the lands. Refugees from Langhammer, Scahill and the elves of Westrich came to Yarberry after their villages had been burned to the ground. Thorne was leaving nothing but darkness and despair in his path.

It wasn't all bad news, though. As predicted by Klavos, his kin, the Ravens from the north, arrived just a week ago. There were only about twenty-five of them, but they were a fearsome-looking group, most of whom had five fingers on each hand, although it was still true that none of them could fly. Gnomeling tribes from Thornhill were forced to flee their lands and joined us three nights ago. There were so many that they had to set up camp just outside of town. Cliff estimated that they numbered in the hundreds, maybe even a thousand. These were mostly farmers, but they were willing to fight nonetheless - a welcome sight for sure.

The biggest surprise came this morning. We woke up to a series of howls and immediately thought we were being invaded. However, it turned out that a species of wolves had arrived in Yarberry. Allies that hailed from the northern end of Second Realm, near the polar caps, a land untouched by Thorne; he would have been a fool to journey that far north. Five wolves joined the fight when they heard of the danger to the Realm. They vowed to stick by us until the bitter end. Their leader, Nora, looked like a husky, only three times the size, with beautiful blue eyes, and to my shock, she spoke Gnomarian. All of the wolves did.

We were gathered around a meeting table in the domed building when Nora spoke through Tubb, who translated for us. "My spies have informed me that Thorne is sending a small unit in our direction," she told the group.

"A scout team?" Cliff stared out the window, stroking his braided beard as the sun rose.

"What's our plan?" I asked, but all eyes turned to me.

"Excellent question," Ava replied. "What is our plan?"

Why were they looking at me? I'm just a kid, I thought to myself.

"A kid with a destiny. A kid who has shown strength in the most impossible of circumstances." I heard Ava's voice in my head. "We follow your lead, Dean."

I looked at the soldiers before me, then down at a map covered in miniature figures representing the entirety of our forces. It was clear we weren't ready. "If the scouts see us like this, they'll charge immediately. They won't hesitate, and I'm not sure that gives us enough time."

"What do you suggest?" Nora asked as Tubb continued to translate.

"We need Thorne to hesitate. We should take out the scout team. That will buy us more time," I said.

"How?" Klavos asked.

"If the scouts don't return immediately, Thorne will be cautious, maybe even afraid. He wouldn't rush in if he thought we had the upper hand. He'd be worried about a trap."

Ava, Nora, Cliff, Tubb, Griff, and Liv nodded in agreement. I felt confidence brewing within me. "Nora," I said.

"Yes," Nora straightened her back, and her ears perked up.

"I need two of your best wolves."

"You shall have them," she turned to her pack. "Alpha, Omega, you're with Dean."

"Tubb. I need you and Griff to ride with me. Bring four others," I commanded.

"Yes, Dean," Griff saluted, the oddest salute I'd ever seen. The salute came from the middle of his forehead; his hand was vertical, with his stubby fingers between his eyebrows as he chopped downward. I shrugged and mimicked his salute back to him.

"Who can train the rest of the Gnomelings?" I asked.

"Leave that to me," Cliff stood and pulled a small axe from his belt.

"The Ravens will prepare the eastern border. If we can funnel them toward us, it should make it easier for our archers to pick them off," Klavos said as he stood and left the room.

"Ava," I said. "You stare into the water stuff in the lab. See if any of the visions are changing. Maybe we've missed something. Something that could help us."

Ava nodded and went on her way.

"And what about me?" Liv asked. Should I ride with you?"

I turned and looked at Liv in her enchanting eyes, "Forever."

She smiled as her eyes began to mist.

"But, bring your bow," I said as I got to my feet, heading to the door.

"What abouts me?" I heard a high-pitched voice from somewhere in the ceiling.

"Who's there?" I asked, searching the underside of the roof just as Pint dropped into view, landing at my feet.

"I'm going to ride out with you. Right, Dean?"

Pint batted his hopeful eyes, putting his hands together and praying.

"I don't think that's the best idea, Pint. It could be dangerous."

"My second name be dangerous."

"I'm serious," I laughed.

"Me too," Pint said as he pulled a small picture ID from his back pocket. "Pint Dangerous Lemon." He traced his fingers over the Gnomarian symbols on the card.

"Your name is Pint Dangerous Lemon?" Liv asked.

Pint shook yes and stowed his ID card away. "So you see, I must be going with you."

"I'm sorry, Pint. We don't know how many there are. We don't know what kind of weapons they have. I can't risk it."

Pint's chin dropped as tears began to overflow from his eyes. "Dean doesn't love Pint."

Liv elbowed me in the gut, mouthing for me to, "Fix this."

"Oh, Pint," I crouched beside him, "Dean does love you." I looked at Liv for advice, but she just motioned to keep going. "It's just... You know how you say that I'm your hero?"

"Yes," Pint sniffled as snot streamed from his nose.

"Well, the truth is, buddy, you're my hero."

"Yeah, right."

"I'm serious. While we were out talking to the troll, I heard you trained all the Gnomeling kids how to fight." Pint started to lift his head. "I heard you taught them how to use swords and shields, and —"

"And don't forget the spears," Pint added.

"Of course. The spears and arrows and axes." I lifted Pint's chin the rest of the way until his bulbous eyes aligned with mine. "I could never do that. Not as fast and as well as you. I was never this brave when I was your age. I'm not as brave as you now, and I'm sixteen."

"You be right," Pint laughed, snorting up his snot. "I remember one day, Miss Ava showed us a moving picture of you being scared of a fanged coiler. Haha! What kind of ninny-muffin is scared of a fanged coiler?" Pint broke out into a full-on belly laugh.

"Alright, laugh it up. But snakes are scary, you know?"

"To a silly gardener, maybe." Pint had stopped crying.

I rubbed the top of Pint's head, messing up his curls.

"I sure do be wanting to go with you, though. The children are ready. And I'm not a baby anymore. I'm a Shire Knight, just like you." This was going to be tougher than I imagined. I looked to Liv for support.

"I have an idea, Pint," Liv said as she crouched beside us. "Dean gave me this when we met. Maybe you could hang onto this while we deal with the scouts?" Liv reached deep into her back pocket and pulled out the New York Yankees stuffed monkey.

"Wow! Is this a soldier from your world?" Pint asked.

Liv looked to me for advice. All I could do was shrug. "Uh, sure, yeah," Liv answered. "A brave soldier indeed."

"You had that with you the whole time?" I asked Liv.

"I did," she answered. "Now I need Pint to keep it safe." She held the stuffed monkey out before Pint. "Do you think you can do that for me?"

Pint stood tall, straightened his shoulders, and took the monkey from Liv's hand. "I can, Princess Liv." He saluted Liv the same way that Griff saluted me. With his hand placed in between his eyes and chopping downward. We stood and returned the awkward gesture.

THE WISE WORDS OF ADMIRAL ACKBAR

Our weapons were slung across the ponies. Once again, I mounted my trusted steed, Horse, as Liv sat atop Stump, whom she was developing a soft spot for. Tubb and Griff followed on their ponies, Jackpot and Captain. For the record, Liv changed their names to Jackpot and Captain, but only after we found out their real names were Mike and Purple. An additional four Gnomelings flanked them, along with two wolves, Alpha and Omega, bringing up the rear. We made our way to the deserted town of Covington, northeast of Yarberry. In the center of town was an abandoned cathedral we'd seen on our trip to the Lagoon. The cathedral had a mostly intact clock tower, though the clock wasn't functional. Liv and I climbed the tower to get a bird's eye view of our surroundings. I ordered Tubb and Griff to hide out in a beat-up diner, which I'm sure they would scour for food before any actual fighting took place. The other four Gnomelings scattered, taking their positions in the town, and the wolves hid in a thick patch of bushes just outside of the south side of the village, hunkering down in the shadows, ready to strike.

An hour had passed. The village lay shrouded in a low, ominous green fog, enveloping it like a thick, eerie blanket. The mist obscured the buildings and streets, reducing them to mere shadows. The atmosphere grew tense and foreboding, and there was still no sign of Thorne's scout team. My nerves worsened. In the back of my mind, I thought I heard Ava's voice, crying out a warning of some kind, but the words were nearly impossible to decipher. It almost sounded like she was yelling at Pint. I pictured him staring into the seeing pool, trying to watch me in action.

"I'm sure it's fine, Dean. We're probably just early," Liv tried to reassure me.

"I'm gonna check again," I said. For the thirty-fifth time in the last thirty-five minutes, I peered over the top of the clock tower, checking the horizon. As far as I could see, the east and west looked clear, though the thick layer of mist limited my visibility. However, the north was a different story. A massive hill descended towards the village where we had taken our positions, obscuring everything on the other side from our view.

"As soon as they reach the top of the hillside, we'll signal the others to be ready," Liv said.

"I have a bad feeling about this," I said, unable to explain the unease in my gut. I descended a ladder to the cathedral's second level and looked out a broken window, where Tubb and Griff were chomping on dried meat. "You two good?" I asked.

"Peachy as a pine needle," Griff replied, giving a thumbs up with a mouthful of food.

I paced to the opposite end of the building, counting the strategically positioned Gnomelings around town. "One," I muttered upon spotting the first Gnomeling, whose helmet was too big and covered most of their face. "Two." The next building was a broken-down stable where a female Gnomeling brushed her pony's hair. I couldn't recall her name--was it Estelle or Stella? "Three." I saw the third Gnomeling, a teenage boy named Coal who had a strange habit of calling everyone Mommy. Coal sat brushing strands of curly black hair from his face. "Four." I looked to our rear where the fourth Gnomeling, Gnolan, should have been, perched on the roof of a schoolhouse. I know he should have been there because I helped boost Gnolan onto the eaves. "Four," I said again, hoping the words would cause him to materialize out of thin air.

"What is it?" Liv asked, peering down at me from the top of the tower.

"Where's Gnolan? Where's the Gnomeling we tossed on the roof?" my voice rose.

"I don't see him," Liv said, squinting and shading her eyes with her hand.

"Coal!" I called urgently. "Do you see Gnolan?"

Coal got to his feet and looked around. "Sorry, Mommy. I don't see him."

I whistled softly, signaling Alpha and Omega to spring into action. But when I whistled again and again, there was no response. No movement from Alpha or Omega. No sign of Gnolan. Only silence. "It's too quiet," I muttered, feeling a sense of dread. As I turned to Liv, ready to climb the ladder, I noticed her eyes had widened, and her face was frozen in shock. "Liv?"

"Dean, we have a big problem," she said as she frantically scrambled down the ladder, missing two rungs at a time, nearly plummeting to the bottom.

I darted to the window on the north side of the building and looked to the top of the hill. Thorne, in Minotaur form, was riding a rhinoceros. He was holding a spear as tall as a javelin pole. To his right, three wraiths dressed in black cloaks -- the real deal, not the Peggs. To his left, a masked soldier in black armor carried a shield with a blood-red X across it. And behind Thorne, an entire army of evil loomed--goblins, Hellions, Mountain Trolls with magnificently horrifying horns, and other beasts in armor.

"We were set up," I said to Liv, my eyes scanning the scene before us. "It's not a scout team. It's all of them. They tricked us."

"Who tricked us?" Liv asked.

I looked back to where Alpha and Omega were supposed to be hiding and said, "The wolves," my voice tight with anger.

"Tubb! Griff!" Liv cried. "Run!"

Tubb and Griff sprang to their feet, their faces etched with confusion and fear. But there was no time for explanations, as I felt the enemy army closing in on us. Thousands upon thousands of enemy troops were marching this way.

"Coal!" I yelled. "We have to move." But I was too late. As soon as Coal heard my voice and stopped biting his fingernails nervously, Alpha leaped out from behind him, sinking his rabid teeth into Coal's neck. "Mommy," he cried. Blood. There was so much blood.

"Gnolan," Tubb's voice quaked as Omega entered the town square, dragging Gnolan's body along.

"To the horses!" I commanded. We sprinted to Horse, Stump, Jackpot, and Captain and mounted them. Omega dropped Gnolan, bore her blood-stained teeth, and charged us. Liv pulled an arrow from her quiver, aimed, then let loose. Thunk! A direct hit. A fatal hit. Omega slid to a halt in the dirt, stopping dead at our feet with an arrow plunged between her eyes. Alpha let out a hideous howl. This just got personal. The female Gnomeling, Stella, tried to run, her tiny legs pushing as fast as they could. She nearly reached her pony when a Troll burst through the schoolhouse - He literally burst through the entire building, picked her up, and tossed her out of sight as her screams faded.

"Ride!" Liv shouted. Goblins, hellions, and orcs climbed over roofs, pouring in through the gangways between the buildings, completely surrounding us. Alpha charged, and Liv pulled another arrow to shoot as we rode straight toward him, but she missed.

"Take him down!" I yelled.

"I'm trying," Liv said. She fired another arrow, but Alpha dodged it. She quickly let out a third shot that skimmed Alpha, slicing into his pelt, but it didn't take him out. Alpha jumped at me, his claws extended, and dug them into Horse, who let out a whimper and tumbled over, landing on top of me. As Alpha got to his feet, I screamed in agony, with Horse crushing everything below the waist. He encircled me like I was prey. What was I saying? I was prey.

I heard Liv cry my name as I saw her and the Gnomelings turning around to come back.

"No! Keep going." I waved them on as more villains started to surround me. "Warn the others."

Liv tried to force her way to me, but Tubb and Griff grabbed ahold of Stump's reins and stopped her in her tracks.

"Go!" I ordered before being completely surrounded by enemies and losing sight of my friends. If this was to be my end, I prayed Liv would at least escape.

Alpha growled, saliva dripping from his fangs. Orcs, goblins, and hellions roared with laughter. Where was Thorne? Were they waiting for him? It turns out the answer must have been no because the troll thundered his way to me and lifted his leg. Horse and I would be nothing more than a stain on the bottom of the troll's foot within a second. My mind was buzzing with thoughts of ways to escape when I suddenly remembered the caduceus and my training. My memory flashed back to when I stopped Chief Troll dead in his tracks. The caduceus was only a few feet away, taunting me with its proximity. Beneath the weight of Horse's massive frame, I squirmed and wriggled, desperate to free myself. My fingertips grazed the hilt of the staff, but I needed just a little more time.

The mountain troll's foot began to descend, and I turned my head away, knowing that this was it. This time, it was all over. But then something unexpected happened. I heard rustling from a satchel on Horse's side, followed by a button popping off. Next, I heard shuffling feet and a loud howl from the troll. A howl of pain. Suddenly, a metallic-tasting liquid dripped onto my face and into my mouth - blood. That's when I heard a familiar voice say, "Get up, Master Dean. To your feet." Even with my eyes closed, I knew the troll had fallen from his commotion upon impact. He must have crushed ten goblins in his collapse. But before I could turn back, I heard another sound - the same voice as before. Pint's voice, crying out.

When my eyes opened, the scene before me was so surreal that my brain struggled to understand it. I was in shock. Part of me didn't want to believe it. Actually, all of me didn't want to believe it. The mountain troll squirmed on his back with a fresh wound on the bottom of his foot and a spear sticking out like a thorn. At my side, I saw the New York Yankees stuffed monkey, and next to the monkey, Pint lay on the ground, holding his stomach with an arrow lodged in it. His hands were covered in red, his face had turned pale white, and his lips were blue and trembling. Seeing him lying on the ground reminded me of the night Liv was shot by Thorne. But this time, there was no magic coin to save his life. "I'm sorry, Dean," Pint said, his voice barely above a whisper.

"Don't talk," I tried to comfort him.

"I'm sorry I couldn't be a Shire Knight like you," Pint said.

"That's not true," I said. "You can be a Shire Knight."

"How?" Pint made a pitiful whimper, and the world around me seemed to stop. The monsters were confused by the commotion of the falling mountain troll and their downed comrades, and maybe they didn't even realize I was still alive, but I didn't care about any of that. The only thing that mattered right now was Pint.

"I'm a knight, and knights can make other knights, right?" I asked.

Pint tried to answer, but speaking was too hard for him, so he just nodded.

"I, Dean Moyers, anoint you, Pint Dangerous Lemon, an official Shire Knight," I said, my eyes watering. "You're one of us now." And with those words, Pint smiled and closed his eyes forever.

For a minute, I just sat there. I didn't react. I didn't know how to react. I expected Pint to open his eyes. To say something, anything. But he didn't. He was gone.

I let out a roar as a surge of strength coursed through me - strength I didn't even know I had. With ease, I lifted Horse off my legs and seized the caduceus. The sudden movement caught the enemies' attention. Despite the swords, spears, and arrows aimed at me, I dug deep, growling in defiance. A nasty-looking hellion charged at me, swinging his curved sword, hoping to slice me in half. Slowly, I turned to face him, pointed the caduceus, and uttered, 'No!' With that single word, the caduceus emitted a bolt of black sparks. Upon impact, the hellion buckled and broke; his bones shattered as his body crumpled like origami. More villains now ran towards me, but I slammed the staff into the dirt. Shockwaves emerged in a ring, throwing the enemies in my vicinity back fifty feet. I reached down, tugging on Horse's reins. "C'mon Horse. Time to go." But Horse didn't budge; Alpha had cut him deep. "Horse," I nudged him. Horse was still alive, but barely.

As the enemies slowly rose, I noticed a helmet with two horns strapped to Horse's saddle. Pint's mother had made it for me. I reached out, grabbed the helmet, slapping it down on my head; it fit perfectly. One after another, the goblins rushed at me. I twirled the staff, taking them down in sequence. A clumsy goblin stumbled past, losing his grip on his sword. Without thinking, I reached out and caught it out of midair. At that moment, something inside me snapped. I unleashed all my anger, slicing through the last two goblins with a savage intensity. The battle had turned me into a bloodthirsty beast, and I reveled in the chaos.

I caught my breath as the first wave of villains passed. I lowered my chin and raised my eyes intently as the dark army before me started to part. Through their formation and the fog, I could see Thorne approaching in the distance with his wraiths and the soldier in black, his personal bodyguard. Thorne was just as I had seen him in my vision. His muscles were ripped, chiseled like a statue, and the amulet hung around his neck on a rope. His face looked like a raging bull, with horns coming out of his skull. But you know what? I had horns too.

I readied the caduceus in my hand and the sword in the other. I planted my left foot, then moved to plant my right when it hit something. That's when I looked down at Pint. Poor pitiful Pint. Why couldn't you just listen? Why couldn't you just stay in Yarberry? I can't quite explain my actions, but at that moment, I dropped the sword. Instead of the weapon in my hands, I picked up Pint and the stuffed monkey, tucking them both beneath my arm. Pint was not leaving my side. He would not be left here with these monsters.

Fear set in. I was outnumbered two thousand to one. I could make a break for it. Do I run? Do I fight? Either way, I wouldn't last long. And that's when I heard the cadence of galloping footsteps. That's when I heard Liv and Stump approaching from behind. Of course, she didn't listen to my orders. Of course, she came back for me. Thank goodness she was hard-headed.

"Moyers!" Thorne growled. He charged in my direction on his rhino, but before he could reach me or before I could make a move, Liv intervened. She grabbed me by the collar and hoisted me onto the back of Stump. Her eyes met mine, then she looked down at Pint.

"Oh, no," she sighed, heavy-hearted, as we darted away. Despite Stump looking like a blob of grape jelly, that pony moved as quickly as lightning, with Liv kicking at his side to make him go even faster. At the same time, Horse seemed inspired by Stump's bravery, or maybe he just didn't want to be trampled by the armored rhinoceros. He struggled to his feet and hobbled after us, but I knew he wouldn't stand a chance of outrunning the army. With a quick aim of the caduceus, another shockwave emitted from the gem, creating a force field of torture that blasted outward from the weapon. Thorne and his troops covered their ears in agony. We left them in a cloud of dust as we rode for Yarberry.

With Pint lying in my arms, we rode back with tears in our eyes. We rode back as failures.

RETURN OF THE KING?

Our ride back to Yarberry was long and grueling, but nothing could have prepared me for what I saw when we reached the shire. Buildings were burning, while Gnomelings were screaming, covered in blood and soot. So many little folk lying motionless on the sides of the dirt roads. As I learned from our ambush in the abandoned town, we were set up. We were tricked. I fell for it hook, line, and sinker. We all did. The wolves of the North played us. A group of goblins lay in wait, and as soon as we rode off, they attacked. A small battalion of Thorne's army sucker-punched Yarberry Shire when we least expected it. According to Cliff's count, we'd lost over one-hundred souls. Nearly as bad, the enemy had burned our reserve food, weapon, and ammunition stashes to the ground. Though, it wasn't a total loss. The free folk of Yarberry were tougher than they appeared. They, along with the Ravens and other misplaced creatures, fought back. They took down Nora, her pack, and the platoon of goblins, but at a cost. And while all of that was devastating enough, nothing could have ever prepared me for the sobbing and wailing of Pint's mother when I handed over his body. No one knew he'd snuck inside a satchel on one of the horses. No one knew he was with us. Yet his mother's tears flowed just the same. Her whole body shook as she laid him on his bed in his room, covering him up to his chin, just below his favorite poster of me.

I didn't deserve to be on a poster.

I didn't deserve to be Pint's hero.

So here I sat in the same room I described at the beginning of my story, peering out the circular window, watching the sunset, watching the once lush green and chestnut fields turn to ash.

The enemies were here. This time, not a small platoon. Not scouts. The entire Thorne army was here.

"Fire!" a coarse demonic voice roared as a massive catapult unleashed its wrath, sending a fireball from its bowl-shaped bucket directly toward me. The projectile roared toward the heavens, hit its peak, and began plummeting downward.

"Take cover," Griff yelped.

I leaned back against the wall, bracing for impact as my attention focused across the room, past the coffee table made from driftwood, littered with weapons of all sorts: swords, arrows, spears, and even a battle axe. Metal clanked and rattled as I shifted my weight to my right side to ease the dull burning sensation that pierced my hip. My sudden movements had toppled over the horned helmet Pint's mom made for me. The helmet had goblin guts splattered on it. I reached for it just as the fireball hit.

The blast crashed down so near that the foundation and plaster on the walls cracked, creating a cloud of dust that danced in the flames and choked the air of oxygen. My lungs wheezed with each inhale as I sucked in deep, toxic breaths. More voices now cried out from outside, voices of all ages. The death rattles of the injured swelled from beyond. I looked upward through dry, bloodshot eyes. I felt it hit me all at once. No, not pain, not fire, or crushing stone, but anxiety, along with a sense of being completely out of my depths and overwhelmed.

"Your army awaits your command, Dean, I mean— Sir!" Liv called out as the front door to the cottage swung open with fury. She entered, marching directly before me. "Dean, you must lead them," she said.

"So many lost. And for what?" I asked, more rhetorical than anything. "There's no point anymore. Is there?"

Liv stooped down low and crouched at my feet. The blaze from beyond the cottage died down for a moment. The ends of her brown hair billowed around her shoulders. "Please, Dean. They need you. I need you."

"And what if I'm not strong enough?" I wiped a lone tear from my cheek.

"There may yet be a day where your strength fails you," Liv said, taking my chin in her hands, turning my head toward her. "But, it is not this day."

"Wait," I said as I recognized this quote, "did you just?" I began to ask.

Liv smiled and nodded. She reached down, grasping my gloved hand, and stood. With her aid, I lumbered to my feet, wiping the trail of tears from my face, so my battalion wouldn't see. My battalion. That sounded so ridiculous, even now at the end of all things.

As the round, blue porthole door shut behind us, we stepped out of the cottage, nestled into the side of a mountain in Yarberry. I clutched my shield tight against my hip and firmly held my weapons. The sky ahead of us had darkened to a gray hue, with streaks of blood-red peeking through clouds, like rips in cloth.

Soldiers stood before me arranged in perfect formation, two lines that stretched to eternity, as straight as arrows. Ravens and Gnomelings saluted us as we walked by and headed down a dirt pathway that led away from the cottage. The Ravens performed a more traditional salute, while the Gnomeling had all adopted Griff's forehead-chopping motion.

We reached the top of the hill that overlooked a valley, and the view was astonishing. Terrifying yet astonishing. Five hundred soldiers stood strong, ready to defend what was theirs, ready to defend hearth and home. They gripped their weapons as if they were extensions of their own bodies. Swords, axes, shovels, knives, picks, and more. And yes, the Gnomeling with the branch that had charms dangling from it. The colors of their lands, the royal blues and the ripe-corn yellows, flew high on homemade flags sewn from sheets, dresses, and suits. The faces of mostly little folk, two platoons of the Ravens, and a few other species from nearby shires, stood shoulder to shoulder, ready to fight, prepared to die.

Beyond what somehow ended up being my army was the stuff from nightmares. Darkness crawled across the horizon as thousands upon thousands of enemy soldiers marched toward us. Mounted and armored rhinos with lacerating tusks led the charge in our direction. Goblins bear-crawled across the fields; some even did so upside down. At least a dozen giant trolls wielded sharpened spears made from uprooted trees. The worst was still to come. A legion of armor-plated spiders with glowing red eyes scampered down the hillside from our left while six dragons with wings like razor blades sliced through the clouds, breathing fire, surveying the feast below. Then, in the center of it all, was the Minotaur. Thorne with his wraiths and his bodyguard.

I tried to block out the sounds of the battlefield - the screams, grunts, growls - but something else soon overtook the chaotic cacophony. I began clanging the staff against my shield in a steady rhythm. Thump, thump, thump. Liv, by my side, the only place I'd ever want her to be, joined in. Thump, thump, thump. Soon, the entire army followed our lead, creating a thundering battle cry that echoed over the hillsides. The uncertainty, anxiety, and doubt that had gripped me were replaced by focus and determination. Fear gave way to a thirst for vengeance.

I scanned the army before me and the soldiers to either side. I looked down at my Gnomeling friends, Tubb and Griff, and nodded. "Thank you both," I said. "For everything."

"We be glad we found you, human," Griff said.

"Very glad indeed," Tubb added.

I knew it was time when I felt Liv's hand rest on my shoulder. "Are you ready?" I asked.

"I think so, yeah," she answered with a familiar response.

"For our friends," I said. "Our companions."

"And your dad," Liv replied.

My eyelids fluttered as they fought a barrage of tears that welled up. Choked up, I only nodded as I looked out at the field, screaming at the top of my lungs, "Charge!" The armies all around me roared in unison, a guttural call, raising their weapons toward the sky. Together we rushed toward our enemies. We rushed toward our certain deaths.

THE BEGINNING OF THE END

It wasn't all chaos at first. No, at first, it appeared we had a coordinated plan of attack. Ava would take a platoon and ride toward the dragons. She would hold them off with her staff. The Ravens would attack the spiders. Their agility, strength, and never-say-die attitude would give me the time I needed. Tubb and Griff were in charge of a battalion of Gnomelings on horseback. They would head off the rhinos, goblins, and hellions. Cliff, with another battalion of Gnomelings from Thornhill, along with some of the refugees from other Shires, would march toward the orc rangers that made up the majority of the archers. As for Liv and I, along with some Yarberry Shire-folk, we rode straight at Thorne with his personal hunters. Liv stuck with Stump while I remained mounted on Horse, who was nearly healed with a little magic from Ava. Say what you will about the uniqueness of his name, but Horse was a legend in his own right. He had battled through a two-inch gash in his leg from Alpha's claws.

Everything in our strategy depended on me getting the amulet away from the Minotaur, away from Thorne. We knew that without the amulet, we stood no chance. Nada. Zero. Not even a fool's chance. Before we rode off, Ava told me a little more about the amulet itself. I already knew it was powerful, and it let me manifest things that weren't there. I knew it gave me super strength. But I didn't know just how much the enemy feared it. She estimated only the closest creatures to Thorne, his most loyal captains, would stay if the amulet fell under my control. Everyone else: The orcs, the goblins, the hellions, the weak-minded spiders, and maybe even the dragons, would flee. They would retreat back to the holes that they crawled out of. Or at least that's what we had hoped. We didn't need to win. We didn't need to defeat every soldier. We just needed the amulet and the fear that it brought with it.

Liv was a natural warrior, firing arrow after arrow while mounted on Stump as we raced towards the enemy. Driven by her need for revenge, Liv started counting her takedowns with each arrow she let loose.

"Seven. That was for Pint," Liv said. "Eight." She brought down another. "That was for getting me shot." She fired an arrow that went straight through two small goblins at the same time. "Ten. Did you see that? It got two of them." She readied another arrow. "Those were for granddad and your mum."

I held my caduceus in my right hand, aiming it forward; its power warded off goblins and orcs almost as if a force emitted from the gem that repulsed most of the villains. I used a small axe in my left hand to fend

off anyone within reach. And not just any axe. This...
was Pint's axe, and I swung it with more anger than I'd
ever felt in my life. Every orc I slashed at was the orc
that fired the arrow that hit Pint. Every goblin that I ran
through was the reason Pint was gone. Every single
monster in my path (at least in my mind) was the
cloaked wraith that took my dad in the mine when I was
so very little.

"Dean," Liv called out. "Look ahead. What is he
doing?"

Directly in front of us, the creatures in our path
had moved into a semi-circle formation. They created
an opening, inviting us right into the middle of it.

"Stop! Fall back. Everyone stop!" I ordered,
pulling up on Horse's reins, but it was too late. When
our steeds skidded to a halt, the enemy flanked us and
began to close in.

I readied my weapons, taking in our situation. The
gravity of our predicament was unmistakable. This was
bad. Really bad. With only fifty Gnomelings
accompanying Liv and me, we found ourselves
completely encircled by Thorne and hundreds of his
loyal troops.

Thorne stepped forward, raising his arm high in the
air to signal his knight in black armor. The knight
retrieved an arrow and dipped it into a container while
an orc holding a torch approached to light the arrow
ablaze. The knight aimed and fired the arrow with
precision, which whizzed past us. At first, I thought he
was aiming for me and missed horribly, but he didn't
miss his target at all. Instead, it hit the ground about
twenty yards behind us, sparking a fire that engulfed our
surroundings. We quickly realized that Thorne had

lured us here, and we were now trapped within a ring of flames.

Smoke burned my eyes, and I could smell fuel burning along with anything in its path, including living creatures. The forces of evil raised their weapons high. They began to dance, celebrating as if they'd already won. Beyond them, I couldn't make out anyone on our side. Not Cliff, nor the Ravens. Not Ava, Tubb, Griff, or the entirety of the Gnomeling army. Only a small platoon of mini-soldiers remained, along with Liv, who would never leave me. I was certain she would find a way through the flames to stay by my side, even if they separated us.

As I surveyed our position and reconsidered our state of affairs, I realized our enemy had severely miscalculated. I hopped off of Horse and marched toward Thorne, his black knight, and the wraiths.

"Where are you going?" Liv jumped down from Stump and followed me. "They have us surrounded."

"You're right." My pace quickened. Liv must have thought I had lost my mind.

"Will you tell me what you're doing?"

"He thinks he's trapped us," I said.

"That's because he has," Liv said.

"Take a closer look." I stopped and opened my arms wide. "He's cut himself off from his army. We're not the only ones stuck inside the flames."

Liv did some quick math and said, "I don't like this, Dean. They still outnumber us."

"Our odds won't get much better." I reached up and lifted the horned helmet off my head, my heart pounding against my chest. I wound up and chucked it towards Thorne, watching as it sailed through the air like a deadly weapon. Thorne stepped to the side, a cruel grin stretching across his face as the helmet crashed onto the dry, barren ground.

"Is that the best you have, Moyers?" While his body and face had changed, his voice did not. The kind of voice that made mothers cry. The kind of voice that made babies fling themselves head-first out of their beds.

"Fight me," I shouted. "Not your wraiths. Not your little friend," I pointed at the black knight, "Just you."

Thorne stepped in my direction, then placed his hand to his chin in thought. "You know," he shook his head no, "I don't think so."

I figured he was too much of a coward to fight one on one. I should have been afraid. I mean, he was a Minotaur. He could probably skewer me like a shish kebab with those horns of his, but deep down, he was still a guy who couldn't do anything on his own. He couldn't take on my dad in a fair fight. He couldn't even beat me with a sword in the hotel. More than anything, I knew that the amulet in my hands was something Thorne absolutely feared. I could smell it. And that is exactly when I saw it glowing. The amulet draped over Thorne's extra-large neck was shimmering, and I felt it calling me. I planted my feet in the dirt, holding my hand out, begging, "C'mon. Come to me. Come home."

The amulet lifted. I swear, I saw it lift from Thorne's skin. It wanted to come home.

It took a second, but Thorne realized what was happening. "What do you think you're doing?" He gripped the amulet, trying to pry it downward, away from my outstretched hand. But it wouldn't budge.

"Please," I whispered. "For the realm."

Thorne would have no more of it. He looked to the wraiths, giving them an order with his eyes. They pulled swords from thin air, pointed them at me, and started to rush us. Before I could react, Liv rode by me on Stump, firing a barrage of arrows, three at a time. The wraiths dodged, narrowly avoiding her shots. As she moved in closer, Liv ditched the bow and pulled out a dagger from her belt that Ava had enchanted with some sort of spell. One of the wraiths swung its sword viciously, nearly taking off her head, but Liv was too quick. She ducked under it and jabbed the dagger into the wraith's side. The wraith vaporized into black ash and was carried off by the wind.

I heard a choir of Gnomelings cheer in the background.

"Liv, look out!" I shouted. The two remaining wraiths converged on her position. They both swung at the same time. Liv ducked again, narrowly avoiding the second wraith's sword, but the third wraith's blade made contact, only not with Liv, but with Stump. The wraith had slashed Stump so deep that the horse was killed upon impact. Liv was thrown headfirst over the reins, skidding face-first on the barren land. The wraiths closed in around her as they glided off of their mounts.

I rushed toward them, sprinting as fast as possible, but it would not be fast enough. The wraiths' blades were already on their way down. Liv struggled to her knees and placed her hands in her lap. Her lip began to quiver as she stared right at me. In a single heartbeat, two things happened, one of which would alter the history of Second Realm. First, I saw Liv mouth the words, "Goodbye, Dean. I love you." The second was the biggest shock of all: a massive club, the size of a large tree, swung into view, taking out dozens of goblins, orcs, and both wraiths, sending them all airborne like an Albert Pujols home run. And the thing on the end of the club, the one who swung so violently to change the tide of this battle… it was Chief Troll.

As blind as he was, Chief looked down at Liv, sniffed, then extended a finger. She was no longer unfamiliar to him. Liv grabbed ahold as he lifted her off her feet.

"Thanks, Chief," Liv said, brushing herself off. She officially had the coolest friend ever.

"Sorry I'm late, feisty human girl," the Chief smiled with all zero of his teeth.

Hurrying over to Stump's side, Liv retrieved her dagger. She gently shut the horse's eyes with her hand. Amid the chaos and violence of battle, she bent down, pressing a sweet kiss to Stump's head, bidding her noble steed farewell.

"What are you doing here, Chief?" Thorne barked with a new level of fear in his voice.

"Someone told me I could be a hero. Thought I'd try that on for size." Chief Troll patted his belly, sniffing the air.

"You'll die alone. Just as you lived," Thorne signaled again with his hand. This time an army of mountain trolls stepped over the ring of fire and into the fray. Thorne looked up at the mountainous mountain trolls and said, "Kill him. Kill the Chief."

The trolls lowered their horns and kicked up dirt as they stampeded toward Chief and Liv. Chief opened his palm and slid Liv behind him to safety, then braced for impact.

Closer. Closer. Closer. The trolls strode angrily toward the Chief. This was going to be the mother of all collisions. Until it wasn't. They stopped short. All of them. Then, they stood upright, each taking a turn saluting, then hugging the Chief.

"What are you doing?" Thorne pouted. "This can't be happening!"

"Boys, let's take out some trash," Chief said as the trolls broke into formation. Each troll took off in a different direction, stomping, smashing, and slapping villains left and right. They broke the ring of fire. They dropkicked rhinos into eternity. One troll even caught a dragon in his teeth, tearing into it, flinging it back and forth until the winged creature had wings no more. It was madness. I loved it!

"Argghhhh!" Thorne absolutely lost his mind. He threw the biggest tantrum, kicking up dirt, punching orcs, screaming, wailing.

"Now's your chance, Dean." Liv had made her way back to me. "You can take him." She gripped my hand, wrapping it around the caduceus and pressing it against my chest. "Go!"

I was off. A full sprint toward an unsuspecting Thorne. He was too busy being a toddler to even see me coming. I used all my willpower, putting all my heart into the caduceus. Its gem was as radiant as the sun. This thing was going to pack one heck of a punch when it hit. And did it ever hit!

I swung the staff upward, striking Thorne right under the chin. The impact was so intense that his amulet and rope flew off his neck as he went head over heels into the air. The earth cracked and split when he landed, forming a crevice between us. A cloud of dust blurred my sight, but I found my way to the divide. It was a chasm. A deep dark chasm that reminded me of one thing. Dad.

A flashback played through my memory. Dad falling. Me being too slow or too small. Unable to help. I stepped backward, now unsure of my footing. I didn't want this to happen, but it did anyway. My confidence drained. Likewise, the caduceus gem's light waned. I froze, feeling powerless. Slowly, as the dust from Thorne's impact settled, he started to rise.

Come on, Dean, I thought to myself, but doubt had crept in too deep. I hung my head, resting my hands on my hips, totally defeated. That was until my twitching fingers made contact with the handle of Pint's axe that dangled from my belt. It was enough to bring me back, to remind me of what I was fighting for. Who I was fighting for. I pulled the axe from my waist and held it in front of my face, looking at the markings on its handle that Pint had carved himself. Time to be the hero...

I took about ten paces backward, then ran, timing my steps and planting off the edge, thrusting forward, soaring across the dark open vat of nothingness. My arms flailed, and my feet ran in place as I flew, but not far enough. My chest slammed into the opposite end of the chasm, and I lost my grip on the axe as I tried to get my footing.

Now I was just like my dad, hanging on for dear life, dangling over the darkness. I didn't dare look down to see if any hands were coming for me. I tried to pull myself up, but the soft ground was crumbling. I was going to fall if someone didn't help me, but who? Liv was across the field on the other side of the gap. The Gnomelings were three feet tall; what could they do, form a Gnomeling chain? Even the trolls, now led by Chief, were too far away. My hands searched for something to hold onto, but it was no use. I was slipping. Within seconds the chasm would swallow me whole. My story would end. It wasn't until the black-armored hand of a knight grabbed me by the wrist that I knew I still had a friend.

"Up," the knight commanded. "On your feet, Dean." He leaned back, pulling me onto solid ground. I caught my breath and dusted myself off. "Here," he continued. "Take this. It's yours." I opened my hand underneath his outstretched arm as he released his grip on the amulet.

"What?" I said, looking first at the amulet, then the knight, and then past him, staring at Thorne. The beast was no more. He was a man once again. A frail, weak man with nothing hanging around his neck

"Who are you?" I asked. "Why are you helping me?"

The knight draped in black reached up, slowly pulling his helmet from his face. "I'm your friend. And I should have never forgotten that."

"Flynn?!" I couldn't believe it. He was here. Flynn was here. Everything he had done. Everything bad. It was all forgotten. Forgiven. I was so happy to see him that I wrapped my arms around him, squeezing him tight. I knew there was more to him. Thorne used him. He didn't have a choice. "I knew you were good, Flynn. I just knew it."

I broke our embrace, and our smiles met briefly. But Flynn's expression shifted from joy to confusion to pain.

"What is it?" I asked as Flynn pushed me away. Then, my eyes followed his gaze downward. Horror gripped me as I saw a blade protruding from his belly. "No!" I yelled as a sword was pulled back through, and Flynn dropped to his knees. Thorne stood behind him, watching coldly as Flynn's body crumpled to the ground.

"I always knew you were too weak to be my son," Thorne spat over Flynn. He stared at the blade. He stared at Flynn's blood on the shimmering silver. "And then there were two."

My teeth ground together as I took the amulet and held it out. "You know what, Thorne?"

Thorne smirked.

"I don't need this to beat you." I stuffed the amulet in my pocket, leaned down, and retrieved Flynn's sword. Thorne extended his weapon. The rapier. The sword he used to fight me in the hotel back in our world. The sword that belonged to my dad. We squared up to begin the final duel.

I would love to tell you this was an epic battle. A battle with twists, flips, and parries. But it wasn't. Thorne was fighting for himself, the only thing he ever cared about. I was fighting for my family. I was fighting for my fellowship. I owned him and every inch of the duel. With each swing, I pushed him back. With each strike, I drove him to the ground. And within the blink of an eye, I had him pinned. What I didn't know was that almost all of the fighting around us had stopped. The trolls had taken out the eastern armies. The Ravens held off the spiders. Ava... Ava had single-handedly taken out three dragons, forcing the others to retreat. Tubb and Griff even took down a hellion or two, this time, proud that they didn't hide in a bucket. And for the hundreds and thousands of orcs and goblins... they were enthralled in the swordplay that was front and center. A first-row seat to the main event.

With a few more strikes, Thorne was out of room. I had backed him into an outcropping of stone. I spun my sword in a spiral, twisting Thorne into a frenzy until he fell to a knee. His rapier was sent airborne. He was disarmed and defeated as he held his arms out in surrender.

I expected a lengthy speech, but all I got was a weak, "You got me, Sport." I turned back and looked at Liv as Tubb and Griff appeared at her side. Liv exhaled, letting her arms rest on her knees, getting a much-needed breather. That was until her eyes opened wide, and she yelled my name at the top of her lungs.

My heart raced as I whipped my attention towards Thorne, and in that split second, I saw him lunging at me with a small, gleaming knife. He had concealed it somewhere, waiting for the perfect moment to strike. I braced for the impact, knowing I wouldn't have time to dodge the attack.

But then, something miraculous happened. As Thorne's dagger came hurtling towards me, I felt a sudden movement in my pocket. I couldn't believe my eyes as I watched a deadly serpent, a fanged coiler, slither out of its hiding place, its eyes locked onto Thorne's. The rope… the amulet chain… now transformed into a venomous weapon.

The snake sprang into action, baring its fangs and sinking them into Thorne's hand. Thorne let out a painful scream as he lost his grip on the dagger. Seizing the opportunity, I struck my enemy, burying Flynn's blade into Thorne's chest. His smirk faded as he let out a final grunt before collapsing to the ground.

Shaken, I reached into my pocket and retrieved the amulet. Holding it over my heart, I watched as the snake wriggled its way up my body, eventually wrapping itself around my neck. Incredibly, it seemed to morph into a chain, fusing together with the amulet. I should have been freaking out, but I wasn't. My dad had specifically chosen this animal for me, and besides, I couldn't let Pint look down on me as a "ninny muffin." A surge of confidence and belonging flowed through me. I felt invincible.

It seemed that the remaining enemies felt it too, because those who didn't flee or fly away quickly dropped to a knee in surrender, leaving their weapons scattered on the ground before us.

THE END OF THE END

A week had passed since the battle at Yarberry (that's what the locals decided to call it). Most of the enemies were captured or retreated to the Dark Lands. Tubb and Griff had been promoted to general and major in the Gnomeling army. Mostly that meant they got extra meat or drinks at birthday parties. Cliff had suffered a wound in battle. Not a mortal wound, but enough to keep him in the hospital for a few weeks. Ava was given the highest honor of the Gnomeling people and the free folk of Second Realm. She was anointed Dragon Queen and official protector. I didn't know what this meant, but it sounded cool. Chief Troll returned to Longwell Lagoon, but he didn't go alone. A group of mountain trolls joined him and agreed to help him renovate, but only after Liv convinced him that his 'home' was in need of a deep clean. Klavos and the Ravens suffered major losses and returned to Raven Town to recoup. Before he left, he met with Liv. He told her that after seeing her skills with a bow, she must have Raven blood in her veins.

As for me, I was welcomed into Pint's home as a guest. No. As a member of the family. I had some scrapes and bruises, but Pint's mother nursed me back to health, feeding me until I was stuffed and then feeding me some more. I gotta admit, it was weird sleeping in a bed with a poster of me hanging above it, but hey… a bed's a bed, and I needed the rest. For most of the past few days, I just sat there, eyes closed, thinking about everything that happened. It seemed like yesterday that Dad and I were reading together, but now I was napping in the home of a Gnomeling in another realm, just days after a battle with a Minotaur, wraiths, dragons, hellions, goblins, spiders, and more.

"Hello?" A knock on the door jarred me from a daydream.

"Come in," I sat up, pulling the tiny blankets to my chin, which yanked them right off of my feet.

"Are you ready?" Liv entered. She wore a black dress with a long train that flowed past her feet. She was so stunning that she took my breath away. "You haven't even changed clothes," she said, noticing my outfit draped over a wooden chair in the corner of the room. She grabbed the black jacket and pants, gently laying them on the bed beside me.

"Sorry. I'll be out in a second," I said

"You okay?" she asked.

"Just thinking. That's all."

"About?"

"What if they come back?"

"Dean," Liv shoved the coat jacket aside and sat down. "We just won a battle."

"One battle. Against one villain. What about the war? The Dark One? What if —"

"Stop." Liv took my hand, squeezing until my fingertips turned white.

"Ouch."

"You can 'what if' tomorrow," Liv said. "Today is about saying goodbye. Nothing more."

"But—"

"No," she stopped me. "No buts, Dean. You're a Shire Knight. Evil will always be on your doorstep, and someone will always need defending. Just not today." Liv released her grip on my hand, stood, and walked off, stopping in the doorway. "Look what Klavos gave me," she said as she reached into a black bag tied around her waist. Liv pulled a silver tiara out and placed it on her head.

"Princess Olivia," I said.

"Apparently so."

"Pint was right," I said.

"Pint Dangerous Lemon was right," she smiled, closing the door behind her.

I got to my feet and got dressed, throwing on the suit that the Gnomelings had stitched for me. The arms were a tad too long, while the cuffs on the legs were too short, but I told the Gnomeling tailors it was the finest suit I'd ever worn. It was the first suit I'd ever worn, but I didn't want to spoil their joy, so I kept my mouth shut.

Another knock at the door hurried my zipping when I said, "Back so soon? I told you I was on my way." Only this time, it wasn't Liv. "Mom?" I said, surprised to see my mom open the door and enter the room. She looked radiant, wearing a gown and heels, and her hair was done up pretty fancy.

"Hi," she said in her motherly tone, opening her arms to me.

I ran into her embrace and squeezed her as tight as ever. I was so happy to see her. "I'm sorry, Mom. I'm so sorry." I wanted to apologize for so many things. For not telling her about the amulet. About Dad. For being too risky with my life. For leaving her at home when we traveled to the realm.

"That doesn't matter anymore," she said. "What matters is you're safe now. And we're together."

"How are you here?" I asked.

"Some small lady named Ava came to me." Mom broke free of our hug with a puzzled look on her face. "I don't know how to say this without sounding crazy, but she came to me in a dream."

"Yeah. They do that here," I said.

"Well, she told me I needed to come, so here I am. But I think I ruined a car."

I flashed back to our adventure in the hearse and wondered if Mom drove through the lake too. "I'm glad you're here." I hugged her again.

"Are you ready?" she said.

"No," I answered honestly. No amount of preparation would leave me ready for this day. "But they're waiting. So I have to do my part."

We walked out of the room to meet Liv, Anders, and Roger. Roger was here. My first new friend in England. He gave me the biggest hug. Roger smelled like beef jerky, which was an improvement over his beer, throw-up, and moldy cheese scent. After we broke our embrace, he backpedaled to Mom's side, getting a little too close to her for my liking. My face must have

400

twisted into a fit of anger because Mom noticed immediately. "Don't worry. He came as a friend."

Roger lifted his arm and tried to hold Mom's hand. "A friend with benefits?"

Mom slapped his hand away. "You wish," she said, which brought me a little satisfaction. Despite his flirting with Mom, I was happy to see Roger. He saved our lives more than once. Plus, it's not often you get to see a drunken dwarf dressed as Gimli sing Mary Poppins songs.

Tubb and Griff opened the door from outside as they entered the home. They were both in their finest suits as well. Only theirs fit. "They all be here," Tubb said as we marched out together, the Shire Knights, minus two. We walked past hundreds of well-dressed Gnomelings, Ravens, and free folk of Second Realm. They lined the dirt paths the way the soldiers did on the day of the battle. Most were crying, wiping their eyes as we passed.

Ava stood waiting for us as we reached the top of the hill. There, overlooking the meadow, the lake, and the Leflorian trees, were markers in the ground with names written on them. Too many to count. Names of the lives lost in the fight. The two markers closest to me were written in Gnomarian and in English. The first said 'Pint' while the other said 'Flynn.'

As a knight of Yarberry and protector of the realm, it was my duty to say a few words to honor those who were no longer with us. So that's what I did. I spoke with pride, praising the Gnomelings who fell defending the realm. I shared stories of Flynn's bravery, telling them how he stood against his father to help us. To save us. I told them about my time with Pint and recounted a story his mother had shared with me. It was the one where he tried to fight a group of pigs over a carrot he had accidentally dropped into their pen. After thanking everyone for coming, I made a promise to them. I pledged that their lands would never fall to the enemy as long as the Shire Knights were there to protect them. In my heart, I hoped I could always keep that promise.

That night there was a celebration of immense proportions. A party made the ball drop at Times Square look like a baby shower in Scranton. I made my rounds, talking to as many curious Gnomelings as possible, but eventually, I grew tired. I made my way back to the markers, where I sat down in between Flynn and Pint. For a while, I didn't say a word. After some time, I told them I loved them and wished they were here with me. I told Flynn that he was right about Jack, Rose, and the wreckage from the Titanic. I just never wanted to admit it. I told Pint some of the stories my dad had shared with me when I was little. More than anything, I spent time with my friends to get all my feelings out. Deep down, I just hoped they knew how I really felt.

"They know," Liv said, almost like she was reading my mind, as she sat beside me.

"How long were you there?" I asked.

"Long enough." She took her crown off and set it on Pint's marker.

"What now?" I asked.

"The Gnomelings will rebuild. And we," Liv took my hand, "we go home."

"There's no way," I said, questioning everything. How does that even work? How could I go back to a normal life, knowing what we know now and seeing what we've seen? And just then, something my dad told me popped into my head. I slid the amulet from the center of my chest to a place where it partially covered my heart.

"What is it?" Liv asked.

As soon as the amulet made contact with the skin above my heart, it began to emit a warm, reassuring glow. "Home," I said, pointing. "This is where I'll stay, as long as you'll have me," I repeated my dad's words, but this time they were meant for Liv. For Mom. For my friends. For Pint and for Flynn. As long as I held them close to my heart, they would always be my home, whether in London, just outside of Pittsburgh, or Yarberry Shire in Second Realm.

The End

EPILOGUE

As I stood on the grounds of Chalice Well, memories of my past visit came flooding back. I closed my eyes, taking a deep breath, savoring the sweet scent of the blooming flowers and the gentle sound of the flowing water.

I felt a surge of emotions as I recalled every detail that took place here just two years ago. I remembered the fear of falling into the well before the world collapsed around me. I recalled the embrace from my dad when he said goodbye. I thought back to the company of my friends on our quest to unite the pieces of the amulet. The same amulet that still hung around my neck on this joyous day.

A soft hum of conversation reverberated across the lush green pasture before me. Rows of white chairs were packed with hundreds of patrons, with a cloth runner dividing the section in half. On the left side of the aisle sat my extended family, with a few old friends.

On the right side was a group of cosplayers adorned in *Lord of the Rings* attire, from Ents to orcs and wizards to elves. Thankfully, there were no wraiths to be seen this time. Not even ones in Converse shoes with high socks.

I stood beneath a white archway at the end of the aisle. Instead of my usual casual attire, I wore a black tuxedo with a blue bow tie. To my left, Tubb and Griff stood wearing their finest Yarberry Shire outfits in shades of blue and yellow. With all the cosplay outfits, it was easy for the *humans* in the audience to overlook their appearance. Mom said they would hide in plain sight. As always, she was right. Standing beside Griff was my little brother, Jackson, who was now a strapping eleven-year-old and, as always, as irritating as ever.

As the flower girl finished sprinkling petals at our feet, my gaze shifted to the other side of the aisle. Directly across from me, three women stood wearing flowing gowns adorned with silver sequins. Among them was a girl around my age, another who seemed closer in age to my mom, and the third was Esther - my former kid-sitter, who was still around despite her age creeping towards a solid century.

Tears started streaming down my face as soon as the violinist played the familiar tune of "Here Comes the Bride."

"You told us you wouldn't be crying," Griff said, tugging my sleeve.

"Wimp," Jackson mocked.

I couldn't help it. Weddings got to me, especially since I was in this one. I tried to hold my emotions under control, but as the crowd stood up, I knew I would be a complete wreck. Seeing her in a white gown would bring me to a full-body sob, but I didn't care.

"Sorry I'm late," I heard a whisper behind me as Liv sneaked across the aisle to join the other bridesmaids. "Grandad got lost again," she explained, her smile lighting up her face. Liv looked radiant in her matching dress bejeweled with silver sequins.

In case you were wondering, this wasn't my wedding. The man standing next to me was the lucky groom - a former night security guard, drunken cosplayer, and a full-time member of my fellowship. He stood between four and five feet tall, with a man bun a shade darker than his scruffy beard. He now reeked of cheap cologne, which was yet another upgrade from his usual odor.

"I am the luckiest man on the face of this earth," Roger said, bawling like a baby as he blew his nose into a soaked handkerchief.

And for his bride... She was coming down the aisle. She looked as beautiful as ever, her black hair curled and her olive skin shimmering.

If you had told me two years ago that my mom would ever remarry, I would have looked at you cross-eyed or likely dreamed of knocking your lights out. But if she had to find another husband, I'm glad she found Roger, especially now that he had kicked his drinking habit and stopped riding wild pigs while wearing maiden dresses.

"I want you to know, Roger," I said just loud enough for only Roger to hear me. "No matter what, I'm never calling you dad."

The Scavenger Hunt

CONCEPT ART

A special thank you to all the brilliant students/artists who contributed to bringing these characters to life.

Concept Art

Figure 1 - Gnomeling by Delaney Kraus

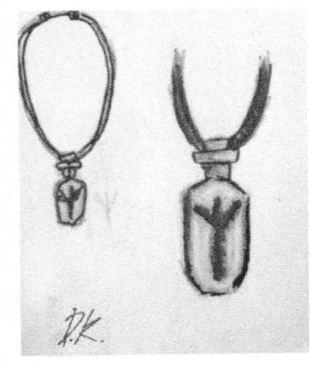

Figure 2- Amulet by Delaney Kraus

Figure 3 - Thorne by Delaney Kraus

Figure 4- Hellion by Delaney Kraus

Figure 5- Armored Rhino by Juliana Riley

Concept Art

Figure 6- Gnomeling inspired by original work of Delaney Kraus as seen below - By Lillian Henry

Figure 7-Hellion by Lillian Henry

Concept Art

Figure 8- Wraith by Kami Carr

Figure 9-Chief Troll by Dan Marino

Concept Art

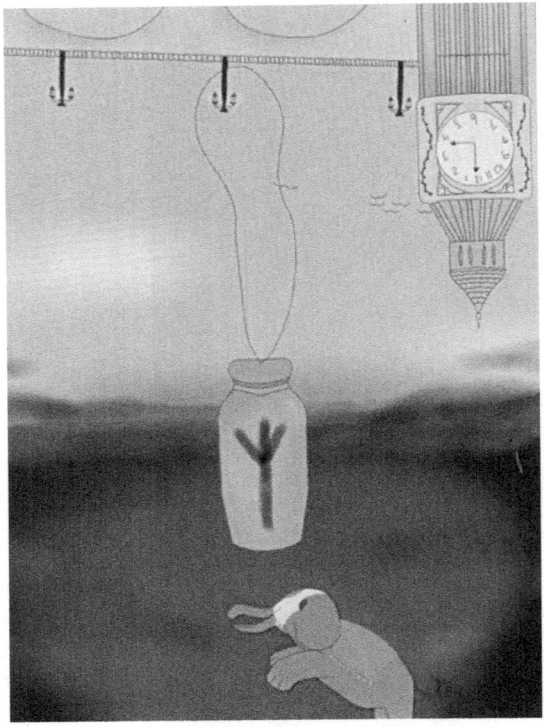

Figure 10-London & 2nd Realm Poster Concept by Taylor Theisman

Made in the USA
Monee, IL
20 March 2023

30222911R00246